11-1-21

Linda Raymond

ROCKING the BABIES

PENGUIN BOOKS

PENGUIN BOOKS
Published by the Penguin Group
Penguin Books USA Inc., 375 Hudson Street,
New York, New York 10014, U.S.A.
Penguin Books Ltd, 27 Wrights Lane, London W8 5TZ, England
Penguin Books Australia Ltd, Ringwood, Victoria, Australia
Penguin Books Canada Ltd, 10 Alcorn Avenue,
Toronto, Ontario, Canada M4V 3B2
Penguin Books (N.Z.) Ltd, 182–190 Wairau Road,
Auckland 10, New Zealand

Penguin Books Ltd, Registered Offices:
Harmondsworth, Middlesex, England

First published in the United States of America by Viking Penguin,
a division of Penguin Books USA Inc. 1994
Published in Penguin Books 1995

1 3 5 7 9 10 8 6 4 2

Portions of this work first appeared in
The Macguffin and *Prism International*.

PUBLISHER'S NOTE

This is a work of fiction. Names, characters, places, and incidents either are the product of the author's imagination or are used fictitiously, and any resemblance to actual persons, living or dead, events, or locales is entirely coincidental.

THE LIBRARY OF CONGRESS HAS CATALOGUED
THE HARDCOVER AS FOLLOWS:
Raymond, Linda.
Rocking the babies/by Linda Raymond
p. cm.
ISBN 0-670-85263-5 (hc.)
ISBN 0 14 02.3254 0 (pbk.)
1. Volunteer workers in hospitals—Ohio—Fiction. 2. African-American women—Ohio—Fiction. 3. Infants (Premature)—Ohio—Fiction. 4. Middle aged women—Ohio—Fiction. 5. African-Americans—Ohio—Fiction. I. Title.
PS3568.A929R63 1994
813′.54—dc20 94-8795

Printed in the United States of America
Set in Adobe Garamond no. 3

For my mother,
Lillian C. Robinson

I would like to thank Linda Riley, Frances Sutz-Brown, and Judith Rose for their criticism and encouragement. Also, thanks to Clarence Major, Elizabeth Tallent, Will Baker, Max Byrd, and Robin Locke-Monda. God bless Elliot Gilbert. For her keen perception and gentle advice, I thank Beena Kamlani. For their faith in me, my deepest thanks to Nat Sobel and Dawn Seferian. Thanks to my husband, Al Raymond, for his insight and inexhaustible patience. And special thanks to Jack Hicks, for opening the door.

ROCKING the BABIES

WANTED: GRANDMOTHERS. Mercy Pediatric Hospital needs senior women to provide TLC in the ICU. Will train. Lunch provided. Call Terese Czajwolski, Child Life Advocate.

Nettie Lee Johnson laid the *Dayton Daily News* on the dinette table next to her cold Pop-Tart. If this were any other day, she'd perk a pot of Maxwell House, toast four pieces of white bread, and fry up two eggs hard, but she didn't have time for that today. She had told the lady at the hospital—What was her name? Sagawoolski?—she'd be there to rock the little babies at nine o'clock, and here it was eight-thirty already. She looked back at the newspaper. She hated to cuss her own child, but damn that Yolanda. When would the girl straighten out? Well, she couldn't worry about that now. Time to leave. She had already packed Little Barn off to Dorothy's house across the street, had just sent him out the door. But now the house needed straightening up something terrible. Little Barn had strewn his video mess in front of the TV. The night before, Nettie Lee had had to cut the TV off herself, since no amount of begging could get him away from those squared-headed street fighters and ninjas he thought so much of. This morning the house would have to wait. Nobody better not come to her house today, because she wouldn't be home. She didn't have time for talking, and she didn't have time for sitting around worrying either. These past five weeks she'd done enough of that. She didn't even have time to finish the paper. She refolded the *News* back to the front page—and there was the picture again: Baby X. Her granddaughter.

In the picture, the paramedics and police stood at a construction site in front of a sign that read FUTURE HOME OF HIP HOP'S CHICKEN JOINT, *Mmmm Mmmm Mmmm!* With disgust Nettie Lee recognized the place. It was about a block up from where Yolanda had been staying with her so-called girlfriend Benji. In the picture (she was getting *so* tired of seeing it) two policemen bent over a tiny bundle of blankets—the victim they were calling Baby X. A paramedic squeezed on a black bag connected to a tube hanging out of the baby's mouth. Her grandbaby. Yolanda's daughter. That girl didn't have the brains God gave a chigger, and she would have told Yolanda that to her face if the little fool hadn't run off—run off and left that baby in a Port-a-Potty, like she thought a child was human waste. Well, she had news for Yolanda. This baby wasn't going to be abandoned. Not *her* grandchild.

Nettie Lee read the headline again: DA . . . MURDER CHARGE. BABY THROWN AWAY. Then, in smaller print, "DA will try for attempted murder charge." She laid the paper down. Yolanda had messed up bad this time. First, she had told Nettie Lee she was pregnant again by that fool Barn. No, she took that back; Yolanda didn't tell her, she let Nettie Lee *guess* it. The day she found out, Yolanda and Nettie Lee had gone to Foodworld with Little Barn. The big warehouse sat far back on a blacktop parking lot jammed with cars shimmering in the heat. They had walked from Yolanda's apartment, only a block away, but the Indian summer day brought back a smack of heat to the city and made all three of them cranky. Tired of Little Barn whining about how he wanted to go back home, Nettie Lee had finally tried to hoist him up to her hip. Then, feeling him squirm, she let him slip back down her thigh to the ground. It seemed to her that every time his mama was around, he took to nervous habits—whining, sucking his thumb, not letting anybody touch him. He was getting downright unsociable.

They had continued walking up the block, Nettie Lee studying Yolanda, who walked a couple of steps ahead of her and Little Barn. She wore a pair of purple leggings and a big *X* T-shirt, Malcolm's face on the back, the sleeves rolled high. Her arms looked thin to Nettie Lee, not as muscular and strong as they usually were. She always seemed to be on some kind of diet, but she was getting too skinny. Even her feet looked bony. They were perfectly pedicured, in strappy gold sandals, toenails polished deep orange to match her long fingernails, yet they looked like the claw feet under a mahogany dining table. Nettie Lee walked behind Yolanda through the warehouse doors, her dress blowing across her bare legs as she passed the threshold. She flashed her membership card at the boy standing by the carts.

The store was huge: fans blew hot air overhead, the aisles were crowded with shoppers and their big wire carts or lopsided flats, and children wandered freely. Nettie Lee threaded their cart through it all, while Yolanda tossed in items from the shelves. After she cashed her welfare check, Yolanda liked to buy the month's groceries all at one time: ten cans of tomato soup, ten cans of beans, ten cans of tuna. Nettie Lee called Yolanda the Tin Can Woman.

When they got to the feminine hygiene aisle, Nettie Lee stopped pushing the cart. "Don't forget your Kotex." She picked up a box. "Want ten?"

Yolanda had just waved them away and looked absently down the aisle, where Little Barn sat on his knees, spilled boxes lying around him. Her face sharpened. "Little Byron! You better get your hands off of those douches."

He looked up, slid a box behind his back while he kept his eyes locked to hers.

"I mean right now, boy! I see you." She scuffled up the aisle, sandals dragging on concrete, bent over him, then jerked him to his feet. "What did I say about throwing stuff on the floor? What did I *tell* you about it?"

He let a small breath out, sniffed. "Okay."

"*What* did I say?"

"Okay." He began to cry.

"I didn't say 'Okay.' Tell me what I said."

"You said, 'Don't throw nothing on the floor."

"That's right." Yolanda jerked on his arm. "How come you can't mind me?"

"Bitch!" Little Barn's face exploded into tears.

"Yo*lan*da." Nettie Lee tried to fix her with a look. "Why don't y'all do that mess at home instead of all up in the middle of this store?"

Yolanda let Little Barn go, but he kept his eyes on her, watching her face. "I just can't hang with this." She turned away, shaking her head. "Let's take this stuff to the checkout and get out of here." She started off toward the checkout lines.

Nettie Lee took Little Barn's hand. "Come on. I see you got yourself into trouble again." She watched his face screw up, tears roll down his cheeks. "Don't be touching nothing in this store," she said softly. "When you going to learn?"

Nettie Lee didn't think too much about Yolanda not wanting Kotex. Maybe she had changed her mind and was going back to Tampax even after that toxic shock scare. Maybe that's all it was. When they got back to Yolanda's apartment, Nettie Lee still wasn't thinking anything was wrong. Yolanda had sat at the kitchen table with her shoes off and her feet propped on a chair. She dragged on a Tiparillo. When she exhaled, her stomach looked like a basketball was stuck up under her blouse. "When's the baby due?" Nettie Lee had joked, but Yolanda surprised her by blowing out a curl of cigar smoke and answering, "February seventh."

"Girl, I know you didn't say you was pregnant?"

"Then you don't know as much as you think you do."

"What?" Nettie Lee pulled out a chair and sat beside her. Almost against her better judgment, Nettie Lee reached out her hand and laid it on top of Yolanda's, which rested on the table.

"Oh, Mama, give it a rest, would you?" She snatched her hand away. "I'm pregnant, okay?"

Nettie Lee felt her skin crawl, from her face down to her feet, like it was being loosened from the bone. "No, it ain't okay. What are you talking about, 'okay'?"

"This is why I never tell you anything, okay? This is *it.* Because you always have to get so stressed. God!"

"What are you talking about? You sitting up here telling me you pregnant *again,* going to have another baby when you just *barely* taking care of the one you got now, and then you got the nerve to tell me *I'm* stressed?"

"I knew it. You never help me." Yolanda stood up. "You know what I wish? I wish you would have paid more attention to me when I was growing up, like ask me where I was going, who I was going with. I mean, you just never seemed interested in me. And now you never come over here to visit."

"What am I going to do over here?"

"See!"

"You over to my house all the time; what do I need to come over here for? You the only person I know who can come to somebody's house, go in their bed, and take a nap."

"Well, you're always asleep on the couch when I come over."

"I'm tired!"

"Can't you wake up to see me?"

"Look, honey, you need to get yourself a life, then what your tired old mother is up to won't look so interesting. You're twenty years old, you got yourself a little family, another one on the way, and you want to cry about how you didn't get everything you wanted when you was a *little girl?*" Nettie Lee laughed, though she really didn't feel like it. "You ain't a little girl anymore."

Yolanda walked over to the kitchen window and looked out. Past the window Nettie Lee could see the crisscross of power lines against the white afternoon sky. Yolanda said, "I just realized I felt this way. I just wanted you to know how I feel. I feel like you didn't pay enough attention to me."

"I *know* that."

Yolanda swung around. "You don't have to say it like that: 'I *know* that.' "

"I *know* that's how you feel," Nettie Lee had said. "But what can I do about it now?"

Nettie Lee put the newspaper on the dinette table and sipped her coffee. She took another bite of her Pop-Tart and let the taste of chemical strawberries coat her tongue. Here it was the middle of December. Yolanda's baby would be five weeks old now, and Nettie Lee thought she had found a way of getting into the hospital to care for the baby without somebody trying to hunt down Yolanda through her: volunteer grandmother in the intensive care nursery where her grandbaby lay. The ad had been in the paper for a week. She *wanted* that job.

When she was done raising children, *if* she ever got done raising children—seemed like when your own babies were just about raised, here *your* babies came with *their* babies—well, when she was done raising children, she'd have herself a fancy breakfast like Eggs Benedict or some such. And she wouldn't worry about smelling like somebody's grandma all the time. She would wear Joop! that new smell she pulled out of a magazine, instead of smelling like baby goop. Or she'd wear Obsession. Think about *that,* honey—a man with an obsession for Nettie Lee Johnson, crazy as a loon for her. Well, maybe it was crazy to think she could get a man's interest up, especially with her turning sixty-one last birthday. Lord, that sounded just about as old as she felt.

At the front door, she stopped to look at herself in the mirror tiles she had glued to the back of the door. In the wavery glass, her eyes were deep-set and tired, and it looked permanent; no amount of sleep could puff those hollows back out to a healthy level. That was just too bad. And she didn't care about the pounds she'd put on over the years; that was God's way of letting her feel loved, by making sure she always had enough to eat. But her head did look a mess, looked like her hair could up and crawl away. She pushed her fingers through it, pulled on the fish-hooked ends. She should get herself a salon appointment, get herself a press before she went out looking for a job. That Miss Sagawoolski would think she was some kind of nut.

Nettie Lee grabbed her hair with both hands and twisted it up into a pigtail, tied it with a red rubber band she got off the dinette table. She straightened out her skirt, smoothing the floral material over her hips, and pulled the hem straight where her stockings grabbed it when she walked. That was the best she could do for right now.

On her way to the bus stop, Nettie Lee admired the silent snow in her small yard and in her neighbors' yards. The street looked like the Lord's Thanksgiving table with the good white cloth laid out. Everything in place. As she stood at the corner pole waiting for the bus, she became afraid. Volunteer grandmother. It must be the first time she had volunteered to do anything for anybody, except Yolanda and Little Barn. Over the phone, the woman had said her job would be to cuddle the tiny little babies up in the intensive care nursery, the ones whose mothers wouldn't hold them, like so many nowadays. Well, like Yolanda. Poor little babies got a ghost for a father and a simpleton for a mother. She couldn't understand it. What was so different about these young people's lives now; what made them lose their common sense, their hope? She had lost hope at one time too, lost it and didn't know where to start looking to get it back, but that didn't make her suck on a crack pipe or drink wine until her head swam, didn't make her want to forget about everything including her own baby. Nettie Lee looked up the street. Two blocks away, the bus slowed down and dipped toward the curb. She could see a dark figure climb in, the bus pull away. *This bus better hurry up and come on, before I lose my wits.*

The streets downtown were slushy after the previous night's snowfall. The Chamber of Commerce had decorated the light poles like oversized candy canes with twists of tinsel. In the evenings, the chamber plugged in the forty-foot Christmas tree on the steps of Courthouse Square, and beneath the tree's silver light, skaters would laugh and fall on a skim of ice. During the day, shoppers crowded the streets at lunchtime and after work. Buses trundled up and down the main roads, occasionally turning off onto a small side street, before heading out to the south, north, east, and finally the west side, where Nettie Lee lived.

From her window seat on the bus, she watched the Christmas displays roll past. In Lazarus's window, a group of motorized "It's a Small World" Christmas elves jerked through the motions of helping Santa in his workshop. The silver and gold ribbons trailing from a five-foot-high stack of presents in Hudson's window seemed like a joke on the people she knew who had lost their jobs before Thanksgiving or had their welfare checks cut. Things were tight for her too. Her social security check just about covered her food and her gas bill. That fool in the White House could read *her* lips, if he ever got interested in what she had to say. And now that Yolanda had left town, Nettie Lee wouldn't be getting any more welfare money for Little Barn.

Yolanda had called her the day after the baby was born. When the operator said it was a collect call, Nettie Lee knew it was bad news. Yolanda's voice had been empty. "Hey, Mama," she'd said, then paused. There was the faint sound of a radio station coming across the wires, some kind of rock-and-roll singing. "You know that baby they're talking about on the news? Well, that's mine." Phone pressed into the side of her face, breath on hold, Nettie Lee didn't know what to say. Yolanda said, "Yeah. I had him last night at the apartment." The phone went quiet; she thought their connection was lost. What was she supposed to do to find her, trace her call? Keep her on the line long enough to convince her to come home? Then, after a long time, Yolanda said, "I don't know," as if Nettie Lee had asked her something. Nettie Lee could hardly get the air to say, "Where you at, girl? Tell me where, and I'll be there right now." Yolanda had said, "I'm no place," then hung up.

She got off the bus in front of Mercy Pediatric Hospital and immediately reared back a step. A flimsy-looking man in a dull black suit jacket worn over a white undershirt almost ran her down with his bicycle. He didn't ride it, he pushed it, strong-armed it past her, muttering, "Got to be there. *Have* to go. Got to be there. *Have* to go." On the handlebars, he had rigged an aluminum star, its fantastic jagged edges like a multicolored bird.

Nettie Lee watched him career his bike up the street. "It sure does take all kinds, Lord," she said aloud. As long as there were people like that, her state of affairs didn't seem quite so desperate.

On the elevator ride to the fourth floor, Nettie Lee thought the hospital was a noisy place, a constant barrage of calls to doctors and department heads, stat messages to technicians. It struck her as odd that the street signs warned this was a quiet zone.

She sat in front of Ms. Czajwolski's nicked-up wooden desk waiting for her to get off the phone. Seemed like the thing rang again just as soon as the poor woman put it down. Ms. Czajwolski, sincere as a schoolgirl, was a thin woman in her mid-twenties; her curly brown hair was pulled back with a terry-cloth band, and she wore no makeup. For the most part, her voice on the phone murmured, soothed, explained. Behind her, through the open door, Nettie Lee could hear other telephones ringing, other one-sided conversations like Ms. Czajwolski's, in which the main point seemed to be (judging from the tone of voice the office staff took), Really, I'll try to get to that later.

Nettie Lee felt impatient. She had *told* the woman she would rock the babies—what did they need to talk about? She clasped her hands in her lap, twisting the ring Yolanda had given her for her sixtieth birthday. It had an emerald stone for May and two zirconium chips, one for Yolanda's birth and the other for Little Barn's. Yolanda had fretted over Nettie Lee's refusal to accept her original present—an obscenely huge diamond ring, the stone in the middle surrounded by ten somewhat smaller diamonds in a heart shape, bought with Barn's drug money. Nettie Lee had told Yolanda there was no way she was going to be a walking advertisement for cocaine, so she could take her tacky drug ring and throw it in the trash can in back of the house, unless she wanted Nettie Lee to do it for her. Yolanda was hurt, but how did she think Nettie Lee felt? What was her daughter trying to say to her, that the life she had provided for Yolanda, the things she had given that girl weren't enough? Sure, she was never able to give Yolanda and her child all the things money could buy, the way Barn could, but she didn't know Yolanda was craving those things bad enough to take up with a low-life hustler.

Hands in her lap, Nettie Lee twisted the ring, watching Ms. Czajwolski uncap a pen with her teeth and scribble on a scrap of paper. The telephone conversation dragged on. Even when Yolanda was pregnant that first time with Little Barn, she could have come to Nettie Lee and got some advice. She'd never kick Yolanda out of the house for having a baby—that was human nature, her hormones talking to her. But a girl gets to a certain age and she wants to be grown, wants to stay with a man and feel like she's part of the world, Nettie Lee guessed. But where was this wonderful Barn, now that he had a family?

The last time she saw Barn was right after this bad newspaper thing came out. Late one evening, she had gone into the grocery down on the corner from her house to pick up some chicken for dinner. Though she really preferred the big supermarket out in Harrison Township because their meat was fresh, she didn't have a ride out there. So she'd put on her coat, told Little Barn to keep the door locked and don't let *anybody* in, she didn't care *what* they said they wanted; then she walked the half block to the little store run by the foreign family, shivering the whole way. While she was in the back of the store choosing chicken from the small refrigerator case, smelling each package, a boy in one of those big black basketball team jackets, the kind that has the big hood and comes way down past the knees, pulled a little gun out of his coat pocket and told the foreign husband to get all the bills out of the cash register and put them in his hand. He laid his hand on the counter, palm up. Nettie Lee looked around the store. The foreign man's wife and their teenage boy weren't there. She was the only customer. She decided if things got serious, if the boy got crazy, she would try to get herself to the door. That's when she saw Barn, sitting outside in his pickup truck, engine running, his ridiculous cowboy hat pulled down low, waiting for that fool to rob the grocery store. What had happened to all his wonderful drug money? The boy with the gun got the bills from the husband, and the two of them took off in the truck.

Nettie Lee heard Ms. Czajwolski say, "I should have that by tomorrow," and hang up the telephone. Smiling at Nettie Lee, she pressed the pen to her lips. "I'm sorry. Sometimes I hate that phone." She grimaced at it and tapped out a quick Morse code on her lips with the pen. "Okay, let's see," she said slowly, starting up again like a stalled car. "You're Nettie Lee Johnson, and I talked to you on the phone yesterday?"

"Day before yesterday."

"Oh, yes, Wednesday." Ms. Czajwolski laid her forehead briefly in her palm, then snapped her head back up again. "Wednesday was the day the Riley baby coded. Then Brown. Two babies on the same day." She shook her head. "But anyway," she said, giving Nellie Lee a long, stretchy smile, "today is Friday, and you're here." She wrote Nellie Lee's name on the top line of a form, speaking it aloud as she wrote. "Address?"

"Three twenty-five Quick Street, Dayton, Ohio." Nettie added the ZIP when Ms. Czajwolski looked up.

"Quick Street." She thought about it for a second. Nettie Lee knew what she'd say next. "I thought that street—well, that whole neighborhood—was condemned?"

"That's right, it was."

"But you live there?" Her hand came to rest on her throat. Her hands were small and square, the nails unpolished, short. She massaged her throat as if there were an ache inside. Nettie Lee looked at her ID badge hanging off the breast pocket of her lab coat. In the picture, Ms. Czajwolski looked like a little girl, the way her eyes stared straight out from under her dark bangs. Although since the picture was taken, she had gotten herself a shorter, more modern hairdo.

"Well, I do live there," Nettie Lee told her. "And I have neighbors, too. It was part of the government Take Over the City Project. They sold us the houses for a dollar. If you had a dollar you could get a house, if you could fix it and keep up with the taxes on it every year." This was what she didn't like about talking to strangers. The part where they got all into your business on some feeble excuse. She made herself keep still in the chair.

"Oh, yes. I do remember the Take Back the City rehab project. I was in high school then." She smiled at Nettie Lee. "Well, from our conversation on the phone, I think you're the type of person the Volunteer Grandmothers program is looking for. We're headquartered here at Mercy, but we service the entire urban and suburban Dayton area. We're looking for women like yourself, who are on a fixed income and do not work, who can relieve the workload our nurses are under."

She cleared her throat, then gazed over Nettie Lee's shoulder, out the open door.

"You see, the nurses have a work/time ratio deficit. The nursery is understaffed, and the nurses at this point must provide all the nursing care; manage the licensed practical nurses, the student nurses, the other health care providers like respiratory therapists and lab techs who come in and out; and there are the X-ray techs, the social workers, the developmental specialists, the physical therapists, et cetera."

Her hand returned to her throat.

"On top of this immense workload, the nurses are expected to provide nurturing to each infant. Studies show that newborns, whether they are full-term or premature, will wither and fail to thrive if they are deprived of human touch. In fact, some studies show that older babies who received regular full-body massage several times each day had an increase in nerve myelination and in the production of growth hormone." Her eyes returned to Nettie Lee's face. "I'm sorry. I guess I was rambling on. It's just that I really feel the grandmother job is so important. But you do know what I mean about the babies needing touch?"

"Mmm-hmm. I know just what you talking about. When a baby don't get the love it needs, it wants to curl up and die."

"That's right. That's *exactly* right, Nettie Lee." Ms. Czajwolski paused, then gassed up again. "So it is the volunteer grandmothers' job to supply the preemies' nurturing needs that our staff is simply too encumbered to address." Her eyes rested on Nettie Lee's ring, watched her twist it around her finger. "Do you have any questions?"

She watched Ms. Czajwolski lift her eyes from her ring to her face. "Yeah, I guess so." This was the part she knew was coming, when the woman would try to judge her intelligence by the way she talked or the way she phrased her questions. "I was kind of wondering about the efficiency of holding the babies. I mean, how efficient do you think it's going to be?"

"Efficient?"

Nettie Lee didn't like the puzzled look on Ms. Czajwolski's face. She wasn't doing so well at impressing her. She was screwing up. Damn. Yolanda had her so she couldn't even think straight. "The holding, I mean. Because I know there's a right way and a wrong way to hold a baby. You got to let the baby know you're in charge, you're *strong,* but you still got a soft heart for them, all at the same time. They can feel it in your touch. They know when somebody don't care, or when they can cry and fuss for no reason and get away with it. Sometimes I think they smarter than we are." Ms. Czajwolski cracked a smile. Good. "I know babies. I know how to make them feel safe. And I'm a grandmother myself, too. I had on-the-job training. I'm efficient. And I just love babies. Don't matter if they mine or somebody else's, I love them all."

Ms. Czajwolski began to speak. The small office was getting hot. There was a curtainless window in the corner behind the desk. A radiator under it blew a hot draft that weakly tufted Ms. Czajwolski's hair. From the window, Nettie Lee could see the yellow brick edge of the hospital's east wing. It rose up eight floors, the top windows glaring in the mid-morning sun. At one window, somewhere about the fourth or fifth floor, a little boy in pajamas leaned flat-palmed onto a pane of glass, then pressed his entire face, white as the moon, into the window. Nettie Lee sat motionless, wanting air. Several seconds passed before Ms. Czajwolski's words seemed meant for her again.

" . . . of course." The woman finished her sentence, letting her smile grow into a question that needed attending to.

"Yeah," Nettie Lee agreed, uneasily. "Of course."

"Good!" Ms. Czajwolski breathed in deeply and placed her hands together, almost in a handclap. "I'm glad we can agree about that. We need you to come in every day. That's the part the volunteers sometimes balk at."

Nettie Lee felt unsettled. "Well, I don't ballcat anything. I'll take the job." She would worry about the details later. What was important now was her granddaughter.

Later in the morning, Ms. Czajwolski sent her to see George Johns, a registered nurse from Antigua (An-*tee*-ga, he called it). He stood at a blackboard and instructed Nettie Lee, the lone student sitting at an eight-foot folding table in the fourth-floor conference room inside the neonatal nursery. Her training was brief. Mr. Johns wore an island-flowered shirt; a picture ID badge pulled down the breast pocket of his lab coat. In the picture, his smooth brown face was rounder, his hair longer. Seemed like everybody who worked here used to have longer hair. Nettie Lee thought his lilting accent strange, comforting. His voice reminded her of the man who ran the corner grocery where she did her weekday shopping: musical in range but crisp as an apple in pronunciation.

Mr. Johns chalked five principles on the board for Nettie Lee to remember, then pointed to them with a ballpoint pen he pulled from his breast pocket. The Five Don'ts: Don't disconnect any equipment connected to the baby. Don't remove the baby from the Isolette unless the nurse says it's okay. Don't give any medication, that's not your job. Don't talk about the babies in front of Mom or Dad. Don't become personally involved with the babies.

"Those are just the rules to keep yourself out of trouble," Mr. Johns said, placing his pen back in his pocket. He dusted his hands on his lab coat. "Now for the rules that will cause you trouble." He smiled at Nettie Lee. "Most important thing to remember: You can love these babies too much. What do I mean by this?" He did not pause for Nettie Lee's answer. "I mean that a premature baby is neurologically fragile. There are individual variations, of course, but—and this is a very important point—they are immature neurologically, just recently pushed from a womb they would prefer to inhabit, and they cannot handle stress *at all.* Now, what do I mean by stress? I mean there will be no handling of these babies that is not extremely gentle and well-considered. For instance." He walked to a file cabinet piled high with papers, on which a dusty breast pump sat, opened the bottom drawer, and pulled out a plastic baby wearing a stocking cap on its head, diapered in a tiny Pampers. "When you are told it is okay to remove the baby from the Isolette, place your palm under his bottom like so—see this?—and slip your fingers under his head for support. Then with your other hand—remember: always two hands, though you will be tempted to pick them up with one, especially if you have large hands, and I see that you do—see this? With my other hand, I add extra support under the thighs." He held the doll toward Nettie Lee. "You see? Okay. Now you try, ma'am."

Nettie Lee gingerly held the doll's head on the edge of her fingertips, her palm steady under the diaper.

"That's it," Mr. Johns praised. "You are doing quite well."

"Mmm-hmm. This comes like second nature to me." Was this as big as the babies got? This little doll couldn't have been more than twelve, maybe thirteen inches long.

"Now, as you are holding the baby, remember his weak neurological system. Do not provide more stimulation than the little one can handle. What do I mean by stimulation?" This time he waited.

"You mean not to bounce him up and down and kitchy-coo him."

"Yes, I mean that and more. For example, some of the little ones cannot take more than one type of interaction at a time. So, although you may want to pick up, talk to, and stroke or even sing to a certain preemie, you'll find he can only tolerate one of these things. You must observe the baby closely to determine what his limits are, then respect those limits. We've even had babies who could not tolerate being fed and held at the same time. One preemie was especially difficult. Only if the nurse laid the infant in the Isolette, turned her head away to prevent eye contact, and did not speak a single word would this child suck the bottle."

"Well, if they so little, am I hurting or helping them by doing things?"

"Oh, you are most definitely helping them. You need only make sure you do it in the proper manner and do not carry it too far."

"How long do they stay?" She knew her grandbaby had been there five weeks.

"It depends on the baby, of course. The more premature the baby, the longer the stay. You can approximate the length of stay like this: for each week of time stolen from the womb, we must keep the baby at least half that amount of time in the hospital. So if a baby is twelve weeks premature—as, say, the Doe baby is; have you heard of that case?—then she will spend a bit more than six weeks with us, barring complications."

Six weeks. Nettie Lee thought quickly. The baby had already been there five weeks, so she had just one week to spend with her grandbaby. Then what? "You know that for sure?"

"We don't," Mr. Johns said. "But we get pretty close in our estimates. We let them go home at five pounds, if all is well. Or, say, a baby is born at thirty-five weeks and weighs five and a half pounds; then we keep her, though her weight says to let her go home. A premature newborn does not necessarily leave the hospital at five pounds. That's only a reference point we go by. Other factors are of importance as we evaluate these babies. As far as your job goes, just remember: For as long as they stay in the hospital, you are their comfort."

"All these rules," Nettie Lee said and looked Mr. Johns directly in the eye. "I never hurt a baby in my life."

"Not to worry," Mr. Johns assured her. "They will assign an

experienced grandmother to be your mentor. That would be Martha. You'll follow her around all day as if you were her baby chick."

Nettie Lee was amazed, then frightened, again and again. The nursery was large and humid as a kitchen, ringed with what looked like microwave ovens lined up in a horseshoe. Two nurses, a tall one with hair so red it was orange, and a short young one in scrub pants and top, named Debbie Foxx (the head nurse, Nettie Lee was told), scooted around the room like they were on wheels. Nettie Lee was afraid she would get in the way. It was hard to think about handling these babies, who looked more like scrawny monkeys than anything else. Yet her yellow scrub gown and the photo ID badge clipped to it made her one of them. She was hospital staff now.

Nurse Foxx took her to each Isolette and showed her each tiny baby, saying in a quick shorthand way, "This is Grant, PCP. This is Gonsalves, crack. This is Whiting, not drug related. 'Baby Doe' "—there was a space there, no Isolette—"mother left her in a Port-a-Potty, do you believe that? Perez, not drug related. O'Neil, crack. Riley, not drug related. Brown, PCP *and* crack. Cruz, crack." She tilted her head at Nettie Lee, lifting her brows high into her smooth forehead. "Crack, crack, crack. Get the picture?"

"Oh, yeah, I got it." What had happened to her grandbaby? Was she too late?

The nursery double doors bumped open. A large plastic box, one of the microwaves, was pushed by two women and a man in scrubs into the empty space in the middle of the horseshoe. "Baby Doe is back!" the redheaded nurse yelled. Immediately, the telephone on the desk rang.

"Okay, come on." Nurse Foxx waved for Nettie Lee to follow her. She walked over to the new Isolette.

"So what you want me to do with all these little babies?"

Nurse Foxx swung her head to the commotion, then back to Nettie Lee. "Okay, well, you just rock them, each one of them every day. Don't worry, though, there's another volunteer who works here too. That's Martha. So the two of you will split up the work." She looked around the nursery. "Where's Martha?"

From across the room the redheaded nurse yelled, "X-ray, Foxx!" and held up the telephone.

Nurse Foxx glanced briefly over her shoulder but continued to instruct Nettie Lee. "Then when you feel comfortable—" she began again, but was interrupted by the other nurse's yell.

"X-ray!"

She called, "*Okay!* I'll be right there," then turned back to Nettie Lee. "Like, there's other stuff for you to do. Like feed them. But I'll get into that later." She ran off in a squish of rubber-soled shoes, leaving Nettie Lee standing by her granddaughter's Isolette, wired up like Yolanda's stereo system.

The baby lay sleeping, her eyes tightly closed against the glare of lights. With her lashless, sunken eyes and black hair worn thin in spots, her face reminded Nettie Lee of a tired old man. A bit of clear tape fastened a tube to the side of her mouth. A feeding tube, just like Mr. Johns had said. Her chest was patched with stick-on leads for the heart monitor. She looked dry to Nettie Lee, dry and wrinkled as a tobacco leaf. If Nettie Lee could take her home she'd use some lotion on her. She'd squirt lotion into her own hands first, rub it till it was warm, then stroke it on that little dry back and on those thin arms and legs, but carefully—the baby's skin looked like it would crumble beneath her fingers.

Nettie Lee lightly tapped the plastic box with the pad of her index finger. "Don't you worry, Tookie," she said. "I'ma get you out of that contraption soon. All you need is a little love and some good food, and you be ready to go home in no time. Your gramma's going to give you everything you need. Just as soon as they train me how to hold a baby." She smiled at that. Nettie Lee Johnson needed to be taught how to hold a baby? Now *that* would be the day.

That same morning, Martha Howard felt depressed as she walked to the bus stop, her low-top Reeboks crunching into the cold glitter of snow. If she had looked out the window before leaving for the hospital, she would have seen that it had snowed the night before and that it now covered the ground and clung to the tree branches. Instead of going out in her sneakers, she would have put on her boots. The wind stung her face, forcing her head aside, shortening her breath into gasps. Hurrying her steps, she passed by houses that seemed all the same, small and brown, squat. They gave no indication of warmth, of who might live inside, of how one neighbor might be different from another. Though Martha had lived in the neighborhood for twenty-five years, she had never really talked to the others. She knew the layout of the houses, as if she had a topography map in her head. She knew what lay under the snow, where the Pringles' rosebushes had been heeled in, the spot where the Dunphys' crocuses would rise up in the spring, and she knew the two snowy, ragged balls by the Robinsons' front porch were sleeping junipers. Yet she didn't know the people inside. They were preoccupied with their own lives, steadying their children on two-wheelers, dashing off to Little

League games, or loading their cars for family camping trips. They did not have time to stop and talk to her, a childless fifty-year-old housewife.

Winter again. Dayton had stern, pitiless winters. Cars sat useless in the driveways, their engines frozen. To touch a doorknob bare-handed was to risk frostbite. So cold. Martha wouldn't be out in this messy weather herself if it were possible to stay home, but she felt her home was no more appealing than the icy street. Since she had retired from the library, filling her days had become a chore. And with the long stretch of days had come the surprising return of her memories of Paul. It was as if he had been waiting for her to slow down, that he might catch up. Sometimes she felt his weight in her arms, or across her breast; sometimes it was the wisp of his hair on her lips that touched her after all these years. She wondered if James—wherever he was—ever thought about Paul, if he ever missed his son. She put him out of her mind.

If Christmas came just once every five years, that would suit Martha fine. In the past she had liked to run around during Christmas season, finding presents for her parents, mailing off gifts to her cousins in West Virginia, remembering to give the paper boy an extra dollar (which he seemed to appreciate more than the cookies she'd handed him last year, though he had held the bill in his fingers and stared at it for a long moment before curling his lips and saying flatly, "Yo, thanks"). Over the last few years she had let the holiday celebrations peter out. Now, only the paper boy expected a gift from her.

She had been sad last Christmas when she realized that her life was dwindling down to nothing; no one needed her anymore. She had her TV shows, *Search for Tomorrow, The Guiding Light, Love of Life,* the ones she'd watched for years. She'd tried watching *The Young and the Restless,* but the people on it were *too* young. They had problems she didn't care about anymore, like if your husband was cheating with his secretary or how to tell your boyfriend you were pregnant. Pregnant! She turned her mouth down. After she retired, staying home and watching her shows satisfied her for a while, then she started feeling antsy, restless. Maybe *useless* was the word she was looking for. No, that wasn't it. Frightened. That was it. She was afraid of everything.

When the bus, sooty and exhaling black smoke, trundled to a stop, Martha stepped up. Only a few other passengers sat inside, disgruntled people on their way to work. Martha sat near the back to avoid the blast of cold air that blew in when the driver opened the doors. The plastic seats were old and ripped, but warm air hissed out of the register by her feet. She untied her scarf and laid it on her lap, pushed her hand through her short gray-brown hair. James had given her the scarf twenty-three years before, and now the indistinct paisley had faded to a rusty brown. She drew a finger over the curves and swirls, trying to trace the pattern, to follow it from one corner, across the silky fabric, to the other corner. She thought about the day James had given it to her.

They were fly-fishing on the Olentangy River, on a mild and breezy river day, not too hot, perfect weather for Martha, who was eight months pregnant. They'd brought along James's sister's six-year-old twin girls, Denise and Shabrice. Although the girls loved picnics, they had no interest in fish and spent the afternoon picking wildflowers on the riverbank.

James stood thigh-deep in the middle of the river, in waders and boots, fly rod raised over his head. He was bare-chested, strong. His hair was hidden beneath a khaki hat that had a strip of lamb's wool at the crown, in which he had lodged his woollybuggers and crickets. He worked the fly rod forward and back, playing out the heavy line in lazy, slow-motion arcs. Martha sat on the bank, her back against a rock, fishing with worms but mostly watching James and rehearsing aloud names for their baby. She felt the baby needed an important name.

"Call him W.E.B. Booker T. Martin Luther Garvey, Jr. X," James offered over his shoulder. He was seven years younger than Martha, and playful.

Martha laughed. "Sure, James." She reeled in her line and propped her rod against a tree, then called the girls for lunch.

They were pretty girls, with dark eyes and frizzy hair their mother had plaited into thick, long braids. They liked James. He made them giggle.

For the picnic, Martha had made fried chicken, James's favorite. She usually saved it for Sunday dinner, but the picnic was a special occasion. Although James was always home when he wasn't working, it seemed as if he was always at work. They rarely had a chance to leave the house together. During the day, James was assistant manager at the Hasty Tasty restaurant on Germantown Pike. In the evenings, he was the night janitor at South Euclid High. He'd come home after eleven and crawl into bed behind her, gently snaking his body to fit hers. She would feel his hand, large and cool, smooth gently across her shoulder, her breast, then cup her stomach, pulling her hips against him, letting her feel his solid thighs, the weight of his arm.

He would talk to her before he fell asleep. Most times she would murmur or sigh but wouldn't fully wake up. She had heard most of it before, his need to hash out his day. "I got me a job for a boy, not a man. All day long it's throw out them trash boxes, all night long it's mop the bathroom floor. I'm telling you, Marth, I ain't being treated in no kind of respectful way. And let somebody know I went to Vietnam, and they all over my case like I done something wrong, the brothers *and* the ofays—same story. Brothers say, 'Man, you sold out to whitey. You some kind of oreo motherfucker.' Then the white boys say, 'You over there fighting for the establishment, man, the military-industrial complex.' He would sigh against the back of her neck, his words warm, sleepy. "I must be some kind of stupid fool." She would murmur, no, what he was, it seemed to her, was patriotic, and besides, he got drafted. What did he think he was going to do, decline Uncle Sam's invitation? Then she would wish he would go to sleep. She was tired with this baby. She would move his arm lower, so it rested on her hipbone, taking the pressure off her stomach. She'd feel the acid recede down her esophagus. "Am I waking you up?" She'd murmur no. "You know why I love you?" he'd ask, rubbing his hand across her belly. "Because you smart like a schoolteacher.

Maybe you going to teach me a few things." She'd turn to face him, telling him to go to sleep.

James sat across the blanket from the girls, plate on his lap, Martha leaning against him for support. Each girl held a chicken drumstick in her fist, attempting to eat it slowly, politely, as their mother had taught, but too hungry for that. James cocked his head to one side, grinning.

"Do you like old dead chicken?" he asked them, bending his arms into wings.

They giggled behind their hands.

"I like old dead chicken," he confided to them, flapping. "Do you like old dead chicken?" He twisted around to Martha, to see if she was laughing too. She was.

"James, I think you're silly," she said. "Don't you, girls?"

"Yeah," Denise said. She was the outspoken twin. "You make a goofy uncle."

Later in the afternoon, Martha lay on her back, on James's army blanket, looking through tree branches to the sky. High in the top branches of an oak, where the air current was stronger, a bird's nest swayed with the breeze, worrying her. She heard soft, slow footsteps on the dry grass. She dropped her eyes from the nest to find James standing beside her, carrying his tackle box, waders dripping over her belly.

"So what's happening under the Big Top?" He squatted down, laying his hand on her stomach. "Thinking of more names?"

She placed her hand on top of his and pressed it against her.

"What do you want his name to be?" she asked. "Seriously."

"Paul."

"Your father's name."

He smiled and opened the tackle box. Inside, a flower wrapped in a red paisley scarf lay upon rows and rows of spiny black flies. He unwrapped it—a Double Delight rose from their garden at home, its center deep white, the petals edged with crimson—and placed the scarf around Martha's neck, pulling her thick brown hair around her shoulders. Martha closed her fingers around the stem, painfully pressing her thumb into a thorn. Though it embedded itself deeply into her thumb pad, below the surface of her skin, she did not tell James about stabbing herself, but later, while he napped on the blanket, she dug the sharp kernel out of her thumb with his knife.

Martha brought her thumb to her mouth and frowned as she looked out the grimy bus window, realizing she was halfway to the hospital and had not yet prepared herself. Every morning when she rode to the hospital she followed a ritual to keep the babies safe. She would picture each baby, thin, fragile, lying on its side in the Isolette, and imagined laying her hand on the plastic top, whispering, "I'm here." As she said this, the Isolette emitted a protective golden light, enveloping the baby within. She would float to each baby, laying her hand upon them. First Cruz, then the glow; then Gonsalves, then the glow; then Baby Doe—she stopped. *I wish they'd give that baby a name.*

She remembered the morning the baby was pushed into the neonatal intensive care nursery on a short metal table, besieged by five people in blue scrubs, their hair shoved up into tidy caps, their faces half covered by masks. One of the five attached a small black bag to the breathing tube protruding from the baby's mouth and began squeezing it between his thumb and middle finger with a supreme daintiness. Her small chest, a fret of ribs, expanded and collapsed with each squeeze. Watching, Martha had felt the labor of her own breathing.

In the scrub room, a small cluttered wash area just outside the neonatal intensive care nursery, Martha scrubbed her hands with Betadine and a hard plastic brush. During her training two months before, one of the nurses had told her to be careful; the thick red disinfectant would stain everything it touched. She dried her hands, then slipped a yellow surgical gown over her clothes, leaving the ties dangling in back. Her sneakers squished with melted snow as she walked to the nursery.

She hesitated outside the nursery's automatic double doors, afraid to go in. Perhaps, as she held one of the babies in her arms, his life might slowly leak out and she would not notice until he was drained. After Paul, she didn't know if she could watch a baby die.

Swallowing back her fear, Martha pushed through the doors. Beneath the glare of fluorescent lights, thirteen Isolettes ringed the room in a horseshoe. Martha squinted against the light. Each Isolette unit was self-contained, with a heart monitor, piped-in gases, an IV alarm, and other equipment hooked to its side. On a tray beneath each Isolette lay a small black rubber resuscitation bag, through which oxygen hissed continuously. The nursery was noisy. Each time a baby's heart beat, a monitor beeped in response. Every time a drop of fluid from an IV bottle entered a baby's vein, a monitor beeped in acknowledgment. The entire back wall was glass, a viewing wall for the babies' relatives. The wall faced a long hall, with access limited to the babies' family members, who wore stick-on identification tags on their clothes. There was no need for them to wear scrubs unless they came into the nursery. The ceiling was tall, and high up on the right wall a set of five windows faced the street. Behind the left wall was the supply room and the conference room.

The NIC nursery reminded Martha of a stage set for a play, where the furniture was larger than life and the glare of light burned out even the tiniest shadows. She pulled the clipboard from its hook on the wall and read the feeding schedule. It looked as if she would be rocking and feeding seven babies today. The other six would have to be handled by the nurses.

In the late morning, when she came back from her break, the nursery was crowded. Two families were visiting their babies. Bowen's mother, her hand inside an Isolette porthole, was trying to get an orange stuffed dog to sit upright in the corner. Martha heard her tell the nurse that she had worn the dog inside her brassiere all night, so Bowen would smell it and think she was there even when she wasn't. The other family was the Perezes. They still hadn't decided on a first name for their baby. The father, a short, stocky man with a full black mustache and a Reds baseball cap, sat in a large rocker. He had refused Martha's advice about how to wrap the baby and loosened the baby's blankets after she had tightened them. Mrs. Perez went into the nurses' conference room to pump her breasts.

Looking around the nursery, checking that each baby was still there, had not died during the night, Martha was surprised to find someone sitting in *her* rocker. The woman held Riley, red-faced and fussy as she rocked her to sleep. She was a big fat woman, Martha thought. Her hips bulged through the rocker's spindles. Her legs were stuffed into beige stockings too light for her skin color. Martha couldn't understand women who didn't care if their stockings looked like sausage casings. When she saw Martha, the woman's eyes widened a bit, but she didn't get up.

"Come on over here, girl," she said. Her dark hand, waving Martha over, seemed laden with such a proprietary conceit that Martha immediately felt balky, like a child.

Martha pretended to look around for a chair—a silly act, she knew, but what else could she do, tell the woman to get up?

"The nurse said she's going to get another rocker in here. She's just waiting on you to get back. I'm Nettie Lee. They told me about you. You the other grandma, ain't you?"

The other grandma? "Yes, I'm the volunteer grandmother in the nursery." Martha sighed. This woman must have answered the ad in the paper. "I can get myself a chair, thanks." She had thought she would be the only grandmother; it hadn't occurred to her that other people might be alone and want to help out. Maybe she would find another rocker in the supply room.

Debbie Foxx walked over to the worktable and dropped a wet Pampers on the scale. She stood looking at Nettie Lee, then looked quickly back to Martha. "I forgot to tell you something, Martha," she said. "You've just been promoted to Head Volunteer Grandmother." She smiled softly. "At double the pay."

Nettie Lee laughed. "Two times nothin' is still nothin'."

Martha's face felt warm. She didn't even want her to make a joke. She turned toward the woman, feeling foolishly furious. "I don't work here for money," she said. "Money's not important to me." Though that wasn't exactly what she wanted to say. It was more like *Get out of here. Let me be their grandmother in peace.* Two doctors, one male, one female, and a very young woman with a ponytail were talking over Isolette number 6. Bowen's. They looked up. She lowered her voice but still felt upset. "I rock these babies because I know they need me." The woman opened her mouth to speak. "And don't miss my point. I don't have a lot of money. And I don't think it's the be-all and end-all to life." Money? Why was she talking about money? Nurse Foxx must think she was a fool. And the other people were looking at her.

"Okay," Foxx said. "That's clear." She leaned in closer to Martha, her gray eyes direct. "Terese Czajwolski called this morning to let us know we got ourselves another grandmother. Her name is Nettie Lee Johnson." She glanced at the woman, then raised her voice slightly to include her in their conversation. "I want you to show Nettie Lee how we do things here." She looked around the nursery. "I can't do it all. And Mary Pangalangan is out sick today. Got a stomach flu. Got it bad, too." She shook her head. "If either of you ever gets sick, stay away! All we need is for some infection to go rip-roaring through here. I was waiting for you to get back from break to show Nettie Lee how to wrap and hold the babies. It's a little early, but you can get started on the twelve o'clocks."

As Martha turned to get the disposable cylinders out of the cabinet under the sink, Foxx touched her shoulder, and some of the tightness left her chest. She told herself to calm down, the woman didn't mean any harm, and she was looking like a foolish old lady. Foxx looked away, preparing to run off to her next task, but she turned back instead and said, "One more thing, Martha. A new baby came in last night. Got some sort of viral infection, they think. Anyway, the baby is in Isolette nine and we're keeping her isolated for now, so you don't have to rock her." The intercom from the doctors' conference room interrupted: *Foxx, rounds consult.* Foxx checked the numbers on the scale and wrote in her chart. "Sure, sure," she said. "I'm coming."

Another grandmother. It wasn't that Martha didn't like Nettie

Lee. Martha couldn't dislike someone she didn't know; she just wanted to rock the babies in peace. Her time with the babies was the only time she really had to be herself. During the day, as she cleaned the house, washed clothes, or watched TV, she felt like she was seeing herself from a couple of steps away, somewhere off to the side. She never lost herself in what she was doing. She always gauged the impression she was making on people, how they perceived her, what they thought of her. Her reaction to working here had surprised her; she found that when she was looking at one of these babies, she forgot herself. Now all that had to change. This woman would expect her to pass the time gossiping, like women do, talking trash about men, home life, children, all things Martha had no interest in discussing. Rocking the babies was her new career. She was a professional grandmother; she was not like this woman.

Rather than dig up another rocker in the supply room, she dragged an orange plastic chair from behind the nurses' desk to the middle Isolette in the semicircle. She'd sit by Baby Doe, and Nettie Lee could do as she pleased. It was only eleven-thirty. If Nettie Lee was so smart, she could figure out how to bundle up and hold the babies until time for the twelve o'clock feedings.

She felt sorry for this baby with no last name. No one knew who her parents were, though the mother was assumed to be a crack addict who delivered her in her sixth month of pregnancy. Since the baby had come into the nursery, Martha had dreamed about her every night: horrible dreams about a mutant baby without a heart, sprawled against a spider's web. In the dream she was paid to free the baby by a skinny woman, hidden in the shadows: the mother, she thought. And there was an urgency to freeing the baby, before the mother changed her mind, snatched the baby away. But each time Martha pulled one of the baby's fingers from the sticky web, one of her own fingers stuck, over and over, until she had replaced the baby within the web. The dream ended with Martha suspended, naked and caught. She couldn't say why the baby gave her nightmares. As she went over the dream in the mornings, she came to the conclusion that the mother was trying to give her a message, to tell her to take the baby home with her. To adopt her.

She stood at the Isolette and unclipped the porthole cover, then slid her hand through. Hot, antiseptic-smelling air drifted out. Pushing her arm in farther, jamming her scrub gown sleeve against the porthole, Martha quickly plugged the leak. Baby Doe was actually a pretty baby, though still covered with dark lanugo hair. Martha liked to stroke her soft furry shoulders and the black monkey hair on her head. A small bandage covered the incision on her upper chest from the cardiac catheterization surgery, performed because of what the doctors called a heart lesion. Foxx had explained it to Martha: The baby's heart vessels were switched. The blood from her lungs was pumped to her heart, then out the wrong artery, and sent right back to her lungs. At the same time, most of the used blood from the baby's body was pumped back out to her body, never going to her lungs for fresh oxygen. Her heart was made backward. Foxx said that while the baby's blood was recirculating that way, her internal organs didn't get the oxygen supply they needed, and her lungs were getting congested. She explained to Martha that the baby had survived because of a special opening in the heart fetuses have before they are born, which mixes blood from both sides of the heart. The opening closed up at birth, but the doctors had made an incision in her chest and reopened it three days after she was born. When the baby got big enough, they would connect the arteries to the proper heart chambers. It seemed to make sense, Martha had thought after Foxx had explained. The baby appeared to be doing all right for now. She touched her dry cheek, pulled a bit of chapped skin from her lips. Poor Baby Doe, she thought. She was a fetus without a mother.

Foxx had told Martha not to feed her; the baby was *npo*—nothing by mouth—because she had spit up her midnight feeding, but they would try her on a nipple again later in the day. Cautiously, Martha slipped one of her fingers onto the baby's palm and, like a small moist flower whose petals close at night, Baby Doe's fingers curled around hers. She studied the transparent hand, the purple tracery of blood vessels, the cell-by-cell pattern of the skin. The see-through nails, thin as razor blades, made her heart ache. She thought she felt a tingle in her breasts, as if they were filling with milk.

Nettie Lee poked her head over Martha's shoulder, smelling stale like some kind of greasy food Martha couldn't quite name. She held her breath against the odor, as Nettie Lee pressed up against her, pushing her large breasts onto Martha's back. They felt soft and loose, like worn-out sofa cushions.

"This little child don't look like she can make another day." Nettie Lee sighed. "Look how her chest is seesawing up and down when she breathes." She poked her face inches from the plastic lid. "Do they know who her mother is?"

"No." Martha turned to look at her, her arm still in the Isolette port. "That was a crazy thing to do, to leave the baby in a toilet. They need to catch that woman and put her away for life."

"Well, there could be some *extenuating* circumstances."

"I can't believe that. There's nothing in this world that could make a person in their right mind throw a baby away." She turned back to the Isolette and felt Nettie Lee lean closer.

"Maybe the girl wasn't in her right mind when she *did* it." Her voice was almost a whisper.

"Well, then she needs a psychiatrist. And her baby needs to be put in a home where people can love her. It's too bad there's not a law to sterilize these women on drugs. They don't have any business having babies. The state ends up taking care of them. And the worst part is these girls make all black people look bad. You know, they get people thinking we all carry on like that, like we don't have good sense." Did she really believe that? Talking to people was a strain. She found herself taking on extreme views, sounding angry, when what she really felt was fear and the possibility of being misunderstood. She knew her insecurity led her to overstate.

Nettie Lee backed away. "Well, seems like this baby is tired. Maybe you ought to stop patting her and let her go to sleep. She looks like she's too sick to be bothered anyway." She cut her eyes from Baby Doe to Martha, and stepped away from the Isolette.

"I do as I please," Martha told her, then withdrew her finger from the baby's palm and shut the porthole. She looked into Nettie Lee's eyes. The whites were flecked with brown spots and reminded her of old hard-boiled eggs. She immediately felt sorry for her unkindness. After all, what harm could Nettie Lee do her, sitting in a rocker, putting a baby to sleep? Maybe she would keep Martha company on the long, draggy afternoons when all she did was rock.

"Honey, it looks to me like you don't know *what* you doing. Now don't be taking offense—none intended—but everybody knows a baby got to get some rest if it's going to grow. You don't have to look that up in a book." Nettie Lee looked back into the Isolette. "You sure better leave *this* baby alone." She turned and walked back to the rocker. Martha watched the side-to-side shift of her hips and the careful way she eased herself down.

"Martha." Debbie Foxx called to her from Cruz's Isolette, where she stood with Dr. Xiang, a female first-year resident, and the doctor's group of medical students. "Mrs. Perez needs to pump her breasts for the twelve o'clock feeding. Would you show her and Nettie Lee how to work the pump?"

"Yes, Nurse Foxx."

Mr. Perez still sat in the rocker, singing to his baby. Martha remembered Mrs. Perez was already in the conference room where the mothers pumped.

Martha followed Nettie Lee into the room and shut the door.

Mrs. Perez sat at the head of the table, hugging her arms to her chest. Here they were, two strangers about to ask the young woman to take off her blouse, expose her breasts. Could Martha have done this at Mrs. Perez's age? She must be in her early twenties.

"Hello, Mrs. Perez," Martha said, trying to sound brisk. "It's really pretty simple." She carried the breast pump from the counter along the wall and set it on the conference table. From a cabinet under the counter, she took out a towel, a funnel, a plastic jar, and a small milk cylinder. She set these on the table too. Turning to Nettie Lee, she said, "You saw where we keep all the equipment?"

Nettie Lee stood behind Mrs. Perez. "Yeah, I saw."

"What you're going to do is place this funnel up against your breast," Martha said to Mrs. Perez, quickly but calmly. "Then I'll flip on the pump and you'll feel it working. It feels like—oh, I don't know. . . ."

"Like a vacuum cleaner?" Mrs. Perez asked, crossing her arms tighter.

"No, no. Not like a vacuum cleaner." She realized how frightened the woman was. Picking up the funnel, she told her, "With a vacuum cleaner, the sucking is continuous. This is more rhythmic, and it doesn't hurt. You'll see." She looked up at Nettie Lee, who stood with her arms folded across her chest, an amused look on her face. Martha felt there really wasn't much to smirk about. "Okay, you help Mrs. Perez get ready."

"Pick up your blouse, honey." Nettie Lee pointed to Mrs. Perez's breasts, hidden beneath her arms. "Mmmm, you don't have buttons on that thing, do you?"

Martha lifted the bottom of Mrs. Perez's blouse while she sat motionless. The blouse was gauzy and loose, with flowing sleeves. Very pretty. "You could just lift the blouse enough to expose one breast. It'll pretty much cover you, if you're modest," Martha said.

"Which one?" Mrs. Perez asked in a small voice.

"It doesn't matter. You'll pump both. Have you been expressing at home?"

Mrs. Perez nodded. "A little. I'm not so good at it, and it kind of hurts."

No one had said that before. "Yes, I know that's true," Martha lied. "You'll find this pump is less traumatic than those smaller ones you buy at the grocery, and you can build up a better milk supply with this one, while your baby's here, than you can with the small pumps or by manual expression. Which breast did you express last?"

"The left one." She lowered her arms, held her hands in her lap.

"Then let's start with the left one." Martha turned to Nettie Lee. "You want to alternate the breast they start with each time. In case there's any difference in the length of time they pump, it'll even out."

Nettie Lee nodded. "Okay, honey, pick up your blouse now, and we'll get started, so that hungry baby of yours can get his food."

Mrs. Perez carefully lifted the flowered material over her left breast just enough to show the nipple. Martha handed her the funnel and cup, attached to a plastic tube that ran to the pump. "Press it on your nipple and get a good seal. Okay, I'm turning it on." The motor began humming. The hum gathered into a sucking sound, then a plop of release. Mrs. Perez watched the funnel grab and release her breast. A stream of milk trickled into the cup. Martha felt a small lift of success.

They were interrupted by the conference room door opening. A tall, bony young woman Martha hadn't seen before walked in. She was long-haired, dressed in jeans and a striped oxford shirt. "Hey," she said, going to the counter and picking up the other pump. She grabbed a plastic funnel and cup from the cabinet. Sitting at the table, she connected the pump and unbuttoned her shirt, flipping her hair across one shoulder. The pump began to hum as she pressed the funnel to her breast. "My baby came in last night because she wasn't doing too good. She's a week old. I used this thing last night." The machine plopped, and milk spilled into the cup. Mrs. Perez watched in silence.

"What's your little baby's name?" Martha asked. The baby must be the one in isolation.

"Dawn Mooney." The milk stopped filling the cup. The mother jiggled the funnel against her breast.

"Here, you've got a kink in the tubing." Martha ran the long tube that connected the funnel to the motor between her fingers, straightening out the loops. She felt the vacuum action tense the tube, then release it. To Nettie Lee she said, "You want to make sure the tubes aren't obstructed. That way you know the pump is working at full capability." She turned to the woman. "Press the funnel against you, tighter."

"It feels tight enough to me." She dropped her eyes to the cup, watched it fill, then screwed on another and pressed the funnel to her other breast. "It's a trip, isn't it?" she said to Mrs. Perez, whose cup still contained only a small sprinkle of milk.

Martha had the sensation of being a voyeur, fascinated at the ease with which Mrs. Mooney could release her milk into containers. Across the table, Mrs. Perez seemed to be closing in on herself, getting smaller in her chair. "Sit up straight," Martha advised her. "Good posture lets the milk flow." She wasn't sure about that, but it wouldn't hurt.

When she finished filling two cups, Mrs. Mooney handed them, warm and brimming, to Martha. "The nurse out there said to give these to you and tell you to freeze them. My baby can't take anything by mouth because she's on an IV for now. You don't have to put my name on it or anything. It's donor milk. Whoever needs it can have it."

Martha poured the milk from the cups into two four-ounce plastic bags, closing them with a piece of tape. Leaving Nettie Lee to finish up with Mrs. Perez, she took the bags to the supply room and opened the lid on the freezer chest. Cold mist swirled around the frozen plastic bags of breast milk, stacked like bluish ice cubes. She placed the two warm bags inside and closed the lid.

Back in the conference room, Mrs. Mooney had left, and Nettie Lee and Mrs. Perez sat studying the funnel and cup.

"Only an ounce of milk," Mrs. Perez said, dejection making her voice sad. "And that includes pumping both breasts."

"Don't worry about it," Martha told her. "When your milk gets in good you'll be pumping out plenty."

Mrs. Perez stood up and adjusted her blouse. "When will I have to do this again?"

"Every three hours is good," Martha said. Then she added, "You probably need to get yourself a pump at home, so you can build up your supply."

"That pump is too expensive!" Nettie Lee said. "You think this little girl is made out of money?"

Martha ignored her. "What you do is, call the Milk Club. They rent you a pump for not too much, maybe a few dollars a month, and if you can't afford that they might not charge you anything. You want their phone number?"

Mrs. Perez seemed noncommittal, walked toward the door. Martha supposed she wasn't interested.

"Well, pump or express that milk every three hours if you want to increase the supply." She felt a little dispirited herself. The pumping had not gone well, though sometimes, she supposed, it wouldn't.

When they were alone in the conference room, putting away the pumps, Nettie Lee said, "What are they going to think up next? I think it's all right for the mamas to express their milk by hand, and I know it's faster to use a pump and such. But, personally, *I* don't trust a machine that can milk you just like a cow. And as far as donor breast milk goes, I just don't trust something that's been in somebody else's body before I swallow it."

Martha felt herself frown. "Well, some mothers might object, but I haven't met one yet." She began to collect the cups and funnels, when she heard the door open.

Ethel Xiang, the resident, leaned into the room without actually stepping over the threshold. She was very young and pretty, though a large pair of glasses with flesh-colored frames covered a good deal of her face. Martha thought she was too young to have all her worries, the responsibility for all the babies' lives. All day and, Martha knew, most of the night, Dr. Xiang walked from baby to baby in the nursery, her enormous black notebook stuffed with frayed papers weighing down her lab coat pocket, giving her a sideways list. In the middle of rounds or during the weekly nurses' meeting, she was likely to pull out the notebook and flip through it, searching, Martha thought, for the correct answer to a baby's woefully complex problems. Martha had watched her at Report but had never had a reason to speak to her.

"You are the grandmother?" Dr. Xiang's delicate question hung in the air.

Martha turned to face her. "May I help you, Doctor?"

"Nurse Foxx says you will assist me with a baby?" Dr. Xiang's glasses flashed briefly at Martha.

"Yes, Doctor. I'm coming right now."

"Baby Doe will need to transfer to a warming tray. You can help with the equipment?"

"Well, I'm not really supposed to do that kind of thing." Martha didn't quite know how to explain it to her. Dr. Xiang fully entered the room, standing close to Martha at the sink.

"What do you mean?" She seemed perplexed.

"I mean, I rock babies and feed them, but if you need someone to do medical things, then I can't." Martha ran warm water over the cups, rinsing off the breast milk. She didn't really want to touch the machines out there. They scared her. So many buttons and alarms that went off if you bumped them.

"This isn't a medical procedure. You just assist, like another set of hands, you know?" Dr. Xiang's voice rose impatiently, annoyed with the effort of explaining. "I'll tell you everything you need to know as we go. Step one, step two."

"Well, they tell me I can't do but what they have outlined for the Grandmother program in their procedure book."

"What you need, Dr. Xiang? I can do it." Nettie Lee put down a pump and walked toward the door. "Just let me wash up."

"You need to go feed Gonsalves." Martha's face turned warm.

"Gonsalves ain't going nowhere." She looked at Martha, raised her eyebrows slightly, let her eyes linger on her face. "You can feed him yourself. Looks like what the doctor wants to do is more important."

Dr. Xiang said, "I am busy, no nurses to help me. I need help at the Isolette. No medical procedures involved. One of you grandmothers be there, please." She left the room.

Nettie Lee wiped her hands against her hips, as if she had been washing up the equipment instead of Martha. "Well, I'm going."

Martha grabbed Nettie Lee's arm as she passed, squeezed the

soft flesh tightly. She felt slightly dizzy. "Look, are you crazy?" she whispered furiously. "First of all, I don't care what the doctor asks you to do, we go by the procedure manual. And second, you do what *I* tell you, because I'm your supervisor. Not the other way around."

Nettie Lee's voice was loud. "Well, honey, it sounds to me like Nurse Foxx said she wants a grandmother doing the job for Dr. Xiang, so that's what I'm going to do right now."

Martha watched Nettie Lee turn from her. Her chest shaking with anger, she gripped Nettie Lee's arm more tightly.

Debbie Foxx opened the conference room door. Nettie Lee looked at Martha, then down at her arm, and snatched it away.

Foxx said cautiously, "Hey, ladies, I found out Dr. Xiang wants to transfer Baby Doe to a warming tray. It'll be easier to work on her that way. We've got one available now, sent over from University Hospital. So I'm going to help with the transfer later. Um, you guys continue with the feeding schedule, okay?"

"Yeah. I'm going to feed Gonsalves right now. What you planning on doing, Martha?"

Martha blew air out of her lips and studied the pumps on the table. She hadn't wanted to work with anyone, and this was why. Co-workers, friends, even husbands, eventually made demands, wanted their way, always. "After I clean this up, I'll feed O'Neil and Cruz."

"Okay," Foxx said slowly, watching both of them. "That sounds fine."

Martha pulled another rocker next to her old familiar one. She and Nettie Lee sat feeding the babies in Isolettes 5 and 8. Martha held Cruz, a chubby four-and-a-half-pound beauty, and Nettie Lee caressed Gonsalves, a few ounces shy of four pounds. Martha couldn't think about the babies' weight in grams, the nursery's standard measurement. She couldn't grasp what a baby at twelve hundred grams looked like, compared to a baby who weighed fourteen hundred grams. The numbers were meaningless. So she just thought of the babies in half-pound weights. She fed Cruz from a cylinder of soy milk, inserting the nipple into his mouth and rocking. Cruz's lips worked against the nipple, pulling out milk. Three feet away, Nettie Lee held Gonsalves against her breast and hummed.

Martha slid her hips sideways in the new rocker Foxx had dragged out of the supply room. She tried to cushion them against the hard wood, but when she sat up straight to relieve the pressure on her tailbone, her feet dangled an inch from the floor.

"You got one of them Papa Rockers," Nettie Lee said. "You know, the kind they make so the daddy can rock his baby sometime." She shook her head. "Don't much of that papa rocking happen at my house. I raise my grandbaby myself. I got Little Barn at home with me, and ain't a daddy in sight. A mama either." She tightened the blanket around Gonsalves. "How many grandbabies you got?"

"None." Martha held the soy milk cylinder up to the light and squinted at the tiny cubic centimeter hash marks inked on the side. They were too small to read, unless she got her glasses out of her purse. That was one reason why she had left her job at the library. All the small print she'd had to read had weakened her eyes. When they switched from the card catalog system to MYSTIC, the new computer screens gave her a headache. She wasn't meant for the computer age anyway. Maybe her time, the era in which she felt comfortable, was over. She slanted the cylinder toward the light.

"He about half through with it," Nettie Lee offered.

"I think I can read." Martha placed the nipple back in Cruz's mouth, feeling her anger rise again. She did not need anyone, especially some stranger, to come in here and tell her how to care for a baby. She'd had her own baby once, though she hadn't done such a good job of keeping him safe.

Martha heard Nettie Lee murmuring steadily to Gonsalves and realized she was telling him a story.

"Know how it ended up that women do all the scut work? Well, I'm going to tell you." Nettie Lee adjusted her hips in the chair and pushed the baby up higher to rest against the mountains beneath her scrub gown. "The story goes like this: After the world was in place, Saint Peter sent a special delivery to John and Mary, and set it down in the middle of the floor. And that's where it stayed. The husband didn't pick it up. The son left it laying, and the daughter just shut her eyes every time she had to pass by it. Finally, the husband's curiosity got the better of him and he started wondering what was in that special delivery box. He tells his wife, 'I know John's woman down the road don't leave no boxes in the middle of the floor. She opens them up first thing. Why don't you do likewise?' The wife says to her husband, 'That old nasty woman? Huh! She can't do nothing I can't.' The wife rips the box open and finds a lifetime of hard work inside. She got up to help her husband and she ain't sat down since." Nettie Lee pushed her head against the rocker back. An expectant silence sprang up around her.

Martha closed her eyes. Another battle of the sexes story. She felt her disdain for Nettie Lee rising. "What kind of story is that to tell a baby? And that's not even how it goes." It was an old folktale; her mother had told it to her when she was little, and she felt it should at least be told right. She pressed Cruz closer and rocked.

"All right, listen to this: Saint Peter sent down two big strong angels with a heavy box from Heaven, to be delivered directly to John and Mary's house. After they flew off, Mary jumped on the box and said 'Me first!' Being a gentleman, John deferred to his bride. Mary ripped the box open and found two key rings. The big ring with fifty or sixty silver keys flashing caught Mary's attention. She chunked it in her pocket. John took the leftover ring: one solitary gold key. He spent the next fifty years sticking his key into every opening, trying to see where it would fit, but he didn't have any luck."

She looked at Nettie Lee, whose head still rested against the rocker back, her eyes focused on the ceiling.

"Mary was more judicious," Martha continued. "She asked herself, 'Now, what sorts of things is it wise to keep under lock and key?' She decided it was gold and silver Saint Peter meant for her to find."

Nettie Lee chuckled and rocked Gonsalves faster.

"After looking all around the house, Mary found a hidden door and used her keys. One after another, she tried them and found they all fit the lock. It was clear to her: whatever was behind the locked door, she was meant to have it. She turned the knob. Inside, she found John and a passle of babies. She took up her burden in disappointment."

Nettie Lee stopped rocking and lifted her head. "Girl, you sure do know what you talking about. We the mule of the world." Gonsalves wrinkled his face in irritation at the sudden movement.

"I didn't say we're the mule of the world," Martha said. "I'm just telling you how the folktale should be told."

"Then you don't believe anything you just said? You believe everything between men and women is hunky-dory?" Her sarcasm stung Martha. Of course she didn't think everything was fine.

"There are problems, of course. I guess I just want to put the blame where it belongs."

"On the victim."

"No, not on the victim. But ask yourself why are there so many victims? This whole victim idea is like poor black folks storming around complaining about whose fault it is they don't have jobs. What are they waiting for, a personal invitation from President Bush to come to Washington and work for him? He'll send his limo every morning? The way I see it, the problem with black people today is they all have their eyes turned backward toward slavery and they can't see their own part in the pitiful way they live. They think it's always somebody else's fault."

"Well, ain't it?" Nettie Lee rocked placidly. "I sure wouldn't live like I do if it was up to me. So it must not be up to me." She slowed her rocker. "And excuse me, honey, but I don't live 'pitiful.' "

Cruz had fallen asleep with the nipple still in his mouth. A thin trail of milk seeped from the corner of his lips and made dark stains on Martha's scrub gown. She sat him up and burped him. He raised his eyebrows in surprise but kept his eyes closed against the light.

"Didn't you ever think you could do something about your situation?" Martha wasn't sure what Nettie Lee's situation was, but she'd seen it enough times: a drunk husband, mice in the kitchen, and squalling children in yellow underpants.

"Are you telling me to go out and get a job?" Nettie Lee looked up now, tilted her head toward Martha, eyes skeptically widened. "Honey, I worked all my life. I'm retired."

Debbie Foxx padded by in thick-soled white shoes. "Martha, would you feed Doe, too? She did okay with the nipple at ten. Just go slow with her. I'm showing Mrs. Baker how to hold her baby. He came in last night." She nodded toward the woman with the ponytail, who nervously patted the top of her son's incubator, as if she hoped he could feel her hand through the plastic.

Martha got up from her chair to put Cruz back in his Isolette. She felt conversations like this one were pointless. She hardly expected Nettie Lee to agree with her. Nettie Lee was the kind of person who thought the middle class had sold out to white society, as if the desire to live a comfortable life, to get along with people, was betraying your race. It was just too easy to say black men were treated like niggers and black women were the mules of the world. That wasn't real to her. Nobody talked to Martha about real things. People looked at her and thought she didn't matter. Or they looked at her and saw an opportunity to vent their opinions. When people looked at her, all they saw was an audience.

"Well, honey, I don't agree with you." Nettie Lee started up from the rocker. "I can feed little Too—I mean *Doe.* Just let me put Gonsalves back in the bed."

A spike of irritation rose in Martha. She quickly raised the hood on Cruz's Isolette. "You go ahead and rock Gonsalves. I'll take care of the Doe baby. She's not sturdy enough for you to rock." Where did this woman get her nerve, her confidence that she was up to anything asked of her? Amazing.

Martha looked at the Doe baby's Isolette. She couldn't see inside through the glare of the lights on the hood. *Faith,* Martha decided. *Her name is Faith. I'll take care of Faith.*

"Oh, wait a minute." Foxx swung by. "Let me change Doe first." She took a Pampers from the pile on the worktable, weighed it on the scale, then marked the weight on the back of the diaper. Martha knew that when the diaper came off, it would be weighed again. "Got to keep track of that fluid," Foxx said. When she was finished, she closed the hood and bent down to the lower cabinets under the sink, pulling out milk cylinders and nipples.

Martha gently unclipped the monitor leads from Faith's chest. She wrapped the baby loosely in two thermal blankets and lifted her out of the Isolette, feeling the weight of the baby's head and behind in her hands. Martha headed for the big rocker, Faith cupped against her breast. After she sat in the rocker, Foxx handed her a fresh cylinder of soy milk with a red nipple screwed on top.

Foxx started to pad off but stopped. "I meant to tell you: this morning, about five? Doe started those apneic episodes again. Boy, she really worries me, but she came around after they flicked her feet." She screwed up her eyes. "You know how to do that, right? Okay, listen. If she stops breathing, just tap the soles of her feet. Like this." She flicked the air with her fingers. "You can do it, it's not hard. Just pay real close attention, okay? And call me if you think she looks funny for any reason." She hurried away. "Mrs. Baker, let me show you something. . . ."

Martha inserted the nipple into Faith's mouth and began rocking hard, more to calm herself than to soothe the baby. Her mind was confused. No baby had stopped breathing since she'd been there, and Faith had been stable all this time, so Martha assumed she was all right. But she knew one of the babies had to get worse sometime. Logically, if babies got better, babies could also get worse. And she did have that heart lesion. What if she stopped breathing? Martha looked at her. Faith's eyes were squeezed shut, her lips pulling milk from the nipple. She seemed peaceful, all her efforts focused on eating.

Across the horseshoe, Foxx instructed Mrs. Baker on how to

wrap her baby in layers of blankets to retain his body heat. Martha looked up. The mother was disheveled, her hair spiking loose from its slicked-back ponytail, as if she had been picking at it. She looked to be around twenty-four, no makeup, still dressed in her hospital patient gown, a yellow scrub gown worn on top, paper booties on her feet. Her thin brown legs touched Martha unexpectedly, as if she had seen Mrs. Baker in an intimate way only a husband or mother should. An ID bracelet still cuffed her wrist.

"Hold him close, keep him warm. We can't have his temperature dropping." Foxx looked at the bundled baby with a nurse's satisfaction. "What's his name again?"

"Bowen," the mother answered, pulling in her upper lip and biting it.

"Well, hold on. I'll turn off the lights; then you can see Bowen's eyes." She padded across the room and flipped a switch.

The nursery was thrown into darkness. As Martha sat rocking Faith, the darkness closed in around her. She felt the weight of it against her chest, the lack of air, the stickiness of her skin. Her heart beat painfully and she couldn't calm it.

"Hang on a minute and let your eyes adjust. Then you can see," Foxx told the new mother.

The darkness grew grainy, then took on a transparency, as light seeped in from the small windows high up in the nursery walls. Martha slowed the motion of her rocker and looked at Faith. In the dim light, Faith opened her eyes. Martha had never seen them before. They were navy blue, so dark they looked pupil-less.

Across the room, the new mother was looking at her son.

"They are the most beautiful eyes I've ever seen," the mother said. "Can he see me?"

Martha continued her slow, steady rocking, drawing Faith closer to her breast. She studied Faith's eyes. Their gaze was steady, directed unwaveringly at her.

"I doubt it," Foxx told the mother. "At this stage of development, it's all pretty much a blur to them. Anyway, that's what the doctors say."

"Hmmm. I could swear he's looking right at me." The mother sounded puzzled.

"Well," Foxx said, "I think you should trust your own judgment. If you think he's looking at you, then he probably is."

"You're my heart, Bowen," the mother murmured. "I'll never let anything hurt you. Never."

Tears slid down Martha's face. She dropped her head to her chest, tried to wipe them without letting Nettie Lee see her do it. She felt an ache in her breast for Paul.

Martha, Nettie Lee, and the mother rocked their babies in the dark.

"You're mine forever," the mother said. "You and me, Bowen. You and me."

The cylinder of milk was only half empty when Faith stopped sucking, her mouth going slack around the nipple, her eyes dull, flat, her body suddenly heavy in Martha's arms. Martha, her heart beating a hard rhythm, unwrapped Faith from the blankets and with shaking hands laid her faceup on her lap. She began tapping the soles of Faith's feet with her fingers. First light taps, then smacks. The baby remained dusky, her eyes half closed, her face loosened into a droop. Frightened, Martha called out for Foxx.

From her rocker, Nettie Lee sucked in her breath loudly. "The baby's dead!"

"No, she isn't!" Martha said. The baby couldn't be dead; she had only stopped breathing, that was all. Between every breath there was a pause; this was just an extended pause. If she tried hard enough, if she tapped Faith's soles in the right way, prayed hard enough, the baby could be saved. Faith could be made to take another breath, then another. They could get her life back.

The lights blazed on. "Doe's black again!" Foxx said, irritated and fretful. She wrested the baby from Martha, who, arms suddenly empty, felt useless. Foxx lay the baby on the warming tray; immediately it was surrounded by a knot of people in blue, connecting the oxygen and the monitors. Martha couldn't see, wouldn't be able to tell if the baby had started to breathe.

"Clear the nursery, please!" Foxx announced, her eyes sweeping the room to rest on the young mother, who had pressed her baby against her breast and started for the nursery door, her face frozen into a look of calm.

"Leave the baby here!" Foxx sang out. "Put him back in the Isolette."

The mother paused, pressing her baby more tightly to her.

Foxx called over her shoulder. "Martha, please help Mrs. Baker get her baby back in the Isolette. Connect up his monitor leads. You know how, right? Then I'm going to ask you all to leave until the code is over." She turned her back to them.

A confused wave of panic rode over Martha. She got up from the rocker and walked toward Mrs. Baker, whose ridged forehead and tight mouth said, *I will not let go of my baby. I will fight you if I have to.* Martha reached out slowly for the child, laid one hand on his back, where his mother gripped him; the other hand she placed on the mother's trembling shoulder. Through her hands, she felt their warmth. She and the mother stood looking at one another for a moment, Martha wanting to encourage her to take her baby and *run.* She wanted to tell her that her child might die in this hospital full of sick babies, and the only fate left for her would be a lonely life without her son. But Mrs. Baker released her baby's weight into Martha's hand. Martha, not sure she had done the right thing but quite relieved, breathed out.

She put Bowen Baker inside his own Isolette, on the folded terry towel that covered a cushion of egg-crate foam, while Mrs. Baker watched in anxiety, twisting her hands, biting her lips. His monitor leads hung into one of the ports like miniature bionic robot parts. Lead by lead, she connected him up, blue wire to blue patch, red wire to red patch, yellow to yellow. As Mrs. Baker watched over her shoulder, Martha wired him up, anchoring him to his life support system, then closed the lid.

Mrs. Baker placed her hand on top of the box. She smiled at Martha, then dipped her head to look at Bowen.

Martha looked across the nursery. Dr. Xiang, Foxx, the other nurses, and a respiratory therapist bent over Faith, their backs to the Isolettes in the horseshoe. She wanted that child, more than she could allow herself to feel. If she were the baby's legal guardian, if she were Baby Doe's foster mother, could she leave her baby here in the middle of all this chaos? Martha walked to the nursery doors. Mrs. Baker followed her.

As the doors swung shut she left the noise behind, the beeping, the hissing, the short-tempered staff wrangling for the baby's life, the other babies. In the scrub room, Martha turned on the faucet full force, letting warm water flood her hands. Mrs. Baker turned to her, nervously holding out a towel.

"Your name is Martha, right?"

Martha nodded, taking the towel. "That's right." She worried about what was happening behind the nursery doors. And where was Nettie Lee? Had she stayed? Martha immediately thought of going back in.

"Well, I'm glad you're here. We can talk when you come in to rock the babies. I mean, if that's okay." Mrs. Baker laughed, then sighed. "It's my first baby." She bit her lip. "Oh, God. I hope that baby in there doesn't die."

Martha looked up from the sink. Faith could not die. She had only stopped breathing, but the doctors would make her breathe again.

"I guess you do this all the time, watching over sick babies," Mrs. Baker said. "But I'll never get used to it."

"You won't have to." Martha took the towel, began drying her hands. "Bowen looks like a big strong boy to me. He'll be leaving in no time." Mrs. Baker smiled, but she shook her head. "I mean that. What does he weigh, four pounds? That's big for this nursery. If he keeps on doing as good as he has, he'll be out when he reaches five pounds."

"How long does that take?"

"I've seen babies gain an ounce a day."

"Sixteen days? That's not too long."

Martha caught herself. She didn't want to tell the mother something that wasn't true. "It could take longer. An ounce a day is what you can expect if everything goes right."

"What could go wrong?"

"Not too much. Don't worry about anything except getting that milk into little Bowen. That's the most important thing."

"Could Bowen do what that other baby just did in there?"

Faith. "Stop breathing? No. No, those apnea spells are something little Doe just wants to do. I'm sure Bowen doesn't have a problem like that." I've got to take the baby home, Martha thought. I can love her, I know how. I can keep her safe.

Mrs. Baker shook her head. "I don't know what I'd do if something happened to Bowen. You know, last night before he was born? When I was in labor and they did the ultrasound and they sent the doctors to talk to me? To tell me what his chances were? Well, I prayed then. To Mary, because she has a son. I prayed to Mary to ask Jesus to save my son. And it's funny, because I'm not really religious and it worked anyway." She smiled at Martha. "You think that's silly, don't you?"

"No," Martha said. "I don't think it's a bit silly. Praying is the strongest kind of medicine there is." Her own prayers hadn't been answered in the past, but she couldn't take away this eager woman's hope. Mrs. Baker wore an expression of mixed trust in Martha, joy that her son was still alive, and relief that the baby who had stopped breathing belonged to someone else.

Mrs. Baker smiled at Martha again. "Do you come here every day? I will. I'm going to come every day and rock Bowen."

Martha nodded. "I come Mondays through Fridays, just in the mornings. That's what I signed the papers for." Faith. "But I'm going to start staying all day, because some of these little babies need more rocking than they've been getting." She supposed that's where Nettie Lee would be valuable. Nettie Lee *was* a willing pair of hands, if nothing else.

"That makes me feel better," Mrs. Baker said, nodding at Martha. "Definitely. Some of these babies really need you."

"I'm going to," Martha said. She would; she'd tell Foxx later on in the afternoon, maybe after the two o'clocks. "I just got a promotion. I have to train that other grandmother."

As if she had been waiting for her named to be called, Nettie

Lee swept through the scrub room door. "I thought I'd like to die in there. I wasn't thinking about babies dying when I signed up." She eyed Mrs. Baker. "Oh, hi, Mrs. Baker. I guess you're getting ready to go on home."

"Did she die?" Martha thought she tasted her own heart, full and beating in the back of her throat.

"Honey, I don't know. They told me to get on out of there. I said if they wanted me, I'd be eating my lunch. Although I don't know what kind of appetite I got left after *all that.*"

Martha tried to give Nettie Lee a significant look, a warning to act professional in front of this mother, who was frightened enough to have seen what she did, without having to think of the hospital staff as fearful as well. "Well, this is one of the things a grandmother has to get used to," she told Nettie Lee. Martha still felt shaky, but she went on. "At any time, one of the babies could stop breathing, or his heart could stop beating. We call it a Code Blue." She handed her towel back to the mother as she continued instructing Nettie Lee. "It's part of your job to notice when a baby's vital signs aren't good. Then you tell the nurse immediately. That way you'll never have a baby code in your arms, and you might save a life." Nettie Lee looked mildly bored; she opened her mouth to speak, but Martha said, "Now wash your hands. What I need right now is a good cup of coffee. You ladies want to join me? It's lunchtime."

Nettie Lee was having another bad night. It seemed like all the past weekend, every time she looked at the TV, there was Yolanda's baby being whisked past that Port-a-Potty into the ambulance. Watching it was like watching the L.A. beating they kept showing over and over until she had finally screamed at the TV to quit it, just leave the poor man on the ground. Now they kept running the same horrible scene: first came that HIP HOP'S CHICKEN JOINT sign; then the camera swooped down to the two policemen carrying the baby from the Port-a-Potty to the ambulance. After all this time, reporters still kept getting on the TV to tack on whatever else they could think of to keep the case going.

That night on the eleven o'clock news, Brian Hayashi shook his head as he interviewed a police detective at the site. His questions made Nettie Lee feel like the top of her head was coming off. "Have you located the mother yet? Is this another crack baby? Will the criminal charge against the mother be attempted murder?" Attempted murder?

The detective told him the Child Protection Agency was preparing a case. When they had decided what charges they thought should be brought against the mother, the police department would release a statement to the public.

Hayashi was persistent. "Don't the circumstances of the case warrant a charge of attempted murder? Is that why you're here investigating?"

The detective shook his head. "Right now we're concerned with the baby's welfare. That's first and foremost. The legalities of the case have yet to be decided."

"But," the reporter said, "if the baby was left for dead, then the charge would be attempted murder, wouldn't it?"

"We don't know if the baby was left for dead," the detective said, turning away.

"Well," Hayashi continued, "if a newborn baby, a *premature* newborn baby, is left in a Port-a-Potty, then . . ." He waved one hand at the blue outhouse behind them and laughed helplessly.

The detective said, "We'll leave the legalities of the case to the DA's office. That's their purview."

The reporter turned toward the camera, his bland face filling Nettie Lee's entire screen. "We'll have live updates as the news continues to break on this story. Back to you in the newsroom, Carol."

The scene changed to a blond woman dressed in a black suit and wearing heavy neck jewelry. She sat at a desk in what Nettie Lee supposed was the newsroom. People walked about, telephones rang. The woman pressed a finger into her ear and spoke to a monitor that displayed Hayashi, his microphone still poised at his mouth. "Brian, it's been over five weeks since the baby was found at the construction site. How soon will the Child Protection Agency have an idea of what charges they'd like to press?"

"That depends on a number of things, not the least of which is the District Attorney's willingness or unwillingness to go forward with the charge of attempted murder. You'll remember several months ago the agency tried to put together a court case to prosecute a pregnant crack addict on charges of child abuse, but that didn't pan out, mainly because of the question of whether or not a fetus is a legal entity with constitutional rights. It looks to me as if CPA is considering whether it wants to become involved in litigating a case it simply cannot win. On the other hand, as with the past case, one of the purposes of going forward with this one would be to test the law—specifically, to test the mother's and the baby's protection under the law. It would be a matter of whose rights take precedence, if you will."

The blond woman said, "Thank you, Brian." She turned back to the camera. "However it all works out, it should be interesting."

Little Barn, dressed in plaid pajamas and hugging an old T-shirt like a security blanket, walked into the living room and laid his head on Nettie Lee's lap. She rubbed the soft hair on the back of his head. His arms circled her knees. "Grandma, I can't sleep." He rubbed his face against her thighs. "The TV's too loud."

"Hush up and go on back to bed." Nettie Lee patted his back. "I'm going myself in a minute."

"That's what you said before." His voice was draggy; his head lolled against her thighs. "Can I sleep in your bed?" She thought about it for a second. She wanted to say yes. Having Little Barn beside her in bed would even comfort *her* some, but what would Yolanda say? You're spoiling him, Mama. He's got to sleep by himself sometime.

"No, a big man like you would take up the whole bed. A man needs a bed to himself."

"I'm not that big, Grandma." Little Barn stood up and gave her a bleary-eyed look. "But I am a man."

"Yeah, you a big man. Now get on back to bed." She watched him move off into the bedroom. "Shut the door behind you." The door closed softly.

She wished she could go to sleep, but she had too many things rolling around in her mind. Yolanda and this baby. The baby almost dying on Friday. Tookie herself, sweet as a dream. Sometimes she felt like it was a dream, the way she had gotten herself into this whole thing with the hospital, being that close to other people dying, intruding on something so personal nobody ought to be allowed to just walk in off the streets and witness it. Yeah, a witness, that's what she was. It seemed like she couldn't control what happened to Yolanda, Tookie, or any of those babies they let her rock, but she could be a witness.

She made herself get up and go into the bedroom, find her way in the dark without waking up Little Barn. It was getting late, and Monday would be another early day in the nursery.

Nettie Lee was on her third cup of coffee from the pot in the nurses' conference room. She sat at the table for a five-minute break. Officially, she had ten minutes coming to her, but she didn't have time to take them. It seemed like things were getting worse at the hospital. When she came in at seven, she had seen Tookie all hooked up to a respirator. Foxx told her the baby was in heart failure and had had emergency surgery over the weekend. The doctors had thought she would do better if they fixed the defect in her heart.

She spent the first half of the morning helping Martha with the eight o'clocks. They managed to feed all the babies who could nipple their milk. The nurses handled the rest with gavage tubes through the nose and down to the stomach. It made feedings go fast, and surprisingly the babies stopped their restless leg pedaling and calmed down as soon as the milk hit their stomachs. Outside the partially open door, she could hear the monitor noise, the nurses calling to one another over the racket. She wondered how any of the babies slept with the lights on and people talking so loud. Maybe that's something she'd bring up at the report meeting—people should try to keep their voices down some, to make the nursery more like a home instead of a video arcade.

She took a sip of coffee and sat back in her folding chair. That first day with Martha had been a trial, Martha being so bourgy and all. Nettie Lee realized she did need training, with all the babies so sick and about to die any second, but sometimes Martha acted like she owned those babies, like they were hers, and nobody else better lay a hand on them. She especially acted queer toward Tookie. Funny. It seemed that every time Nettie Lee tried to do something for the baby, help the doctor or just touch her, Martha got an attitude like a little brown turd and tried to stop her. At least Nettie Lee didn't have to go off on her the first day.

That was a blessing, because Martha would not want to see Nettie Lee mad.

Nettie Lee had spent the early part of the morning letting Martha tell her how to hold a baby—again. Every time she picked up a baby, Martha rushed over and showed her some minor adjustment to make with her hands, or maybe Martha thought she was sticking her elbow out wrong. Then there was Martha checking up on the milk cylinders, checking to see if Nettie Lee could read the number of cc's stamped on the side of them. Nettie Lee had to tell her, "I can see just fine. *You* the one wears glasses."

She checked the clock over the door, got up, tossed her cup in the trash, and went back into the nursery. Martha had gone down the hall to the Child Life Advocate's office for something. Nettie Lee wasn't the least curious about what it was. She was happy to have a minute in the nursery without Martha correcting her.

Outside the conference room door, the long horseshoe of Isolettes stretched across the room. Nettie Lee decided to take a walk around the nursery to check on each baby. Isolette number 1, Riley—a little girl, she thought; she'd have to make sure later—was rolled up to the glass viewing wall. A woman, probably the grandmother, and a little girl about six or seven stood on the other side of the glass, bending in to see the baby. Inside the nursery, Riley's mother, a curlyheaded thirtyish woman, pushed the Isolette closer to the glass and mouthed the word "Okay?" She nodded enthusiastically at the little girl. "Okay? Okay?" The girl placed her palms on the glass, bent her head against the glare, and looked into the Isolette. She glanced up at the older woman, who looked down and smiled.

Nettie Lee looked down the horseshoe: Lewis-Morley, Perez, O'Neil, Cruz, Baker, then, lying on her warming tray, Tookie. Up the other side of the horseshoe: Gonsalves, Mooney, Whiting, Brown, Grant, and Derrick in Isolette number 14. There were only thirteen babies but, Debbie Foxx had explained, no one had the nerve to call a baby's incubator Isolette 13, so they just skipped that number. Nettie Lee stood by Tookie's warming tray. She had the coffee jangles. Her stomach kept trying to burp itself into her throat. She swallowed. *Dear Lord.* Maybe if she prayed at the baby's bedside every day, He would protect her and Yolanda. *Dear Lord, I don't know Your plan, but—*

She felt the air move behind her. Dr. Shapiro, an intern newly assigned to the nursery, stood beside her and was looking down on the baby. He was short and thin and wore glasses like the other doctor, but unlike Dr. Xiang he sent out what Nettie Lee called bad vibes. Maybe it was his lack of experience—he was just an intern—that caused him to act so curt and bossy.

"Let's get Baby Doe examined, then change the bandages on that incision. Where's the other grandmother?" The way the doctor said *Baby Doe* made Nettie Lee stop and think. He sounded like he thought he owned Tookie. "Can you assist me, Grandmother?" She wasn't his grandmother. "I want you to hold the baby."

The baby lay naked on her side, a plastic respirator tube drooping from her mouth. She was swathed in gauze to protect the incision where the knife had sliced through her chest to her heart.

Shapiro reached under his yellow gown into his lab coat pocket and pulled out an instrument he put into Tookie's ears: first the right, then the left. Nettie Lee held the baby's skinny arms out to her sides, pinning them in place with just the weight of her index fingers. His head bent low, Shapiro finished looking in one ear; then he held the baby's head between his thumb and forefinger and flipped it to the other side and looked in the other ear. "We're going to have to take this bandage off. Where's Foxx?" Nettie Lee saw Debbie Foxx bent over the Baker baby's Isolette on the other side of the room. The other nurse, the redheaded one, was feeding one of the babies with a syringe. "Okay," the doctor said, "your hands are as good as anybody else's. Let's get this bandage off."

"I can't be doing this," Nettie Lee told him.

"You can do anything I tell you to," Shapiro said. "Are your hands clean? Go wash up real quick." He gestured to the sink by the nursery door.

Nettie Lee squirted Betadine on her hands and rubbed it into her palms, across the backs of her hands, and up her wrists. She looked around the nursery to see if Martha had come back from

Ms. Czajwolski's office yet. Martha had told her not to do what the doctors asked because they didn't care if a grandmother got in trouble or not, and you could get in serious trouble for doing things that weren't in your job description. The hospital could fire you. She rinsed the red disinfectant down the drain and walked back to the warming tray.

"Okay," the doctor said, "hold her hands down." Nettie Lee pinned Tookie down again, pressing the baby's palms to the mattress. She felt like a bully, her victim a Tom Thumb sissy. "You're doing a good job, Grandmother. The other woman always seems so shaky. I don't completely trust her." He slipped a pair of scissors under the bandage against the baby's ribs and began to cut through the gauze and tape. When he pulled the bandage away, the baby's chest lay exposed.

Nettie Lee forced herself to look—Tookie had a two-inch incision over her heart, stitched with neat black thread, just like a trussed-up turkey. Her skin had been painted orange around the wound, probably with Betadine. Shapiro brought out his stethoscope and placed the tiny disk on the baby's chest. Nettie Lee's head felt full of gas She watched Tookie's face wrinkle and smooth as if she were trying to make sense of what they were doing to her by weaving the sensations into a dream.

Later in the afternoon, Nettie Lee sighed and closed her eyes. "Girl, if I wasn't so tired today I could put up with your foolishness better. I got me some problems I just don't know what to do with."

She sat alongside Martha, rocking the babies after the four o'clock feeding. Nettie Lee held Riley; Martha rocked Gonsalves. Each baby was wrapped in three rough-feeling receiving blankets; their small faces were the only part of them that showed.

"Problems?" Martha looked up from nudging the nipple into Gonsalves's mouth. "What did you do while I was down the hall?"

"*I* didn't do anything. Why it's always got to be me that did something? What did you go down there for?"

"I was just checking on my application to be a foster parent."

"Oh." Nettie Lee began to rock a little faster. "Well, I'm talking about something you don't know about. I'm talking about my own child. My daughter." She stopped. Maybe it was okay to talk to Martha. Maybe she would understand. Martha looked away from Nettie Lee, yawning. Nettie Lee guessed she would be tired from the way she hopped around the nursery. She had seen Martha cleaning up before the four o'clocks, flinging a towel over the babies' Isolettes. Nettie Lee half expected her to snap her towel, like some up-and-coming shoeshine boy.

"You know how some people always got the answers?" Nettie Lee said. "You tell them, 'Now, I don't think you better be doing all that mess. Look like trouble to me,' and they say, 'No, don't be bothering me with no commonsense advice. I got to go ahead and make a fool out myself.' So all you can do is say, 'Go ahead on, make all the mistakes you can. I won't say I told you so.' " Martha nodded slightly, as if she did not know exactly what she was agreeing to. "Well, Yolanda's just like that, hardheaded as the day is long. And I seen it coming from a *long* way off."

"Who's Yolanda?"

"That's my daughter. I told her, 'Yolanda, you got to take care of yourself now. You and Little Barn are a little family.' That's exactly what I said, 'a little family.' I told her, 'You got to keep this family of yours little, because if you think one baby's hard, then don't try two.' Two is more than two, if you know what I mean. It's like in mathematics, what they call opponents. You know, how one number times itself equals some big number you wasn't expecting, like two times two times two can equal almost a million if you keep multiplying it over? Well, that's what I told Yolanda—don't make your family into opponents like that. I know what I'm talking about."

"So she's got a baby?" Martha wrapped Gonsalves's blanket over his feet. "How did that happen?"

"Same way it happens to everybody. But for her, I expected her to know better because I taught her good. But she can't take advice." Nettie Lee looked at Martha. That woman would never understand this Baby X mess. But maybe she would understand Little Barn.

❧❧

One time I got home from work and here's Barn laying up in Yolanda's bed like he owns the whole damn house. He's got a reefer in one hand and Yolanda's left titty in the other. When she sees me standing in the door, she pokes out her bottom lip and crosses her arms. I say, "Yolanda, you got to be crazy because I know you ain't stupid. I ain't running no whorehouse." She sticks her lip out even further and takes a drag off of the reefer.

If I wasn't so mad I would of laughed. Here's these two kids doing everything they can think of to be grown, sitting up naked in that child's bed that's got the purple balloon sheets on it I bought her when she was six. I look over on her dresser and she's still got the Easy Bake oven her granny gave her when she turned seven. Her floor is strewn with Barn's clothes—the black trousers I thought he never took off, since every time I saw him back then that's what he'd be wearing, and there was that fancy black cowboy hat of his that seemed like a total contradiction to everything else he was, and it's laying right on the floor. A trail of his underwear is heading from the bedroom door to the bed, the tail end of it being one silk sock hanging off of Yolanda's mattress. I look back at the bed, and now Barn's puffing reefer smoke out his nose. He squints at me through the haze with his pale gray eyes, and I'm just tongue-tied up in knots. I don't know what to say. I don't suppose you can believe that, can you? I look in his face. Barn's eyebrows are smooth, every hair going the same way, like he lines them up by size with a fine-tooth comb. His nose is straight and short. Underneath it he's got a thin mustache curling down over his top lip. His mouth is pooched into an old-maid frown that says he's looking at something he don't like. Those nasty gray eyes look right at me. He takes another hit off of that reefer, blows smoke out, and his nostrils flutter like paper. I stand there letting the smoke go up my nose; then I've had it.

"Yolanda, what you got this raggelly boy sitting up in your bed for? You fifteen years old. He ain't nothing but fourteen."

She scratches her head like she got to think about it. "Mama, you know Byron's old for his age."

"This boy ain't old enough to be in nobody's bed, and particularly not in yours." It's common knowledge that a boy is two years behind a girl in the teenage years. Now, with Yolanda being fifteen and him being fourteen, that means that to her he's really twelve, or to him she's more like seventeen. You see what I'm talking about?

Yolanda crosses her arms again and huffs. Now Barn's taking another toke off of that reefer.

"Mama, I am old enough to conduct my life in the manner in which I see fit," she says. Her skinny little arms barely cover up her titties. "I can make my own decisions, thank you." Barn pokes his elbow into her ribs, hands her the reefer. "Thank you, Byron," she says, like she's the Queen of Timbuktu.

So what am I doing? I feel like taking him by his nappy head and pulling him out the bed, then kicking his butt on out the back door. And slam it. But I don't do none of that. I'm too tired. I'm going to do like those TV talk show people say—I'm going to *communicate* with these children.

"Barn, do your mother know where you at?"

I don't even know why I ask him. He looks like he ain't got no mother. He don't look dirty or nothing, that's not what I mean. He looks like he's missing something, and he's looking around trying to find out where he left it. I know he ain't finding it in *my* house.

Barn looks up from Mr. Reefer, but he don't talk.

"Do you want me to call your mama and let her know where you at?"

"No, ma'am. We don't have a telephone." He takes another drag off the reefer, and I watch his little hairless chest inflate.

"You want me to talk to her? Where do you stay?"

Yolanda starts squirming in the bed.

"If that's what you think you got to do," he says, in that stingy little voice boys use when they trying to talk, but they want to keep their reefer smoke down in their lungs too, where they think it's doing them some good. "But really, Nettie Lee," he says, "I don't see that this involves either one of you-all." He finally blows out and his chest goes down to normal. He looks like a kid again. Fourteen.

I go over and sit on the bed, on Barn's side. It sinks down and he almost slides into me, but he straightens himself up. He sets his back against Yolanda's pillow, looking like a king sitting up there, Yolanda's ruffled pillow fanning out behind him. With his left arm, skinny with a hard little muscle knotted on top, he nudges Yolanda up straight.

I can see I need to try something different, make them act like they got sense.

"You plan on marrying my daughter when she turns up pregnant?"

Yolanda busts out a laugh at that, then covers her mouth and says, "Oops."

Barn looks from Yolanda to me. "I don't think marriage is a viable institution."

"You don't think *what*?"

"I think marriage is dead."

"It's still going strong in *my* house."

"Not as practiced in the West." He stops talking then, like what he just said made sense.

Now what is he talking about, "the West"? We live in Ohio. Last I checked, that is the Midwest. I know that reefer is doing the talking now. And he just goes on and on like he's Ed Bradley on *60 Minutes.*

"And if I decide to formally commit myself to a female, I wouldn't do it now. I'm not old enough to even consider restricting my opportunities for—"

He stops blabbing and looks at Yolanda. She's got her hand up to her forehead, wiping away sweat. I know I make that girl nervous, because I don't put up with no b.s. She barely turns toward that little boy and she mouths, Chill. With the tip of his middle finger he smooths first one eyebrow, then the other.

I feel like I can't breathe right, like something is itching inside my heart. This was probably wrong on my part, but I grab that boy by his hair, put my hands into that permanent wave mess on his head, and I yank. I jerk his head down to his chest. Then I do it again. He winces and takes it, but all I can think is, *It's soft.* His hair is soft and fine like a baby's. So I let it go. I can see he's squinting back tears.

I get up off of the bed, stand over them with my hands on my hips—that's my "you in deep shit" pose—and I look at them *hard.* Let them know I'm really analyzing the situation. Barn and Yolanda sit side by side, like two of the same thing, but they don't touch each other. Yolanda has a scared look I've seen too many times. Barn's face don't look like nothing to me. I tell her, "Yolanda, I'll be talking to you when you get your clothes on." Then, "Barn, you better go on home and don't show yourself around here no more."

I stand at the foot of the bed waiting for them to do what I say. When Barn notices I'm not going anywhere, he says to me, "Would you leave so I can get dressed?" Like he's got something under that sheet I ain't never seen before.

That little punk thinks he's a grown man.

Yolanda sits on the couch next to me, plucking up a little piece of the sheet I use for a slipcover between her fingers. This couch was where I slept because I knew a teenage girl needs a bedroom to herself. Someplace she can go and plan her future or just dream. When I told her I was moving out of the bedroom so she could have it to herself, at first she said, "No, Mama. If you're not here I'll get lonely." But after I put my things in the hall closet she started to like having the room be hers. Now she pulls up another piece of the sheet and rubs it with her thumb. I suppose she's waiting for me to start.

"Yolanda," I tell her, "honey, you are a fine young lady now. Almost grown." She doesn't answer me. "You have to take care of yourself, because a boy ain't thinking about doing it for you." She studies the piece of sheet in her hands, turns it over, and rubs the other side. "Do you hear what I'm saying to you?"

"Saying the same thing you always say."

"And just what is that?"

" 'Men are no good.' "

"What?"

"Oh, Mama, I'm sorry, but every time we talk about anything it always comes back to 'Men are no good.' We can be talking about something as stupid as dinner, and it turns out we can't have what you'd like to eat because we don't have the money, and we don't have the money because of Daddy, who left you because 'Men are no good.' We talk about your friend Dorothy. I say, How is Miss Dorothy today? and you, 'Men are no good. Her boyfriend left her in the middle of the night, got right up out of the bed, left her hugging the pillow.' Everything we talk about has the same conclusion. I just get tired of hearing it sometimes."

"I wasn't *about* to say that. If you could wait a minute and listen, you'd find out what I was *about* to say."

Oh, my feet hurt. My bunions like to kill me, hurt worse than they ever did. I work eight hours every day at the tire plant, bending over a conveyor belt with my calipers, trying to see if the tread measures out right, and I got to come home to this mess? I kick off my shoes, push them back under the couch, then bend down to rub my bunions. My corns are hard and dry. I'll use some lotion on them tonight, I'm thinking; rub the sore spots out. But for now I got this problem on my hands.

"First of all," I say, "I was talking about birth control. You got any?"

Yolanda looks back at the hank of sheet in her hands. "Mama, that's personal."

"Not if you have a baby!"

"It would be *my* baby."

"Not in this house!"

"Would you please give me some credit for having common sense? I wouldn't have a baby if I didn't want one. I'm smarter than that. Byron doesn't want a baby anyway. He said so."

"At fourteen I should hope not."

"Mama, I keep telling you that age doesn't matter. It's just a number, like on a lottery ticket. Some people act older, some people act younger, and their birth certificates say they're the same age." She looks so sincere about what she saying, it makes my head hurt.

"Do y'all think you're in love?"

"I love him, yes."

"He love you back?"

She don't say anything, puts her hands in her lap. She got hands like fresh-baked sugar cookies: plump tan skin, nails buffed pink. I just hate to see those hands go to waste patting Barn on the behind. Yolanda's smart and could be a teacher if she wanted to. I just don't know why she don't want to.

"He loves me," she says. "He hasn't said it yet, but I know he does."

"His hair that short you can read his mind?"

She gives me that exasperated look she's so good at. "No, Mama. I don't have to read his mind. He *treats* me like he loves me. He lets me talk when I need to. He doesn't tell me what to do. I feel like I can take a deep breath around him."

"Girl, if you want to breathe, there's a whole big world full of air right past that door. Go outside and knock yourself out."

Yolanda sighs, sucking up our words and pushing them out again.

"I knew you wouldn't understand," she says and gets up. "And do you know why? Because you don't know who I am. You don't have a clue."

She slams the front door, and I can see my old yellow sheet has a dent in it where she's been sitting.

I don't catch Barn at my house after that, but I know when he's been there. I can smell him in the air in Yolanda's bedroom and on her sheets and pillowcases. It's a sharp odor that comes off his head and gets into everything, not a bad smell, just different from Yolanda's. When she was a little girl, three or maybe four, I'd lay my cheek down on top of her head just before I washed her hair. I'd lay my cheek flat against her braids and smell that smell. I could get drunk off it. A smell like fresh dirt. Barn's smell is like that too, but different somehow, not pleasing to me at all.

That smell was around so much, I started feeling like there was a ghost in the house—the ghost of Barn. Seemed like if I turned around fast enough I'd catch him disappearing around a corner, maybe going to my bathroom to pee or sliding in my kitchen to empty his ashtray. But the place his shadow grew clear was in the smirk on Yolanda's face. I wanted to tell her, Girl, you don't *have* a secret, but that smile wasn't an invitation to talk.

I watched her when I was home at night. She didn't go out too much, especially on school nights. By the time I got home from work around five-thirty or six, she'd have dinner started. She made pretty good spaghetti sauce from the *I Hate to Cook Book,* so that's what we'd eat. When I walked in she'd already be at the kitchen table with her schoolbooks spread out in front of her, hunched over in her chair, arms crossed, a frown pulling her face down to a point. She never asked me for help. She'd just look up from her books and say hi. Then I'd say, "What'd you do after school today?" and the ghost of Barn would slide around the corner and flush the toilet. I'd go lay down on the couch for just a little while to rest before dinner, but ninety-nine times out of ten I'd fall asleep.

What goes around comes back. Yolanda started missing school, started staying in the bed, stopped having dinner ready when I came home. Said she must have the flu.

One morning, about three months after I caught them in bed that time, I finally figured something out. It's already eight-thirty, snow on the ground, and I'm running from the bathroom, pulling on my coat, trying to make my bus to work. I look in the bedroom on my way out.

Yolanda's laying up in the bed with the blankets pulled over her head. She looks small, just a little lump under the covers. I go to the window and yank her drapes open. Thin December sunlight, the kind that don't warm nobody, comes in. Them drapes been closed so long, dust is flying all around. I lean over Yolanda, pull back the blankets, and press my hand against her forehead. Feels like touching myself.

"Yolanda, you sick again?"

She turns over so she's facing the wall and says, "Yeah," like she's half dead.

"What you think is wrong with you? I never heard of no flu lasting three months." I'm trying to keep the sarcasm out of my voice, but there it is anyway.

She sits up, squeezes her face into a frown, boosts herself out of the bed, and runs for the bathroom, groaning. Oh, hell, my job can wait. I sit on her bed trying to figure out what I'm going to say. When she comes back, she lays flat on the bed and stares straight up.

"Go ahead and ask me," she says, looking at that same spot on the ceiling. "Go ahead."

"How far along are you?"

She darts her eyes at me. They say this is not the question she expects. I smooth the hair back from her forehead, away from her eyes. Her face is a blotchy jigsaw puzzle; the pieces are all there, but if I'm not careful, they can be shook loose. Her hair feels rough under my hand, so I smooth it down and smooth it down, until she closes her eyes and says, "June."

Men are no good. And it's too damn bad, because they don't have to be that way. They do things just to be doing them. When Sweet left me and Yolanda, I asked him over and over, "Why? Why you going?" His smart reply was, "Why you got to be so nosy, Nettie Lee? I'm going because I feel like it. That all right with you?" I stood out on the sidewalk with Yolanda in my arms. I never even thought of answering him back. I didn't want to waste my breath.

I hear Yolanda in the bedroom talking on the phone. First little whispers, then she's screaming like she's trying to talk to somebody lives in the next state without the benefit of a telephone.

"You trifling nigger, you!"

I block it out, shut off my ears. I look out the window, out to the road. That's where I'd rather be. Out on that road that leads away from here.

One night in May I come home from work, and I smell him when I sit down to take off my shoes. I reach under the couch, and instead of my house shoes what I pull out from under there is one of his black Dunhill's loafers. The way it feels light, weightless, makes me throw it across the room, against Yolanda's bedroom door. From inside I hear her say, "Mama?"

She is in her nightgown, sitting on her bed, resting her back against the pillows, her skinny arms crossed tight over the hump of her stomach. She likes to sit like that, says she's hugging the baby. Barn is sitting right beside her smoking his reefer, his legs stretched out on top of the blankets, drinking a Colt 45 right out of the bottle. When the smoke curls from his nose, Yolanda fans it away with her hand.

"Byron says he might move in," she says, looking at him, coughing a little.

"Yolanda, you don't have the sense you was born with."

She takes her arms off of her stomach and says, "I thought you'd be pleased."

I swear I don't know where she'd get a notion like that. So I ask her, "Why do I want that boy here? I already got a child messing up my life."

"Why do you think?" She's getting hot now. "My baby will have a father. Byron's here." She looks at Barn like he is her salvation.

"Where's the baby's father been up till now?"

"The baby hasn't been born yet. And you don't have to talk about Byron like he's not here."

I look right in his gray eyes and I say, "All right, Barn, you answer the question. Where you been all these months Yolanda been pregnant?"

Barn puts his reefer in the green bubble-glass ashtray my mama gave me when she died. It's the only thing I have left of her. He's got it laying on the blanket beside him like it belongs to him now.

"I realize you don't like me—" he starts up.

"Boy, it don't matter if I like you or not. You don't put food on my table."

"And I know you think I'm too young to take care of your daughter."

"You got that right," I say. "Little fourteen-year-old I-don't-know-*what*—"

"I'm fifteen now. And I know you think I don't know how to be a good father."

"Well, you seem to know all about what I'm thinking." I put my hands on my hips and stand over the bed, right on top of him. "*Do* you know how to be one? Doesn't look like it to me. Where you been for five months, on vacation? In the Bahamas? It ain't been no Bahamas around here."

"I was taking care of my family." He raises his hand. "Just let me finish, all right? Just let me tell you something. I don't have a father, I never did, and my mother left us when I was twelve. Do you understand me? Ain't nobody raised me. I raised myself and Nathan."

"Who's that?"

"My little brother."

"All by yourself?"

He nods his head.

"How'd you manage with no mama or daddy?"

He looks like he ain't going to say no more. He reaches for his reefer, then changes his mind. He looks at Yolanda, who's giving him the message with her eyes to go on, tell it.

"Well, at first Mama's sister, Cheechee, she stayed with us. She used to live with us when Mama was there. She even looked like Mama sometimes, like how she walked, the way she laughed when she talked on the phone. Sometimes after Mama left, if I wasn't paying too close attention, I thought she was Mama. Nathan was worse than me. He'd be curled up on the couch with Cheechee watching TV. Have his head in the crook of her leg, laying there till way past midnight. I'd have to half carry him to bed. He never even knew she was passed out drunk." He smooths his eyebrows with his finger.

Yolanda is looking at me to see if his words need embroidery, if he is getting through to me. I sit down on his side of the bed. They scootch over to make room.

"What happened to Cheechee? Where did she go?" I want to know.

He shrugs. "Wherever Mama and Daddy went."

I don't say anything. I don't have any answer for it.

He shakes his head. "I don't really care, either. They're not necessary to my life. I already proved that. Cheechee stayed about two months; then she said she had some important out-of-town business to take care of. She had on that old red knit dress she thought made her look cute, and wobbly high heels. She told me, 'Y'all be fine, I have no doubt.' That's the last thing I heard from her: 'Y'all be fine.' I had to explain that to Nathan, explain what was wrong with Mama and Cheechee. I said they're a little mixed up. They'll be back later."

I can't tell if he believes it or not, believes they're coming back. Can't tell by his face.

"After she left, we just stayed on in the apartment, pretending like she was there. That lasted about two weeks; then Mr. Winn came over, hollering about the rent. Said it hadn't been paid in three months and he wanted his money right then or he'd put us out in the street and beat the money out of us. What was I supposed to do? I got no job at twelve. And here's this okey-doke-looking motherfucker handing me eviction papers. I almost went off on him.

"I got me a job that night catching for the dealer in my building. Everybody knows Marquis does business upstairs. So I ask him if he'll hire me. He said yeah. All I had to do was hang around outside from nine at night to five in the morning. Somebody funny-looking come by, I tell Marquis. Or if I miss that and they get up to Marquis's apartment, then I go around back and wait at the bedroom window. Lots of hustling and shadows on the curtains, then the window scrapes open and out flies Marquis's duffel bag full of pharmaceuticals—you know, cocaine mostly. So I catch it and run. I bring it back to him later."

"Barn, you going to get hurt doing that mess. How you go to school in the morning if you're up all night?"

He just shrugged again, but he looked hurt. I could tell the school thing was bothering him, since he was the kind of boy who liked to sound educated. "It was a job, and it paid. That's all I cared about then. Now I'm looking for something more; I got my own business. Anyway, the point is I know how to take care of my family, been doing it too long not to. I can take care of Yolanda and the baby, and I can take care of you too."

And me too. Somebody wanted to take care of me too. Well, I kind of liked that idea, except he tacked me on like he was adding another raggelly ribbon to the tail of his low-flying kite.

Barn and Yolanda were outside looking up into the gray sky, checking for thunderheads. They're standing beside their cardboard grocery boxes loaded up with stuff from my house. Barn wants to take them to the new apartment now. Yolanda wants to wait, says rain will come down any minute. She has her hands on her hips, her face thrown backward while her maternity blouse blows like laundry on a clothesline.

"One just hit me on the face!" she says to him and wipes her cheek with her finger. "See that? That is a raindrop." Barn, like a long tree branch, bends over to look.

I can't see her raindrop, but other drops hit the living room window and I know I'm not going to move all this stuff now. The couch is sitting in the middle of the floor, waiting for us to carry it out the door, but I lay on it instead. That way I know it's not going nowhere.

Yolanda says Barn's new apartment is so fine it's got two bathrooms. She wants me to move out of this house, to stop working and stay with her and Barn, be like a mother-in-law on TV. I told her they'd have to get married first, but then I said all right, since I owe it to her. I want to see my little girl happy just once. But I been thinking about it. I have to break my promise, because I don't want to move.

Rain or shine I want to stay in my little old raggelly house.

From way before Yolanda can remember, this was *my* house. *I* saw the boarded-up windows and the condemned sign. *I* read the warnings posted on the front door. *I* paid the dollar it cost to take it off the city's hands. *I* signed my name. *I* borrowed tools. *I* bought lumber. *I* stole bricks. *I* ripped out, tore apart, hauled away. *I* hammered and plastered and wired until they told me I could quit. The day the county inspector ripped the condemned papers off the door, he looked at me and Yolanda with unnatural pale eyes and said, "This is the worst thing you could have done, lady. All the houses on this block are boarded up except yours. You'll have rats for neighbors, and that's all!" Yolanda buried her face between my legs. I pulled my hand out of my coat pocket and poked my middle finger at his back and told him, "I'm getting rid of the rats right now!" because he was already driving off in his truck.

No, I didn't want to move from there. That house was too much like me—used up. If I moved away to a new apartment with big old square white rooms, where could I lay down? Where could I be myself?

Barn and Yolanda come in with a man wearing a maroon windbreaker splotched up with rain. The man says, "Yeah, I'm here for the couch and shit," and stands over me. "That it?"

"Yes," Barn says. "It makes out into a bed."

"How much you want?" He squats down and runs his bony dark fingers across the fabric on the arms. "Looks kind of worn. Looks real worn. How much?"

Barn and Yolanda are standing there with this man, looking down at me. Barn's mouth twists up, ready to sell my couch.

"Not a cent," I say, standing up. "This couch ain't for sale. What fool said it was?"

He looks at Barn. When he turns, the water on his kinky head drips down his neck.

"Look," he says to Barn, "I ain't here to waste time, yours or mine. This shit for sale or not?"

"My shit ain't for sale and never has been," I say. "Get out of my house."

He looks over at Barn and snorts. Before he goes out the door, he bumps into Barn and whispers, too loud, "Boy, you shoulda asked your mama first." Barn don't answer; his eyes don't flicker, his lips don't twitch.

As soon as that man is out the door, Barn and me will *talk*. I got things to say about how no fifteen-year-old little something can sell my furniture out from under my behind. How I don't need a new apartment—I got me a house. I'm going to tell him how I don't need him—I already had a man once. I'm going to tell him how I'm not moving anywhere. Ever.

But Barn don't wait around to talk. He pulls on Yolanda's hand and they both walk out to his truck, rain hitting their heads, their shoulders. Yolanda's blouse sticks to her back, and I see the sharp edges of her shoulder blades. They both know they could catch their death of cold, but they go on like you can't tell them nothing. They get in his new black pickup truck. Barn sticks his cowboy hat on his head and drives off.

Once Yolanda yelled at me, "Mama, I am my worst self around you!" And I said, "Girl, you know it don't take no special occasion for you to act a fool."

But I'm sorry I said it, and if I could take it back, I would. Yolanda is like a voodoo doll—full of needles. If I could, I'd pull them all out one by one, but wouldn't that hurt her too? Maybe once you got a curse put on you, the best thing is to just go on out and do your magic.

Yolanda is on her hands and knees, crawling across the labor room floor. She says she can take the pain better that way. First she crawls forward, screaming the whole way, then she crawls backward. That's harder; she can't see what's behind her. Nurses are looking at her through the open door like they think she's crazy.

"Yolanda," I say, "why don't you let me help you get in the bed? You going to wear that baby out."

She sits in a heap, legs splayed out in front, her hospital togs open in the back. "Oh, Mama," she says, and I can hear all the weary in her voice, "I can't stand this. How long do I have before the next one?"

I look at the clock over her bed. "Look like twenty-five seconds to me."

"Oh, shit." She puts her head in her hands.

"Why don't you go on back to bed? You'll feel better if your stomach don't hang down so far."

"No, I feel better this way, when the baby hangs out, like it's just part of me, not all of me. How many seconds?"

"Five," I say, "four, three . . ."

"Oh, Mama, don't be funny. I don't have time to laugh right now." She gets back up on her hands and knees.

The nurses come in and out. They pick Yolanda up off of the floor, get her back in the bed. They strap a monitor around her stomach. Later, they take her to the delivery room. They know I'm the labor coach, so they let me come too.

And where is Barn? I'm thinking this when I stand beside Yolanda at the delivery table, my hands under her knees, spreading her thighs apart so the baby can come out. She's got her hands on top of mine, gripping me like she ain't got nobody else. I tell her to pant, wait for the contraction to get good and strong, then take a deep breath and push. I pant with her until I get lightheaded. We're together like that, me trying to help deliver this baby, her trying to push it out. I'm thinking things are so different in the hospital now. I was asleep when Yolanda was born. I didn't know anything about panting, helping the baby come out in its own time, having to be patient with the birth. I guess I'm just surprised I didn't mess it all up myself.

Then here comes the baby's head. I see it shiny wet, coming out between Yolanda's legs. She cries, says, "Help me, Mama. Help me!" And I say, "No crying. Take a deep breath and push hard. Push real hard." The baby slides out in one wet plop. When they lay him on her stomach, Yolanda says, "Oh!" They clamp him off and hand me the scissors, saying, Cut between these two clamps. I open up the scissors and get the cord in there, then cut through like I'm cutting raw steak. I remember something I heard on TV once. I think it was Michael asking Archie on *All in the Family:* If two people you love are drowning and you can only save one, who would you save? Well, my answer is: I just don't know.

❧❧

Martha shook her head. "I think you have to save yourself."

"But I love my child like I love myself. More."

"And you think that's a good thing?" Martha looked down at Gonsalves, pulled his blanket in closer to his face. "If you love your child more than you love yourself, when something happens to her, then you'll die. You won't have any reason to live because everything you thought was yours will be gone. It's like when you plan the future with him at the center of it. You see yourself doing everything. In every single picture you have of yourself in the future, your child is there too. Then, if something happens to him, you have to go through and rip out the part of the picture where he was. And that's not possible. So you have to think of yourself as a separate person, always."

Riley jerked in Nettie Lee's arms. "Who are you talking about, exactly? That don't sound like me and Yolanda." She rocked slower to keep the baby asleep. Sometimes Martha didn't make sense, though Nettie Lee could see she was trying hard to tell her something.

"All I'm saying is, how can you help somebody else when you're drowning yourself? I think if two people are drowning—say, you and Yolanda—then if you have any hope of saving the other person, you have to know you are strong enough to save not just yourself but that other person too. You have to have the strength of *two* people."

Although Nettie Lee wasn't sure what Martha was talking about, she did think maybe Martha was right. Maybe nobody had to drown if she was strong enough to keep all their heads out of the ocean: hers, Yolanda's, Little Barn's, Tookie's. If she could be Hercules, things might be all right.

CHAPTER 4

In the scrub room, Martha quietly listened to two student nurses who stood by the sink, talking. Their yellow gowns were cinched tight at their waists, and below the long hems the girls wore white sweat socks and high-top sneakers. They looked like new pledges to a convent. In one continuous movement, they lifted their arms behind their heads, twisted their hair into knots, and tucked it into blue paper bonnets. The gesture was young and synchronized, like a well-practiced dance move. Martha pretended to busy herself putting on her scrub gown as they spoke.

"I totally blew him off," one said, fingering the last bit of blond hair into the front of her bonnet. "He pretends like his wife doesn't work on the second floor."

The other one, less pretty now without her frame of hair, looked at her friend and shrugged. "Yeah, he's married, Kristy, but he's still a doctor and he's cute. So what's it going to hurt?" They leaned in to the sink, taking turns washing their hands in disinfectant.

"You're probably right," the first one said. "I guess I'm just old-fashioned when it comes to men. I'd rather go out with somebody who can stay the night." She looked up at Martha, then blushed. "We better hurry up and get to labor and delivery," she said to her friend. "We've got that lecture on preemies, then the delivery room tour."

Martha felt a small turning in her stomach, an acid displeasure. Since she didn't want to be the last one in the scrub room, she wiped her hands and quickly left before the students did.

She stood looking through the small window in one of the nursery doors. Beyond it, the nursery played like a television soap opera with the mute button on: Debbie Foxx skirting Dr. Shapiro, an X-ray tech ponderously hauling his equipment from one Isolette to the next, the electronic monitors silently drawing their fluorescent green graphs of the babies' heartbeats—all of it muffled. She paused to collect herself. Was this really what she wanted to do, to rock these babies, fragile, dangerous as ticking bombs? With dismay she felt her own beating heart. Worried it could be heard by the doctors, the nurses, she imagined her chest stuffed with cotton swabbing to deaden its strikes. She stepped on the door pad, flinging the double doors open, and there was the noise: hissing respirators, beeping monitors, nurses' chatter, and an occasional yell.

"Martha!" Debbie Foxx waved impatiently from across the room.

Martha felt queasy, wished she had at least eaten a piece of toast before leaving home. Now it looked as if the nursery would be too busy for her to eat breakfast during break. She walked to where Foxx leaned against the worktable, writing in one of the charts. Foxx straightened up and put her hand on Martha's elbow.

"Come on. We're late for Report, but we can say we got hung up talking about a case with the mom and dad." She laughed a little. "That's partly true, since *I* did. Where've you been?" She gave Martha a long look, her eyebrows raised.

With a sigh, Martha remembered it was Tuesday. On Tuesdays and Thursdays the nurses' Report began half an hour early. Afterward the social worker from the Child Protection Agency reported her progress on the cases she was assigned. Three babies had been added to the caseload while Martha worked there. Two were born exposed to drugs, the third was Martha's Faith: drug exposed, then disposed of in a toilet. She hoped the woman from CPA would place the baby with her. She loved holding the babies, these tiny ones especially, and she took care of all the babies every day; didn't that prove she was good enough? Maybe they would let her take Faith home.

She took her place at the conference table next to an empty chair. Nettie Lee, wearing deep-brown lipstick, her down-turned mouth accentuated, gave Martha a sour look, then turned away. She looked like a disgruntled Happy Meal clown. Foxx sat in the empty chair beside Martha. The other staff members circled the table. Martha's chair was on the table's curve, her feet unable to find a spot to rest flat. After hitting her shins against the table legs, she folded her feet under her chair.

She thought again of Faith, lying several feet away beyond the open door. Poor baby. How was it possible for girls who had all these services available to them—welfare, Medicare, drug abuse clinics, counseling of all sorts—how was it they could still make such a mess out of their lives, do something as trashy as throwing away a baby in a toilet? She shook her head. With the government playing husband to these girls, what did they lack? They got money for a place to live, and they got food stamps to feed themselves and their kids. She looked around the table at the hospital staff: Dr. Xiang and the intern, Shapiro; four nurses; a social worker; the director of Respiratory Therapy; the Child Life Advocate; and *two* grandmothers. Here sat all the help anybody could ask for. Any problem could be solved. But some of these girls were on their second and third baby. Why did they keep messing up? Some of the babies didn't even have anybody to go home to, would have to be released into foster care. She shook her head. Some people just didn't *want* to be helped.

The new social worker leaned forward in her chair. Dressed in a cream-colored jacket with matching miniskirt, cream stockings, and flat-heeled shoes, she had a hopeful smile that Martha chalked up to youth and good intentions. A triangle of pink lace showed on her chest beneath her buttoned jacket. Lace underwear instead of a blouse? Martha checked the buttons on her own oxford shirt, drew her sweater tighter across her chest.

"I'm Barb Hunter, the new Child Protection Specialist for the nursery unit." Hunter looked full circle around the table, then laced her fingers together. "The former specialist for Mercy Ped, Lorna Patterson, got married, and now she's on maternity leave. So I'm the one you'll contact if a baby has been drug exposed or if any other type of abuse or neglect is suspected." She paused. Martha thought her voice sounded little-girlish and jumpy. "You can get in touch with me the same way you did with Lorna, okay? Right now, I'm catching up on the casework that's been turned over to me, but I'll be able to give you a report on what I'm planning for the families by next week. And that includes a request I have from one of your volunteer grandmothers to be a foster parent." She looked at Nettie Lee. "Are you Martha Howard?" Nettie Lee turned down her mouth further.

"No, I am," Martha said, feeling a quickening in her chest. "I put in the application."

"Have you made a decision?" Terese Czajwolski asked. Martha felt hopeful about being approved. Ms. Czajwolski said they would come out to her house before the final determination, but unless Martha had some sort of serious problems, like a criminal record, things should go smoothly.

"Well," Miss Hunter said, "I will tell you that normally we try to find a couple for placement. You're an older woman and you aren't married or currently employed, and these could be strikes against you." She sat back and nervously touched her fingers to her mouth. Martha felt embarrassed and shamed. She angrily thought Miss Hunter was too young to decide on what was best for the babies.

Foxx said, "Well, that's fine, Barb. Welcome to the nursery, by the way. Okay, I have just one thing to add before we all head back into the chaos." There were groans and a small amount of laughter. "I've, uh, got a change in personnel plans." She looked at Martha, then at Nettie Lee. "Nettie Lee Johnson has completed her training, and since she's done such a good job with the babies, the nurses agreed that she and Martha should share the position of Head Grandmother." She smiled at Nettie Lee and Martha, then sat down.

Nettie Lee smiled at Martha as if she could now afford the expense.

"May I ask a question?" Martha said it before she could stop herself. "How can there be two Head Grandmothers? That's like a two-headed monster."

Nettie Lee frowned. "That sure is a funny way to put it."

"Martha," Foxx said, "there's no reason to feel upset—"

"I don't feel upset."

"—because what I see is you and Nettie Lee working together as equals, like the nurses do in the unit. You divide up the work equally anyway, don't you?" Foxx asked cheerfully.

Martha said, "Doesn't the unit have a head nurse anymore?"

A few seconds passed before Foxx spoke. Martha's mind raced forward to what she herself would say next in her own defense.

"Well, yes, of course the nursery has a head nurse, but what we do is so complicated and we've got so many patients and personnel providing care that we need someone in charge." She looked around the room as if searching for someone to hand her head nurse position to. "Don't get me wrong. I think the work you do, both of you, is wonderful. I just thought—we all did—that since you two are the grandmothers who answered the ad and agreed to the workload, you could be equal partners. And besides, I noticed that sometimes you have a little difficulty finishing up the tasks I assign. I'm sure it's because there's so much work to be done. But if you and Nettie Lee kind of checked up on each other, you could both make sure that no baby assigned to a grandmother misses a feeding or a diaper change. It's just a way to make sure things get done and make it easier on you. I hope it's not going to be a problem." She picked up her clipboard.

Martha felt a pang in her chest. Had she forgotten to feed a baby? What had she done wrong? "No. It's not a problem."

In the early afternoon, the sun slanted palely through the nursery's high windows. Martha stood at Baby Doe's warming tray, watching the windows become blank with reflected light. She had completed the housekeeping chores she had assigned herself: straightening the babies' blankets and cleaning the Isolettes by rubbing an alcohol wipe over each one, polishing off the fingerprints and spilled oily medicines. Now came the time she wanted to enjoy—holding her babies, one by one, and lulling them into a dream of the womb they had left behind.

Before Nettie Lee came, Martha had tried to rock every baby every day. That didn't work. With only ten or even eight babies in the horseshoe, Martha couldn't rock them all. Some couldn't be picked up, like Faith now; she had to stay on her warming tray, lying flat or sometimes lying on her side but never held; her condition was too critical. Foxx said they had cut open her chest for heart surgery on Saturday morning. Even if Martha had the nerve to pick her up, there was also the problem of what to do with the respirator tubing, and the tube down her throat the respirator was connected to. Was it all right to just let them droop or would that hurt the baby? Beside Faith's tray stood a Baby Bird respirator, an IV monitor slung from a pole, a heart monitor mounted on the partition behind her tray, and a set of bilirubin lights, brilliantly fluorescent, poised just a foot over the baby. Faith lay on her back, her eyes bandaged against the light. For her, Martha just stroked her arm or lifted her leg, then gently put it down on the mattress.

Before Nettie Lee came, she couldn't spend too much time on Faith or any of the other babies. They got ten minutes for a morning rock and that was all. She could barely get that done, even with so small an amount of time for each child. The babies deserved more attention than that. Maybe it was good to have Nettie Lee there, an extra pair of hands, another set of eyes, more rocking time for the babies. But then, she knew her babies had gotten used to *her,* looked forward to being held in *her* arms and rocked, not somebody else's. Babies were funny that way. They preferred the person they got used to. Now they had to let a stranger hold them. They wouldn't like that. She traced her finger along Faith's thigh, ruffling the sparse lanugo hair.

In the supply room, Debbie Foxx was unloading linens off the laundry cart and storing them. Martha could see her through the half-open door. Bracing a pile of folded laundry against her chest, Foxx walked to where Martha stood beside Faith's warming tray. They both watched the baby sleep, her bony chest rising, taking in measured drafts of respirator oxygen.

"She's a cute baby," Foxx said, resting her chin on the towels. "Sometimes before I go home, I go over to maternity and look in the nursery. I can't help it, but I stand there looking at all those rows of newborns, and I can't quit thinking that regular babies are such big gazoos. You know?" She rested her finger on Faith's shoulder. "When my husband and I decide it's time to have one, I'm going to be so used to these little guys I won't know what to do with a full-term baby."

"I think you figure out what God gives you pretty quick," Martha said. "No matter what you end up with, you can't imagine your children being any other way but the way they are."

"Yeah." Foxx lifted her head from the towels. "How many grandchildren do you have?"

"None." Martha turned from the warming tray. "I'm going to start the afternoon schedule by feeding Riley. All right?"

"All right," Foxx replied quickly. "Would you change her first? I've got to put this stuff on the supply cart. Then save the diaper for me so I can record her output." She headed toward the back room.

Martha flipped the latch on Riley's Isolette and slid her arm through the port. On the inside corner, Riley's mother had taped a green and red plastic Christmas tree ball. Martha bounced it with the tip of her fingers. Occasionally a mother brought something from home, a little stuffed toy or a tiny pillow stitched in bright thread and dotted with her perfume, just to let the baby smell her when she wasn't there, for comfort. Riley's mother was obviously in the Christmas spirit, Martha thought. With Christmas only two days away, she sadly realized her holiday would pass unacknowledged: no tree, no Christmas dinner. What would be the point? She unclipped the wires from sticky patches on the baby's chest and sides, untangling red, blue, and yellow strands. She removed Riley's diaper, put on a fresh one, folding it down twice to expose the black scab over her navel. It took longer than she wanted, her stiff fingers stumbling over the diaper tapes. She couldn't fold the diaper right. It didn't want to stay beneath the baby's navel. She looked up briefly, saw Foxx moving around in the supply room, occupied with stocking the linen carts. "I'm leaving the diaper on the scale for you, Nurse Foxx," she called.

Foxx's voice drifted out from the supply room. "Fine. I'll weigh the evidence before it evaporates."

The double nursery doors bumped open and Nettie Lee walked through. She strolled around the horseshoe, looking into each Isolette, lingered at Baby Doe's tray, then stood beside Martha. The warmth from Nettie Lee's body seemed to rise in waves. Martha already felt hot: the nursery lights were too bright, the Isolettes emitted their own heat, and, with all that, the yellow gown over her pants, shirt, and sweater was too much.

She wiped perspiration from her forehead, saying to Nettie Lee as politely as she could, "Would you go ahead and get the bottles ready for the two o'clocks?"

Nettie Lee stood looking at her, making no movement toward the conference room where the feeding supplies were stored.

"I'm doing Riley, and then Cruz after that. You can get Whiting and Mooney." It occurred to her she should consult Nettie Lee on this arrangement instead of simply announcing which babies she'd rock and which ones belonged to Nettie Lee for the afternoon, but she couldn't force her mouth to say, Sound all right to you? She didn't really feel like discussing it. Sliding her hands into Riley's Isolette ports, she balled the paper diaper into a small package, secured it with the sticky tabs, and placed it on top of the Isolette. Hands back inside, she began straightening up the lamb's-wool mattress and waterproof padding.

"I'ma rock that little one over there." Nettie Lee pointed to

Gonsalves. Her hands were puffy-looking, chapped, the nails bitten off. She was wearing a wedding ring, but it was on the wrong hand. "I know you had patting this baby in mind, but I think little Baker is getting ready to wake up and start fussing. He over there squirming in his sleep right now, like he got worms or something. You need to go pick him up." She looked at Martha expectantly, as if waiting for her to close Riley's incubator port and carry out *her* instructions. Nettie Lee's face looked tired, puffy like her hands. Her mouth, naked of the lipstick she had worn during Report, added to her washed-out look.

"I've already decided which babies I can take care of today. Riley for now, then Cruz when it's time for the four o'clock feeding," Martha told her.

"You're not going to have Baker to feed. By four o'clock, his mama'll be in here," Nettie Lee said. Then she added, "Her husband gets off his job then, and they come straight here. They like to see the baby before they go home to eat their dinner. And see them two over there?" She gestured toward two visitors, a thin long-haired girl and a shorter fat—no, pregnant—girl talking to Debbie Foxx near the supply room. "That's Cruz's mama, the tall one. She can feed him."

Martha had forgotten about Mrs. Baker. And she had never seen Cruz's mother. Now her slip made her look forgetful, maybe even incompetent. Would Nettie Lee tell anyone she couldn't handle the schedule? She would worry about that later.

A silence was born between them. Martha turned back toward Riley's Isolette, slid her hands out of the ports, and opened the lid. Riley lay on her back, her eyes squeezed shut, her forehead wrinkled with the effort to close out the light. Martha knew she wasn't asleep. She wriggled one hand beneath Riley's back, then scooped up her sprawling weight. With her other hand, she steadied the small head, lifted the baby up. The baby felt awkward in her hands, her tiny legs and arms flinging up, pulling the rest of her body off balance. Martha had the dizzying sensation of dropping her. She braced her hands around the baby's body, stiffening her elbows yet cradling her gently but firmly, the way she would a camera, trying not to shake. At the same time, she moved the baby toward the blanket she'd thrown over her shoulder, then neatly stepped around Nettie Lee.

"I see my opinion don't count for too much." Nettie Lee turned to follow Martha's progress to her rocker. "You know I'm in the same position as you now." She raised her voice. "We got *two* head grandmothers in this nursery."

Martha turned quickly, said in a low voice, "I didn't say a word." She laid the baby against her shoulder, sat in the rocker. "And, as far as two grandmothers in the nursery goes, anything Nurse Foxx decides to do for these babies is all right with *me.*" She covered Riley with the blanket, first draping it over the baby's back, then laying her on her lap to tightly crisscross the blanket flaps in front. "I don't pretend to know more about what's good for the patients than the nurses do themselves." Finished with the swaddling, she laid Riley over her shoulder and began to rock quickly, letting the motion of the rocker quiet them both.

Nettie Lee disappeared into the conference room, returning several minutes later with a cylinder of milk. "I told Debbie I'ma feed Gonsalves, and she said go on ahead."

She took her time at Gonsalves's Isolette, unclipping and wrapping him. After she sat down with him and he began to suck his bottle, Nettie Lee stopped rocking and looked at Martha.

"Did I ever tell you the story about why the dog hates the cat?"

Martha felt her mouth tighten.

"I didn't, did I? Well, I meant to. See, the dog and the cat loved to dress up and go out together every Friday night. The trouble was, they both liked to wear the same kind of clothes.

"The dog was partial to silk and lace boudoir outfits and she wanted to borrow the cat's fine red chemise.

"The cat says, 'All right, Sister Dog. You can have the outfit for Friday night, but I want it back for the party I'ma go to on Saturday.'

"The dog says, 'Trust me, Sister Cat. I won't get nothing on the dress.'

"On Friday night they're at the club and Sister Dog is doing what dogs do best: rumbling through the garbage cans looking for leftovers, chasing Brother Skunk through the fence, tussling around the alley with that fine-looking Brother Dog. Pretty soon, the red chemise ain't red no more.

"The next day, Sister Dog comes trailing up the walk with Sister Cat's tattered dress. 'Excuse what happened to your clothes, Sister Cat. I was careful as I could be. But you know I can't help myself, seeing how I'm a dog.' "

Martha stopped rocking. "And just what is *that* supposed to mean?" She got up unsteadily, carrying Riley into the conference room. Another cylinder of soy sat warming in a small basin of water in the sink. She picked it up and shook it in her hand, the milk foaming up. She had hoped her days weren't going to be like this, with Nettie Lee taking over the work, getting her own way with the nurses, dominating her, and doing a good job of it too. She felt helpless, faced with the total confidence others naturally assumed when in her presence. When they got around her, people could not seem to mind their own business. They immediately became experts on whatever it was she was doing, from holding these babies to telling her she was selfish. If she *was* selfish, whose business was it anyway? Certainly not this woman's. And at fifty, she was too old to be told what to do. She walked Riley back to the rocker, sat down, worked the nipple into her mouth.

"It don't mean a thing," Nettie Lee said placidly, as if Martha had never left. "Except what you get out of it." Nettie Lee looked up at her.

She felt a queer nervousness edge her anger. "I don't need you telling me my business." Why did everything she say sound like a kid's retort?

"Well, who said you did?" Nettie Lee patted Gonsalves's bottom. "My idea about stories is this: You hear one, you take what you can from it. Now some people you can't talk sense into. Tell them one thing, they hear another. Other people are always thinking you talking about them. No matter what you really saying, to them you talking about their personal business. Now those kind of people make me tired. I can't be worrying about somebody's hurt feelings all the time. I got to say what's on my mind and then let it go. What other people do with my speech is their own business."

Martha hissed air through her teeth. "In my family, people try to mind their own business. Not stick their nose where it doesn't belong. I suppose you never learned how to do that."

"I suppose I didn't."

Martha and Nettie Lee rocked silently, their chairs facing each other but in no danger of touching. Nettie Lee was close enough to talk to without Martha having to raise her voice. The rhythmic push of their rockers kept back the racket of the intensive care unit. It seemed if they rocked hard enough they could create a quiet space around them that would expand like a balloon they were blowing up. They rocked like that, getting up every half hour or so to change babies; then both would sit down again with a new one and begin rocking and feeding all over again. After their argument, Martha thought she'd welcome the silence, but surprisingly she did not.

The two student nurses Martha had seen earlier in the scrub room walked into the nursery a little after five. They came immediately to where Martha, LaRone Cruz, and her friend Shavonne, in her last month of pregnancy, stood talking.

"Oh, look at this little guy," one student said, bending over Cruz's Isolette. "Isn't he cute?" She turned to Martha. "Can I hold him?"

"You better not wake my baby up." LaRone stood sullen-mouthed beside her son.

"Oh, is this your baby? My name is Kristy Williams, I'm in nurse's training. I just want to rock him for a little while. That's one of the things we do on the neonatal rotation."

"I just put him to sleep. He don't need rocking."

The student looked at her friend. "Well, okay. Maybe I'll get to rock him tomorrow." She shrugged.

Martha felt the girl's disappointment. "Derrick and Grant are done eating. You can rock them." She nodded toward their Isolettes at the far end of the horseshoe.

The students walked over with a slightly knock-kneed shuffle.

"They're pretty girls," she told LaRone and her friend. "I like to see girls training to be nurses. It's a good occupation, like teaching. And it pays well enough until they find a doctor to marry. I know they're looking. I heard them talking about it." She was sure they never meant to get involved with married men. The doctors weren't being honest with them, that's all. Some men were like that with young girls, always leading them on.

Shavonne snorted. "I don't believe I'm hearing this shit. Why you got to be looking all up in white girls' faces? If you want to talk about somebody being pretty, look at LaRone. She's beautiful. I mean, I for one don't need no picture of some pasty-face blond to show *me* what *I* need to look like, know what I'm saying? That shit is too old."

LaRone *was* pretty, but too skinny. She looked Polynesian, dark-haired, dark-eyed, but Martha didn't like her style of dress—a stretchy black minidress that showed her long legs to be hinged on the boniest knees Martha had ever seen. And her head looked too large for her body. She looked as if she didn't eat. She thought LaRone wasn't married, and decided that was the reason why. No man wanted a skinny woman.

"Well, I don't apologize for my views. I don't think there's anything wrong with saying what everybody knows is true. If you were impressed with your own nappy head, you wouldn't take offense when I compliment somebody else."

"Oh, Lord. Who rang your doorbell?" Shavonne rolled her eyes at LaRone.

"My generation grew up during a time when we tried to fit in, my whole family did. I'm not one of your politically correct black nationalists, but I don't need to justify myself to a little girl who doesn't know which end is up."

"Excuse me?"

"What y'all talking about over here?" Nettie Lee held the schedule clipboard. She looked at Shavonne. "What you got your eyes rolled up for?"

"I don't believe some of this shit I'm hearing."

Nettie Lee swung to Martha. "What?"

Somehow, she had gotten herself into trouble.

LaRone looked at Martha. She opened the top of her baby's Isolette. "I'm going to rock him some more, okay?"

"Sure, dear. Go ahead." She watched LaRone try to work the monitor clips with her long red nails. "Here, let me help." She wanted to keep her hands occupied, busy her mind.

"It's okay," LaRone said. "I got it."

She let LaRone take the blue clip out of her hand. She felt heartened to see another mother, besides Mrs. Baker, who was not completely afraid to touch her baby. "All right. You go ahead, you're doing fine." Her anger was lessening; she felt more in control. She was, after all, more experienced than Nettie Lee or any of the mothers in the nursery. Only the nurses surpassed her capability.

"Get the rockers out," Martha announced. "It's time to rock these babies." She tapped Shavonne on the arm. "Come on and help me—being pregnant isn't a handicap."

Shavonne disappeared into the supply room, returning with a small wooden rocker, which she scooted along the floor. Martha found the rocker she'd used that morning for Riley pulled up next to Brown's Isolette. She held it out in front of her and duck-footed to where LaRone was settling down with her baby. She unhooked Whiting from his monitor leads and sat down with him.

"I need me a new baby this evening." Nettie Lee scanned the horseshoe. "Who have I been neglecting?" Her eyes rested briefly on the Doe baby, then passed on. "Who needs a special rock from their designated grandma?" She turned to Martha. "Who you got?"

Martha looked at the baby in her lap. "Whiting." He was flat-faced, puffy-eyed, only eight days old and weighing three and a half pounds. His face had the smooth look of a half-empty leather pocketbook. He grimaced, breathing out in gentle pants. "And you've got your little baby," she said to LaRone. "What's his name?"

"Daquille," LaRone said.

"So Daquille is getting his rock." She looked at the student nurses. "And those two got Derrick and Grant."

"Well, I guess I'ma take Mooney," Nettie Lee said. "I never rocked her before."

Shavonne got out of her chair. "I can rock a baby."

Martha waved her back into the chair. "I know you can, dear, but you either have to be a parent or be a volunteer grandmother."

"Why? Grandmothers ain't the only ones who know how to rock. There really ain't that much to it."

Martha grew impatient. "You're not insured by the hospital to rock somebody else's baby unless you're in the program."

"What are you getting so stressed for? I guess I could sign their papers. I'm not doing anything all day. If I get to be a volunteer, I could help y'all out when I come here with LaRone."

"You can't do that."

"Why not?"

"You're not old enough to be a grandmother."

"I got to be a *grandmother* to be a grandmother?"

"You have to be fifty to be a grandmother."

"Shoot, I ain't nowhere near fifty." She laughed. "And glad of it."

"Well, when you get to be fifty you can be a grandmother."

"LaRone going to be a grandmother before she forty."

"Shut up, Shavonne."

"No, think about it, girl. Okay, here you are twenty, and you got Daquille. Then he gets some girl pregnant when he's sixteen—"

"Shut up."

"You be thirty-six, got some little kid calling you Granny."

"How old will you be when *your* grandchild is born?" Martha looked at Shavonne.

"I don't know."

"You younger than me, Shavonne."

"Shoot."

They rocked in silence for a while, Shavonne apparently satisfied to be quiet. Martha began to feel restless; the silence weighed on her. She found it surprising to want to hear her companions talk. Across the horseshoe, the student nurses laughed a little at something one of them said; then they stopped rocking while one girl pointed to the baby in her arms, and the other girl leaned from her rocker to look. Martha watched them, then turned back to her circle. She drew Whiting against her breast, tilted back, and rocked. A sad feeling welled behind her eyes. This story poured out.

When I came home from my sixth-grade health class with comic books from the Kotex company on menstruation, my mama didn't say anything. There was that hesitation she had, that compression of her lips, then the turning away. I curled up on the couch looking at my pictures of yellow-haired girls with pink eggs in their uteruses and question marks over their heads to show they were wondering about menstruation, what it was going to do to them. I turned the page to see the cartoon girl's mother, hand resting on her daughter's shoulder, smiling and holding a box of sanitary pads. While Mama swept the living room carpet with a broom, her strokes especially hard in front of the couch where I lay, I wished passionately for my monthly to come, for the blood to start; then I could use the clean sanitary pads like the girl in the book.

The next day, even though my monthly hadn't started, I walked down to the Rexall and bought myself a plain blue box of Kotex with my allowance. The clerk, a middle-aged man who stopped his conversation with an older woman standing at the counter, couldn't understand me when I whispered that I wanted Kotex. "What?" he kept saying. "You want a box of *what*?" until the woman flatly told him, "She wants a box of Kotex, John." Rather than being embarrassed because I'd asked for it, I was embarrassed for not having said it loud enough. *Kotex,* I should have yelled. *I want Kotex!*

I saved the box in my dresser drawer for months, waiting for my monthly to start. When it finally did, I didn't recognize it. I was walking home for lunch on one of those overly bright February days when the sun made the snow on the ground glittery and sharp in my eyes. I felt heavy in my crotch and wet between my legs. Squinting, I opened the door to my house. Inside, it was so dark I couldn't see at all. I was snow-blind. I felt my way from the front door, down the hall to the bathroom. In the dark, I pulled up my dress. On my panties I could see the floaters in front of my eyes and big dark-green spots. My heart caught. It looked like blood, but I couldn't be sure what I was seeing. It was hard to wait to get my eyesight back, to stop being snow-blind, to find out if I had finally started my monthly. Meanwhile, I got bad cramps and threw up. Just that quick.

I called Mama at her work to tell her. A man answered the phone and said she was in the rest room. I thought it was odd we were doing the same thing at the same time, only she was in Springfield at the air force base, and I was at home. When she got home at five-thirty, Mama didn't ask me about it, but she swatted my butt with her hand to feel the pad.

Even though Mama was a good woman deep in her heart, and told me when I was little that she loved me more than tongue can tell, I knew my teenage concerns were petty in her eyes. She loved babies, not teenagers. She simply didn't have eyes for me anymore.

When my brother, Michael, was in the tenth grade, and I was in the sixth, he told me that nobody was thinking about a silly little colored girl like me. I wasn't a threat to anybody, not important enough to worry about. But wait until I got to high school, he said. People would look at me differently.

Since sixth grade I'd had two friends, Kathy and Karen, who spent most of their time lying across my bed reading fashion magazines and, when my mother was at work, smoking cigarettes. Karen liked Winstons because the high school boy she was after had the same name. I didn't like him too much, though. He called Karen a nigger lover, and he spat on her face sometimes, though she liked it. She said it was as close to sex as you could get. I'd never been inside Karen's house. I'd only stood below her bedroom window while she climbed out to meet me. Her mother didn't like to have strangers in the house, including Karen's friends, but sometimes she got away with sneaking Winston in through her bedroom window. In back of the house they had a screened-in porch I admired just because it looked like it might be cool to sit there in the summertime. Karen would meet me beneath her window dressed in tan shorts and a sleeveless white blouse. I'd wear black shorts and a black short-sleeved blouse, hot as hades; then we'd walk to the corner store to buy a pack of Winstons for her and a Sugar Daddy for me. I had such a sweet tooth Mama was forever telling me I was about to catch diabetes.

The summer between eighth and ninth Karen wouldn't come out of her house. She'd say she was on punishment or she had to clean out the fireplace or *something.* Kathy started doing the same thing too. All that summer I lay on my bed and listened to the radio at night, a wobbly fan blowing hot air from the floor, too hot to sleep. I didn't really see them again, except to pass them in the hall in high school. I decided to forget my eighth-grade friends and to make my own high school life. Custom-make it to suit me, made to fit.

When high school started in the fall, I met a girl in algebra class named Angelbertha. She and I were the only black girls at Fairlawn High. Four other black people went to the high school, but I didn't know them. Two were juniors on the basketball team, one was a senior on the football team, and one was running for student council president. Angelbertha was in the drama club. Because she was so fat she mostly got to play middle-aged mothers, or the great-aunt who is eccentric but lovable and encourages people to sit down to the table and *eat;* once, to her embarrassment, she played a mammy to a Civil War family in the South.

She said it was okay because she pretended she was Hattie McDaniel in *Gone With the Wind,* a real actress, though no one knew it. When I told her I was planning to try out for Fairlawn High's drill team, she said, "I hope you're not disappointed when you don't make it." We were walking home from school together. We both lived about two miles away.

"Why do you think I won't make it?" The closer we got to home, the smaller the houses got. Angelbertha lived another half mile from me.

"Well, you're too mousy." She was quietly panting. "You've got to speak up for yourself and let people know what you want." I didn't say anything for a moment, just listened to the rustle of Angelbertha's stockings beneath her dress.

"That's what I'm doing," I said. "I want to be on the drill team, so I'm trying out." I was thinking that it never failed, people always thought I was too quiet, even though I tried to seem loud and funny.

"Don't get insulted. I didn't mean anything. I'm just saying you have to know what you want out of life to get it."

It really surprised me back then when people saw me that way, because inside I was alert. I watched people, kept score. I learned how not to make the same mistake twice when all around me I saw fools who added two plus two and got twenty-two. A big number, certainly, but wrong.

"Angelbertha, don't judge a book by its cover."

"You're mad at me." She looked down as she walked, her round face doubling in on itself. Her skin was the same color as mine, a light shade of medium brown. I liked to gauge the darkness of people's skin, trying to connect them to me by way of family color. Angelbertha would fit into my family.

"I'm not mad at you, Angelbertha."

It just seemed to me that mostly everybody I knew didn't really know what they were talking about. But on the other hand, they were right about *everything* in a way that I wasn't. So I decided I had better change my personality before the tryouts. I had six weeks; that was enough time. The tryout committee had never met me. Mr. Peterson, the band director, had never spoken to me, didn't know who I was yet. For all anybody on the drill team knew, I could be an extrovert.

The girls who went to Fairlawn High School had last names that were exotic to me. Names like Schlosser, Baumer, Wonka, Van Zlike. They seemed so different from me. When I told Mama how delicately they stirred the pancake batter with a *wooden* spoon in home economics class, not a teaspoon, Mama set her mouth. "That's because they got a maid to do everything for them. They never mixed up pancake batter before." I doubted that. These girls had mixed pancake batter. They knew the right spoon to use, and they were careful with the batter, as Mama did not have the patience to be.

In my social studies class I sat behind a little girl named Mindy Madigan. Mindy's yellow hair fascinated me in a way that Kathy's and Karen's mousy brown hair had not. Mindy's hair lay flat to her head and curled up at the tips. I studied her hair like a minister studies the Bible. Instead of correcting homework with the rest of the class, I kept my head down low, pretending to mark my paper, but my eyes were rolled up to Mindy's hair. I'd count the number of gold strands, the number of white ones, the yellow ones. To me her hair was the same as the hair on the baby dolls I'd gotten for Christmas, the hair of the angel on top of our tree.

Those nights, before I went to bed I put my hair on pink sponge rollers. I smoothed my hair below my ears, then rolled it pinch-tight, so tight I couldn't sleep. But in the morning, the result was perfect: my hair lay almost flat to my head, then curled in a sausage roll all the way around my head just below my ears.

One afternoon when we corrected homework, I felt something crawling through my hair. At the front of the room Mrs. Walker dragged chalk across the blackboard, explaining what she called the "colonization of the subcontinents," for the benefit of the students who had missed the question on the previous night's homework. I looked up from Mindy's hair just in time to see Mrs.

Walker looking at me, stabbing her chalk at the thing she had drawn on the board.

"Martha," she said, in that I-know-you-don't-know-the-answer-but-in-all-fairness-I'll-call-on-you-anyway-and-be-kind-when-you-make-a-fool-of-yourself voice, "please tell us what continent this is."

I felt a fly walking around on the back of my head, barely moving my hair. I swatted it. My hand brushed against something hard sticking out of my curl. A pencil.

"Ummm, continent?" I pulled out the pencil, but I felt something else, two paper clips. The boy who sat in back of me laughed softly. "Well, maybe it's Australia?" I felt the back of my head. I wanted to tell her, Look at Dave! See what he's doing to me!

"No." Mrs. Walker was impatient. That voice of hers lied. "Would you like to make another guess?" She ran the chalk around the outline again, emphasizing the hump on the left side and the tail at the bottom.

I could feel Dave's breath on my neck. "Hey, hey. How do you get your hair to do that? It's like a shelf."

Mrs. Walker waited, chalk pointing to the board.

"Ummm, continent?"

She drew an emphatic X on the hump of her creature. "Don't you recognize this?"

From behind, Dave whispered. "Hey, hey, is your hair real? What do you do to make it so hard?"

"Ummm, is that a continent?"

Mrs. Walker tossed her chalk in the tray. "Yes, it's a continent! One you need to study."

That night I didn't put my hair up in the pink rollers. I lay with my head on my feather pillow, instead of feeling the rollers digging in my scalp. I prayed to God to please, *please,* change me. Or at least change my hair. If only He would change my hair, that would be enough. Make it straight, make it long, make it lie flat on my head. I'd do anything if only He would change my hair. I prayed, *Please, Lord, I have faith. Amen.*

When I woke up in the morning I still had nappy hair. I was disgusted.

❧❧

"Disgusted with what?" Shavonne asked impatiently. "Your stupid little prayer or your stupid little wish for straight hair?"

"Praying ain't stupid, honey," Nettie Lee said. "Many's the time saying a prayer was the only thing I could do."

"What good did it do you?"

"What you mean, what good did it do me? You see I'm sitting right here, still alive. That's proof enough prayer did me some good."

"Please."

Martha tried to explain. "I was disgusted with myself. I guess for asking God to perform such a ludicrous miracle." And there was something more. "I was disgusted with God for not performing my silly miracle anyway, because I needed it so badly."

"God ain't no fool," Shavonne said. "He ain't about to give you something as stupid as straight hair just because you can't deal with your own black self. I mean, if God was as stupid as you think He is, then I could ask Him for a million dollars and get it."

"Haven't you ever asked God for anything?"

"I *said* I woulda had a million dollars already. Ask LaRone if she ever prayed."

"Shut up."

"Go on and ask her about the time she *thought* she was pregnant."

From her chair, LaRone sighed loudly.

"Turned out to be more than just a thought, didn't it, girl?"

"Maybe you ought to stop talking so much and have some more *thoughts,* Shavonne." LaRone sounded uninterested in what she was saying.

"Excuse me?"

"You heard me. You talk too much."

"I was quiet during the *story.*"

"Well, you're not totally rude, then."

"Mmnh. Well, I see the way this conversation is headed."

Nettie Lee said, "I never did have a notion to get something a white person had. You know, blond hair is going to look kind of foolish sitting on top of my head. When I was that age, I guess I was wishing for the same kinds of things, like a better head of hair. I just wasn't thinking about no white people. Of course, everybody in my school was colored—or black, like they say now—but changing my looks just never was a notion I held."

"African American," Shavonne said.

"Well, it don't matter what you call us, we know who we are."

"Nuh-unh. Some black folks, African American folks, don't act like they know who they are. They so busy trying to get what the white man got they can't appreciate their own culture. Then somebody like Vanilla Ice or Marky Mark come along and rip us off *and* get paid for it. And on top of that, here come our own men with those same old blond girls on they arms. Tell me that ain't some shit."

Martha looked over to the two student nurses rocking Grant and Derrick, their rockers moving together in the same rhythm.

"Can't nobody tell you nothing once you get started, Shavonne."

"Shut up, LaRone."

"I've got another story for you then, since you didn't care for the first one."

"What's this one about?" Nettie Lee said.

"My brother."

"Well, let me get a fresh baby. I done wore this one out."

While Nettie Lee put Mooney back in her incubator, Martha continued rocking Whiting. He slept now, his small hard head cradled into her breast. His chapped lips made drowsy sucking motions. Shavonne stood up and began stretching her legs. Martha got up and laid Whiting in his Isolette, then went through the ritual of unclipping Brown. Nettie Lee returned to the rocker with O'Neil. LaRone still held Daquille.

After bending over in a complete rag doll flop, Shavonne came back to her chair and sat down. "Okay, Granny," she said, "I'm going to be quiet. Continue on with your marathon storytelling session."

❧❧

My brother, Michael, used to save ants. First he'd try to kill them, then he'd try to save them. If it worked, he'd keep them in an aquarium full of dirt in his room. Sometimes he couldn't save the ants, but he always tried, and that is what's important.

My family moved to Amberley Oaks Drive on the Tuesday after the Fourth of July, since Daddy couldn't wait until the weekend. Mama packed up the dishes and all the household things you'd expect, but one thing she tried to wrestle onto the moving truck just didn't fit: her rusty trash barrel from South Euclid Street. Most of the green paint was scorched off from all the trash Mama burned. Rain had gotten into the barrel and rusted it down the sides, and the bottom had finally fallen out. She told Boo, Daddy's friend, to put the barrel in the truck with the lawn mower and tools, but Daddy said we weren't taking any junk.

"How'm I suppose to burn my trash without a can?" Mama's voice rose up. She leaned into the truck, examining what Daddy had already loaded.

"You won't need no can where we moving." Daddy looked at me with that smile he always used—like he and I knew more than Mama. "You can't take the country out of some people," he said, looking at me. "Can't *force* it out of some people."

Mama ignored Daddy and took the barrel anyway. She said Daddy wasn't practical. She put the barrel behind the peony bush in our new backyard. It was hidden way out back by the privacy hedge that closed off our yard from our neighbor's. The bush's leaves were soft green and fresh, the flowers pink. The first time I stuck my face into one of them, six or seven big red and black ants ran out onto my nose. Feeling their feeble legs scooting across my face made me scream and slap them off. As pretty as the flowers were, I knew not to bother them after that.

Amberley Oaks Drive was a wide clean sweep of blacktop that I could follow to a rise at the end of the block. Our neighbors' houses were big. They looked like libraries or schools. Though our house was a good size, we lived in the smallest, plainest house on the block. Directly across from us sat a two-story red-brick fortress with black shutters, the yard neat as a checkerboard. Two little round bushes guarded either side of the front door. I could see the front tire of a tricycle peeking around the side of the house, the only sign that people lived there. The house next to that one looked like a picture I had seen in Mama's *Redbook,* a bald-faced red-brick square set on a rise of clipped grass parted precisely down the middle by a strip of sidewalk. I was afraid the doors would open and the people would come out, ask me why I was there, ask me what my family was doing moving onto their street.

The night before we moved, at dinner, Daddy had folded the newspaper and waved at Mama. "Look at this, Lil. We in this paper tonight."

Mama didn't get up to look. "What's it say?"

He tapped the paper against the dinette table twice. "About us moving here. Telling the people, Don't panic! Don't sell your house! Stay put!" He laughed and slapped the paper against the dinette table, knocking over his water glass. The water seeped under his plate.

Mama sat at the end of the table, elbows planted on top, waving her fork in the air. "Don't panic!" she said and laughed with him.

The first time Mama burned trash at our new house was a Friday evening after dinner. We'd lived there a little over a week. From a stool I'd pulled up to the kitchen window over the sink, I watched her hump along the backyard, carrying grocery sacks of garbage out to the privacy hedge. As she disappeared behind the peonies, I could hear the tin cans in the bags rattle. I heard her dump the sacks in the barrel, then she must have put a match to it. Smoke drifted over the top of the peony bush, carrying the smell of burning newspaper, then scorching tin. A minute later, Mama came back into the house and let the fire burn by itself. When she passed through the kitchen, she said, "Keep away from that fire, girl. It'll burn your behind!"

Even though I had planned on going out to the fire as soon as she left, I said, "All right, Mama." The minute I heard her in the living room, setting up the ironing board, I took off my gym shoes and socks and left them by the sink. Mama didn't hear me go out the back door.

The lawn in the backyard was nothing but mown weeds. Prickly. I scratched the tiny, stinging cuts around my ankles while thick smoke curled from the trash barrel. I looked around for something to burn, trying a few peony leaves, tossing in a couple of twigs. The fire suddenly burned hot, the smoke all but gone as the air shimmered with heat. Tin cans popped, and sparks burst out from deep inside the barrel. I stepped back from the heat to watch the fire grow and consume the trash, then die back to a steady ashy glow.

Twilight changed to dark; a few lightning bugs came out. Mama turned on the lights in the house. Behind me, I heard the privacy hedge rustle. Michael moved up close behind me, placing his hands on my shoulders, watching the fire.

"Hey, little sis, where Mama at?"

"She's ironing." I turned to look at him. He was in his same old clothes: tan chinos and a light blue shirt with a button-down collar. Unless he was going out on a date, he never wore anything else. He hadn't had any dates since we moved. He pulled a folded-up white envelope from the back pocket of his trousers and smoothed out the creases.

"What's that for?" I said.

"Salvation."

I didn't know what he was talking about.

"Who wrote you a letter? Carnette?"

"It ain't no love letter." He bent back the flap and spread his dark fingers inside to show me it was empty. "Don't do no good to be in love with somebody you never going to see again." He pulled a peony off the bush and shook it over the pocket of the envelope.

"You can't shake them out," I told him. "They run in the middle and hide." He kept on shaking. "Why do you want to catch those things?"

He pulled the pink petals from the outside of the flower and threw them on the ground. "Come on out of there," he said. An ant ran onto his hand. He grunted, dropped the flower and the envelope, brushed at his hand. "Here." He gave me the envelope. "Hold this open."

I cupped it open while he picked the ants from the center of the peony and dropped them in. They ran up the sides, their black butts swinging with the effort of trying to escape. Michael frowned as he touched them.

"Are you going to keep them in the aquarium in your room?" He hadn't unpacked his bug collection since we moved.

"No, that's kid's stuff. I might throw all that junk out." Since he got a steady girlfriend, he worked hard at leaving what he called "kid's stuff" alone. When Mama found out about Carnette, she said Michael was acting too mannish. Daddy grinned and said, "Go on, son. Show 'em what you got."

"Here, Marth, give me that thing now." He rubbed the last ant off his finger and dropped it into the envelope. Then he wet his finger and ran it along the glue on the flap, sealing it shut.

He tossed the envelope into the barrel. It lay on the ashes for a few seconds, then the heat ate brown half circles into the edges; smoke trickled out of the corners. Michael stared into the can, hands hanging at his sides, but before the envelope caught, he reached in and plucked it out. It still smoldered. Only the edges had burned.

"I saved their lives," he said. He blew on the envelope, then stuck the ants in his back pocket and walked to the house. Mama didn't like ants in the house; she'd already told Michael that. She said a house that had ants in it meant the people who lived there were nasty.

"Mama's going to whip your butt."

He turned around. "Mama can't do nothing. So don't be squealing."

There was a message on the side of our house the next Saturday, glopped on in red paint: NIGERS ARE TRASH! A red drip hung at the bottom of each letter. I rubbed my hand over NIGERS, to smudge it out before I had to read it twice, but I only ended up with chalky white paint from the bricks scuffed into my palms. I don't know why that word made me so mad. I'd heard Daddy say it plenty of times. He'd say Boo was a "stupid nigger" or "You can't tell niggers nothing." When Daddy said it, I didn't think anything about it. But this mess on our house was different. I slapped my hand against the bricks.

Michael's window scraped open. He stuck his head out, squinting.

"Marth, what the hell? Why you always got to get up so early?"

"Read this."

He looked down the wall, craning his neck sideways, but I could tell he didn't get it. He slammed the window shut, and a few moments later he stood beside me in his pajama bottoms, reading the message on the wall.

He was quiet for a moment; then all he said was, "The stupid son-of-a-bitches can't even spell," before he went back into the house.

When Mama saw the paint she didn't say a word. She stood in front of the wall, big and silent, and didn't speak. I wasn't surprised. By then I'd heard her stutter on the phone to bill collectors, or seen her wrap her lips around her teeth in embarrassment, when all she really wanted to do was simply smile. I was used to her plugged-up silences, her unwillingness to let go of her thoughts.

"Do we have to move?" I asked her. It seemed like I was the only one who was happy there, and that seemed like a thin thread to sew things together with. Still, her eyes were on the wall.

"We ain't moving. We ain't going nowhere." She went back in the house.

Mama bought a can of white paint to cover up the red, but no matter how many coats she slathered on, the words bled through. Not enough to read, but enough to remember they were there. Those words bothered me all summer; then in September school started and I forgot about it. The smudge just became part of the house.

October came. The air turned sharp; the leaves on all the trees fired with color: reds, purples, oranges. Michael was late coming home from school the Friday before Halloween. Mama was at work. Daddy, too. I was lying on the couch reading Mama's *True Love Story* magazine when I heard the front door muffle closed. Michael was sneaking in. I held the magazine to my face, pretending to read it, in case he wanted to check on me. After I counted to thirty, I went looking for him.

He was in his bedroom, leaning toward the long mirror on top of his bureau, his back toward me. His shirtsleeve was ripped at the shoulder seam, torn half off. Dirt smeared the back of his shirt and trousers. I watched him gently finger his bottom lip, then his right eye, the motion soft and hesitant. In the mirror, his expression hardened and he swung around.

"What you staring at?" His shirt front was stained bright red, his lower lip swollen and shiny.

"Who'd you fight?" I kept my mouth tight to keep from throwing up.

"I didn't fight *nobody.*" He punched the air with his fist. His shirt gaped open at the shoulder. "Motherfuckers ran away."

He was crying, so I started to cry too.

"Go on out of here," he told me. "Go on back downstairs and read your magazine."

I was so afraid, I did exactly that.

"Go out to the tree and get me a long switch."

I looked up from *True Love Story* to see Mama standing over me like a giant. She drew out "long" so I'd know I should break off a big branch. She still had her work clothes on, a pink housekeeping dress from the air force base, and stockings, and crepe-soled shoes. Her hair still held its workday curl, a sausage-roll that touched her shoulders.

"Who are you going to whip?"

"Go do what I said or you'll be next."

From the maple tree on the left side of the lawn, I chose a long sucker branch sprouting from the bottom of the trunk.

When Mama heard the screen door slam, she called out for me to come up to Michael's room. They were both standing in front of the mirror, looking at each other: Michael, tall, thin, and sullen, his chin thrust out, and Mama, dressed for work, arms folded over her chest, her lips mashed together in a hard frown.

Without looking at me, Mama reached back her hand. I put the switch into it. She snatched it, raised it into the air, held it over Michael's head.

He lowered his eyes halfway, still looking at her. "Go on and do what you gonna do."

"Don't you sass me in this house!" she said, bringing the switch down on his shoulders. "I will not tolerate sass in this house! I told you to stay away from that girl." With every word she spoke, her arm raised and the switch sounded. *Whup! Whup!*

"Mama, I don't go near those people. That simple-acting sister of theirs *lies. They* follow *me*! They jump *me*; then the cowards run away. I didn't fight nobody." Tears were in his voice.

"You better hush that sass. I told you and told you till I can't tell you no more, stay in your own yard. Leave those people alone."

I'd heard the other girls in my class talking about it, about what color gowns they had, how they'd wrap their hair around their heads, the pink lipstick they'd wear. Everybody wanted to be a fairy princess for trick or treat. I decided on the same costume.

Dressed in Mama's old crinolines, I leaned in to her mirror and puffed her face powder against my skin. I was still too dark for a fairy princess. I shook some of Daddy's white foot powder onto the puff and covered my face, lips, and eyes. I redrew my mouth and eyes back on with Mama's black eyebrow pencil. I painted a crusty silver star on my forehead with my bottle of glitter. Tilting my head forward and back, I watched the lamplight strike glisters from my star.

Michael showed up behind me, laughing his goofy brother laugh.

"Girl, you look like some kind of monkey. Don't ask me which kind."

"Then you're a monkey's brother."

"Come on, little sis. Since you so hot to get your candy ration, we better go. Have to hike all the way over to Euclid."

"We have to walk there?"

He yawned. "What do you think? The President heard you want to go trick-or-treating so he sent out his limo?"

"I thought Daddy would take us."

"You know Daddy's working overtime."

"Michael, I can't walk that far in high heels."

"Wear your sneaks."

"I'm supposed to be a fairy princess!"

"You got that right." He ran his hand over his hair, making a bristly, electric sound. "Oh, for chrissake, let's go before it gets too dark." He started for the bedroom door.

"We can just go around here."

"Who you think's going to give you candy around here?" He raised his eyebrows.

"Everybody," I said. "The whole damn neighborhood. They're all waiting for me. Okay?"

"Shut up, Marth. And get your coat." He shoved his hands in his trouser pockets and waited.

"You think you're pretty bossy," I said. "You're not Mama or Daddy. You're nobody."

We were almost out the front door before I realized he wasn't dressed for trick or treat. He had on his same old chinos and shirt. I said, "Why don't you put a costume on? At least look like you know it's Halloween."

"I ain't in the spirit of it," he said. "I'm just taking you out because Mama told me to keep you out of trouble."

"Will you put on a costume? Please?" I pulled out one of his hands and held it against my face.

"Don't get that shit on me!"

"Please?"

"Oh, for chrissake, all right. You damn sure are a fairy princess." He took the stairs two at a time. "I'll be down in a minute."

In a few minutes he came down dressed in black trousers and a black undershirt, with one of Mama's black stockings pulled over his face. He'd tied the end of it up into a Woody Woodpecker topknot. His nose was smashed to the side like rubber.

"A cat burglar," I said, admiring how he could change himself into something he wasn't. "That's a good one, Michael."

"Yeah, I'm a second-story man, if you can get ready for that. Let's go."

He pulled his jacket on and we went to the door.

"No, wait a minute." He yanked the stocking off his face. "I can't breathe with this thing on," he said, and stuffed it in his pocket.

While we'd been talking, it had gotten dark. A lot of kids were on the streets—ghosts and skeletons and hoboes and princesses, swinging their flashlights, squealing and running—yet our doorbell hadn't rung once. I thought about what Michael had said. The only reason I went up to the first house was to prove he was wrong. He waited on the sidewalk while I walked through the yard to a small porch. I climbed the steps, passed between two long white columns, and stood in front of a huge door painted glassy white. A brass plaque in the middle of the door said THE HAVERFORDS. I saw them every day on their way to work. He dressed in gray suits. She was a high school teacher.

Mrs. Haverford opened the door with a silly, surprised, wide-eyed welcoming look, as if she were expecting a pirate or a vampire, as if prepared to scream politely before she handed over the candy. But when she saw me, she wiped her face clean and swung the door closed with a *thunk.*

Back on the sidewalk, I could barely make out Michael in his black shirt and pants. I couldn't see much more than his movements; he kept looking back at everyone who passed him. I balled up my pillowcase to make it look like there was candy inside.

"So what'd you get?"

"A Milky Way," I said. "Big one."

"Oh, yeah? Well, they got a lot of money. They can afford to be nice. Let's keep going then."

The next house belonged to the Koenigsbergs. I would babysit their little girl sometimes. I knew Mrs. Koenigsberg would open the door for me, smile at me, say something nice. On the day we moved in, Mr. Koenigsberg came into our yard to shake my father's hand.

Their house was dark, all lights out; I felt let down. I didn't want to go to the other houses on our block. What was the point? When I told Michael, he shrugged and said, "You doing all right. You got that big candy bar. Why stop now?"

"Let's go someplace else, someplace we've never been."

He looked interested. "You want to go over a couple of streets? I know where some really big houses are. More candy for you."

My empty sack was light in my hands, and I didn't want to go home with nothing.

We walked three streets up, then one over. I'd never had a reason to go this far; school was the other way. The houses rose up high, shadowed by tall trees, but dim lights glowed, and I took comfort in that. Our house sat right out on the street; anybody could look in our windows anytime and see what we were doing. These houses hid their owners behind brick walls, trees, shrubbery, deep lawns.

At the first house I went to, an old man with colorless eyes opened the door and said, "Who are you?" I watched his Adam's apple bob in his skinny throat. I felt the dark porch furniture hulking around me on all sides. I jumped down off the porch and ran out of his yard, back to the sidewalk.

"What's wrong with you?" Michael stood alone, his hands jammed into his pants pockets. It must have been late. The other kids had gotten their candy and gone home.

"Let's go home now. It's cold and I'm scared."

"Of what? Ain't nobody here."

"That makes it worse. Let's go home."

"All right. Got your bag?"

I didn't have it. I looked at the old man's porch. He had gone back into the house. "I dropped it back there."

Michael looked at the house. "Dang!" he said. "I can't see nothing up there. What'd you drop it for?"

"I don't know! Let's just go."

"Stay here." He started up the walk. "By the porch?"

"Yeah. In the grass."

He disappeared in a couple of steps, like the dark opened up and let him in. I stood on the sidewalk for a few moments, feeling jumpy. I wanted to get out of there, to run home, but instead I ran up the walk, through the dark to Michael. Before I could get to him, the yard lights blazed on, the house sprang forward, and I stopped. In the grass, Michael crouched over my empty pillowcase, his head lifted toward the porch, his face alert.

I heard a pop like a cap gun. Michael fell backward out of his crouch, as if someone had placed a finger against his forehead and given him a little push.

I ran through the old man's yard, across the grass, straight to Michael. He was stretched out in the grass, one arm resting on his chest, the other flung out to his side, holding the pillowcase. I leaned on my knees beside him, afraid to touch him. On my knees, I bent over him, my ear to his mouth. I prayed to hear him breathe, but I couldn't hear. And I told him that—I said my ears were roaring and I couldn't hear him, and he had to get up and leave before the old man got us. We had to hurry up and get out of there. We had to *go.*

We got to be in the newspaper again. This time, there was a picture of Mama and Daddy, staring straight into the camera. Beneath it, the caption said, *The Harrises lost their son.* I've still got that picture in an album at home. I don't take it out too often, but sometimes I do, and I think about that time when everybody seemed so mute: Mama, Daddy, even Michael.

Sometimes I can still see Michael in his room, pretending to have a girl in his arms, dancing. Eyes closed, he'll swing her out, to the tips of his fingers, then curl her back into his arms, tuck his head to fit hers on his shoulder, and dip forward, letting her feel the weight of his chest.

Sometimes I wonder if things have really changed.

❦❦

"Naw," Nettie Lee said. "Ain't nothing changed."

"I don't know." LaRone drew her baby in close. "I hear so much talk about prejudice being on the rise. But I hope for the best, then usually that's what I get. My philosophy is: I just try to take people like I find them."

Shavonne cleared her throat loudly. "What about skinheads, LaRone? They'd take you somewhere *nobody* would find you."

"I just want to raise my child in an environment where things like race don't matter."

"Shoot. What planet you going to live on? Wait, I know. You going to live on Planet Peaceful, where people call each other brother and sister, and they got wild animals for pets because lions and tigers don't bite. LaRone, you got to stop living in the Age of Aquarius."

"Well, maybe we should all be hopeful for the world LaRone wants," Martha said, though she didn't feel hopeful herself. She felt exhausted. "Ladies, I'm done for the day. You can solve the world's problems without me. I'm going home."

"See you tomorrow." Nettie Lee looked tired too, Martha thought. As if she were—well, plagued by some problem. Martha thought about this on her way out of the nursery to the locker room to get her coat. And she thought about Nettie Lee in the elevator, but by the time she had clutched her coat to her throat and walked outside to the bus stop, Nettie Lee had slipped from her mind.

Nettie Lee stood at her granddaughter's Isolette, watching the baby twitch in her sleep. She lay on her side, one thin arm flung across her barrel chest, the other arm wedged beneath her on the mattress. A respirator tube trailed from her mouth, trembling with the force of compressed oxygen. Nettie Lee found herself breathing with the respirator's rhythm: a prolonged inhalation, then a quick release of air. She stood for a while breathing in and out, panting almost, with the baby, but she couldn't keep up with the respirator's fast pace without feeling dizzy. She sighed aloud and resumed her own slow rhythm. The baby looked okay, not critical like they said she was, although Nettie Lee was willing to admit she couldn't tell a critical baby from a stable one in this place. That was all the more reason to name the baby, she thought. Even if she was the only one who knew what the name was. To come up with a good name, she'd have to think on it. *But for now, I'ma keep on calling you Tookie, because you so sweet. You just like a piece of candy.*

With a cotton ball, she dabbed at a drop of water collected in the corner of the baby's eye. *Got to keep you comfortable and dry. Got to keep your oxygen level up, your breathing quiet. Got to keep your heart calm and beating strong.* Nettie Lee sighed loudly. Who was she kidding? She was falling apart. She wanted nothing so much as to gather this baby into her arms and get the hell out of there, especially since it looked like Martha had designs on her. But if she took the baby away from all these machines, all the doctors and nurses, she was sure to die. Then again, if Nettie Lee stayed here, how long could she pretend she had nothing to do with the baby? As it was, she felt like she was giving herself away every time she looked across the nursery to the warming tray, every time she sat at the table while that social worker talked about foster care for Baby Doe, every time some hospital worker came to the nursery asking if that was Baby X over there on the tray. What had she thought she would accomplish by coming here? What good was it doing her, the baby, or Yolanda?

It was hard to tell if she had done the right thing, answering the ad for grandmothers. What she had hoped for—seeing her granddaughter, letting her know she wasn't alone in the world—went off okay. Here she was. But—Nettie Lee sighed with exasperation—it wasn't *enough* for the baby somehow. Tookie deserved more than to lie on this table like some kind of sick experiment. She wanted to take her grandbaby home.

Nettie Lee thought of what Martha had said in Report the day before, that she was looking to be a foster parent for a preemie. It was clear to her that Martha had only one baby in mind: hers. She'd seen Martha mooning around Tookie's bed, looking at her, touching her. It would be too crazy if the hospital gave her baby to Martha, while she had to sit silent and never tell anybody she was Tookie's grandmother.

Debbie Foxx had been standing at Cruz's Isolette, talking to his mother and her friend, and now she came over to Nettie Lee. She looked at the baby. "I know. She looks kind of peaked, doesn't she?"

Nettie Lee didn't answer.

"You're not getting too attached, are you?" Debbie placed her hand on Nettie Lee's shoulder. "That's like a rule we're supposed to have around here. Don't get too attached." She laughed as if truly delighted. "I'd just like someone to come in here and specifically tell me how to avoid that. Someone could give us all a lecture on it. Some nonattachment expert."

"Yeah, I could use some expert help."

"We all could," Debbie agreed. "Well, back in the real world. I have an extra job for you today."

"What's that, honey?" Nettie Lee balled up the cotton into her hand.

Debbie let her eyes trail away from Nettie Lee and fall on LaRone Cruz, her friend Shavonne, and a man Nettie Lee didn't know, all standing by Daquille's Isolette. The man kissed LaRone on the cheek and walked to the nursery doors, his yellow gown hanging far above his knees and straining at his chest. LaRone stood by awkwardly while the redheaded nurse lifted the baby out.

"He's going home as soon as he reaches five pounds," Debbie told her. "That's his grandpa leaving. He comes in sometimes, even when Mom isn't here, usually during the night shift." Debbie looked back at Nettie Lee. "Mom needs to be shown how to give the bath. Would you do it?"

"All right." She left her thoughts of Tookie behind and followed Debbie over to the two girls.

LaRone sat down in a rocker, then stretched out her arms to receive her baby from the redheaded nurse.

"Miss Cruz, Mrs. Johnson will be helping you with the bath," Debbie told her. "Just take your time and ask her anything you want to. If she doesn't have the answer, she can ask me. Both the grandmothers are here to help you in any way they can, just as if you had a grandmother at home to show you how to care for your baby."

"That'd be a joke," Shavonne said.

"I beg your pardon?" Debbie looked at Shavonne, confusion spreading across her face.

Shavonne, still standing at the Isolette, puckered her mouth and nodded.

She said, "Having my grandmother at home wouldn't work out too well, since my mother put her out of the house."

"Oh," Debbie said. "Well, that's what *our* grandmothers are here for—they can fill in the gaps our own relatives leave. I want Nettie Lee to show you how to bathe Daquille this morning."

"I was going to feed him now."

The clock read 9:30. "You're actually a little early for the ten o'clock."

"I know, but Shavonne got an appointment at WIC, and I told her I'd go with her since it's her first one."

"What's Wick, some kind of welfare?" Nettie Lee asked.

LaRone looked at Nettie Lee for a long moment, then said yes and rolled her eyes up to Shavonne. Daquille had settled into his mother's arms and now peeked out from his hood of blankets. His face was alert, cautious.

"WIC is a program to give extra nutrition to mothers and their children," Debbie told Nettie Lee. "The mothers can get more milk and formula if they go in and take parenting classes."

Nettie Lee nodded. "It sounds like something beneficial." She asked LaRone, "Won't Wick wait for you to take care of your child? You can't be two places at one time."

"She told you I got an *appointment,*" Shavonne said. "I miss my appointment time, they won't make another one for me until next week."

"Mmm-hmm," LaRone said. "Them people don't care what you have to go through to get there. They got so many people down there trying to apply, they don't care if you had something else to do and that's why you're late. They just tell you to go on home and come back next week. You'll just be one less person they have to deal with."

"That's how those people are," Shavonne said. "They all the same." She turned away, pretending interest in a large group of noisy medical students coming in for rounds.

"You go ahead and show LaRone how to give a bath," Debbie

told Nettie Lee. She took the nurser from LaRone. "I'll defrost some more breast milk when you're done."

"What's wrong with her?" LaRone said. Then she said, raising the pitch of her voice, " 'You go ahead and do like I told you to. Your opinion ain't shit.' "

"She ain't usually like that, honey. I guess she got things on her mind this morning."

Nettie Lee pushed the bath cart over to the sink. All the equipment was on it—the plastic tub, liquid soap, body lotion, several large towels, a facecloth.

"You can stay put in your chair and hold Daquille on your lap for the bath." Nettie Lee filled up the washtub in the sink. The water felt warm, just right. "Daquille is a nice name for your baby. Where did you get it from?"

"Thanks." LaRone smoothed the hair on her baby's head with a long fingernail, pink this time. "I made it up."

"That *is* a cute name," Shavonne said. "LaRone's going to help me with a name for my baby. I want a name that expresses her individuality."

"You having a girl for sure?"

"As sure as they can be." Shavonne sat down next to LaRone, in the rocker Martha liked to use, and began to rock, pushing off with her toes. "The doctor said with a girl the ultrasound isn't for sure like it is with a boy. He said with a boy you can actually see his little thing, but with a girl what you're looking at is the absence of a thing." She laughed. "It sounds wack but it makes sense, don't it?"

"Yeah, it does," LaRone said. "It's kind of a shock, isn't it? When you see the baby moving around on that TV screen, and you think, All that's inside of me." She smiled down at her baby. "I liked that."

"It made me sick," Shavonne said. "I looked at that TV and I said to myself, "Nuh-unh, girl. No way. That baby is in there and swimming around, and swallowing that nasty pee it's swimming in, and growing big, and then it's going to want to come out. No. Shavonne ain't playing that."

"Who do you think is going to play it?" LaRone said flatly. "You going to have that baby, Shavonne. You and nobody else."

"I know. I be tripping about it sometime. Sometime I think I'll beg the doctor to give me a C-section, so I can have the baby when I'm asleep."

"You don't want a C-section. They hurt too much after. I was in a room with a girl that had one, and she kept us up all night with her complaining."

"You better show up when I'm in labor, girl. I better not call you and you say you going to miss."

"I said I'd be your labor coach. Stop worrying about it."

"Where's your mama?" Nettie Lee asked, setting the basin of water on the cart. "Can't she help you any?" She wheeled the cart back to the rocker.

LaRone and Shavonne cut their eyes to each other. Shavonne snickered. "You don't want to hear nothing about *my* mother," she said. "That lady don't know her behind from a hole in the ground." She turned to LaRone. "And *she* got the nerve to say that about *me.*"

"Your mother's wack," LaRone said, without enthusiasm.

"Tell me about it." Shavonne looked at Nettie Lee. "I don't mean to disrespect you—what's your name—Nettie *Lee*, but I think I'm best off figuring out my life for myself. Considering the great job you so-called grown-ups have done so far."

"Mmm-hmm," LaRone said.

"And let me tell you something else. Everything I got now, I got on my own, didn't have Mommy and Daddy helping me, because, girl, I don't even know where Mommy and Daddy are half the time, unless I see one of them out on the street. And I *do not* care. I know I can take care of myself. I know what's best for me better than anybody else. So if you got some advice for me, save it." She leaned back in the rocker and closed her eyes. Nettie Lee watched her belly rise and fall in great heaves, imagined the baby turning inside.

She pulled the cart close to LaRone's rocker, dipped the washcloth in the warm water, and wrung it out. "Here." She extended the cloth. "Start with his face and head, then go on to the rest of his body."

"Do I need soap?"

"Not on his face. We'll put some soap on the rag when you get to his body, but then we got to remember to wash it all off so it don't irritate his skin. His skin is going to be really sensitive to things like soap and maybe even lotion and the detergent you wash his clothes in. Any baby is sensitive, but he's a preemie, so you got to worry more when it comes to life on the outside."

"He couldn't stay inside me forever. Had to come out sometime, even if it was a few weeks early."

"Yeah," Nettie Lee said. "But I was talking about outside the *nursery,* where you got to protect him from germs and chemicals. You got to make sure he eats right—you see he eats every two hours in here, don't you? You got to keep up his schedule at home too. And you got to make sure he gets his rest. All he's going to want to do when you get him home is sleep, so let him. Keep your apartment quiet and warm as you can. Make sure his crib don't sit in a draft. Here." She pulled the blanket over Daquille's chest and arms. "After you wash a part, cover it up so he don't get cold during the bath." LaRone nodded. "Later, when he's got more fat on him, you can give him a regular tub bath. For now, just think of him being uncontaminated, and it's your job to keep him from getting exposed to things he just ain't up to."

During the ten o'clocks, as she rocked and fed Gonsalves, Nettie Lee watched LaRone prepare to feed her baby. She had told Shavonne to go ahead to WIC by herself, since she had to take care of Daquille, but Shavonne stayed. Martha sat in a rocker with Riley. The redheaded nurse—Callie Hart—handed LaRone a fresh cylinder of donor breast milk. She tentatively nudged her baby's mouth with the nipple, and he tensed his forehead in concentration, opening his mouth wide, his head jerking toward it. He latched on and sucked the milk in quick little pulls. Sitting beside LaRone in a rocker, Shavonne watched her friend feed the baby and absently kicked her foot against the IV stand Daquille no longer used.

Nettie Lee cleared her throat. "Martha, did I ever tell you about how I came to live here in Dayton?" She said "Martha," but she looked at LaRone and Shavonne.

"No, ma'am," Martha answered. "But you look like you might do it now."

"I wasn't too much younger than these two young ladies right here. We were sick of where we stayed and how we lived, but we couldn't make the move until my mama got herself some courage."

Shavonne looked at LaRone. "She be telling stories just like my grandma. Granny got to tell you her old-timey stories or she bust."

"Yeah," LaRone said.

"They be talking about things that happened way back when, like it got something to do with right now. And she thinks she sly, slipping something she wants you to know into the story, like you can't tell that's what she doing." She sat forward in her chair. "Okay, listen to this: My granny be trying to tell me about sex one day when I was fourteen, and she said, 'Now don't stay out on the street at night because a boy will grab you and knock you down and try to put his finger up in your panties.' His finger!" I said, 'Granny, that's weak. Boys do more than that if they catch you.' Then she's looking all flustrated with me, trying to get me to tell her if anybody done anything to me yet. That's none of her damn business. Besides, by the time I was fourteen I knew more about sex than she did. She thinks if you don't talk about sex it means you ain't doing nothing. I kept on telling that lady to wake up and smell the cappuccino." She snapped her fingers. "It's the nineties."

"I thought you ain't seen your grandma since your mother put her out," Nettie Lee said.

"I'm talking about before then." She gave LaRone a look. "My grandma get so senile she be talking about something, and she can't remember what she said in the middle of it. You have to finish it for her because her mind drifts away from her point."

"Your grandma trips a lot, but she's okay," LaRone said. "I thought you said you were going to WIC?"

"Shoot, I can go over there some other time. I'm tired."

LaRone shook her head and turned to Nettie Lee. "So what happened that made you move here?"

"Oh, Lord. What you want to get her started for, LaRone? I'm telling you, once they get their mouths on something, grandmas don't even know when to stop."

❧ ❧

I'm going to tell you about the time my mama got herself some courage. Up until then, she'd was a mealy-mousy person. Real meek. If somebody say, "Boo!" she'd jump ten feet in the air. If somebody say, "Give me the draws on your behind," she'd snatch those panties right off. And feel bad about it too, like she can't say nothing in her own defense. M'Dear thought people took advantage of her. But she always had this saying, "The worm will turn," that she'd end her conversations with. Stop everybody cold, don't matter who running their mouth, laughing at her, telling her she backwards or whatever. "The worm will turn," she'd say. "The worm will turn."

M'Dear came from a poor little country town called North Kenova, stuck in the north corner of West Virginia where it meets Kentucky and Ohio. She talked about that place like being there was some kind of paradise and heaven rolled into one. She'd call it Down Home. Everything good be happening Down Home. "Down Home we had us some kinda good food. Collard greens, sweet-potato pie, fresh-killed bacon. Can't get us none of that in Chicago." And she'd say, "Wondering what Ruthie Mae up to Down Home? Betcha she in that ol' garden patch of hers right now. Girl probably hoeing the weeds out her snap beans."

Big Daddy Walter always told M'Dear to shut up about Down Home. He don't want to hear no fuss about someplace country. He came up from Clarksdale, Mississippi, and couldn't get out of there fast enough. Clarksdale, Mississippi, the birthplace of the blues, though it seems to me he brought the blues with him when he got off the train. Didn't want no reminders of home, neither. He said he'd seen all the cotton fields he was going to in his lifetime, and he sure didn't want to see them in hell. Seen too many lynchings, beatings, castrations, till he can't see no more. He figured his turn was coming up, better get out of town. Before he hopped the train to Chicago, his brothers and his sister came up, one by one, on that same train. Daddy Walter was the baby of the family, the last one to stay and make sure his daddy was provided for. When the old man died, Daddy Walter put on his Sunday suit, got himself a train ticket, and was gone twenty minutes after his daddy was laid in the ground.

He saw M'Dear at church up in Chicago. Sometimes he'd laugh and say, Church is the only place to meet a good-looking woman. Oh, you can meet them in a bar, but they'll be just as hard-drinking as the men, and as tough too. Bar women are the ones who got the roaming urge, don't want to stay home and cook or watch their kids. Now church, that's where all the women who care about God sit. You can just pick one off the pew.

Not that Daddy Walter cared about God. He said God is just another white man, the biggest one you ever run into, tell *everybody* what to do. But when it came to a wife, he wanted a woman used to minding a man. He figured bending down to God's will was good practice for a woman. He saw M'Dear sitting on the church pew when he was out on one of his Sunday cruises, her hair combed back into a French roll, a white tailored dress buttoned up to her neck, her legs pale and shiny in white stockings, feet crossed nice at the ankles, and he thought, Damn. Dearly beloved, gather together and let no man put us asunder because *I do.*

M'Dear was thinking the same thing when she saw him: Here's a nice-looking redbone man—yellow skin, light brown eyes, intelligent-looking. He even had nappy hair, and M'Dear liked that. She had good hair herself, from that French blood in her, but she thought it was better for a man to have naps. You can't trust a man with wavy hair; he's too stuck on himself, thinking he's more beautiful than you are. One day after they got married, Daddy Walter surprised her; he let their neighbor, who ran a beauty parlor out of her kitchen, conk his hair. When M'Dear saw his slicked-back head, she like to take a skillet after him. But that's how he wore his hair from then on. You want to talk about somebody being handsome, then you got to talk about Big Daddy Walter; he was so fine he had four girls on his arm. And M'Dear said that was the whole problem with that son-of-a-bitch. "Your daddy got three damn women too many."

Like so many, they started having their children before they got married. M'Dear was pregnant with Brawley at the altar. After that she had her babies right quick: Lenis and Lenetta, my older sisters; then here come my other brothers, Acie, Egg, and Too Much. Then me, the baby. We all lived in a two-bedroom apartment on Thirty-second and Indiana Avenue.

I liked to hear M'Dear talk about her life. Way Back When she called it, but I knew she wasn't that old. She may have felt like she was old, but she was only thirty-four. I used to curl up with her on the couch while she read the newspaper. I combed her hair while she laid with her head leaned back against the armrest. I'd start at the hairline and pull the comb through till it reached the ends, curling her hair down over the couch arm. She liked that. She'd say, "Knock the dandruff out," and I'd scratch up all the dandruff on her scalp, then comb through real fast to make the flakes fly off her hair.

When I was in the sixth grade I saw that M'Dear had some gray hairs in the front and a small patch of it on top. The longer the year went on, the more gray hairs I saw, till soon they were all over her head. But those gray hairs didn't take away none of her beauty, just added to it. That year was a bad year for my whole family. Maybe all the same old things was happening, but we just took it different.

One Sunday morning early in June that year, M'Dear was standing in the living room picking up from the night before. She liked to go on a cleaning spree every Sunday before church. Seven o'clock in the morning. Had me out the bed cleaning too. Mostly Daddy Walter's stuff and hers; pint whiskey bottles his friends brought over in their back pockets to be sociable, M'dear's run-down house shoes laying by the couch, some plates with oily sardine tails and cigar ashes on the coffee table. The drapes were already pulled back and the sun was just beginning to show around the top of the apartment building across the street.

"Open up that window and air this place out. Smells like a whiskey factory in here." M'Dear was standing with a little trash can in her hands, clinking the bottles in, and Daddy Walter was in the bedroom snoring as loud as he felt like, since he just got home at five. Daddy Walter spent his nights all up and down Forty-third, listening to Muddy Waters and Little Milton sing the Delta blues and play their guitars. Mama was getting real mad, listening to him snoring.

The window was stuck like always, almost painted shut. I jiggled it hard till it finally gave way and slid up a few inches. Outside, there wasn't nobody on the street. The only car parked in front of our building was Big Daddy Walter's new red Buick, the thing he was so proud of. On the windowsill was a picture of M'Dear and Big Daddy Walter taken when M'Dear was still pregnant with me. They're sitting in a nightclub at a long fold-up table with M'Dear's sister Mary Catherine on one side of her and Daddy Walter on the other. There's all kinds of people in the background, sitting at other tables and standing up talking. Mary Catherine got an evening dress on, looks like it was made out of watered silk, and cut low so it shows her bosom. M'Dear's got on something like it, you can't see it too good in the picture, same fabric, but the straps are frilly instead of straight like Mary Catherine's. M'Dear's got her pocketbook up on the table, and it matches her dress. They both have their hair done up real nice and their faces all made up, their lips painted on. M'Dear is still skinny, and she got one elbow on the table, between the beer bottles, with her wrist bent and her fingers just barely touching her neck. Her head is cocked off to the side, but her eyes look right at the camera and a smile is on her lips. Big Daddy Walter is sitting beside her in a white suit, and his face is almost as white as the suit. Big Daddy Walter's got a thin mustache, a bald spot on top of his head, and a little smile on his face like he's enjoying himself real good. Everybody in that picture looks like they feeling good and sexy, except Mary Catherine.

"Seem like every Sunday it's the same old six and seven," M'Dear said with her back to me, and I couldn't hear what she said next. Then she turned around again. "I get tired of having him all over my behind when he do decide to come to bed." Then her back turned again. I already knew what this meant. I heard it while it was happening the night before. Pretty soon she went into the other kids' bedroom and got them up and dressed for church while I scrambled eggs in the iron skillet. When they were all ready, we ate our eggs at the dinette table, then walked to church.

Our church was down on Forty-ninth Street, a few doors down from the Ace of Clubs. It was a little storefront church that didn't hold too many people. Reverend Cosgrove preached there, and sometimes his assistant reverend took over if Reverend Cosgrove had to work overtime at the bus station. That Sunday morning when we walked in, Chester Applewhite, a big gangly man with womanish-looking hands, was playing on the piano a tinkly little church song made for listening to, not singing to. He had a habit of chewing bubble gum even when he played, and his mouth was going then. We sat in the middle, like always.

Up in front of us I saw Hubie Owens and his mama and daddy sitting. Hubie was in my class at school, Mrs. Thompkins's sixth grade. Him and his friend Dairy Jones was always trying to look up my dress. Dairy's daddy was my daddy's boss at the Carlton Hotel restaurant, where Big Daddy Walter worked as a dishwasher on the day shift. Mr. Jones was what Big Daddy Walter called a "real cracker." Big Daddy didn't appreciate being told what to do by nobody. He said somebody owned his daddy down south, but nobody owned *him,* down south or anywhere else. In Clarksdale, Big Daddy Walter was known as a "bad nigger." That means he was hard-drinking, loud-talking, and made it a point never to say "sir" to any man. Folks was scared of him, glad when he left town; no telling what he might do. He was still like that in Chicago from habit. Dairy's daddy threatened to fire Big Daddy Walter many a day, said he was sleeping on the job, got drunk before lunchtime, was too hung over to work some days, picked fights with the other men. Mr. Jones said Big Daddy Walter was just too unreliable.

Reverend Cosgrove walked in through the front door a few minutes after nine, when everybody was seated. He was a tall, dark man, kind of round-headed, which was nice. And talk about sweet—that man had the nicest temperament I ever saw. Never a harsh word for nobody. But if you needed a good talking-to, the reverend could make you straighten up and fly right with his words. He had a gift. The reverend took the short trip up that little aisle with the people sitting on folding chairs brought out of the side closet for Sunday meetings. The place was always full; all in all about thirty or forty people were there every Sunday. Even though he had already got up to the podium and was standing there waiting for silence, the two women in front of me and M'Dear didn't notice he was standing up there, so they didn't quiet down like everybody else, and one of them was left with the last word. She looked at the other woman, embarrassed, and restuck the hat pin in her hat. The lady next to her was wearing a fox stole that kept staring at me over her shoulder. We all rose to sing "The Negro National Anthem," then "Look Up for a Brighter Day Is Coming." M'Dear didn't have much of a voice, but she was loud and the reverend appreciated it. I mouthed the words so people couldn't hear my bad voice.

Reverend Cosgrove thanked us for our strong voices that Sunday morning and made us sit down.

"This Sunday is a *special* one," he said, "because this Sunday we are going to honor those students graduating from high school. Now, I didn't go on to higher learning myself, so I don't share their honor, but that don't stop me from knowing how important higher learning is."

"Amen," somebody said.

"I said, we as parents may not have passed though the annals of education ourselves, but that don't stop us from knowing how important education is."

"Mmm-hmm. Tell it, Reverend."

"And it don't matter in these times now if you graduate summa cum laude. No, sir. I said, it just don't matter how you graduate in these times the Negro is having right now. If you can't graduate summa cum laude, the next best thing is Thank you, Lordy!"

"Amen, Reverend."

"And I know some of you young people out there who have not completed your high school education are wondering, Shall I continue? Shall I keep climbing the mountain of higher learning if I can't see the mountaintop yet?"

"That's right."

"I said, you're wondering if you are going to see any benefit from all the hard work, all the toil you going through, all the mental gymnastics you performing in the name of higher education. Did I hear an amen?"

"Yes, Reverend. Amen."

"But you don't have to wonder anymore, because the answer to all your questions is sitting right beside you. Look at your fathers." Reverend Cosgrove let his eyes sweep the room. "Well, then, look at your mother if your father ain't here. See that this man or this woman is one of the pillars of the community."

I looked up at M'Dear. She had a special light coming from her eyes. I knew she felt in the spirit that morning, her hands folded in her lap, her head tipped back, the pheasant feather on her hat pointed straight up and trembling with her heartbeat.

"These are the people who raised you up from nothing. Who formed you from clay, just as the Lord God made Adam and Eve from the dirt beneath His feet."

"Amen."

"Preach it, Reverend."

"So it would behoove you to take the time to thank your parents. Get down on your knees and thank the men and women who gave you life, and look to them for your answers." I heard a commotion in the back row. One of the older boys, dressed in a hairy-looking brown suit and tie, was jerking his arm away from his mother's hand. He said, "I didn't ask to be born!" and got up and left out the door. His mother was a lady I saw at church every Sunday, but I only saw him every once in a while. She put her hand on her bosom and lifted her head to listen to the reverend. We all turned back to the front.

Reverend Cosgrove pretended like he didn't see what happened.

"These are the happiest days of your lives, when you're young. Now I know you may question—"

I heard a ruckus in the row ahead of me, up to the left where Hubie Owens was sitting. In the front row, Hubie was turning around to look at me, twisting up his face to make me laugh. I looked at M'Dear. Her head was still held high in its listening pose, so I turned my head toward Hubie, just the slightest, and stuck my tongue out. M'Dear jabbed me in the side with her elbow pretty hard. She had her some bony elbows, though she wasn't a little skinny woman anymore. I knew not to even look her in the face; that would just make her mad. Even though Hubie stayed twisted around in his chair, buckteeth showing, sitting right beside his mama and daddy, who were pretending not to see him, I kept my head turned forward. As quiet as M'Dear was, she could kill you if she felt like it.

Reverend Cosgrove kept on preaching his sermon, through bad kids twisting around pinching each other and babies wailing and whatnot, through boys trying to talk about "Let me have some, baby," right there in the row behind me. The more I think about it, the more I admire the reverend's concentration. And he went on like that for an hour; then he passed the plate.

When we got home M'Dear opened the door to the apartment. I could smell whiskey. Leaving the window open didn't help; it just always smelled like whiskey in there. Big Daddy Walter was still in the bed. Even so, that didn't stop M'Dear from clanging her pots around while she made Sunday dinner: fried chicken, potato salad, and deviled eggs, ready at two o'clock. She took off her Sunday shoes and slipped on her house shoes. Still wearing her good clothes, she got a whole chicken out the refrigerator and chopped its head off with a cleaver. Next, the feet came off. She saved those, but she threw the head away. She cut the chicken up into nine pieces and rolled them in flour and fried them in lard. Still, Big Daddy Walter slept on. But I knew that sooner or later he was going to smell that chicken and wake up.

M'Dear turned on the radio to the *At Home with Brother John* program and began to sing "Everybody's Talking About Heaven" along with the choir while she cut up the potatoes to boil. I watched the way her hips swayed when she sang that song; first she shifted to her left foot, paused for a beat, then swayed to the right. When the water got hot on the stove she dropped the potatoes into the pot. She saw me leaning on Big Daddy Walter's card table, watching her.

"Go change out of your good clothes," she told me. "Then see if you know how to do something besides stand in the middle of the floor."

"Like what?"

"Like what?" She could sound just like me. "Like sweep it. Get your behind in there and change your clothes, then sweep the dirt off of the floor. I got to do everything myself. Get so tired of it. Everybody else act like they blind."

I heard Big Daddy Walter roll over in the bed. M'Dear was talking too loud again.

"Every Sunday, the same old thing. Some people get to sleep, and some people get to clean up after the ones who get to sleep. Well, they can sleep till they can't do nothing else *but* sleep, because the worm will turn."

"Damn." Big Daddy Walter was still mostly asleep, but he was awake enough to be mad. "What you hollering about now? Bad enough you have to go to that church and sit there with them Sunday Christians who can't act no better than they do come Monday." The bedsprings started squeaking; then I heard his feet thump on the floor. "The only time you catch me in church be to pray to the Lord to keep those kinda people away from me." His footsteps got closer; then Big Daddy Walter was standing in the living room in his underwear. I tried not to look at his privates, but I couldn't help myself. I wondered what they looked like in there, what a man looked like, but I was scared of how big Big Daddy Walter was. He saw me not looking at him. He put his hands on his hips and strutted over to M'Dear.

"Walter, put some clothes on your behind!" Mama put her knife down on the counter. "Run around half naked in front of the children like you ain't got good sense." She still had four more potatoes to cut up, and they caught her attention again. She sliced the knife through them like she was deadheading a chicken.

"Why you always got to be thinking about somebody's behind?" Big Daddy Walter stuck his hands in his pants and started to scratch with a bristly, itchy sound. "Ain't nobody care about my underwear!"

Mama chopped up potatoes so fierce you could hear the knife scrape the Formica.

"I'm going back to bed. Wake me up when you got dinner ready to eat." He turned and walked back into their bedroom, the soles of his feet slapping the floor like wet bath mats.

Going to school on Monday was something I liked a whole lot, just because I knew the week had got started. I got the feeling on the weekend, especially Sunday, that I was stuck in my life. Time didn't just drag along then, it stopped dead in its tracks and refused to go on. When I felt like that, I didn't want to be home with M'Dear and them. At least on Monday things got going again. I had to hurry up to get out the bed to get to school; teachers expected to see some work from my mind. That's the way I felt on one particular Monday that same June, like my life had wound itself back up and started ticking again. I was sorry school was about to end for the year, that this was my last week with someplace to go.

Walking up Indiana Avenue where all the shops were, on my

way back from school, I turned down Forty-ninth, thinking I'd go over to the Forty-ninth Street beach instead of home. It was one of the hottest June days we ever had in Chicago. Later, M'Dear read in the paper that people were dying of heatstrokes that summer. I didn't know anything about that, I just knew I was hot and didn't feel like going home. So I turned down Forty-ninth and headed toward the beach, about a mile away. On the street, people was sitting out on their stoops playing cards and music, mostly Leadbelly wailing like a cat caught on a roof at night, and of course Muddy Waters. Walking along that street I could smell dinner drifting out through their screen doors; cabbage, which made me sick, and liver and onions, one of my favorites. I started thinking about M'Dear's dinners, that when she came home from work around four there'd be something good to eat.

Forty-ninth Street was solid tenements, just door after door, as far down the block as you could see. Then there was a stoplight at the corner and the tenements went on up the next block. They were tall buildings, reached way over me. Right on the sidewalk was a row of basement windows that marched on up the street. Those windows would be people's only light. A man was sticking his head out his basement window, talking to an older man squatting on the sidewalk. I saw him just as I was fixing to walk by, his head right by my feet. He smiled at me really nice, his face friendly. Look like he was about thirty or so. But when I walked by he looked up my dress and said, "Those sure are some pretty panties." Now that made me mad. That fool thought he was giving me some kind of sneaky compliment. I told him, "You can get yourself a pair just like them at Kresge's," and swished right on by him *and* that old fool he was talking to. The older man laughed and said, "That little girl don't want none of your candy, Archie." He got that right.

Behind me I heard somebody puffing, out of breath.

"Nettie Lee, wait up!" It was Dairy Jones, Big Daddy Walter's boss's son, running with his bookbag thrown over his shoulder. His face was red from running, his socks run down into the heels of his shoes. He didn't worry about tucking the tail of his shirt into his shorts or pulling up his socks, and I liked that. He impressed me like he had better things to think about than how he looked and how other people was taking him. He said, "Want me to walk you home?"

"What for?"

He looked confounded for a minute; then he said, "You're walking through a bad neighborhood."

"I live right up the next block." I pointed to where my building was. He started walking in the direction I pointed. "I'm not going home anyway," I told him. "I'm going to go see the beach."

He stopped. "Which one?"

"The one over there." I pointed over my shoulder. He followed my finger with his eyes, then squinted and shook his head.

"That's not a good idea."

I laughed at him. "What you talking about?"

"Going to the Forty-ninth Street beach is not a good idea."

"Who said?"

"My parents. You could get killed over there."

"No," I said. "*You* the one could get killed over there."

"Then what's the point of going?" He stopped walking and looked at me.

"Maybe for you there ain't no point, but for Nettie Lee Johnson there is a point."

"So lemme walk you home, okay?" I liked the way he dragged it out: Okaaaaay?

"Okaaaaay."

We turned around in the middle of the sidewalk and headed the other way, down Drexel Avenue.

"You ever see *The Wizard of Oz*?" he said.

"The who of what?" I wasn't paying him no mind. He liked to talk about movies he saw on the weekend at Loew's. M'Dear said going to the movies was something white people like to do. I thought I might like it too, but I didn't want her to accuse me of trying to act white.

"*The Wizard of Oz.* In the middle of the movie, Dorothy and the straw man start out walking to Oz. First they go one way, down this yellow brick road, then they turn in the middle of a step, just when they're ready to put their feet down, and they go in the opposite direction. Like we just did. Almost. The difference is they do it at exactly the same time."

"So?"

"So we could do that. Walk in perfect step, then switch around and walk in perfect step the other way."

"Boy, you crazy! Why we want to do something like that? And if we did do it, which one would you be—Dorothy?"

"I ain't a queer!"

"Then you made out of straw."

He looked disgusted. "Forget it."

"Forgot it."

We kept walking, passing by the businesses on Drexel. He edged me with his shoulder.

"Boy, what you pushing for? Quit."

"Go down there. Let's go that way."

"I don't want to walk down no alley. Get my shoes dirty."

"It's a shortcut to your street. You act just like a girl. All they think about is, 'I might get my shoes dirty. I might muss my hair.' "

"I know how to get to my own street. And my hair don't get 'muss.' Or ain't you noticed?"

"Wait a minute." He stopped and put down his bookbag. "Let me feel it." I thought about how his hands would feel in my hair. Nobody ever touched me like that before. "Let me feel what it's like."

He was standing close enough for me to smell his clothes: smelled like green beans cooked in bacon grease and spilled milk. Looking at his face I got scared, worried to death that he might try to kiss me out on Drexel Avenue in front of all them people. I pushed his hand away.

"Don't be touching me, boy." I thought of what M'Dear would

say if she caught me and him in the street touching each other. "You got filthy hands anyway, probably been playing with your thing."

Dairy's mouth opened. "Don't talk like that, Nettie Lee. Nice girls aren't supposed to say that kind of thing."

"Who said I'm nice?" I started down the alley. At least down there nobody would see me with Dairy Jones.

He turned and followed me.

"If you're not a nice girl, I bet you done some things, like let boys into your panties." It was kind of a question, his voice rising up at the end and quivering on "panties."

"I don't have to tell you what I done. It's my private business." We were coming up on the back door of the church. Three doors down was the bar Big Daddy Walter went to all the time, the Ace of Clubs. I kept walking up the alley, but I was scared. I had a yearning to find out what he was like, what any boy touching me was like. The other boys in my class didn't bother with me too much. I think they were scared of me, to tell you the truth. Then again, the thought of Dairy touching me, *any* boy touching me, was repulsive.

The door to the bar peeked open a little and a lady in a tight red chemise strutted out. Her dress had wide straps and a row of tassels hanging across her breasts. On top of her bare chest she had a long rope of pearls. She was laughing at somebody still in the club. "I told you, Big Daddy! I done told you I want a ring to prove your love. Talk is very, *very* cheap."

Daddy Walter rushed up behind her and grabbed her arm. "Aw, baby," he said. "Didn't I tell you I already bought the ring? Got it in layaway over to the jewelry place on Michigan." She strutted her tail on up the alley. I thought he looked my way for a minute before he hurried after her. I saw them get in his Buick, parked behind the butcher's.

"That's your daddy," Dairy said, like I ain't got eyes.

"I know it."

"Who's he talking to? That ain't your mama."

"Shut up."

Dairy put his bookbag down in the gravel. "Only thing shut me up is a kiss."

He pushed his lips against mine so hard I felt the outline of his teeth, and the point of his nose smashed up against mine. I couldn't breathe. I knew right then and there why that woman told Daddy Walter he better give her a ring for all her trouble. I decided I wasn't going to give nothing away either. Every time somebody put their hands on me, I was going to come away with something. Dairy had his eyes squeezed shut and was pushing me so hard I leaned backward and stumbled over my own shoes, and we fell on the ground. But he didn't stop pressing his mouth on mine and trying to push his hands under my dress. I squeezed my legs shut so his hand wouldn't find my coochie. I just wasn't ready for him to be forcing himself on me. Now if he had *asked,* that might have been a different story. I couldn't breathe and the rocks in the alley was pressing into my butt, so I got sick of being underneath him, and I pushed him off.

"What's wrong?"

"I can't breathe. You too heavy."

"Oh."

I looked up the alley, toward the bar. "Let's go."

He seemed relieved, like he didn't have plans on what to do next anyway. "Okay."

I heard a car start up, and then I saw the Buick move off down the alley.

Big Daddy Walter was sitting on the front stoop waiting for me when I got home. He sat on the top step with his legs splayed open, his shoulder against the iron rail. I concentrated on the top of his bald head while I squeezed past him. I thought, If he says anything to me, I'll just turn around and run as fast as I can. Just take off down the street and fly—he's so drunk he couldn't catch up with me nohow. My leg hit his shoulder while I was trying to turn the doorknob, and he grabbed me around the ankle. I shook his hand off and ran into the living room. M'Dear was in the kitchen making pintos and fatback. A whole row of bean cans sat on the counter with their tops open in a little salute. She said, "Hello, what took you so long coming home from school?" She slid a pan of cornbread batter in the oven.

I turned toward the door. Daddy Walter swayed in the doorway, a mean look on his face, but something more was there. He looked scared.

"Nettie Lee," he told me, "go on to the bedroom and do that homework you so crazy about." He looked at me so intense it was like he was praying to me.

"Why, Daddy Walter?"

"I said *go.* Don't want to start no arguments with me today. I ain't but two minutes off of your behind. You ain't as grown as you think you is."

"What'd I do? Besides, I ain't got no homework today. I did it all at school during recess."

"Well, get in there and clean the room, then."

That was something I did *not* want to hear. All of us children slept in that room. Acie, Too Much, Brawley, Egg, the girls, and me. M'Dear had two beds and a mattress on the floor crammed into that room. The boys was about as bad as you can get about not picking up their clothes and hiding food under the beds. Last thing I wanted to do was go in there and pick up their mess.

"Daddy Walter, that room a mess and it's not my fault. I'm not going to clean up something that a bunch of slobs made."

He took a step toward me, his face pleading with me to get in my room. "I told you to get that sassy little black behind of yours into that pigsty you sleep in and clean it up. Now."

"Big Daddy," M'Dear said in her nice voice, "don't be getting mad at the child. She going in there right now." M'Dear gave me a look. "She going right in. You go on outside and get yourself some air. I'll call you when your dinner's ready." She looked at me and jerked her head toward the bedroom.

"Naw, I ain't going outside." He jerked his arm from M'Dear's hand. "And don't be using that voice on me. I ain't no public aid lady listening to no lies you telling."

I was trying to figure out what was going on. Daddy Walter was drunk, but that didn't account for all this kind of loud talking.

Daddy Walter caught me by the head and pulled me over to him. He pushed his mouth into my ear and said, "Keep your mouth shut." After a little pause he said, looking right into my face, "Okay, Nettie Lee? Can you do that for Daddy?"

"Your breath stink, smell like you been kissing some stinky old lady who drink too much." I don't know why I said that. I knew he would slap me silly.

His face turned so mad I thought he was going to drool at the mouth. He put both his hands around my neck and squeezed till I couldn't breathe. I knew he wouldn't choke me for real. He wouldn't do such a thing. But I was getting dizzy waiting for him to stop.

"Damn, Walter, let loose of that child!" M'Dear grabbed Daddy Walter by his arm.

He didn't answer her, just kept on grunting and trying to strangle me. I guess when you're drunk it takes some of the strength out of your hands. Still, those hands felt like cats' claws digging into my neck, giving me the worst headache I ever had. In back of me I could hear M'Dear screaming, "Walter! Walter! Don't kill that child!" I wanted to tell her this was none of her business, this was between Big Daddy Walter and me. Besides, I started thinking that if he did kill me, I wouldn't mind. *He'd* get in trouble, not me, and boy, would that be worth it to see Big Daddy Walter get his. The more he choked me, the more I thought it. Let him kill me. It would serve him right.

I heard *thong, thong, thong!* and I knew the bells was ringing for me up in heaven, that I done passed over to the other side. Then I hit the floor, and it woke me up right quick. M'Dear was standing over Daddy Walter with her big bean pot held over her head with both hands; she was bringing it up again smack over his head, until she saw he was passed out from the first blows. She dropped the pot on the floor and grabbed me by my hands. I looked into her eyes, as serious and scared as I had ever seen them.

"We got to leave here quick before that son-of-a-bitch wakes hisself up," she told me. She called out the door for all the rest of them to run to the Buick, don't worry about taking no clothes or nothing, just get in the car *quick.* She told Brawley to drive us out of Chicago. She don't care where, he just supposed to get the Buick on the road and keep going till we somewhere else. Then she changed her mind and said, "Brawley, head this car Down Home where we belong."

And that's how we ended up in Dayton. That's all the gas the car had in it.

"Your family trips a lot," Shavonne said to Nettie Lee. "I couldn't handle a family like that."

Nettie Lee didn't feel like replying.

"Do you miss Chicago, miss where you grew up?" LaRone asked.

"Naw, I don't miss that place." Sadness pushed up her throat, followed by a short little laugh. "I sure don't miss that time in my life. But you know what I do miss sometimes? My family. After M'Dear got rid of Big Daddy Walter, I never saw him again. Mean as he was, I do miss my daddy."

"So when your mama had enough of your daddy telling her what to do, she told the fool to step?" Shavonne said.

"Yeah. Something like that."

"Sometimes people are crying out for help. They don't even know it themselves," Martha said. "They hide what's wrong with them so nobody could help if they wanted to."

"Yeah, maybe that's true."

Shavonne said, "Don't your story have some kind of a moral or a point to it?"

"There's no explaining human behavior, honey. You just look at it." Nettie Lee continued rocking Gonsalves, who had fallen asleep.

Martha sat across the conference table from Nettie Lee on a dreary Thursday morning. It was Christmas Eve. Everyone was assembled for Report: Barb Hunter and Terese Czajwolski; the nurses Mary Pangalangan and Callie Hart; George Johns, the nurse who had instructed her on her first day—she hadn't seen him since then; Dr. Ethel Xiang, the neonatology resident; Nettie Lee; and Debbie Foxx's empty chair. Barb Hunter shuffled through a stack of legal-sized papers. The smell of coffee and chocolate steamed from a take-out Lava Java cup set beside her smart black briefcase—a graduation present, Martha assumed. Through the open door, Martha could see Foxx scuttling around the nursery, giving quick instructions to the other first-shift nurses, who had already taken over the duties from the night shift. Sitting in rockers and holding their babies, Mrs. Baker and LaRone Cruz, who had come to the unit more in the past week than she had during Daquille's entire hospitalization, fed their babies and talked. Perhaps LaRone finally realized she would be the sole caretaker for her baby in a week or so, and she wanted to get used to him before she took him home. She cradled him in her arms, her finger tracing a circle around his face.

"Shall we start the meeting now?" Dr. Xiang looked impatiently at the nurses, folded her hands on the table. "Nurse Foxx may catch up with us when she arrives."

"I've arrived," Foxx said, closing the door. She sat down.

Dr. Xiang nodded to Barb Hunter. "I believe you have some information about our mystery Baby Doe?"

"That's right," Hunter said. "But first I'd like to hear an update on the baby's medical condition."

Dr. Xiang pulled a metal-cased patient file from the stack in front of her and read from it. "Baby is suffering from transposition of the great vessels and subsequent heart failure, as you know. The corrective surgery performed last Saturday was successful; the prognosis is, of course, guarded. Her condition is critical." She flipped through the thick chart. "Bloodwork is looking as expected—blood gases fair, moderate hypovolemia, moderate pulmonary hypertension, high bilirubin, for which, if it does not lessen in twelve hours, I will order an exchange transfusion." She looked briefly around the table, her expression grave. "I examined her this morning to check her skin color. Definitely more jaundiced than yesterday. Baby was born with a positive tox to cocaine and is receiving the appropriate drugs."

There were murmurs around the table.

"How is the drug treatment coming?" Hunter asked.

"Of course, we can't really treat cocaine addiction. All we can do is tranquilize Baby to moderate the manifestations of the addiction: increased tone, crying and jitteriness, staring, scissoring of the legs, that type of thing. But Baby seems stabilized. No further episodes of seizures since Tuesday, when I upped the meds." Dr. Xiang took off her glasses and rubbed both eyes. "That *was* Tuesday, Foxx?"

"That was Wednesday, Doctor," she replied, then looked across the table to Barb Hunter. "Wednesday the baby had a mild seizure. Her right foot and eye were primarily involved. Dr. Xiang upped the seizure meds."

Martha remembered what had happened. She had just finished wiping off the warming tray and looked at Faith. Her chest rose rhythmically with the respirator breaths; her arms, raised above her head in a seeming gesture of mock surprise, and her legs, sprawled apart, twitched randomly. She was sleeping as peacefully as Martha had ever seen. But then her right foot began trembling in a finely tuned vibration that Martha had almost missed. She had stared at the baby's leg, watching the trembles travel upward to affect her hand; then her eyelid danced briefly. Foxx had come over to the warming tray and stood beside her.

"What's wrong, Martha?" She looked at the baby. "My God, that's all you need, you poor little girl." To Martha, she had said, "She's got the shakes." Foxx picked up the chart and clicked her pen. "This is why your mother tells you not to do drugs."

Now Foxx said to Dr. Xiang, "The meds are controlling the seizures for the most part. But occasionally one breaks through."

"Perhaps I will order an increase. Trial and error."

"Well," said Hunter, "I'm wondering what you think the baby's chances for survival are, Dr. Xiang."

"Baby's condition is as expected. But percentagewise I would say the odds are not on Baby's side."

"Oh, Lord have mercy."

Dr. Xiang looked briefly at Nettie Lee, who looked terrible, stricken.

Barb Hunter went on as if she hadn't noticed Nettie Lee's prayer. "My office is ready to go forward with charges against the mother," Hunter said. "The DA is looking for attempted murder since the child was abandoned in a portable toilet, and after talking with him I'm all for it. I mean, when is this ridiculousness going to stop? But CPA won't go for it. All my office hopes for is child abandonment, and, since the baby is so premature and was found still attached to the placenta, we could probably do delivering drugs to a minor."

"I think you'll have a rough time on that one," Terese Czajwolski said. "It's been tried before, and the judge decided that even though a pregnant mother *can* addict her baby in utero, the fetus is not legally considered a baby. And that's the law. You can't prosecute."

"I realize that. I read the cases," Hunter said. "But the difference this time is, the prosecutor wants to go on the fact that after a baby has been delivered, but before the umbilical cord is cut, the mother still pumps cocaine to the baby through the cord. In this case especially, since we found the baby still attached to the placenta, the prosecutor feels there was no effort made to protect the newly born child from the cocaine ingested by the mother."

George Johns sighed impatiently. "You have to prove the mother had medical knowledge of cocaine's ability to cross the placenta, yes? You would have to prove a young girl has an understanding of anatomy and physiology, of pharmacology."

"Not really," Hunter said. "And who says it's a young girl?"

"Who else could be so foolish?" replied Mr. Johns.

"We're not talking about foolish," Hunter said. "Leaving your car in the rain with the top down is foolish. Leaving a baby to die is murder. But actually, George, if you read the literature, you'd know the majority of these babies are born to women with more than one child. They are not young girls."

Mary Pangalangan nodded. "It's very cruel. They should know better."

"It's cruel, and it's becoming more common," said Callie Hart. "I can't believe this is the second time it's happened in the last couple of years. And it's not even summer. Leaving a baby in a public place is usually a warm-weather thing."

"Well, maybe that's why the mother called nine-one-one right away," Mary said. "It's too cruel."

"Do you think they'll be able to find that mother?" asked Nettie Lee.

"We have some information," Hunter said. "The call in to nine-eleven reporting the baby's location was made by a female who sounded black. It was pretty typical."

"What do you mean, 'typical'?" Nettie Lee crossed her arms, lifted her head.

"Typical situation. I mean, I wasn't surprised when I heard it. Black female, sounded high as hell, calling from a pay phone, crying. Incoherent, almost. And when the baby arrived at the hospital, they got a positive tox screen on her."

"And that's typical?"

"Well, what I mean is, the crack problem is pretty much confined to that area of town. Let's just be honest, okay? The west side is where the most severe drug use takes place. Following that use is a multitude of problems: child abuse and neglect, criminal activity, poverty, homelessness."

"Some of every evil, is that right?" George Johns said.

"Yes, basically. And I'm not ashamed to say it. It's a fact. And it's horrible. I get so tired of people behaving like animals."

"Well," said Foxx, "I really don't think prosecuting a mother who obviously needs psychiatric and substance abuse help is going to accomplish much. And how do you expect addicted pregnant mothers to go for prenatal care when they're worried about being thrown in jail?"

"Then you wouldn't do anything to stop these people from throwing their babies away?" the social worker said. "That seems callous, Debbie. Where's your heart?"

"I guess I left it in the nursery." Debbie got up and walked out.

The table was uncomfortably silent for several moments. Through the door, Martha watched Foxx talk briefly to one of the nurses who had stayed in the nursery during Report; then Foxx went to the phone.

"Well," Hunter said, a bit sarcastically, Martha thought, "let's go on. Of course the baby's condition isn't stable yet, but barring an extraordinary turn of events, I expect that she too will recover and need a foster placement. Martha"—she looked right at her for the first time—"I am prepared to set up a home visit for you, if you're still interested. We can talk about it after Report."

Martha's heart jumped. "That sounds fine."

"Now for Baby Gonsalves. His mother was contacted and her position is, basically, that she doesn't want to see him and wants him signed over to adoption services. If they can't get a placement there, I suppose we'll try for a long-term foster placement."

Martha let Hunter's talk drift past her. A home visit for evaluation. She could become Faith's foster mother. For the first time since Paul died, her heart really lifted.

LaRone Cruz had been at the hospital all morning. Martha watched her bathe and feed Daquille. A little before four, her friend Shavonne came in to meet her. Shavonne said they were just going to see a movie, though she had tried to talk LaRone into going to a club with her that evening. LaRone said she was too tired. Now, in the late afternoon, LaRone sat rocking her baby, listening to the grandmothers talk. Shavonne sat in a rocker beside her, anxious to leave.

"I think I'll adopt that little Baby Doe myself," Martha said. "I know they'll have a hard time finding a home willing to take in a crack baby, and I'll already have her as a foster child."

Nettie Lee blew air through her teeth. "Don't count your chicks before they hatch." She stopped rocking and looked at Martha. "You know, folks get paid money to take those babies in. I thought you said money didn't interest you. Guess you say anything that suits you at the time. Being a foster is a paid job, just like anything else."

"I don't think anybody's getting rich being a foster mother," Martha said carefully. She didn't understand Nettie Lee's anger but had seen it pop up so often when the baby was mentioned that she wasn't surprised. "They use that money to feed and clothe the kids."

"Some of them do. Then again, some of them don't."

"You're too cynical, Nettie Lee." She paused. It was the first time Martha had said her name. She looked at Nettie Lee to see if she had noticed. Nettie Lee rocked Gonsalves back and forth, with fury.

"What's the matter with you? You've been touchy since the meeting. Though I can't say I blame you."

"Ain't nothing wrong with me. You want to talk about somebody hard and cynical, then talk about that Miss Hunter. I never seen somebody who wanted to throw a mother in jail as bad as that woman does."

"Don't you think Baby Doe's mother deserves it? That's what you said before."

"Well, I don't think she deserves what *they've* got planned for her. I don't think she had murder on her mind when she left the baby behind. The girl was probably high or something, like the social worker said, and didn't know what she was doing."

"That's no excuse."

"I'm not trying to excuse her. I think what she did is against God's law. But He will judge her. It's not up to us."

"I was getting angry at that Hunter girl myself," Martha said.

LaRone said, "Who are you-all talking about?"

"Oh, just a smart young lady from the Child Protection Agency." Martha didn't want to say more. What they talked about in Report was confidential.

"What did she do?"

"She's in charge of Baby Doe, that's all," Martha said.

"The one they call Baby X? Well, that mother better look out for *her,*" LaRone said. "You don't want to play with a woman who's got helping poor folks on her mind."

"What did you hear about Baby X?" Nettie Lee asked casually. Martha thought she sounded too casual. Nettie Lee took a sudden interest in folding down the hand cuffs on Gonsalves's shirt, covering his fingers.

"I've been hearing about her for the past month. You can't turn on the TV without seeing somebody talk about it."

"What do you think is wrong with the mother?" Martha asked. "The way she just disappeared?" She shook her head. If it were her, she would miss the baby so much she couldn't possibly stay away. "Do you think she's hoping to get her baby back?"

"I don't really think about it," LaRone said. "I mean, how do I know what she was feeling? How can I judge? I'm just happy I've never been that desperate."

"Maybe she had post-delivery depression," Shavonne said.

"You heard of that? Where the mother goes crazy and thinks her baby is the devil or something? I saw that on *Oprah.*"

Martha said, "It's not just being desperate that has me worried. It's being misunderstood. I think Miss Hunter looks at people and she sees the pictures, the explanations, already in her mind, and she doesn't see what stands right in front of her. That's what worries me."

"You know what else I saw one time?" Shavonne said. "They had this woman on who didn't even know she was pregnant. So she has labor pains, right? And she thinks she's got appendicitis, so she calls a cab to go to the hospital and the baby plops out of her, right there in the cab. When she was feeling it, all she thought was she had to go to the bathroom."

"That's pretty dumb." LaRone looked unimpressed.

"Then another time, they had a show with this girl who looked like she was about twelve or something, I don't remember how old she said she was. Well, this girl lived with her grandmother, who was real strict and made the girl go to church all the time, and everything like that? So this girl turns up pregnant anyway, and she hides it from her grandmother by wearing big old shirts and staying in her room a lot, so her grandmother won't notice anything. Then she has the baby one night in her room, while her grandmother is asleep. She wraps it up in a bunch of towels and puts it in the toy chest so nobody can find it. Only, her grandmother is cleaning up, like days later, and the baby is in there dead. So the girl claims she didn't know the baby was in there. Then they get a psychiatrist to examine her, and he says she had that same kind of post-delivery thing that the girl on *Oprah* had. I don't remember what show this one was. It could have been *Montel.*"

"Oh, for Christ's sake," Martha said, feeling curiosity and disgust. "That garbage is going to rot your mind."

"It really did happen," Shavonne said. "Don't you want to know what's going on in the world? Unless you're just like that grandmother, who thought making that girl go to church all the time was all she needed to do."

"Well," Nettie Lee said, "it's a fact you can't control your children these days. Don't seem to matter how hard you try. They go on out and do as they please and let the devil take the hindmost." She shook her head. "You disagree with that and you're just living in denial."

"Yes," Martha said. "People need to face up to what they know is the truth."

"Like who?" Nettie Lee said quickly.

"Anyone. I was just talking in general. But if you want to get specific, I know about a man who was the king of denial. He was one of my relatives."

"Where your people from?" Nettie Lee asked.

"Oh, we come from a long way, over in West Virginia," Martha said. "And before that, North Carolina." She closed her eyes and leaned her face against Brown's back and shoulder, nuzzling the warm, loose skin on the baby's back, grazing the fine hairs on the baby's shoulder with the tips of her fingers before tightening the blankets to keep her warm. Brown stirred and squeaked, then opened her eyes. Large and dark, they gave her face a worried expression.

"How y'all end up in Dayton?"

"Moved here. Took the bus."

"Girl, talking to you is like walking down a brick road in the middle of January—got to do it one brick at a time. You afraid I'ma sell your story to the *Enquirer*?"

"I'm not studying about you."

"Because you ain't got nothing to be ashamed of. Or especially proud of. Far as I can tell, you the average woman. Got a average life. You not going to wake up some bright morning and find out you married to Donald Trump, so you don't have to worry over your image like you been doing."

"What are you mumbling about?" Martha rubbed her cheek against the baby's coarse blanket.

"Your airs. You got too many," Nettie Lee said. "Now don't get me wrong. A few high-flung notions is a good thing. You know, give the world something good to chew on about you. But, honey, I know you ain't no Ivana Trump." She laughed and shook her head. "Ivana ain't got to use no Vaseline on *her* head."

Martha stopped rocking. "I don't use Vaseline, old woman."

"You grease your head up like anybody else got nappy hair. Myself included. I'm just trying to say—"

"You're just saying too much. Leave me alone. I changed my mind. I don't feel like discussing my private business today."

"You ashamed of your people," Nettie Lee said simply, then bent her face down to Gonsalves, humming the theme song from *The Waltons.*

Could that be true? Martha's mind flew off in a race of worry. She loved her mother but had felt sorry for her, and as a child she had wanted to protect her. She'd walked behind her, throughout the house, watching her hips hump beneath her dress, wanting to be her mother's second voice, loud as a bullhorn. She'd tell her father why Mama used sweet potatoes in the pot roast that time, instead of the carrots he was expecting: *None of your business! Next time make dinner yourself!* She thought of her big brother, Michael, angry and dusty and bloody. And then her father's rage, likely to turn to soft tears. A terrible thought—what could she do about a grown man's tears?

Ashamed of her people? Her grandmother Adele, a tiny-boned woman with a white frizz of hair around her face, lying in a coffin. She'd seemed like a giant when she was alive. When Martha heard the story of David and Goliath in Sunday school, she had imagined David was Grandma Adele and Goliath a strong black man with her father's face. She knew Grandma could pick up a slingshot and pitch a rock hard enough, far enough, to knock Goliath down.

Her mama was the oldest, Uncle Chillie the baby. There were six other children between them. Back when Martha was growing up, Uncle Chillie was a grown man with a job at the air force base. Once, Martha came into the front room of Grandma Adele's house and found Uncle Chillie lying with his head cradled in her lap, his legs hanging over the rolled arm of the couch, the tips of his shoes grazing the carpet. Grandma bent over him, her face almost touching his, and dabbed at his eye with a twisted bit of toilet paper. She had said, "Chillie's got an eyelash up under his lid." She held his lashes between her fingers and turned the lid inside out. Even so, Uncle Chillie lay still, his arms drooped over the couch, his hand resting palm up on the floor.

Her people: they were unpredictable, rough. Was she ashamed of them?

Martha watched Nettie Lee bending over Gonsalves, swaddling him tighter in his blanket.

"My people came from North Kenova, West Virginia. And before that, for five generations back, from North Carolina. My first relative, born a slave but died a free woman, was my great-great-great-grandmother, Armella Moses."

"We talking about after the Emancipation?"

"She was born before the Civil War even started."

"Then how come she wasn't a slave? And who was this king of denial you talking about?"

❧ ❧

My great-great-great-grandmother, Armella Sykes Moses, was born on a big tobacco plantation in North Carolina sometime in the late 1830s. I don't have any pictures of Armella, but in my mind her face is clear as the moon at night. Her nose was broken so badly it lay flat to one side. Her daddy was an Indian brave who took up with black folks. They say the Indian in her made her willful, disinclined to take orders, and along the way she got her nose smashed for it. But I don't believe in that kind of stereotyping. I think she was strong because she had to be. No such thing as a weak slave. She could plow up a field good as any man. When she planted her big feet in the dirt, you couldn't budge that girl from whatever she was trying to haul.

Sykes ran a big plantation, more than three thousand acres planted mostly to tobacco, but he grew cotton too. To work the place, he had over three hundred slaves doing all kinds of jobs, from cooking to valeting to working as carpenters, seamstresses, and blacksmiths; some were also singers and poets. All that the plantation needed, they provided.

Armella lived there with her brother Geoffrey. She remembered three things about the Sykes plantation. The first was Christmas dinner, when Sykes would have the men clear out the tool barn to make room for thirty or so long tables groaning with food. The women spent the week before Christmas cooking in the Big House kitchen. While they cooked, they used to sing a song that went:

Christmas for the master
The food laid out so neat.
Darkies cooking dinner
For the master's treat.

New Year's Day is coming.
Together we shall rest.
Cooking for the master—
Cook up a hornet's nest.

Mrs. Sykes had a fireplace that took up one whole wall, with cast-iron pots hanging at the sides, kept sparkling clean by old Granny Ivory. That was her job, to cook for the Sykes family. None of the cooking for the slaves took place in the Big House kitchen. Instead, Sykes had a separate building where the children's cook kept a fire going, cooking up cornbread and roasting potatoes. Pa Joe's job was to watch the children while their parents were in the fields. He helped the cook dump cornbread and buttermilk into a trough that stretched across the whole front of the kitchen building, for the young ones to eat breakfast and lunch.

Most of the time they got just enough to keep the gripe out of their stomachs, but on Christmas there was food and more food. Plenty of roasted turkeys, of course, and hams, roasted chickens, and sometimes deer meat, though Armella didn't care for that. She and Geoffrey lived with Granny Ivory, who baked pies of every sort: apple, grape, sweet potato, sticky on top with brown sugar. She made plenty of desserts all by herself, but some of the women would get a contest going to see who could make the best sweet-potato pie, get the sweetest grape juice, the lightest biscuits. They let the men judge. They cooked up all the usual winter vegetables too, turnips and carrots and dried corn soaked in milk. Out in the barn, they had the braziers heaped with hot coals. When all the people gathered together, they made their own warmth. After dinner, they lined up at the back door of the Big House while Sykes handed out the Christmas treats. The men got a plug of tobacco to keep for themselves. Sykes said the slaves grew it, so they ought to get a little piece of it. The women got a length of cloth to make a new dress, and the children got a bit of rock candy to suck. They had their dancing and singing all the rest of the week until New Year's Day. That was the day they got back to work.

The second thing Armella remembered from the Sykes place was Peggy Dear. She lived in the cabin next to Granny Ivory. Peggy Dear didn't have a husband but she had four light-skinned children, all of them too little to work. When Armella turned twelve, Peggy Dear had another baby, just as light as can be. Everybody knew those were Sykes's children, but nobody said anything in front of Peggy Dear, since she felt humiliated as it was, though she loved her children the same as anybody else. But with this baby, the burden was too great. She lost her mind. Try as she might, Granny Ivory couldn't get her to nurse the child. Pretty soon, Peggy Dear ran off without confiding to anybody what she was planning, and she didn't take her children, not even the newborn. Granny took up all the kids into her cabin, the same as she did for Armella and Geoffrey when they arrived without a mother. That was too many people for one cabin, so Granny put Peggy Dear's children back in their own cabin, just across the way, and put Armella in charge of them, like a little mother. Around a week after Peggy Dear was still missing, Armella was sitting out in the yard with Granny Ivory, shelling peas for the

Sykeses' dinner, the baby sleeping in a wood box next to Armella's feet. She looked up the road, and here comes one of Mr. Sykes's tobacco wagons rolling down to the cabins. All of Peggy Dear's children were sitting in the dirt, making mudpies, watching the wagon come. Granny Ivory got up slowly, her eyes on the wagon still off a ways yet, and she turned to Armella and told her, "Take those children inside and close the door. Don't you let me see that you done gone and opened that door, not even a peep."

Armella got them into Peggy Dear's cabin, but as soon as Granny Ivory turned her back, she opened the door a little peep, just enough to see the driver—a big strong man—pull Peggy Dear out of the wagon, her dress front torn down to her waist, her bare chest as bloody as could be and flat as a child's. Her mouth was torn, her earlobes were gone, and her legs were bloody. He carried her into Granny Ivory's cabin, her body drooping out of his arms, and Granny Ivory shut the door after him.

Armella helped nurse Peggy Dear, helped wrap her bloody chest with a larded cloth, helped clean off her face, her ears. Granny Ivory washed carefully between Peggy Dear's legs, though Granny wouldn't let Armella see what she was doing under the covers, what produced so many bloody rags for her to bury. Armella fed Peggy Dear broth until she got her strength back, then she went home and took up being her children's mother again. Granny Ivory never explained to Armella what had happened. The wagon driver's wife told everybody that after Peggy Dear ran away, Sykes sent the overseer with the dogs out after her. They sniffed her out, found her hiding in a ramshackle hovel some nasty people had abandoned. She was lying unconscious on the dirt floor, rats crawling all over the poor woman, eating off her delicate parts. The overseer sicced the dogs on her. They began to cry, scrambling over each other to get to her, and the rats just flew off. The driver told his wife he thought the overseer was slow to beat those dogs off Peggy Dear, but Armella said the dogs saved Peggy Dear's life, in a way. They saved her from being eaten by rats.

The last thing Armella remembered was when she was thirteen, Granny Ivory called her over and said, "Go on up to the Big House and see what's up there." Granny looked like she'd been crying, but she didn't say anything about why. She just stood nodding her head up and down, over and over, as if it were broken. Armella went, and found Geoffrey sitting in a strange tobacco wagon, his legs swinging off the back. Sykes, standing beside the driver, told her to get in too, told her the man driving the wagon was Smith, their new master. The man was young-looking, his hair reddish, tattered. A puny look hung around his shoulders. He didn't say anything, just started up the horses as soon as Armella sat.

They rode until the Sykes place disappeared and there was just tobacco fields for miles. For hours they rolled along, Armella next to Geoffrey, neither settled enough to speak. Their hands weren't tied, their legs were free, and the wagon hobbled; they could have jumped off the back and run. But it never entered little Armella's head to do such a thing, though she did notice that if she extended her foot down a little bit, she could drag her toe on the dusty road. The wagon jerked along until darkness fell. Through the dark, Armella thought she recognized a stand of oaks they had passed a few hours before, but she wasn't sure.

Not too much later, Smith turned the wagon onto a rutty road that traveled up to a small house on a rise, and down to a cabin, which lay in a depression fronted by a stand of trees. They swayed down the road and along a field to the cabin, which smelled of fresh-cut pine boarding. The wagon rolled to a stop and shook as Smith hopped off. He stood before them in the moonlight, pale, one-sided as a paper doll, the cabin posed darkly behind him. Armella knew she and Geoffrey were supposed to get out of the wagon; they were, after all, slaves. Their obligation was to do anything the man wanted. But they sat, until Smith told them to hurry up and slide on down; they were at their new home.

What you get used to feels like what always was. Armella got used to the farm. It was dangerously small; she and Geoffrey were the only slaves on it, and Smith worked right alongside them in the field. Occasionally, Miz Smith did too, though she spent most of her time in the modest Big House. Miz Smith was a big-boned, dark-haired woman, not pretty, not even handsome, but impressively, commandingly, feminine.

On this little farm, Miz Smith didn't have household help. Smith claimed he couldn't spare Armella from the fields but one day a week to work in the Big House. Unlike her husband, Miz Smith had a natural proprietary gaze; whatever she looked at suddenly seemed *owned.* Armella followed Miz Smith's eyes around the house, jumping when they came to rest on *her.* The house had pine floors. A mistake, Miz Smith said; the wood was too soft to last. The little furniture they had sprinkled around the house was made of dark waxed wood and brocade and looked old and handed down, maybe from Miz Smith's family in Virginia.

Miz Smith was tight-fisted. She knew how to squeeze money until it bled. Her daddy gave her a dowry when she married Smith but told her to keep control of it herself, given the Smith family history with money. She kept the whole bundle buried in the yard on the south corner of the house, underneath a cape jasmine vine that crawled up the chimney flue. She was scared about that little bit of money, terrified somebody wanted to take it from her. Alone, she tumbled an onerous boulder over the spot to hide it. Armella and Geoffrey knew all about the money, but they didn't touch it. What would they do with money? Anytime Smith wanted some of that money, even if it was to buy Miz Smith something (he was always having to give her peace offerings), she made him dress up in his clean clothes and apply, the way you would to a bank.

Some years their small cotton and tobacco crop got them by, but some years it didn't. Smith thought of himself as an imitation Thomas Jefferson—inventor, grand estate owner. In his mind, things were always about to hit big, and what he saw right in front of his eyes simply didn't count. The special cash crops Smith dreamed up always cost them money. But they didn't suffer. They ate out of their garden patch all year, whether the food was fresh or put up. Wild hog meat usually hung in the Smiths' smokehouse, though in the spring Armella and Geoffrey might have to catch squirrels and rabbits to keep a hot meal on their poor table.

Those two drank peanut coffee and cottonseed tea. On Sunday, they ate cabbage, boiled peanuts, cornbread, greens, potatoes, and hog meat, or sometimes chitterlings. If they got worms, Miz Smith dosed them with sorghum syrup and Jerusalem oak. Their cabin had two beds, a bench, and a fireplace. Beside the fireplace sat a box of pine knots.

Armella and Geoffrey kept their own garden in back of the cabin, where the sun shone fully all day. They had to wait until evening and a full moon to see by, to tend their own vegetables. In front, Geoffrey had planted flower seeds he got from Miz Smith's dooryard patch. Cooking smoke wisping from the chimney, vegetable garden out back, orange and yellow flowers in the dooryard, Armella's cabin sat on the dirt road, a smaller and shoddier version of the Big House.

Miz Smith doted on Palsy, her snappy little yapping dog. She got it from her father as a coming-out present, before Smith married her in Virginia. She carried on about Palsy like it was a baby. Miz Smith carried Palsy around in her arms while she went about the house, sat it in her lap while she and Smith ate their food. Palsy slept on the bed, between the Smiths. Miz Smith had tufts of Palsy's fur clinging to her, bringing on a threat from Smith to build a kennel out in the yard for both of them.

One day an old coon dog, probably used to hunt runaways, came limping through the oaks to the Big House. Smith took a liking to the skinny, scroungy thing and fed it enough for it to hang around and try to ingratiate itself. The dog gave Smith an idea for an experiment. He told his wife to bring Palsy into the yard; he wanted to breed her to the coon dog and see what kind of puppies would come out of it. Miz Smith took on like she was fit to be tied. Nobody was going to breed her Palsy to a beast like the coon dog—Palsy would die from it; she'd shoot the coon dog first. She made good on her threat. As soon as Smith was back in the fields with Armella, hoeing tobacco, they heard a rifle shot. Sure enough, when they were done that evening, Miz Smith called Geoffrey to the house. The coon dog lay dead in the yard, flies swarming. Miz Smith said, "Take it out behind the smokehouse, Geoffrey, and bury it deep, where the wild pigs won't dig it up." Smith didn't say anything, just walked into the house. Years later, when Palsy died of old age, and Smith buried the dog under the cape jasmine, Miz Smith carried on like she wanted to jump in the grave after it.

Armella and Geoffrey got lonely. They missed the company of the younger people on the Sykes plantation. They missed Granny Ivory. Smith never let them leave, never handed out passes for them to visit friends. He said, with some nervousness, that everything they needed they would find on his farm. When he wanted a certain tool made, or a bolt of cloth, or shoes for everybody come winter, Smith would say, with hatred in his voice, he'd go over to the Sykes plantation to purchase them. Miz Smith performed what she called a "darkie check" every night. She would show up with a lantern anytime between dark and midnight, her bedtime, to shine the lantern in the cabin window, to make sure her property remained where she had placed it.

Armella felt warmth in the air, felt spring coming. The leafing out of the oaks, the tobacco pushing up through the black soil, gave her an optimism she hadn't felt since she left Granny Ivory. Along the end of April, when the weather turned warm for good, Armella started her monthly period. And that brought on a whole new set of problems. Now that Armella was fourteen, Smith looked at her more than he did his own wife.

Geoffrey got bigger and stronger, but he wasn't keen on the work and had to be coaxed along. He'd want to stop in the middle of a row and rest, or go down to the kitchen patch and dig himself a potato. Laying down his hoe, Smith would quietly guide Geoffrey back to the spot he was working on.

———

When Smith came to visit Armella down in the cabin, she wouldn't let him lie down on her real bed. She kept her slave duties and her womanhood separate. The difference between her real bed and the one she used with Smith was, for one thing, her real bed was stuffed with moss, not weeds, and for another thing, her real bed didn't smell like the master's behind, and she wanted to keep it that way. But Smith thought he was lying on the bed she slept in, and that mattered to him. He was looking for intimacy, possession. She just wanted to get it over with.

She'd back up as he walked in.

His eyes would sweep around her cabin. "Where's Geoffrey?" he'd want to know.

"Out to the barn, tending the milking," would be her answer.

He already knew that. Out in the barn was where Smith told Geoffrey to sleep.

When Smith noticed her belly growing, felt his child like a hard stone beneath him, he grew kinder, demanded loving less often. In the fields, he'd take her hoe, chop the weeds himself. When she got big, he told Armella to lie under the stand of oaks separating the cotton field from the tobacco, to rest. Inside her, the child elbowed and stretched, unhappy, cramped. When she sat, she could track the movements of the child across her belly: a sudden knee jut, or a long rolling wave across her abdomen when he turned, exploring the confines of her womb. When she became weary of his antics, Armella would bend her head to whisper, "I see you're impatient, but the world is a bigger place than you think. You'll find out when the time comes."

The baby was late. Geoffrey accused Armella of trying to hold it inside, to protect the child from his fate. Geoffrey placed his hands on her belly, gave her the only advice he could think of. "You better let go of that baby soon, before he knocks his way out."

Knocking his way out was exactly what the birth felt like to Armella. Her pains exhausted her. When Geoffrey held out the baby boy, wrapped in a cotton sheet, his name came to her immediately—Amber. He was the clear brown of amber glass.

Miz Smith refused to attend Armella in labor or have anything to do with her when she found out about the pregnancy. The same night Amber came into the world, Miz Smith sneaked into Armella's cabin. Geoffrey woke to find her holding a fancy pillow over Armella's face with one hand, the other hand clamped over the baby's nose and mouth. He knocked her down, dumped her in the dooryard, bound their door tight with a piece of rope. When morning came, Miz Smith left the master and the farm, raving about how it was killing her to stay there, suffocating her to stay; she couldn't put up with half-human animals living right alongside her. Smith left to hunt her down. He returned her to the house. He bought new furniture he had to send for all the way to New Orleans, and that seemed to quiet Miz Smith for a time. But that fight went on for years—Miz Smith leaving, Smith tracking her down, then buying her something to own, to dust, to polish, to keep her attachment to the house.

At first, the Emancipation was a rumor. All over the South there were whispers that war was coming. Sometimes the slaves couldn't talk about it but gave each other a look that held a moment or two longer, and it felt good. But the way Smith acted had Armella, Amber, and Geoffrey frightened. Smith started toting his gun around. He ate with one hand on the rifle stock; he slept with the rifle lying next to him, as if he were its nervous lover. He sat on the porch looking out to the road, the rifle on his knees.

Miz Smith got downright nasty with her slaves. Wouldn't turn her back on them. Made sure her rifle was in plain sight. She told Armella, "If you so much as look me in the face, I'll snatch you bald-headed, then shoot you dead." That's the way things were going with all the rumors flying around. Armella better not turn her eyes toward a newspaper or any little word written down. That would be the end of her. Geoffrey or Amber better not look the Smiths in the eye. They would be hung from a tree, meat flayed off their bones, bodies thrown in the woods for the animals to carry off. Miz Smith told them what was what.

At night, Armella sneaked to the farmhouse and eased up a window, just a crack. Master and Miz Smith's voices drifted out. Lying in the dirt, under the cape jasmine, she heard Miz Smith say, plain as if she were sitting in a chair across from her, "Ain't nothing to do for it. Nigger lover up in Washington going to set all the niggers free. I hope one comes right in his bedchamber and rapes his wife!" Miz Smith began to cry. "I hope she feels the degradation white women in the South have been subjected to all these years. And we never cringed from our duty. Why, that Lincoln is more like a soft-hearted woman himself! Don't have the sense of a pig mite. Free the niggers, and we all live like they do!"

Miz Smith exhaled loudly. She was carrying on, in a state. When she got like that, her voice screeched. "I am not ready to have niggers in my face without the least bit of control on them! What will happen to us?"

Smith mumbled something Armella couldn't make out.

"Oh, for the love of God, Aubrey! It's one thing being humane to dumb animals. But we ain't talking pure animals. The niggers act half human. They ain't going to appreciate any crying and studying you do over them. They are scheming liars. Stick a knife in your back soon as say, 'Yes, Massa.' Don't start feeling soft about them. Especially not Armella."

Armella's breath caught. Miz Smith went on yelling, her voice like small darts hitting a target, bull's-eye.

"If she ever turns out another halfbreed, I'll kill it soon as I see it. And I'll kill you too."

More muffled talk.

"Oh, go away! I don't want to talk about it anymore. Go on outside and make sure those niggers ain't trying to break in here and cut our throats, while you sit around drinking whiskey."

Right before she left for good, Miz Smith took Armella aside. It was the first and last time Miz Smith said anything important to her. "Armella, I don't understand how you can turn against us this way. I nursed you when you were sick. Remember the time you and Geoffrey both came down with pneumonia?"

"Yes, ma'am." She remembered the first winter, lying in her cold cabin, a single wool blanket pulled up to her nose, Geoffrey in the other bed, not yet driven off to sleep in the barn, the fireplace dark, rain outside. Miz Smith blew in on a gust of wind, slammed the door shut, poured a swallow of bitter-tasting elixir down their throats, slammed the door shut again. When old Miz left, both she and Geoffrey prayed out loud. Prayed that pneumonia would be the feather that could float them to heaven. But now they didn't have to die to get their freedom. President Lincoln signed the Proclamation and it was finished.

Miz Smith ran off and didn't come back. She dug up her Palsy's casket and took it with her.

Did you ever have to steal back something that was already yours? Some precious thing, like a ball or a baby doll? It wasn't worth much to anybody except you, but oh, how you treasured it, how you wrapped your heart around it! It wasn't just a plastic doll anymore, it was your baby. Then a bully gets ahold of it. He steals it and holds it high over your head, your baby in his large ugly hands.

Smith decided the Emancipation Proclamation didn't apply to his slaves. He'd refuse to tell them about it, simple as that. If anybody trespassed onto his farm, white or nigger, he'd shoot them dead. If any of his slaves tried to leave, he'd shoot them dead too. Besides, they were happy where they were. He treated them right. He was fond of Armella and his Amber. Owning that boy was like having a son. Somebody to help him break apart the beaver dams in the creek, do a man's day of planting in the fields, fill up the smokehouse with hog and rabbit meat. Smith felt old, and the feeling wasn't going away. He needed Amber to keep back the loneliness. No. It was impossible for him to tell his slaves about the Emancipation, then watch them walk off.

Armella and the others already knew about freedom. They knew more about freedom than a free man. It was a presence and an absence in their lives. The more confined he kept them, the deeper their knowledge of freedom became.

After Miz Smith was gone, people started leaving the Sykes place, too. They'd get onto Smith's property by accident, lost, trying to walk their way north or to other plantations, looking for mothers and wives, sisters and brothers, and children who had been sold away. One old man with four grown children had set off looking for his wife, sold to a speculator ten years before, and got his directions fouled up in the far end of Smith's tobacco field. Amber met the man while hoeing the first weeds of summer. Wiping sweat from his eyes, the old man told Amber about the Yankee soldiers coming to the Sykes plantation a few days before. How the soldiers told them they were free, while old Mr. and Miz Sykes looked on. They had a meeting down in the cabins to plan what to do about the freedom. Some wanted to stay, to help Sykes work his place for pay, but most grabbed their children by the hands and walked. So here he was trying to locate his wife. Did Amber ever know of a Florence Sykes? Before Amber could answer him, Smith came down from the porch at the Big House, raised his rifle and shot the man where he stood, then turned and went back to the house.

They decided they weren't up to a confrontation with Smith. They'd take the few little things they needed from the cabin and leave in the early morning, way before the sun was ready to come up.

They walked through the side yard, hoping to get past the farmhouse, then out through the cotton field, and finally onto the road. When they'd gotten as far as the boulder and the cape jasmine vine, its trunk thick as the devil's walking stick and its leaves crispy brown with neglect, Amber heard a creak on the porch. Smith rose darkly from his sentinel chair, his shadow blacker than the surrounding night. Amber watched him step off the porch, arms raised in the familiar gesture of taking aim.

Smith's "Where y'all going?" sounded almost pleasant, like a question to pass the time. Armella answered before either of the men could.

"We going on down the road, Master Smith. Just going on down the road."

"What you doing that for?" The rifle stock rested high against his shoulder.

Amber heard Geoffrey take in a breath. "We know about the Emancipation," Geoffrey said. "We're going to take our freedom now."

Smith swung the rifle to Geoffrey. He complained, "You think you a slave? You want to be free? I'll free you from slavery." He swung the rifle to Amber, raised it high, taking aim at his head. Smith talked slowly, as if he was thinking over every word. "You want to be free. I think I can help you. See, I don't think a stranger can free my slaves, even if that man is the President of this sad country. No stranger knows what my niggers mean to me, no stranger can take my family away from me. No stranger can free you." Smith lowered his rifle. "You *do* want to be free?"

Armella spoke. Her quiet voice spread through the yard. "Yes, Master. That's what we want."

Smith hefted his rifle to her, steadied it at her head. "Then I'll free you myself. Like I'm that 'salvation' you're so fond of singing about."

"Freedom!" Amber shouted.

Smith held the rifle steady on Armella.

"Freedom!" Amber shouted again, frightened. "That's something you can't provide. You ain't got the power to give it or take it away. You ain't got the power to hold on to a slave or free him. Only a man can do that. And you ain't been a man in a long time." The rifle swung to Amber.

"Amber, hush!" Armella said.

Amber couldn't keep silent. "It takes more than what you got between your legs to prove you a man, Smith. Mama told me that, and she's right."

"All right, Amber," Armella said. "Stop talking now. Let the master have his say."

"No. I been listening to the master since before I knew I had ears. I been looking at his farm, his cotton, his tobacco. I been listening to his ideas, his plans. I got plans too. Did you know that, Smith? I got me some plans. And I can't carry them through, living on this farm with you. I can't stay here and be your nigger boy no more."

From the edge of his mind, Amber had a vision of his mother, armed with a stone, poised to strike. He saw Smith swing the rifle to her, saw him aim lower, the rifle like some horrible extension of Smith, his true form, an elephant's trunk, a bestial deformity that Amber had finally glimpsed.

His creep to Smith took an eternity. His breath, a thread, unraveled into the night air and then spooled back. He wanted only for the rifle to remain still until he could quiet its master.

Amber circled Smith's neck with his hands, felt its loose skin beneath the stubble of beard, and broke it quickly. He let Smith sway against him, felt his weight sag into his arms, then let the body slip to the dirt.

After Armella, Amber, and Geoffrey walked off the farm, they all took the name of Moses, from the Bible, and settled down in Mt. Airy, North Carolina. Armella got work with Miz Eveleen Richmond, who was married to a lawyer. Geoffrey worked as their gardener, and Amber went to a school for colored children through the eighth grade. He moved to Philadelphia and became a merchant, selling whiskey and cloth. He married a woman from Mt. Airy, Pless Higgins, who gave him five children, Mary being one of them.

Geoffrey never did get married, and neither did Armella. They lived out their lives in a little house in town, with a small garden patch in back for Geoffrey's vegetables and flowers. When they got too feeble to do for themselves, Amber moved his family back to Mt. Airy and took Armella and Geoffrey into his own house.

Amber Moses turned out to be an odd man. He put all his faith in his business dealings and left his wife, Pless, to herself. He had a habit of shunning his relations or anybody who claimed to be related to him. He said he knew Armella and he knew

Geoffrey, and that's as far as he wanted to take it. I think killing his own father addled his mind.

Armella wouldn't talk about slavery days until she got old; then she could remember some of the things that happened to her, way back then, just as clear as if she had lived them the day before. Armella told my Great-great-grandmother Pless, Pless told my Great-grandmother Mary, Mary told Grandma Adele, Adele told Mama, and now I'm telling you.

❧❧

"I see what you mean about not living a lie," Nettie Lee said. "It sure will mess you up. So Smith was your great-great-*great*-grandfather?"

"Yes. Mother's side."

"You think it does you any good to retell them old slavery-days stories?" Shavonne said. "It just makes me feel mad about the whole mess all over again."

"You think we should forget what happened?" Martha said.

"Yeah, if it's something that happened way back that far. If black people want to hold on to the time they was slaves, then white people be holding on to the time they was masters. What kind of sense does that make? *I* wasn't a slave. I don't hold a grudge toward nobody. You treat me right, I'll treat you the same. You don't treat me right and you got a problem go by the name of Shavonne. But the way I feel about it is this: Forgive and forget."

Martha said, "And the way I feel about it is this: Forget where you came from, and you're bound to head back to the same place." Then she added, "People tend to walk in circles."

Nettie Lee hated dinnertime. It wasn't just fixing the food in her little rundown kitchen, it was eating it in front of the TV with Little Barn and wondering if his baby sister would show up on the set while he was sitting on the floor watching. When she got home from the hospital on Christmas Eve she was tired; her bunions ached. Standing in front of the apartment-sized stove with its four tiny gas burners that could only hold three pots, if she placed them just right, didn't inspire her. She took a package of chicken wings out of the refrigerator. The meat looked pale with fat, was still slightly frozen. She turned on the tap to trickle out lukewarm water, laid the meat in the sink, still wrapped in Styrofoam and plastic. She took the giant bottle of warehouse barbecue sauce out of the refrigerator and set it on the counter, then sat for a moment in the kindergarten chair by the stove. She'd bought it for Yolanda at a yard sale so many years ago. Now she let Little Barn sit on it to watch her cook, or she'd stand on it herself to reach up into the high cabinets.

Little Barn was in the living room, playing Nintendo and watching Barney. She could hear him switch over to the video game right after the TV said, "We'll be right back right after these messages!" Then she'd hear the mechanical wind-up music from Super Mario Brothers or the deep-throated men's chorus singing "Teenage Mutant Ninja Turtles! Turtle Power!" That's fine, she thought. Let the boy have his fun. He'd find out quick enough that life wasn't like those games. She was glad his daddy bought him all that mess, though at the time she had shaken her head and told him—right in front of Little Barn because she was speaking the truth and the truth doesn't need to be hidden—that a boy needs his *father,* not a load of guilt toys.

Sitting in the chair, she bent low into a cabinet and rummaged through several boxes, finally pulling out the Rice-A-Roni. She wet a paper towel and wiped off a rusty circle on the cast iron skillet, then dug two soup spoons full of margarine out of the little yellow tub and melted them in the skillet, turning the skillet around to season the bottom. After a few minutes, after the rice turned white and the spaghetti pieces turned brown, she added two cups of water and the contents of the seasoning package, turned the heat down, and covered the skillet with a lid. She sat on the little chair again.

She had been awake since three that morning and finally got out of bed at five, when she figured it was no use, sleep wasn't going to come; lying in bed turning over all her problems wouldn't produce any answers. Tookie wasn't getting better. In fact, now that she was having seizures, the doctor acted pessimistic. Nettie Lee overheard Dr. Xiang telling the redheaded nurse that the next few days would determine the baby's prognosis.

She went to the sink and unwrapped the chicken. She began massaging the cold wings between her fingers until the joints loosened and thawed. She put the chicken in a bowl, then ran warm water over her hands to warm them up. If Tookie's yellow eyes didn't clear up, the doctor said, they would take the blood out of her body and replace it with different blood. Nettie Lee worried maybe Tookie would catch AIDS from the blood. She heard about that happening all the time. But they *must* test blood for AIDS now, right? Since they could test people.

She arranged the wings on a cookie pan covered with Reynolds

Wrap and poured barbecue sauce over them, the sharp smell making her hungry for the finished meat. She slid them inside the cold oven, shut the door, turned on the gas.

Nettie Lee stared out the kitchen window, counting the bare branches of two intertwined maples in the front yard, their canopy a chaotic outline against the sky. Christmas was the next day, December was coming to a slow close, and a new year waited for her. But she didn't feel up to it.

Little Barn sat crossed-legged on the living room floor, three feet from the TV. Nettie Lee sat on the couch behind him, her feet propped up on an ottoman. Her dinner plate, full of chicken wings and Rice-A-Roni and two pieces of sliced bread, rested on her thighs. The portable TV they watched sat on top of a console TV that was broken. Little Barn's chin pointed up to the working screen, his jaws in motion eating the rice. TV light played over his face faintly.

"Move on back from that set, Little Barn. I don't want you getting in the magnetic field."

"What magnet, Grandma?" Little Barn turned around to look at her, his face open and curious.

"Just don't sit right up on the TV. Move back. Here, come sit by my feet."

He settled by her feet with his back against the couch, but he complained. "I can't *see,* Grandma. The people are too far away." On the screen, a group of friends who met in a bar every day were scheming to break up the wedding of the bartender and his barmaid girlfriend. One of the drinkers said something, and there was a roar of laughter.

"It's almost time for you to go to bed anyway," Nettie Lee told him. She wanted to watch the six o'clock news, but she didn't want him in the room. He had to go to bed now, before the news came on. She knew she couldn't make it to the eleven o'clock news. She was too tired after a string of long restless nights. She'd be asleep before nine.

"It's not bedtime," he said. "It's only dinnertime! I want to stay up for Santa Claus."

She had forgotten to buy him Christmas presents. "Stop whining. I know what time it is." She picked up her fork. "Eat your food." Maybe she could put him to bed, then go out to the toy store. It wasn't too late.

"I don't like chicken things."

"Yes, you do. Eat." She didn't like leaving him alone at night, but she couldn't let him wake up on Christmas with nothing under the tree.

"No," he insisted. "I don't like this food. My daddy says you don't have to eat stuff you don't like."

"Well then, tell your daddy to get over here and make dinner."

"I don't know where he is," Little Barn admitted.

"You and everybody else. Now hush up and eat. Let the food stop your mouth." She would just have to tell Little Barn to get in bed and stay there until she got back.

Little Barn picked up a wing carefully, licking the sauce from it, but didn't bite into it.

"I hope you don't call that eating. What you doing don't put food in your stomach."

"I don't like the chicken part. It makes my stomach hurt." He threw the wing onto his plate and turned back to the television, his back pushed furiously against the couch. She hoped he wouldn't start his crying again. Tonight she just wasn't up to hearing it. It was really too bad for a boy as sweet as her Little Barn to have to act like such a brat. She knew what was going on. When children don't get the love they need, they act up enough to get on their parents' nerves.

Nettie Lee tried a different tack. "Your daddy likes chicken wings."

"How do you know?" He turned around to look at her, his face interested.

" 'Cause I seen him eat my chicken wings enough times. They his favorite."

Little Barn looked suspicious. "How come I never saw him eat them?"

"What have you seen him eat?"

He was silent for several moments. "Nothing," he finally said. "I don't remember."

"Chicken wings are his favorite."

Little Barn bit into one, then chewed in loud smacks meant to keep his taste buds uninvolved.

"Now you like them?"

"I guess so," he said. "They taste kind of good." He put his plate on the rug. "Grandma, how come you so mad all the time?"

Nettie Lee felt herself suffocating, her chest caving in. If only it were possible to die right then of natural causes, she wouldn't feel like killing herself. No, she'd never do that. Little Barn needed her. Tookie needed her. "Boy, pick that plate up off of the floor. What did I tell you about that?" Her words were slow and half-hearted.

"You said the floor ain't my table." He put the plate on his knees. "The floor ain't my closet or my bed neither." He turned to look at her. His round head needed a good brushing. Good Lord, she guessed she let him go out of the house looking like that, with lint all in his hair. Now here she sat arguing with him until she got his face all screwed up for tears. "You hate me, don't you?" he said.

"Why you say that?" Nettie Lee immediately felt her breathing return like a jolt of oxygen. "Look here, you live here, don't you? How can I hate you if you living right here with me? That means I love you."

"Yeah, but Mommy used to live here with you, and you told her you hated her and she had to move out."

"I never said that." She didn't *remember* saying it, anyway. Or maybe she did. Sometimes she said things to Yolanda she didn't mean. The last time she had seen Yolanda, the girl was on her way out the door to live with that so-called friend of hers, the one with so many kids she couldn't count their daddies. And that apartment they had—no furniture except that couch with the baby piss and what-all on it, a throw rug, and that old TV Yolanda used to keep in her bedroom when she lived in this house.

"When Mommy comes home with her new baby, we going to find us an apartment where we don't have to listen to no bitches." He picked up his plate and began to eat again.

"Well, your mommy may have a problem with *that* if she opens her own mouth."

"What you mean, Grandma?"

"I don't mean nothing, honey. Eat your Rice-A-Roni. And yeah, I love you. I love you more than tongue can tell. Now don't ask me that mess no more, you hear?"

"You love Mommy?"

"I said don't ask me that mess." Nettie Lee's stomach flopped in a sudden wave of nausea. "I love your mommy."

"And my daddy?"

Now he was pushing it. "Honey, I ain't seen your daddy in some time. Your birthday, I guess was it. I can't love somebody I don't know." She couldn't tell him she had seen Barn robbing the grocery store over a month ago. Much as she hated his daddy, she couldn't hurt Little Barn like that. She got up from the couch. The travel alarm clock on top of the TV said five-thirty. "Give me your plate, then go on in to bed. Put on your pajamas. No, take a bath. Take a bath and *then* put on your pajamas."

Half an hour later, Little Barn came out of the bathroom in a Dallas Cowboys T-shirt that hung past his knees. He looked like a little girl going to sleep in her nightdress.

"Where'd you find that thing?"

"In my room. Daddy said I could have it."

"Well, that's not what *I* said to put on." She took him in his room, opened his bottom bureau drawer, and pulled out a set of red plaid pajamas creased so badly it hurt her to think she hadn't told him to wear pajamas since she folded these and put them away weeks before. "Here." She thrust them in his direction.

He frowned. "Those are lame."

"*You* going to be lame if you don't put these on *now.*" Weeks of not doing laundry. How could she forget him, let him go over to Dorothy's every morning with his dirty clothes and linty hair? Yet the bedroom they shared was as neat as if she'd been picking up after him. "Where's your dirty clothes?"

He pointed to the bed. "Under there."

Nettie Lee leaned against the mattress and squatted down to get a look under his bed. Sure enough, there were his clothes in a heap, everything he owned: pants, pullovers, underwear, socks, towels, *everything* jumbled up in a heap on the linoleum. And smelling like a rat's behind. But how could she yell at him?

"Grandma," he said, holding the plaid pajamas and stretching his voice into a soft whine, as if unsure exactly how he should tell her this, "I know the floor ain't my closet." He patted her on her shoulder, in quick little flutters. "I didn't want you worrying about the bedroom being dirty. See how I cleaned it up?"

"Yeah, I see." She felt his soft hand come to rest on her shoulder. "Get on in the bed now."

He pulled the T-shirt over his head, folded it carefully into a lumpy square that stuck between the mattress and the metal bed frame. "This is where I keep it," he said simply, and put on his pajamas and got into bed.

On the six o'clock news, Brian Hayashi interviewed a woman whose thirteen-year-old daughter had been missing for two days. She held up a picture of her daughter, a smiling blonde with braces, or maybe not: Nettie Lee couldn't tell with all the snow on the screen. She adjusted the rabbit ears on top of the set. Better. But now the woman and her picture were gone, replaced by another reporter, Rosie Gomez, who held a microphone to her mouth, which worked unnecessarily hard, Nettie Lee thought, to shape the words that poured out. Live at the downtown ice skating rink, breath gusting around her head, Rosie described the skaters, the hot apple cider, the *fun,* all created by the local chapter of Children's Wish. Then back to the newsroom to Carol Smith, a nice-looking woman with a big head of hair, who said that, on a more serious note, a local doctor had been wounded in front of the birth control clinic where he worked. The doctor had been stoned by seven women and one man, all under arrest now, who had surprised him as he left the clinic the previous evening. The group called itself People for a Better Tomorrow. A commercial came on.

Nettie Lee grew impatient. She sat through the rambling questions of a man in a white jacket asking her about constipation, then a woman who confided that she knew what to take for that time of the month when she just didn't feel herself. That's all right, honey, Nettie Lee thought, I don't feel like myself, either. I don't know who I feel like.

The news was back on again. George Watson, a handsome man in a plain, inoffensive way, said it was time for sports. Nettie Lee said "Shit!" and cut off the set. The news was over. All that was left was the weather, and she knew what that would be: cold.

In the kitchen, she ran hot water over the dinner dishes. Scraping pieces of greasy rice off the plates, then sliding them into the water, she suddenly felt a revulsion to getting her hands wet. It seemed too much like scrubbing up in the nursery. Her hands were chapped from all the scrubbing. She worried so much about contaminating one of the babies, especially Tookie.

She cut off the lights and went into the bedroom. Lying on his back, body tucked neatly under the blankets and quilt, Little Barn was still awake. Nettie Lee leaned over him.

"I told you to go on to sleep. Santa Claus don't come until everybody in the house is snoring." He immediately closed his eyes. "I got to go somewhere right now, but I'll be back in a little while. Stay in the bed and don't get out for nothing, you hear?"

"Okay, Grandma."

"Can you kiss Grandma good-bye?" She touched her lips to his forehead. "Good night, honey."

In the living room she counted twenty-seven dollars in her wallet. What kind of toys could she buy for that? One of these days she was going to get it together. Next Christmas there wouldn't be a little tinsel tree with no presents beside it. Next year she would have her entire family around her, eating a big dinner and singing carols. Santa Claus would be on time; she would make sure of that. She put on her coat, hat, and gloves, closed the front door behind her, and walked up the cold street to the corner grocery. Maybe she could find some toys for Little Barn there.

When Nettie Lee came into the nursery the following Monday morning, a small group of people were leaning over Tookie's Isolette. This was how she could always tell things were going wrong: too many experts. Dr. Xiang, Debbie Foxx, and the redheaded nurse bent over the baby. Martha moved to the side, letting them crowd in close, then came over when she saw Nettie Lee.

"She all right?" Nettie Lee felt anxious. "What are they doing?"

"They decided to do the exchange transfusion," Martha said in a low voice, her eyes worried. She pressed her lips together. "The jaundice got too bad. The light therapy they tried didn't work, and now they're worried about brain damage."

Nettie Lee had the sensation that Martha's words weren't real. They lost their meaning as they spilled from her mouth. Jaundice? Brain damage? She couldn't make sense of the words. "What-all they going to do to her?" She wasn't sure Martha's answer would make any more sense.

"Well, I'm not positive about everything they're going to do, but they want to take out the jaundiced blood and put in fresh blood."

"I already know that!" Nettie Lee looked around, then lowered her voice. "What I want to know is, how do they plan to drain her blood out?"

"I don't know; I've never seen it done." Martha seemed jumpy, unwilling to look straight at Nettie Lee or at the baby's warming tray. Behind her glasses, Martha's eyes kept sliding away from Nettie Lee. "Why don't you just go over there and watch?" she said. Instead of going with Nettie Lee, Martha walked off in the opposite direction.

Nettie Lee wasn't afraid of blood, as long as it didn't belong to somebody she knew and it wasn't spilled on something. As she approached the Isolette, she smoothed out her scrub gown with her hands. Nobody told her to go away, so she stayed. Debbie wheeled over a machine that looked like a mechanical vise with a large syringe of dark blood clamped in it. She was hooking up clear plastic tubing to the syringe, her face pointed in concentration. Dr. Xiang held the tube that came out of the baby's navel. She attached the tube Debbie handed her to the baby's plastic tube with a silver stopcock. Dr. Xiang said, "All right, Nurse?"

Debbie turned on the machine, which hummed, then clicked. The click depressed the plunger on the cylinder. The humming stopped. Dark blood crawled through the tube to the stopcock and waited there. Dr. Xiang twisted the stopcock valve, and the blood traveled on, winding its way to the baby's navel.

"Looks fine to me." Dr. Xiang looked at Debbie. "We will give it a few minutes before we extract." Debbie nodded and looked back to the baby.

As the blood entered Tookie's navel, Nettie Lee studied her face closely for signs of pain, alert for any indication that she felt the blood moving through her. Was it warm? Did it make her feel stronger? Or did it feel wrong, like mixing oil and water? Tookie slept on. Her face sometimes twitched, the corners of her mouth momentarily pulled up into an odd smile, or her eye flickered in a closed wink, but Nettie Lee couldn't relate Tookie's expressions—were they expressions? were they even the gas she had told Yolanda that Little Barn's smiles were?—or any of her movements to the slow snake of new blood into her body. After several minutes, Dr. Xiang closed the valve, attached a small empty syringe to the stopcock, and withdrew blood from Tookie with a mighty pull. "This is not easy," the doctor said to herself. She held her breath and grunted a little as she pulled again. When the syringe was full, she shut the valve and said, "All right, that looks fine. It's time to wait." She left the Isolette.

Debbie stayed beside the baby, writing notes on her chart and checking the equipment—the respirator, the heart monitor, the mechanical vise with the cylinder of blood. After each check, she wrote more notes. Nettie Lee stood silently, feeling only the feet she rested heavily on, the rest of her light as air. She had the brilliant sensation of floating, expanding beyond the nursery, leaving the large hot room.

Debbie grabbed her by the arm, her warm fingers gripping tightly through the scrub gown. "Nettie Lee, would you like to sit down?"

"No, ma'am," Nettie Lee told her as she felt herself being maneuvered to a rocker. Her fall into the chair knocked the air out of her lungs. Debbie squatted in front of her, one hand on her knee. She pushed a piece of hair from her own face. "You stay in this chair for a couple of minutes, you hear? I'll get Martha to bring you some o.j."

Nettie Lee closed her eyes. Damn tears, welling up and falling out. Damn tears. And yet she didn't have the strength to wipe them away.

Martha stood over her, a small Dixie cup of orange juice in her hand. "Are you feeling sick?" She thought Martha looked at her strangely.

"I got dizzy," Nettie Lee said quickly, and wiped her eyes.

"Well, drink this and you'll feel better."

"You ever get sick looking at some of the things they do in here?" Nettie Lee asked.

"All the time. I think for me it's the smell of alcohol or whatever that smell is. Soon as you walk in the hospital you can catch a whiff of it. I used to think it was embalming fluid, but I smell it everywhere I go. Except the cafeteria. Now *that* smells like SpaghettiOs."

Nettie Lee smiled, though she felt weak. "Don't you like SpaghettiOs?"

"Not for breakfast, lunch, *and* dinner." Martha looked at her. "Mind if I'm honest with you?" She put her hand on the back of the rocker, dipped her head in closer.

"I got a choice? You ain't nothing *but* honest."

Martha smiled and took the cup from her. "Want some more?"

Nettie Lee shook her head.

"Why don't you go home? Nothing out of the ordinary is going to happen this afternoon. LaRone's coming at four to feed her baby. And Mrs. Baker already came this morning since she had the day off, but she'll be back, so little Bowen's taken care of." Martha paused. "Who else? Well, some of the babies get their milk through a gavage tube. The nurses will make quick work of that. And I'll be sure to spend some time with each baby before I leave, especially that poor little thing over there getting blood." Martha looked away to where the baby lay.

Nettie Lee felt much stronger. "I'm not going anywhere. I'm staying right here. I got work to do." She raised up from her rocker and was deeply sorry she did for about five seconds, but by the time her head cleared she was over to the sink washing her hands, looking at the clock and planning to rock Gonsalves. She just hoped they would finish with Tookie soon. It was horrifying to keep looking over there and seeing all those experts huddled around her.

The baby's exchange transfusion went all right. Smoothly, Dr. Xiang said. She had added a small amount of donor blood to the baby's total circulation, then removed a same amount from her, then repeated the process until all the blood was given. Nettie Lee understood that the transfusion was an effort by Dr. Xiang to lower the chemical in the baby's blood that caused jaundice, but she hated to see them torturing her granddaughter. That's just the way she felt about it. She briskly carried out her jobs in the nursery, but she felt mopey inside. Or maybe defeated was more like it. She had never let the trials of life get her down before, but this whole mess seemed like more than she knew how to handle.

Right before the four o'clocks, LaRone and Shavonne came in to see Daquille. LaRone looked dressed for a party, and Shavonne, in her big maternity sweatshirt and baggy purple jeans that sagged into a puddle around her ankles, was talking trash.

"And I told him he's working my last nerve, and that ain't

something he want to do." Shavonne grabbed her belly on either side and rubbed. "This baby is kicking me." She rubbed in deep circles, groaning. "Every time I talk to that fool the baby acts up."

"What did he say about a job?" LaRone leaned closer to the Isolette, hand resting on the lid. Inside, Daquille slept.

"Job? I got to spell the word for him. He act like he never heard it before. He says he's not ready to get married, but he'll be here for the baby. Meanwhile, I got to pay his rent."

"Don't get caught. You know that case worker *will* look in your closet to see if he's keeping his clothes in there." LaRone looked at the nursery clock.

"She already did that. That nigger don't have no clothes anyway. What he does have, he keeps at his mama's."

LaRone rubbed her hand across the top of the Isolette. "I want to feed Daquille now."

"He's asleep. Don't be waking him up to feed him."

"Look how his blankets are all messed up like he's been kicking around." She straightened up. "I think he got hungry, then went back to sleep. I don't like him going to sleep hungry."

Martha went over to them. "Where's your scrub gowns, ladies?"

LaRone touched her hand to her forehead. "Oh, yeah. I'm going to put it on right now."

"Why we got to wear them things? My clothes are clean," Shavonne said loudly, while walking to the scrub room.

When they got back, Nettie Lee told LaRone, "You want to feed your baby now? Tell the nurse. It's *your* baby." She saw LaRone hesitate. "Go ahead. See Debbie Foxx over there?" Debbie stood at Tookie's tray, looking at Tookie and talking to Dr. Xiang. "Go tell her your baby is hungry and you want to feed him. It *is* four o'clock."

LaRone walked over to the nurse.

Nettie Lee watched Shavonne rubbing her stomach down low. "So how's your baby today? Looks like it's kicking."

"It's doing somersaults," Shavonne told her. "I used to say I was glad I got pregnant, just so I won't have to mess with no periods every month, but this is starting to be aggravating. And I got acid on my stomach." She groaned. "You got a Tums?"

"No. Go on down to the gift shop and get yourself some. I know I saw some down there."

"That'll work. I'll go later. I know LaRone's going to take her time feeding Daquille. She wants to get used to him before she gets him home and don't have all these nurses and doctors to ask questions to."

"She's a smart girl."

LaRone came back. "She said to ask you to get the feeding out of the freezer for her."

Nettie Lee pulled a four-ounce bag of breast milk from the freezer and ran warm water over it in the sink. She poured two ounces of it into a nurser and handed it to LaRone, who sat in the rocker talking to Daquille.

"Here, just the right temperature."

LaRone took the bottle, worked the nipple into Daquille's mouth. He took several soft smacks of milk, then stopped, the milk spilling from the side of his mouth.

Shavonne blew air out of her mouth. "You letting him waste it, LaRone! See, I told you to let the nurse do it."

Nettie Lee interrupted Shavonne. "He's doing okay, LaRone." She stood behind the rocker. "He just too anxious. Hold him real close to you." LaRone tucked Daquille against her breast. "Now, put your face right in his. Look that boy right in the eye and put the bottle in his mouth. Now tell him you know he's hungry and you got just what he needs."

LaRone's murmurs were soft at first, directed quietly at Daquille. Milk still drooled from his mouth.

"That's all right," Nettie Lee said. "That's just what you want to do. Tell him Mama's got some food for his stomach, and he's doing real good getting it in his mouth, but now he's got to swallow it."

"Okay, baby," LaRone said, louder this time. "You doing okay. That's right. Take another swallow." Daquille's eyes locked on

LaRone's, his mouth pulling at the nipple. She bent closer. "That's right. You doing it just right, Daquille. You doing fine."

"Babies need encouragement, even for something as simple as eating. Especially little babies like yours. They're laying around the hospital all day, maybe they forget they supposed to be held and loved."

"Well, when LaRone gets Daquille home, she'll be missing these nurses," Shavonne said. "She be doing all this work by herself."

"That bother you, LaRone?"

"It's all I worry about."

"See, LaRone got insomnia," Shavonne said. "She don't go to bed until three in the morning." LaRone looked at her. "Don't be looking at me. I see you up in the bed reading that Mr. Spock book." Shavonne turned back to Nettie Lee. "She trying to figure out how to raise a baby by reading a book. I told her ain't no book going to be doing the two A.M. feedings. Of course, she be up anyway since she can't sleep."

"You'd be surprised at all they tell you in that book," LaRone said, keeping her eyes locked with Daquille's.

"Keep on reading it then," Nettie Lee said. "A little knowledge is a dangerous thing to waste."

"I'm too sick of *school* to be reading books," Shavonne said. She rubbed her stomach and groaned. "I'm going to find me a chair."

A little after four o'clock, Martha had pulled her rocker next to LaRone's. Nettie Lee asked Martha whom she planned to feed.

"I'm planning on Riley," Martha answered, then said, "Unless you have other plans?"

"No, that's fine with me. I'ma rock little Gonsalves. I haven't really talked to him since this morning, with everything that's been going on." She looked to Tookie's spot in the horseshoe. No one stood by the warming tray and respirator. The baby slept peacefully, alone.

The four of them sat opposite one another, rocking babies and giving the four o'clock feedings. Nettie Lee and Gonsalves, then Martha and Riley on one side, LaRone holding Daquille and, next to her, Shavonne with no baby in her arms on the other side. Gonsalves and Daquille Cruz were next-door neighbors, of a sort. Gonsalves would be considered the loud neighbor who partied too much. He stared from his incubator with wide, alert eyes, scissors-kicked his legs constantly, often cried inconsolably. Nettie Lee found him hard to feed. First she had to calm him, hard to do with his hypersensitivity to touch, but she figured out that he liked to be wrapped in two receiving blankets, swaddled so tightly he looked like a bullet. She had to rivet his attention on her eyes to encourage him to eat—really, she thought, to convince him that living was worthwhile.

Nettie Lee coaxed Gonsalves into taking extra swallows of breast milk while Martha soothed Riley into drinking more soy. She could feel LaRone watching her, imitating the movements she made with Gonsalves—the little pats and adjustments—with her own baby. Nettie Lee thought briefly about Yolanda. Thinking it could be her own daughter she was showing how to take care of a preemie. It could be Yolanda and Tookie sitting with her at home.

LaRone sat Daquille on her lap to burp him, just like Nettie Lee did Gonsalves. Daquille's chin rested in the V between LaRone's forefinger and thumb, his head slumped sideways, his fat cheeks pushed against her hand. LaRone patted firmly on his back, using the same rhythm Nettie Lee patted out on Gonsalves. LaRone was going to do okay. She just needed to have faith that she could do the right things for her baby when the time came. Shavonne was another story. Nettie Lee looked at her. She'd gotten a little wooden rocker with no arms from the supply room. Rubbing her belly, her short fingers meeting deep in her groin, Shavonne rocked along with the other women. With nothing to occupy her hands, Shavonne seemed fidgety, kept playing with gauze pads or little Band-Aids she picked up from the utility tray next to Gonsalves's Isolette. She was just a bored kid with nothing to do except have a baby. Nettie Lee shook her head.

"Martha?"

"What?"

"Did I ever tell you about the time I got pregnant with my daughter?"

❦❦

Yolanda was my change-of-life baby. At first when I turned forty I wondered what all the fuss was about. You know, you hear from everybody whose business it ain't, "Forty? You're too old to pass the mustard." I didn't feel old, but I knew something was off. When I turned forty, I'd been without a man for ten years. They say a woman's prime is those years in her thirties. Well, I guess I had my prime all to myself. Then all of a sudden everybody else got the same idea and started doing what I been doing. It was women's liberation time, time to cut loose from men. All over the place I saw women who said they burned their bras. I heard one woman say on the TV that a woman without a man was like a fish without a bicycle. Well, I didn't have a man, and I wasn't looking to climb up on top of no bicycle neither. I felt like the things I didn't have, I didn't need—or I would already have them, right? I didn't need liberating because nobody was holding me prisoner. Then Sweet came along, and all of a sudden what I thought I needed changed.

I got into forty a little ways, then something in me went haywire. I got scared when I looked in the mirror. My hair was short and kinky, my hips were too big, my face too round. I started thinking I needed negligees and lace brassieres. I thought I had to buy me some perfume from the grocery store, to try those recipes in the *Family Circle* magazine that tell you how to cook a fancy meal. I read the *Reader's Digest* articles like "Fifteen Things a Woman Should Never Say to a Man." It turned out I had already said fourteen of them, and the fifteenth was on my lips. I was trying to step outside myself, trying to find out if what a man saw when he looked at me was anything he'd want. I got scared.

I started noticing when I went anywhere—downtown, the grocery, getting on the bus, anywhere I was—I saw nobody would look at me. Their eyes would slide right past. Then I would try to be those other people, try to figure out, from their side, what they saw when they looked at me. I figured it out—they're the center of their world, so I was just scenery, not important. I was the fat woman buying pork chops at the corner grocery. I was the heavy-set woman with the bad feet at work. I was the husky woman with the thin hair at the beauty parlor, the one they had to use the little tiny rollers on. For years, I paid good money for a frizzy head of hair, but it wasn't what I wanted. I wanted to be sexy. Before I saw Sweet, I was reduced to ugly in my own eyes. I knew that's why I had to have him, to prove I still existed.

I don't know what made him want me. I could give him the usual motive, that he was a man and I was a woman and men always got to try, but that wouldn't be fair to him. Yolanda is always telling me to be fair to her daddy. In her eyes, that man can do no wrong. But to be fair, this is what I know:

At forty I didn't know nothing about going out on a date, so I kept Sweet home in bed. If I had thought about it for any length of time, we would've gone out somewhere, a walk in the park, a cup of coffee on a Sunday morning; maybe we should have sat in church a few Sundays. I see people do that all the time—just sit around and be with each other. But I felt nervous with him, like I couldn't look him in the face without my own face twitching, like I had to be more than I was to keep him interested. That's the thing about men, that's what kept me away from them for ten years. They have a short attention span. They need to be entertained or they get bored.

It wasn't a mystery to me how Sweet got his name. That man was sweet as an all-day sucker, always smiling, face dark and smooth, cheeks round, belly round too, but that didn't matter a bit because, like I said, I was ten years without a man. Now don't get me wrong, I wasn't settling for less. By the time Sweet Smoaks saw me in the street, walking past the pawnshop where him and another man were leaning in the doorway fussing at each other, it took a different kind of man to get my eye. I wasn't interested in looks by then. I wanted a man with some weight to him, a man who wouldn't blow down in a stiff wind.

He stopped fussing long enough to look at me, real sweet, with his eyes just on me. I knew that ignoring him would cause me more trouble than just saying good morning. I knew I should just speak to him and be done with it. I turned my head real quick, and said, "Hi," and he said, "No," like I asked him a question. By the time I figured out the joke, I was past him, and the smile on my face belonged to just me.

He started calling after me, "Hey, Miss Lady, you in a hurry?" The smile came off my face. I was forty years old, and I didn't want somebody yelling after me in the street. I wasn't some child, still afraid of boys on the one hand and boy-crazy on the other. I stopped walking, turned back to the man, and really gave him a good look. I mean, if he wanted the job as my boyfriend, then I wanted to see who I was hiring.

He looked like he was about thirty-eight or so, pleasant-looking. The only lines on his face came up around his eyes when he smiled, and to be fair, he kept that smile on his face for a long time, until things went bad between us. Now that smile, I got to explain it. It was all natural. It was the expression God wanted man to have on his face all the time, if man wasn't so busy making trouble. Standing out on the street, I studied him from his Jheri-curled head to his red platform shoes, and honey, every time I got back to his natural God-given smile, I knew that man had the job.

He could talk about anything, I found out later, from the presidential primary to that movie about that funny girl, Barbra Streisand, but he didn't know how to talk to a woman. It still surprises me when I think about it, makes me wonder how I fell so hard for a man who didn't know how to talk me into it. After I was done looking at him, I remembered his answer to me saying hi. I said, "You into drugs?" and he looked offended. He hemmed and hawed; then he said, eyes brown and clear as a German shepherd's, "No. I told you I wasn't high. That's not my bag." He cleared his throat and said, "You into pharmaceuticals, Miss Lady?" in some kind of hip way, like he was supposed to be groovy.

The whole thing tickled me, him making such a lame effort to be cool, trying to get my attention, while life was passing through my body like I wasn't any encumbrance to the flow of people around me, like I didn't exist. Here was a man who stopped me with his smile and pinned me down to the moment we were living in. Well, I guess I was impressed.

Sweet was a hard-loving man. Not physically hard, because he was gentle in that way, but he was mentally hard for me. Loving him took up all my thoughts, no room left for me to think things through. Before he came along, I was worrying about where my life was headed—did I want to continue with my job at Dayton Tire and Rubber or did I see something different for the future? When I thought about what I wanted to do with myself, I got scared. I knew working on the assembly line at the tire plant wasn't leading nowhere. It paid all right, but it wasn't nothing spectacular. I knew I'd never get promoted out of that job. I wanted a change for myself. I thought maybe I'd retrain for something at the community college, like a licensed practical nurse. That's back when the college was brand new. I'd lay in the bed at night trying to figure it out. Did I have enough money, did I want to work at night and go to school during the day?

But having a man around was so arousing for me that I got overly optimistic. All of a sudden I just knew everything was going to be okay, and I slipped out of the habit of thinking about my future. I let the school calendar get buried under newspapers and old *Family Circle*s. When I was straightening up one day, I must have thrown the calendar out. You get a lazy, fat feeling when you think things are okay. I cooked up recipes from magazines, smiling the whole time because he was going to be eating them. I arranged the chairs in my house to the best spot in front of the TV because I knew he was going to be sitting in them. I went around the house sitting in chairs, looking out windows, laying in the bed, pretending I was Sweet, testing out everything for him, seeing life with his eyes, feeling love with his heart. In the hours I was at work, Sweet's face would roll up in my mind, the way his eyebrows met over his nose, the flat space on his forehead. I said his name over and over in my mind: Sweet Blanford Smoaks.

I got him in my bed real quick, before he could drift away. Sex can be like that: one minute you think you got to do something about the longing in your heart, the worse longing between your legs, then the next day you don't remember why you cared. Let that careless attitude settle in for ten years, and you really got a mountain of indifference to climb. I wanted to get him into my bed while I still felt roused up, still cared about what his mouth would feel like on my neck, what his hands would be like on my breasts. I realized I had missed being touched all those years.

And Sweet knew what to do. He was just lovely, I'll say, and I'll have to leave it at that. The rest is my business.

Now, what usually follows after lovemaking is a love child. Being forty didn't make that any different for me. I missed my period that first month.

I didn't tell Sweet right away, since I didn't know how I felt about it myself. I loved babies, always planned on having one someday. In my twenties I guess I was lucky I didn't get in the family way, for all the carrying on I did. Since I didn't get pregnant then, I just assumed I couldn't have a baby, that I was barren. So there I was, forty and pregnant. On the one hand, I was facing my dream come true; on the other hand, I didn't know that man from the man in the moon.

I started dreaming in sepia tones, like the old brown photographs M'Dear set on our mantel in Chicago. In my dreams the landscape was brown and cream, the people dark and slow. I dreamed about sailors riding the ocean, whales sliding underneath ships. About shrimps and catfish scooting across the ocean floor, looking for trash. About bathtubs with babies in them, overflowing, flooding out the houses they were in, the water traveling down streets, rushing through gutters, stopping at my feet. I'd wake up at two in the morning, crying for M'Dear, only the words weren't coming out, they were stuck in those sepia-toned dreams. It went on for two months, got so I wouldn't go to bed at night.

I waited for Sweet to leave at six, headed for his job at Dayton Power and Light. I'd take my blanket off my bed and head for the couch. Laying on the soft lumpy couch, I remembered something M'Dear said to Daddy Walter when I was five, and M'Dear and him had all of us kids. She said, "Water dreams. I'm having me some water dreams, Walter. Guess I'm having me a baby."

I was laying on the couch half asleep, the air crawling into my throat and me huffing it out without thinking about it, my mind just dead. I didn't want to sleep, but I was too tired to wake up. My throat felt sore and rough, and my head hurt. I sat up with the thought of being pregnant rolling through my head. I laid on my back and felt my stomach between the hipbones, ran my hands over the loose skin, pushed my fingers into the crotch hair. Nothing. I just didn't feel nothing. But the thought of a baby growing inside, like some fish, some crawdad, made me sick to my stomach. Outside, the air was getting hot. I could feel it when I walked past the living room window to the bathroom. I stopped and pulled the window down across a sheet of hot air hovering just inside. Hanging over the toilet bowl, retching till it hurt my stomach, I thought if it was true, if there was a fish baby in there, I could retch it up, spit it into the toilet, flush it away. I guess I knew right then what Sweet would say about a baby. *Water dreams. I guess I'm having me a baby.* Daddy Walter had told M'Dear, "No, you ain't."

He was right. M'Dear didn't have her baby. When I was a child, I wondered how Daddy Walter knew. I came out of the bathroom, back to the couch. I tried to lick the sour taste out of my mouth, then sleep. *Water dreams.* A sepia man standing on the prow of his ship, riding the waves. Shrimp on the bottom of the ocean. Whales sliding underneath. The ship. The waves. *Water dreams. I guess I'm having me a baby.*

I kept checking between my legs for blood, the sign I wasn't pregnant. I felt sore and full down there, knobby from all the wiping I did with toilet paper, all the checking I had done in the past couple of days. No blood. Nothing yet. But I was having water dreams, and I was having me a baby.

Sweet sat on the couch, his hands folded in his lap like he was saying his prayers. I hoped he was praying for a new family.

"Okay, I'm here, so what you want?" He let his hands loose from his lap, folded his arms. The way he was sitting, legs crossed, foot jiggling up and down, so impatient, turned my stomach hard. I made my face into a mask he couldn't take off. No use for him to see what was underneath.

"I got to talk to you about something important." I watched him fidget, brush his nose with his finger, look away from me to the wall behind my head.

"What?" He made it sound so easy. What? A little tiny word.

"A baby." I said it, and I watched the understanding of it fly across Sweet's face. He opened his eyes wide, let his mouth drop. "Don't try to act surprised about it," I said. "I ain't ready for no games."

"What you talking about a *baby*? You sound like you think that thing is mine."

Oh, no. Here it starts: I know that ain't my baby, since you done slept with every man in the neighborhood, and I'll call them in to say so, if you make me.

"How you know it's mine?"

"Fool, who else's do you think it is?"

"Now *that* I don't know, because your personal life is your own damn business."

I felt my hand twitching to slap that man. "You want to repeat yourself?"

"You heard me. Every woman that says, 'I'm pregnant, you the father,' be getting away with murder. Who's going to disprove it? Naw, don't put that stuff on me. Not me. No. Lot more than you saying I'm the father got to happen before *I* become a daddy."

The man was being so typical, I got embarrassed.

My stomach cramped up. I think a baby knows what's going on around it even before it comes out of the womb. Here's this little tiny baby getting a good taste of what her daddy is like, a close firsthand look into the soul of that man. I put my hand over my stomach to rub her quiet while I said to Sweet, "Get out of my house. Don't never think about putting your foot on my doorstep again."

He did exactly that.

Later on, months later, he came talking about he wanted a second chance. I had already had my baby. It went like this:

Sweet said, "I want to ask you something."

I said, "What?" That little tiny word.

He said, "You still mad at me?"

I said, "What difference do it make?"

He said, "I don't want to marry nobody who's already got her lip stuck out."

I said, "What you trying to say?"

He said, "Will you marry me?"

"No," I said.

He said, "Why not?"

I said, "It's too late."

"But we got a baby together," he said.

"It don't matter," I said.

Then he had the nerve to get mad.

"God, woman! I don't know what you want. I try to do the right thing as a man, and all you do is put me down."

I said, "You had your chance to be a man. You want to do the right thing when it suits you, that's all. What am I going to do when it don't suit you no more?"

He said, "So, it's like that?" and turned away. "Look," he said, "you got every right to be mad at me. I was disrespectful to you. But I'm sorry. I just love you and I want to be a father to my girl. I knew I was wrong not to stand by you. I was scared, Nettie Lee, that's all. I want to stand by you."

I said, "I don't know what to tell you."

He said, "Then don't tell me nothing right now. Think about us being a family. Think about us being together. Okay? Think about it?"

I said I would think about it. I felt so sleepy I couldn't hold my eyes open.

He went on about his business and I flopped in the bed. I never been so tired. Through all the months I was pregnant with Yolanda, I wasn't as tired as I was on that day arguing with Sweet. Yolanda was sleeping in her bassinet in the bedroom. I slept beside her all that afternoon. When Yolanda woke me up crying to be fed, I knew the answer to Sweet's proposal was no.

After he was gone for a year, he had the nerve to call me and tell me where he was: Toledo. I reported him to the Montgomery County district attorney. After I did that, Yolanda's sixty-dollar checks started coming in, with a four-dollar collection fee taken out by the county. I never saw him again, just talked to him a few minutes on the phone every once in a while when he was calling for Yolanda.

He told me once, during one of his let's-be-friends phone calls, he wanted to take that sixty dollars the court ordered him to pay and put it in a bank account until Yolanda was ready for college. My answer was, "What's she going to eat off of until then?" Then he got married. With his first wife, he told me he was going to electronics school to get a better job. He said money was tight right then, with him just getting married. Would I defer his child support payments until he got out of school? I said, "Oh, you going to *school* now? That's funny, so is Yolanda. Is she supposed to starve until you get smarter?" It just didn't make sense to me that he thought whatever little bit he did was good enough and he should be congratulated for it. But the simpleminded part, the part I just can't get my mind around, is that Yolanda agrees with him. "Mama," she says, "he's doing everything he can. You know he doesn't have much money, Mama."

He's the one who calls her up maybe once every six months and tells her he's thinking about her. Never calls on Christmas, never calls on her birthday, never sent her a cent over what the court said to pay, that pitiful fifty-six dollars a month. Never sent extra money for school clothes. But here's what that tells me: he was going on with his life. I guess his life wasn't measured off September to September, the way it is when you got kids. I guess he didn't think about June being the time to get summer clothes,

September being the time for school clothes and books, Christmas being the time for Santa Claus, Easter being the time for new outfits and the Easter bunny, Valentine's Day being the time for those little heart candies for kids, October being the time for trick or treat. That wasn't how he measured off time.

He got married more than once. The first time, he wanted me to be friends with his wife. I had to talk to her on the phone when she stepped in to take his place inquiring after Yolanda's health every six months or so. When she divorced him, when Yolanda was six, she sent me a bus ticket so Yolanda could go visit her in Georgia. There were some letters for a year or so after that; then she faded away. Next, he had a girlfriend that gave him trouble. He would call, and I was supposed to listen to his grief. I must say I slammed down the telephone on those calls. He got married again to another woman, and they had a baby right away, then another one. I guess those kids are around ten and twelve now. Yolanda still talks to that wife now and then. Yolanda told me once the woman told her that her daddy prays for her a lot. I said it would do more good if he prayed less and did more, and Yolanda liked to have a fit. She told me I was a jealous old woman who didn't have a man and took it out on everybody I ran into. I told her to look around and see who was there taking care of her and who was in Toledo praying. She told me not everybody could be as *mature* as I was. Lord have mercy, I never heard the word "mature" sound so much like a cuss word until it fell out of Yolanda's mouth.

You know how you think your life belongs to you, it's *your* history? You think back on how your mama and daddy did this or that to you. Maybe they didn't think much of kids' feelings, didn't take them seriously, or maybe one of them drank too much whiskey and scared you all the time, or whatever their faults might have been. Then you get grown and you realize that the whole time you were growing up, you were just a little tiny part of your folks' lives. And here you'd been thinking you were the center of attention.

One day I'm talking to Yolanda and it hits me. I'm just a bit actor in her movie. Depending on Yolanda's mood, I play the part of either the mama who ruined her daughter's life when the poor girl was growing up or the mama who ain't been young in so long she don't understand anything about how a young woman today feels. It's like Yolanda thinks love and passion, and even common sense, got handed out this morning, and I slept late. Either way, to her I'm not real. I'm only made up of what makes her mad on a certain day. On all days, I'm an old lady, tired and not worth a second look. According to Yolanda, I'm a sexless man-hater, I scare men away. But I think I can live with that.

I got my daughter and my grandbabies, and that's what counts to me. The rest I can work out.

❧❧

Nettie Lee turned to Martha. "So that's how I had my daughter."

"When did all that happen?" LaRone asked drowsily, eyes closed, as if the story had lulled her to sleep.

"Twenty years ago."

"Hmmm."

"I wasn't even born twenty years ago," Shavonne said. She was playing with Gonsalves's disconnected heart monitor, absently twirling the lead wires.

"You old enough to understand what you heard, even if you didn't live it," Nettie Lee said. "Put those wires down before you mess them up."

"Understand what? That you got dogged by some freak?" Shavonne shook her head. "I don't allow nobody to dog me the way Sweet did you."

"What about Joe?" LaRone said, still lazily rocking.

"I told him he could take his tired ass home. I don't need *two* kids to raise. What do I need him for? All he's good for is making a baby. Now he's all tripping because he don't want to raise a kid. He wants to go to school. Shoot, I want to go to school too. But I know my responsibilities. Children got to come first in this world. Never mind what the *parents* want to be doing, they got to do what's best for their children." Shavonne stood up. "I got to get me some Tums. This acid's about to burn a hole in my stomach. I'm coming back."

Nettie Lee watched her go out the nursery doors.

"Shavonne don't mean half of what she says," LaRone said.

"She makes perfect sense, honey," Nettie Lee told her. "I hope she's listening to herself."

Martha hadn't said anything since before Nettie Lee began her story.

"You pretty quiet today, Martha," Nettie Lee told her, watching Martha's thoughtful look grow into discomfort and something else, maybe sadness.

"I'm just tired," Martha said.

"You ain't got any thoughts on my story?"

Martha looked like her mind was on something else. "Well, maybe you were too hard on Sweet," was all she said. She cupped Riley against her chest in an effort to look at the watch on her left arm. "It's five already. I'm about to go home." She got up slowly from the rocker and took Riley to her Isolette. Nettie Lee had the feeling something was wrong with Martha; there was some problem on her mind. She watched Martha and Debbie Foxx connect Riley back to her monitors. Maybe her almost fainting at Tookie's Isolette had got Martha suspicious.

When Martha was finished putting the baby back and was headed for the nursery doors, Nettie Lee called out to her, "I'll see you tomorrow," but Martha didn't turn around to answer.

Martha woke up late. Lying on her stomach, gripping the edge of the mattress, her face in the pillow inches from the bedside table, she felt herself sailing into consciousness on the tail of the spider-baby dream. Faith. Eyes open now, still groggy, she thought she was looking into a hospital supply cabinet at some yellow demon head, round and bald, peeking back at her. More awake, the head turned into a design on the Picasso coffee mug sitting on her bedside table.

She felt angry. No, depressed was closer to it, she supposed. Half depressed, half unconscious and dreamy, a bad feeling. Bad dream. Vague, mournful thoughts turned over in her mind. She lay on the bed, her face pushed into her pillow, letting the thoughts turn, hold tenant, as if they had a right to be there. She couldn't get at their meaning; they held themselves off from her, waiting to catch her unawares. She rolled flat on her back, crossed her arms over her chest.

December. It was the anniversary of Paul's death. Now she was waking up. Her face felt less heavy and pulled down, her chest less scratchy when she breathed in. She began to think about getting up and going to the hospital, imagining the cold, gray sky outside her window, how it hung above her street and above the hospital too. She breathed deeper and sat up in bed, rested her back against the pillow. She would stop by the post office downtown for stamps to pay her bills, then wait for the crosstown bus to take her to the nursery where the babies were waiting for her in their Isolettes.

The bare wood floor numbed the soles of her feet, turning them a waxy yellow. In the bathroom she ran warm water into the sink for a sponge bath. Because she hated getting wet, she had never lain in a bathtub. She buried her face in the wet, rough nap of the washcloth. It was sweet and warm, like the crevices of Paul's soft neck shortly after he was born. When she couldn't stand the thought of him anymore, she pushed Paul from her mind and dressed.

In the kitchen, Martha wanted something to drink, something cool and fruity to ease the tightness in her throat. A plastic bottle of red juice she had mixed the day before sat in the refrigerator. As the cold juice traveled through her chest, she opened up more and breathed deeper. She smoothed out the pants and shirt she'd worn throughout the night, too exhausted to change, got her shoes on, put on her parka and scarf, and went out of the house to the hospital.

Martha just made Tuesday morning Report. Just as the crosstown bus had pulled away from her stop, before she had even sat down, one of the trolley poles slipped from its wire and the bus went dead. Probably ice on the line. The driver had opened the doors, letting in cold air, then run out to the rear of the bus and spent several minutes hauling up the fallen pole by its pulley to make the connection. From her seat, Martha could hear sparks fly as the pole made contact with the wires. Oddly, she felt kin to the stalled bus, and each crackle startled her. Finally, the bus began to shake and the lights blinked back on; then the heaters started up. The driver boarded, took his seat, and headed the bus down Main Street, Martha got to the hospital late.

Debbie Foxx slipped into her seat at the head of the table, directly opposite Barb Hunter. Martha felt some measure of sympathy for the social worker. Of course Hunter would be nervous all the time, and maybe a little brusque; after all, she was just out of school with her master's degree, and now she was suddenly in charge of all the babies in the nursery. She seemed so *young* at times to have all that responsibility. Yet Martha supposed from looking at her that she was no younger than Nurse Foxx. Martha remembered her own twenties as a time of absolutes and having complete confidence in her own judgments. Now it seemed every truth that had appeared so simple was somehow tied to every other so-called simple truth, threads crisscrossing, entangling, until the world looked to her like a hopeless knot. Barb Hunter's faith in her own conception of right and wrong touched Martha and saddened her.

The others were present for the meeting: Dr. Xiang, Debbie Foxx, the three other nurses, including George Johns, who could be spared from the nursery for the time it took to meet, Terese Czajwolski, and Nettie Lee.

George Johns spoke first. He looked nervous, and he rose from his chair to stand, as if he found lecturing from a height more comfortable than carrying on a level conversation. George was close to Martha's own age, tall, a little thick through the middle, and starting to bald, but still handsome. Though his dark face was completely smooth, he had to be over fifty, though no worry lines showed around his eyes. His West Indian accent pleased her ears yet commanded respect.

"We've been in the midst of a controversy here, and I'd like to be direct," he said. "Now, what do I mean by controversy? I mean simply that the nursing staff has a small but significant disagreement brewing, and I'd like to turn the fire off under the pot." He looked at Mary Pangalangan, who pointedly returned his stare. "I do not feel the staff has an adequate understanding of what our role is in helping the mothers of these crack babies born to them."

"What do you need to know?" Barb Hunter asked.

Martha saw Nettie Lee's head whip to Barb's end of the table, flinging aside her usual composure. Martha immediately became wary. She still hadn't figured out what it was about the mention of crack and Baby Doe that upset Nettie Lee. Now she watched Nettie Lee listen to George and the social worker talk, watched the way her shoulders and chest rose shakily with each breath.

"First of all," Barb Hunter said, "I would suggest we stop calling them 'crack babies' and start referring to them as 'babies exposed to drugs'. They are babies first. Their medical condition comes second. Then, I'd caution you all to remember that the *baby* is your patient, not the mother."

George glared at Hunter. "Miss Hunter," he said emphatically, leaning on the table, drawing out his words, "these unfortunate children are the end result of a tragic progression of human events. If we can help the mothers, we can prevent the suffering all of us at this table see every day. Can you inform us on what our duties are to refer the mothers of these infants to a drug treatment program?"

Hunter screwed up her mouth, letting George know she barely tolerated his questions. "Well, actually you don't have a *duty* to refer them to a program or to talk with them in any way about their drug use. But if you want, I can provide you with the telephone numbers of the treatment facilities I sometimes deal with. Of course, what drug they're using has a lot to do with where you would refer them. There's a methadone program downtown. Also, I know there are a couple of support programs for pregnant mothers who are using. This doesn't involve my department, but I can refer you to the director of the drug and alcohol program."

"Can a mother call up and admit herself to one of these programs?" Debbie asked.

"Yes, of course. She'd have to be evaluated for suitability. And most of the programs won't take the mother's children in with her, so she'd have to make some sort of arrangements for child care during her stay in the program. But if you give the women a telephone number when they present here in labor and tell them to call, they can get into a program within a month or so."

"A telephone number?" George turned down his mouth, laced

his fingers behind his back, and stared off above their heads. "I was hoping for a more useful answer." He looked back to the table, to Barb. His face spoke of angry frustration. "What shall I do for these women *right now*? You know, they come to the hospital in labor, probably the first time they will have seen a doctor during their entire pregnancy, and they aren't feeling good—they are after all in labor. Oh, let's be honest, ladies, they are feeling *evil.* They are, in all likelihood, jonesing, or they are high and will be wanting their next taste very, very soon. Then the baby is delivered. We do the tox screen, and 'Ah ha!' we say, 'drug exposed.' Then I'm supposed to say, 'Shall I give you the telephone number of a rehabilitation program? Perhaps they can see you in a month.' " He laughed. "Do you know what this woman says to me?"

"Don't say it, George, it's not becoming for a gentleman to speak that way." Terese smiled.

"Exactly." George returned her smile. "She will tell me, in colorful language, that I should step out of her business, and that she doesn't have a telephone anyway."

"And you accept that as an excuse?" Hunter asked.

"Excuse? How can you make a *telephone* call without the telephone?"

"Go down to the corner store and put your quarter in?" Hunter raised her eyebrows into two sarcastic parentheses.

"Lady, you are living in a dream world of safe convenience stores with working pay phones." George fanned his hand through the air.

There was a silent moment in which Martha heard the fluorescent tubes in the ceiling flicker.

"What would you like to happen, George?" Hunter asked. "I always hear that the system is bad, but I never hear a plan to fix what's wrong."

George flamboyantly placed both hands on his hips. "I want to see any woman who asks to be placed in a treatment program be referred straight from the hospital, discharged from here, then taken by car directly to a residence program with her baby."

Hunter tossed her pen on the table. She looked disgusted. "Then *you're* dreaming."

"This is the only way to do it." George raised his hands, palms up in supplication. "When the woman asks for help, help her immediately. These people are not about waiting lists. They are *right now* people. They want relief *right now.*"

"Well, it doesn't work that way. We are here to help the *children* of these 'right now' people. They are the victims. They are first in line to get whatever limited resources the county has." Hunter turned away. "Let's move on to the Baby Doe case. May I have a report of her physical condition?"

George blasted out a sigh, like a curse, and sat down.

Dr. Xiang spoke softly from her chair, head bent as she read from the baby's chart, her face partially covered by a swath of black hair. "Baby's condition remains critical. Her prognosis is very poor, due mostly to her response to surgery—she is still comatose—and also due to her propensity to retain bilirubin, which has been quite damaging to her neurologically. I think the exchange transfusion will give her a few more days, but I am not hopeful beyond this." She raised her head. "We must wait and see."

An electrical current began to run along the surface of Martha's skin, up and down her body. She felt electrified on the surface but hollow inside, a hollow woman-shell.

"So what happens to Mom if Baby dies?" Mary Pangalangan asked.

Dr. Xiang angled her face toward Mary. "My report will state that Baby's birth defect, transposition of the great vessels, was severe enough to prevent the child from living had she not received extraordinary care. Now that Baby has received the care, even if she does die it will not be due to neglect or abuse on the mother's part."

"What?" Hunter looked incredulous.

"This is my opinion," Dr. Xiang said.

"I think that's ridiculous. When this baby was left in the toilet, there was total negligence on the mother's part, possibly an intent to kill it."

"Do we *know* that?" said George.

"What do you think?" Hunter's pen hit the table again.

"*I* don't know. I find this whole police affair hard to swallow."

"Well, if you can't swallow murder, then you can certainly taste abandonment," Hunter said. "If the baby dies of natural causes before the mother can be found, that is no reason to let her off the hook for abandoning the baby."

"Yes," George said. "The mother needs to be 'on the hook,' as you say. But let's be clear for what reason."

"Murder."

George leaned forward on the table. "If the baby dies for a reason that could not be helped?"

Barb was silent, then opened her mouth to speak.

"People," Foxx said, "this is getting us nowhere. Yelling at each other doesn't make the baby better or worse. It doesn't find the mother or excuse her." Foxx looked at Barb. "It's all just talk, and I suggest we go on to another case."

"Fine." Barb crossed her arms on her chest.

The others seemed relieved, but as Martha's gaze traveled around the table, she found Nettie Lee helplessly looking at her, her eyes wild with restraint.

After the meeting, Martha continued her chores in the nursery: the cleaning, the rocking, the feeding. She expected Nettie Lee to approach her, to tell her what had gotten her so crazy at the conference table, but Nettie Lee stayed far away. When the meeting broke up, Nettie Lee had been the first to leave. If Martha got close to her, Nettie Lee immediately hurried off, saying she had to go over to someone's Isolette, or she simply left without saying anything at all. That was fine with Martha. She was learning a new word when it came to Nettie Lee—whatever. There was just too much that Nettie Lee did or said that couldn't be explained.

The morning passed tensely, the nurses slightly on edge. Martha's empty feeling wouldn't go away. As she rocked the babies, the morning drifted into afternoon. It was probably the worst day she had spent since coming to the nursery. No matter who she held and rocked, she couldn't replace the hollowness inside, the longing for Paul. And that had been the point of coming here.

Martha was surprised to read late afternoon into the sunlight that runneled through the windows. It was four o'clock. LaRone hadn't come for the four o'clock feeding. Martha automatically told Debbie she'd prepare the formula and give Daquille his bottle. He felt warm and heavy in her arms, different from Riley, whose weight was more a surprise of lightness, or little Gonsalves, who squirmed and kicked without his tranquilizers.

Nettie Lee silently sat down in the chair beside Martha, holding O'Neil, who, Debbie said, had lost three ounces since the beginning of the week. She wanted the grandmothers to make a special effort to get extra nutrition into him. Martha felt a cynical wave rise within her. What good would it do to fatten up O'Neil? He had no home to go to, not even a foster home. No one wanted a crack baby, or should she say a baby exposed to drugs? Whatever the correct term was for them, nobody wanted much to do with these infants. And now she seemed to be losing Faith, unless the baby did pull herself together in the next few days and start to mend, instead of tumbling farther away from life. If she did get well and Martha did become her foster parent, what would the Child Protection Agency do about her mother? It would be a legal nightmare, with no peace in sight. Not that she was up to thinking about taking a baby home. Paul had her cowed today, back to where she had started. It was good that Nettie Lee was silent, didn't want to talk. Martha felt if she opened her own mouth she'd weep.

LaRone hurried into the nursery at four-thirty. Martha saw her hesitate at Daquille's empty Isolette, then approach her. She was dressed in jeans and sneakers, her glasses on, her hair pulled into a ponytail that fanned down her back.

"I got tied up down at WIC." She quickly tied the strings on her scrub gown.

"Where's your little friend Shavonne?" Nettie Lee asked her.

"She's too messed up to be here," LaRone said, as if that were a complete explanation. She pointed to Daquille, her fingernails polished in beautiful red. "You feed him?"

"Yes." Martha patted his bottom. "He ate like a truck driver."

LaRone smiled shyly. "I don't know where he got that appetite from. I didn't give it to him."

Nettie Lee said, "Maybe he can give some lessons to little O'Neil here. He's still working on his first ounce."

"Sometimes it takes them a while to get used to sucking the nipple," Martha told her. "When they first try it, they wear themselves out. These drug-exposed babies use up so much of their energy kicking and crying. It's not surprising he's losing weight." Her words struck her as sounding false, spoken by somebody else.

"This ain't O'Neil's first time on a nipple," Nettie Lee said. "This boy been sucking a bottle since I got here."

"Maybe they need to go back to feeding him by tube until he's up to the extra effort of sucking." Martha turned to LaRone. "When do you take Daquille home? It's got to be in a week or so."

"They told me I can take him on Thursday. He gained enough weight."

"That make him five pounds?" Nettie Lee asked.

LaRone nodded. She reached out to take Daquille, her long fingers splayed into a safety net. Martha handed over the baby and switched places with her. She walked to Riley's Isolette, then changed her mind. Riley had parents. She wanted to rock a baby no one cared about. She looked at Faith, lying on the warming table, tranquilized.

"You nervous about it, honey?" Nettie Lee said.

"I can't keep my mind on anything else," LaRone answered.

Martha opened Gonsalves's incubator.

"A first baby is enough to worry anybody," Nettie Lee said. Martha thought she heard a lecture coming on in the pitch of Nettie Lee's voice, a lecture or one of those folktales with a hidden meaning. "Martha didn't have children. I guess that's why she's in here every day rocking these little babies, since she didn't have any babies of her own."

"That just shows your ignorance, old woman. I had a baby," Martha said, settling down with Gonsalves. The hollowness had returned to her full force, the electric drone.

"Well, where's your grandkids? Or maybe you raised one of these Buppies that don't want to take the time to have no kids of their own."

Whatever, Martha thought, but then she said, "No, that's not what happened to my child."

We had a baby named Paul. You couldn't separate us. He spent the first month of his life in my arms, sleeping and eating. He slept with me curled around him. And James, that was my husband, curled around both of us. That's the way we slept. When Paul woke up late at night, hungry, he'd press his face against my breast, smelling my milk; his soft lips would open, searching for my nipple. When he found it and pulled it into his mouth, I felt hot flutters in my stomach, like a hundred tiny butterflies drifting up from a rose bed.

In the late afternoons, waiting for James to come home, I'd lie on the couch with my feet up, pillows behind my back, feeding Paul. His hard little head rested in the crook of my arm, his body pressed against mine, his face was buried in my breast, sucking. He'd stretch his hand across my breast, as if he were claiming it. I'd fall asleep that way, every afternoon, with Paul in my arms.

One evening when Paul was five weeks old, I woke up on the couch in the dark. I don't know how long we'd been asleep, but it must have been a couple of hours. My chest felt heavy, weighted. In the dark I could barely see Paul lying in my arms against me. But his weight felt strange, unfamiliar. He wasn't warm, and his hand still lay on my breast, but his fingers were bent backward, stiff, away from my skin.

I can never remember how I got off the couch, or who told James, or how we got to the hospital. I just blocked it out, I guess. But I do remember that when we got to the hospital, the doctor, some anonymous man in blue scrubs, said my baby was dead.

❧ ❧

"Oh, my God." LaRone put her hand to her mouth. "I'm sorry, Martha."

"What you trying to do, scare her?" Nettie Lee sounded angry. "What kind of thing is that to tell a little girl with her first baby?"

"Well," Martha said, squeezing her eyes against the droning, "I didn't mean to frighten you, LaRone."

"And you not blaming yourself, I hope?" Nettie Lee said. "I heard things like that happen all the time. Doctors don't know what causes a baby to up and die like that."

"Oh, God." LaRone looked at Daquille, sleeping in her arms. "How am I going to take him home? What if it happens to me?" She drew him against her body.

"It won't happen, LaRone." Martha felt sure of this. "What happened to me, I guess I deserved." She thought about it. It seemed dangerous to get too attached to the people you loved. You always ended up losing them, one way or another.

"Well, I know I couldn't handle it if Daquille died."

"I just ended up worrying you to death with that story." Martha felt bad.

"No," LaRone said, sitting up straighter in the rocker. "I'm glad you told me. I want to know everything I can about taking care of my baby."

"I guess the truth ain't always pretty," Nettie Lee said. "Everybody's got something in their life causing pain."

"I suppose you're right, as usual," Martha said, rocking. Although she kept her voice neutral, she felt angered to be the recipient of Nettie Lee's easy sympathy.

When Nettie Lee left her house the next morning it was still dark outside, the sky full of wet snow that deadened the light. If it kept up, by afternoon the snow trucks would come out and clear the main streets for the ride home from work. They hadn't had a bad snowfall yet, when the schools closed and the downtown workers stayed home, but with the look of the sky that morning and a weather forecast for eleven inches by nightfall, this might be the first bad storm of the year.

Nettie Lee arrived at the hospital forty-five minutes early. She wanted to get there before Martha waltzed in and set up the day. Nettie Lee had her own plans today. She would tell Martha, point-blank, that she was Tookie's grandmother, and she'd tell her as soon as she walked in the door. Having decided to admit the truth the night before made her feel calm, clearheaded, and with the calm came the certainty that whatever storm might blow up from her admission, whatever rough tide might wash over her, she wouldn't drown, and so she calmly spent the extra time stacking towels, washing cylinders and nipples from the night feedings, and straightening up the diaper pile, as she ticked off the minutes until Martha came in. Debbie was busy at the nurses' desk, talking to a night-shift nurse who had stayed over a couple of hours. Both held Styrofoam cups of coffee poised against their lips, lowering the cups only when they spoke. Nettie Lee assumed they discussed how each baby had fared during the night.

If she had to, Nettie Lee would tell the administration, the child welfare, anybody who thought they had a right to know, that she was Tookie's grandmother. After what Martha had said the day before, how she had talked about her baby dying, Nettie Lee felt sure of one thing: a family had to acknowledge itself. Every member of a family had to claim every other member, no matter what trouble might boil over from admitting who belonged to whom.

Martha came in a half hour later, at eight forty-five, her scrub gown flapping around her knees.

Nettie Lee walked to the supply room, stood just inside the door, and looked at Martha. Her hair was dampened from the snow falling heavily outside. She said "Morning" to Nettie Lee, then busied herself in the back room stacking towels on the supply cart, a job Nettie Lee had just finished.

Martha picked up the work schedule hanging on the wall and looked down the list of chores for a moment. "Looks like Daquille's going home tomorrow morning. We have to show LaRone how to set up his feeding schedule this afternoon."

"I'll do it." Nettie Lee began straightening up gauze packs and syringes, felt her hands tremble, then told herself to calm down. First she would tell Martha, then she would tell the Child Protection woman. She pointed at the schedule. "What else you got on there?"

"Well, everything else looks like yesterday's schedule, although they're taking Baby Doe for some kind of test in the cardio lab later on." She looked up. The flick of her eyes over Nettie Lee's face felt like an examination. *What was she looking at?*

Nettie Lee tried to stay calm as she arranged the needles on the cart. "I feel so sorry for that baby. She's just been through too much."

"Well, God has a plan for every life." Martha sounded like a TV evangelist. "Nobody, no *mortal,* has any business questioning the wisdom of God."

"I'm not questioning God. I just wonder what's going to happen to the baby. Do you think you're going to get her or what?"

Martha's eyes narrowed. "You're always the one with the answers. What do *you* say?"

"God is a mystery I can't explain. I don't even try to figure it out. And as for what these social service people might decide, I know even less about that." She was worried, and she didn't like the feeling. Worry didn't change anything, it only had the effect of making folks—*her*—unsteady, weak. "Could you have a baby and then figure things was so bad you had to leave her? That she would be better off without you?"

"How can you ask me that?" Martha turned away, then quickly turned back. "Think about it yourself. Could you give birth to a child, then dump her?"

Nettie Lee hesitated. "I don't know what I might do if the conditions were wrong." She walked toward the door. "I can't say what God might lead me to do. I can only do the best I can under the circumstances I got." Her hand shook as she closed it around the doorknob. When the door banged shut on the frame, she realized she didn't feel calm at all.

Out in the nursery she chastised herself for lacking the courage to tell Martha. But she just didn't have the opportunity yet. Maybe after the ten o'clocks.

At ten, Nettie Lee and Martha fed and rocked two babies apiece, a short amount of attention for each baby but all they could spare. Debbie was called to the regular newborn nursery to evaluate a problem the nurses there were having with a small baby, born full term but feeding poorly.

At eleven-thirty, LaRone came in to feed her baby on his last full day in the nursery. Nettie Lee sat her in the conference room, where they could talk without interruption.

LaRone had taken to wearing more comfortable clothes to the

nursery and sat today in a pink sweatshirt and jeans underneath the scrub gown. She had pulled her hair up into a ponytail. Now LaRone looked like a young high school girl, almost too young to have had a baby. She laid a steno notebook on the table and took a pen from the black backpack she'd thrown on the floor beside her chair. Nettie Lee handed her the papers Debbie said to give every mother going home, including a sheet on feeding schedules. Nettie Lee was supposed to go over the sheet to see if LaRone had any questions. LaRone was her first discharge. It felt good to see a baby going home.

When they were done, Debbie was back and it was time for the twelve o'clocks.

LaRone joined Nettie Lee and Martha, sitting in the rockers.

"Who's going to tell the story today?" LaRone asked. She shook up the milk in Daquille's bottle.

"Why don't you give it a try, dear?" Martha said. She was fussing with Brown's scalp IV, trying to stick the tape back down to his head.

"No, not me." She looked scared. "I don't know how to make anything sound interesting. I think it's Nettie Lee's turn."

"I don't really feel like it today, honey." Nettie Lee had dragged herself through the ten o'clocks. Now O'Neil lay in her arms, noisily sucking his soy formula. After the feeding, Nettie Lee knew she would have to struggle with a gassy, crying baby.

"You *have* been pretty quiet all morning. Is something bothering you?"

"No."

"Come on, Nettie Lee. I like hearing about your life. Martha's too. It's like I never knew what happened before I was born. I never hear about it. There was a whole other world that happened before time got to me."

"That's right," Martha said. "But it's not so much a whole other world as it's the same world just continuing. Nothing ever is done and gone. It just spins itself away, then spins itself back."

"Remember my daughter, Yolanda?" Nettie Lee said.

"Of course," Martha answered.

"That's your change-of-life baby," LaRone said. "And her name's Yolanda?"

"Yeah. I told Martha another story about her one day, about how she had Little Barn. That's my grandson. I guess you wasn't coming in here yet. This time I'ma tell y'all what Yolanda did after she had Little Barn."

❧ ❧

Some people don't have the brains they were born with. Yolanda fits into that category. You think she would have had enough of Barn and his mess after their first baby was born. Don't forget, that fool missed the delivery. Didn't do Yolanda no good trying to get him into Lamaze lessons. No, sir. I guess he figured he didn't need no lessons to have a baby; he already did his part in getting Yolanda pregnant. Well, I guess he proved his point, since he got her pregnant again. And he still didn't say nothing about marrying the girl.

He figured he gave Yolanda and Little Barn everything they wanted—a big house over in Upper Dayton View, big-screen TVs, shiny black Toyota pickup with the leather interior, all that stereo mess he liked to play with. If they needed a refrigerator, Barn had to go out and buy the one with electronic buttons that didn't just make ice but added the whiskey and put the glass in your hand. He even tried to buy me a Niagara bed that vibrated and carried on. I thought about it for a while because I really could use a good night sleep, my bones get to aching so bad at night, but I turned that boy down because I don't want nothing to do with drug money. And that's all he had in his wallet. Money he got from those poor fools who got to stay high. You know, he had all that money and didn't know what to do with it. Couldn't do anything legitimate like buy a house; they had to rent. What bank is going to believe a sixteen-year-old boy got enough money and a job to put the down payment on a big house? I don't know how he rented the one he did. That house was like rich folks' houses—all brick and a lawn been to the manicurist. Still, there he was standing at my door waiting to take Yolanda. Drive her away in his new black pickup, like he's the King of England and Yolanda is Princess Di. I told that girl it wouldn't last.

Barn couldn't find his way to the hospital when his own child was born. He said he had business to take care of that night, a big deal to close. It was always something with him, always a reason why. That went on for years. After the baby got big, Yolanda was back on my doorstep, crying. Said she left Barn, he was too cold-blooded for her tastes. All he thinks about is work, work, work. Never spends time with her and Little Barn, and when he's home he's got his business associates around him. She won't say who they are. Then his beeper goes off and he's on the telephone, then he's out the door. All day long, the same thing. She was knocking around that big house like a loose marble. I saw their place a couple of times. It looks good from the outside, very respectable, but on the inside it was just walls and floor. Sure, it had a big TV in the living room, always on. (That's Yolanda's bad habit—she can't stand the sound of quiet.) That's why I never went over there too much—I caught a headache that took me a week to get rid of every time I stayed there more than a minute. Only thing in the living room was the TV and a black leather couch sitting smack in front of it. In the kitchen, he got his fancy appliances, three ovens (like he thought he could get more out of Yolanda than a peanut butter sandwich), a gas cooktop *and* an electric one, a trash compactor. (I told Yolanda, "Make sure the baby don't get caught in that. That thing'll crunch him up good.") The kitchen's got all glass cabinets, and skylights, and windows all around so you can see out to the backyard pool. (I told Yolanda to make sure she kept the back door locked. A baby can drown in a pool quick as you can turn your back on him.) She said don't worry about nothing, she got it all under control. But that's a bald lie. All she did was sit up in front of the TV and let Little Barn do what he pleased. One time I came in there, and he was running around naked leaving a brown trail behind him. She was laying on the couch with a blanket up to her chin. She said, "Oh, Little Byron's got the runs." I said, "So I noticed. Why don't you put a pair of underwear on him and save your good carpet?" Now, here's the dumbest answer I ever heard: "Because I ran out." So I said, "What's stopping you from doing the laundry?" And she says, "Money. I'm broke, Mama."

"Broke?" I felt like shaking her off that couch. "What you mean, broke?"

"They turned my electricity off. I don't have any money for the bill." She scrunched down further in the blanket.

"Where's Barn at?"

"Byron is out. I haven't seen him in weeks."

"So what you doing laying up here all by yourself?"

"Mama, leave me alone. I'm tired. And I don't feel too good myself. Me and Little Byron got the same thing."

"Well, pack up your stuff. You can come home with me. You don't have to take this shit."

"What shit? I just don't have any money, and I'm sick. That's all. When Byron gets back he'll give me some money for Little Byron."

"What makes you so sure?"

"He loves his son. Our relationship is a different matter, a private one, okay? But the man does love his son."

"Loves him so much he just walks off and lets him starve? Lets him be sick?"

"Mama, it's okay," she says, like she's so tired she can't talk. Then she falls asleep right in my face.

I took Little Barn home with me while Yolanda was asleep. I thought she'd call me up as soon as she noticed he wasn't there. She never has said a word to me about why he's at my house. So I just kept him. I took him home, washed him up, gave him some burnt flour and water for his diarrhea, put a pair of *my* underwear on his behind till I could wash up his dirty pants. Then I took him out to K mart and bought him some little pants, and shirts, and underwear, and a bottle of Kaopectate.

Time passed, like it always does. Then here comes Yolanda dragging her butt up to my front door, and she looks terrible. Like she been on a month-long toot. Clothes look like the same ones she had on when I was at her house. Girl ain't never heard the words "Comb your hair, wash your clothes." She smelled so funky, she out and out stunk. I said, "Yolanda, what is the matter with you?"

"Nothing," she says, and pushes her way past me, plops herself down on the couch. "What you got to eat?"

"Nothing extra. Go look in the kitchen and see what you can find."

I didn't think she looked skinny, so I didn't think she was starving or nothing. I guess Barn didn't come by and give her money for Little Barn yet. She rummaged around in the cabinets for a minute, then came out of the kitchen with some Cheerios.

"Them's the baby's," I said.

"I'm not going to eat the whole box." She flopped on the couch. She kept digging her hand in like she was going to finish off the whole thing. I guess it takes a kid to eat them like that, right out of the box. A kid or Yolanda, because she went to town on that box. Then she scootched down on the couch and fell asleep.

When Little Barn woke up he went over to where she was passed out. First, he just looked at her with her mouth all open, snoring. Then he laid his head on her back and hugged her. Didn't even wake her up. So now I'm starting to get suspicious about her. I'm thinking she's got narcolepsy—you know, that sleeping sickness where you can't help when you fall asleep. He's hugging her and crying too, he's so glad to see her. Still, she sleeps on. Then out of the sky it hits me. My daughter, who was always clean and careful, always good, my daughter is using drugs. Now how did it come to this?

I always said there ain't nobody in this world I hate. Maybe I don't like you, maybe I don't want to have to deal with you, but there ain't nobody I hate. Well, I had to stop saying that, because I hated Barn so bad I didn't know what to do with it. I had all this hate jamming against me on the inside, trying every minute of the day to get out. Hate had me acting evil. I couldn't keep my mind on nothing, except how I was going to hurt that boy for hurting my daughter. Every time I went out to the store, I was looking up and down the street, trying to catch a glimpse of his pickup. When I rode the bus, I was looking out the window, searching the streets for him. The only thing that made me feel calm was telling myself that one day I was going to put my hands around his neck and squeeze until every last bit of my hate found a way out.

Time passed some more. Yolanda got herself a welfare check and moved in with her so-called friend Benji. Still, I kept Little Barn with me. Yolanda didn't fight me on it, neither. She knows what's best for her child. Besides, Yolanda's not the kind of person who can let a child watch her get high. I know some girls, like Benji for instance, get their kids to help them. Benji got two kids old enough to play outside. She give them some money, say, "Run on down to so-and-so and get me a bottle." Now what kind of example are you setting for a child with behavior like that? I certainly don't know. And here we are laughing at the government for telling us to have more family values. That ain't nothing to laugh at. More people should be paying attention to good advice, even if the source is questionable.

Now Yolanda got a place to stay and a welfare check. You think she's going to try to raise her boy? No. She's living with somebody else's children but not her own. I said, "Yolanda, does this make sense?"

"Yeah," she said. "I don't want Little Barn to live in the environment I have to live in. I want my child to have better than that."

"Well, your child needs his mother," I told her. But she was right. The way Benji and them carried on, you'd think they lived in an insane asylum. People coming over all hours, and roaches, brave as a SWAT team, attacking your food right on the table, while you'd be sitting there trying to eat.

Every first of the month I took Yolanda grocery shopping. She'd spend all her food stamps in one day, stocking up on everything she thought she was going to need for the month. Of course, she gave me some of the food for Little Barn, since he was staying with me. And I'm glad of it. Benji's two kids ate up Yolanda's food like it belonged to them, while their mother got a welfare check bigger than Yolanda did and more food stamps too. They went through their food, then started in on Yolanda's. All she said about it was, "I don't eat that much myself. They're growing kids, anyway." Well, I think their mother could have had a little more control on how long that food lasted. Yolanda just bought herself big cans of tuna, beans, some dry soup mix, stuff like that. Nothing fancy. Sometimes I took Little Barn over there, and Benji's kids would be eating steak and artichokes. I said, "Benji, you wasting them food stamps. You got to make them last. What you going to do when the end of the month comes?" And she said, "We ain't starved yet, Miss Johnson." Then she looked at Yolanda and said, "I got me a friend that takes care of the end of the month." Yolanda said, "Only if you take care of him first." Then Benji waved her hand and said, "It ain't nothing. He knows if he wants it, he got to compensate me for it." Yolanda nodded her head. "Nothing in this life is free."

Yolanda and me went shopping on October first. She cashed her check, then went down and bought her food stamps. After that, we walked over to the warehouse, did our shopping, and called a cab back to my house, since all the heavy things go there. After shopping we was both tired, sitting at the kitchen table, both of us with our feet on a chair. She got one of them stinky cigars for women out of her pocketbook and lit it. That's when I saw her stomach looking like she got the official NBA basketball stuck up under her T-shirt.

I said, "Yolanda, when is that baby due?"

She said, "Ain't no baby. You looking at a water tumor on my ovary."

I said, "What kind of fool do you take me for?"

"I don't take you for no kind of fool, Mama," she told me. "The doctor said I got a water tumor on my ovary. Believe it or not." She crossed her feet. "I feel like I'm all bloated inside. I'm going to have him take it off soon as I get some time."

I got up and stood over her chair. "I know I'm looking at a baby." I put my hands on her stomach. Felt hard as a brick. "You ever feel this baby kick you?"

"No, Mama," she says and gets up. "Water tumors don't kick." She picked up the phone. "I have to go home. Have to call me a cab." She started telling the cab company my address.

I knew why she was so anxious to get home. Her pipe was calling her. She had to go get a hit. But she couldn't stop with one. Yolanda was going to be wasted all night long.

I said, "Just tell the truth. When's the baby due?"

She said, "February seventh." She went over to the window to wait for the cab.

I was so disappointed in her, I couldn't speak. I felt like I had been through all that mess before, and I just didn't know if I could do it again. I just sat there looking at her back.

Late one Saturday night in the middle of November, the phone rang. Only I didn't know it was the phone since I'm in the middle of a dream. There were birds tweeting in my dream, soft pretty little mockingbirds in a tree outside my house. I was telling myself I never even *have* dreams, so what was I doing dreaming? Then the birds started screeching, flapping their wings and fighting with each other. The screeching got worse and I dreamt I couldn't wake up. Then the birds were screeching to a rhythm, like they were singing to each other *Screech! Screech! Screech!* Turns out it was the phone. Now, I don't like answering the phone at night, not when I can't see nothing in the room and I'm liable to fall down and break my neck trying to get to it. The clock said it was three-twenty. Got to be bad news.

It was Yolanda. "Mommy?" Her voice was whiny.

I said, "What? What you calling for?" I knew I sounded mad, but scared was what I felt.

"Mommy, that you?" And I heard her crying. "Mommy, Mommy, Mommy."

I hate to be called Mommy, and she knew it because I told her that a long time ago, when she was a little girl. It sounds like what some bourgy black kids have to call their mother. I told her to call me Mama. So I knew something was up with all this Mommy business. She got me real worried. "Girl, what you calling me on the phone and whining at me for?" I was trying to make her come to the point.

"Mommy?"

"Yeah, it's your mommy," I said. "What you want?"

"Mommy?" Now she was getting on my nerves. "Mommy, where am I?"

"How'm I supposed to know that? You the one making the phone call. Where does it look like you are?"

"Mommy, come and get me. I'm bleeding bad, Mommy."

"You bleeding?" She doesn't answer me. "Yolanda, what you say about bleeding?"

"I'm bleeding, Mommy, and the baby is coming. What am I going to do?"

I was trying to put my clothes on, but I was tripping over the phone cord. "Where are you at, girl? You at home?"

"The baby's coming, Mommy." And that's all she says, over and over.

"Yolanda, call yourself a ambulance," I told her firm. "Dial nine-one-one. You can do that, can't you? Where are you?"

"I'm no place, Mommy," was all she said, then she hung up on me.

All I could do was hope she dialed the ambulance, but to me it sounded like she was out of her mind. I got my clothes on in the dark, since Little Barn was in the bedroom, sleeping. I didn't feel right about it, but I had to go over to Yolanda's quick and help her with the baby, so I had to leave him in his bed.

Outside, the wind was blowing and snow was flying. And I'm running up the street like some kind of crazy fool, just trying not to slip and fall. Before too long, I lost my wind and had to slow down, but I was hurrying to get over to her apartment, about two miles away. There was nothing on the street except me and the snow. My hands went numb. No gloves, no boots. Every now and then, a gust of wind caught me in the face, took my breath from me. But I kept hurrying. I wanted to catch Yolanda before the baby came out.

Finally, I got to Summit Street. My lungs hurt so bad, they felt like they'd been cut up with a knife. I walked up to Yolanda's four-plex. She was on the top floor on the left. I climbed the stairs, puffing all the way. When I got there, I saw the door was standing wide open, not a peep coming from inside. I went in, calling out her name. Nothing. But the mess in that place was enough to turn me back into the street. There was junk all over. Her and Benji didn't pick up nothing off the floor. Once something got thrown there, it had a home. I went back to the bedroom, calling out Yolanda's name. No answer. There was glass exploded on the bedroom floor—her bureau mirror was busted out. In the bathroom, the mirror was busted in the sink. I went back to the living room and, yeah, the mirror on the antique wardrobe she thought so much of was broken out too. Back in the bedroom, the bed was a mess of heaped-up raggelly sheets, and—this scared the wits out of me—in the middle of the bed was a lot of blood. Pale, runny-looking stains. But Yolanda was nowhere to be seen. "Dear Lord in heaven," I said out loud. "Where has that child gone?" I waited around for two or three hours, but nobody came, not Yolanda, not Benji or her kids. Down the street I heard sirens, ambulances and police cars. I thought they done found Yolanda's body in the road. Naturally, I picked up the phone and tried to call the hospital, but the phone was dead. It was plugged in, but it wasn't working. So I sat there convincing myself she was going to walk in that door any minute. When I got tired of slapping cockroaches off my legs, I left and walked on home in the daylight, just the way I came.

At home, I called every hospital in the city. They all said, no, they ain't seen nobody look like Yolanda. Then all I could do was wait by the phone, thinking she'd call and tell me where she was. And I ain't heard yet.

❦ ❦

"Summit Street is where she lives?" Martha asked.

"Yeah."

"That street where they're putting up the Hip Hop's Chicken Joint?"

"Yeah."

Martha got up from her rocker, Brown's blanket unraveling behind her. "Nurse?" Nettie Lee watched the redheaded nurse come over.

"Here." Martha handed Brown to her and walked out.

"What's her problem?" LaRone said.

"She don't like the story I told."

"What do you mean?"

"Forget it, honey." Nettie Lee took a slow breath in and out. *I did it,* she thought.

The automatic doors flung open in front of Martha. She walked through, then turned to watch them close on the nursery, muffling the beeps and exhales.

Faith belonged to Nettie Lee? Was that possible? Why hadn't she said anything? Martha leaned her back against the doors. Why hadn't Nettie Lee told her before now?

She felt a hard rapping against her back. Debbie Foxx appeared in the window. Behind Foxx, Martha could see the horseshoe of babies, and Nettie Lee and LaRone sitting in their rockers. Nettie Lee held O'Neil upright on her lap, patting him impatiently, while LaRone rocked Daquille in her arms. It all looked so normal. But Foxx's expression was urgent; she pointed at Martha and spoke in exaggerated tones. "Move back, Martha! I have to open the door!" When Martha stepped away from the doors, they sprang open.

"You were blocking the door." Foxx looked puzzled. "I need you in there. You weren't going for a break, were you?"

Martha shook her head.

"Okay, good. While I was over in Newborn we got backed up with the feedings, and now I have to get Dr. Xiang here for Baby

Doe. She had another seizure. Her monitor went off, and when I watched her she stopped right away, but that makes three times today. I think she's going to keep it up. Go check on her while I call Xiang, okay? It would just make me feel better if somebody was close by until the doc gets here. Oh, wait. I've got to write up the evaluation on that baby in Newborn, then get a nutrition consult for Baker. Maybe you'd better change Gonsalves's diaper for me, first. I'll have Callie watch Doe. Just leave the diaper on the scale. I'll weigh it when I get off the phone. Or you weigh it. Just write down the weight on the output sheet in his chart." She waved Martha in through the doors.

The nursery seemed too hot, the air too humid, the smell too antiseptic. If there was a perfect time to leave, to resign as a grandmother, this was it. Faith wouldn't be going home with her, not if she belonged to Nettie Lee. Martha's eyes stung with tears. Though Hunter had told Martha that her chances of adopting the baby were slim, she had still hoped. But Faith would not be going home with her. At the sink, she washed up with a squirt of iodine soap.

Martha took a paper diaper from the stack on the worktable, along with a couple of Tucks. She opened the portholes in Gonsalves's Isolette. Sliding her hands into the heated air, she pulled apart the sticky tabs on his diaper, exposing his genitals, which looked huge for such a small boy. Diaper loose, he immediately sent out a thin stream of urine. Feeling awkward holding Gonsalves like this, in an odd, once-removed embrace, she remembered working one of those toy-grabber machines at the fair when she was little. She would put a nickel in, then the mechanical hand started up, hovering over the toy she wanted. But when she pushed the button to make the hand drop, it always grabbed up the wrong toy. She had never won that game. When she was finished cleaning Gonsalves, Martha slid the diaper from him, rolled it into a neat ball, secured the sticky tabs. She laid it on top of the incubator, then walked over to check on Baby Doe.

Faith, her dream baby, lay on her back in the warming tray. Tumescent with oxygen, her respirator tubes jerked slightly with every breath. Her leg jerked, or her arm did, or she'd grimace, her mouth stretching into a look of pain, her eyes squeezing tight; then her face would go slack, as if she hadn't felt anything after all. It wasn't that Faith *frightened* her, it was as if the baby *accused* her, lying in the tray with its high plastic sides, hooked up to all her lifesaving machines. *Where were the machines that could have saved Paul?* Her eyes stung. Best not to think about it. What good did it do?

Martha's dream came to her—the naked baby, connected to all her tubes and wires, the baby caught in a spider web spun by *herself,* she realized. She was spinning the web herself. She felt the helplessness of the dream Martha, caught, trapped, just like those babies. The life she'd chosen for herself after Paul's death was like an Isolette, a plastic box. She had felt safe at first, insulating herself from other people. Until James claimed her grief was suffocating him, that he was helpless to do anything about it. He had left the same year. Alone, she'd lived a quiet life, thinking she had buried Paul deep inside. Then she saw the ad in the paper to rock these babies. When she first saw the nursery, it had seemed frightening, all the Isolettes lined up, full of squirming babies that needed to get out but would die without the incubators' protection. She was afraid of everything in the nursery: every piece of equipment, every procedure she was asked to perform, every baby. It all terrified her. Yet she was also comfortable with her fear. She recognized it as belonging with her. Maybe she would never lose it.

Faith's entire body jerked convulsively; then she lay still. Martha grazed her index finger along the baby's left thigh, which trembled gently. Was this Nettie Lee's grandchild? Could it be true? And why was Nettie Lee blessed with yet another baby? First Yolanda, then Little Byron, and now this one. But surely, if this were her grandchild, Nettie Lee would have named her, and she had never heard Nettie Lee call this child anything.

She brushed her finger across Faith's cheek, soft and fuzzy as a kiwi, her nose a flawless bud, her mouth slack around the respirator tube. And still her left leg trembled. She picked up Faith's leg in her hand, then laid it gently on the mattress, where it continued to tremble. A seizure. The baby was having a seizure!

"Nurse Foxx!" Martha shouted over the noise, one hand on Faith's leg, the other waving when Foxx finally looked up from Baker's Isolette. Foxx hurried over.

"What's wrong?"

Martha pointed to the leg. "I think it's another seizure."

Foxx silently watched the baby's leg shake. She sighed. "I guess Dr. Xiang will up her seizure meds." She looked at her watch. "Where is she? I called her pager five minutes ago." She turned toward the reception desk. "Louise, page Dr. Xiang again, stat." She turned to Martha. "Thanks. Way to watch 'em."

Martha took the soiled diaper from the top of Gonsalves's Isolette, charted its weight, and tossed it in the trash. At the sink, as she washed her hands again, she heard the intercom page Dr. Xiang to the NIC nursery, stat.

Martha tipped back her rocker. Cradled loosely in her arms, Gonsalves sagged against her stomach, his head lolling gently to one side before she could right it. Nettie Lee sat beside her, burping O'Neil, a thoughtful-looking pout on her lips. LaRone had got up and left, saying she had to go clean up her apartment in preparation for Daquille's homecoming. Nettie Lee got up from her rocker and told Martha to follow her into the supply room.

As she partially closed the door, Nettie Lee seemed restless and kept shifting about on her feet. Behind her, Martha could see Foxx walking back and forth through the nursery, checking every Isolette. "So you figured out about Tookie." Her question was a challenge.

"Is that what you named her?" Martha laid Gonsalves on her shoulder. Anger rose up in her; she pushed it down. She didn't want to talk about the child she had tried to think of as her own and now knew she couldn't have.

"No, Tookie is just her cradle name." Nettie Lee stood silent for a moment, then said softly, "I did name her something, though. What you think about Maria Christina Johnson?"

Martha rocked her body from side to side, Gonsalves's head tucked in the cup of her shoulder. "That sounds all right."

"I think it's got some music to it." She looked at Martha expectantly, holding O'Neil in a jittery embrace.

Martha was growing intolerant of their conversation; it was like watching a dog scratch its eye with a hind foot. She sighed, exasperated, then turned to leave the supply room. Knowing that Nettie Lee and Yolanda had abandoned Faith made her furious. She couldn't listen any more and she didn't want to talk. Words had left her.

"Look," Nettie Lee said. "I know you had plans for the baby, and I know what you're going to think—that I ain't got no business telling Tookie's secret, but I'ma tell the administration about her today."

Martha stopped rocking on her feet and faced Nettie Lee, who looked sorrowful. But Nettie Lee's sadness didn't matter; it was the baby who counted. If Nettie Lee told the hospital who the baby belonged to, she would put the child in jeopardy of returning to a dangerous home situation. Nettie Lee was a liar, Yolanda wasn't fit to be a mother. She headed for the half-open door. "Do what you think is best. I'm just sick of all the abuse that baby is constantly put through."

"Abuse? Abused by who?"

Though she wanted to be done with it, to get out of the tight, crowded room, the overcrowded hospital, to leave grandmothering—she didn't need all this excitement, this grief—Nettie Lee's words called her back. Yes, the baby was being abused by those closest to her. "By you," she said to Nettie Lee. "By you and by everybody who has had anything to do with her."

"Me? I'm right here taking care of this baby and every other baby in the nursery, every day. So what are you talking about, abuse? I don't abuse nobody."

Martha reconsidered. "Well, maybe it's not intentional, but look at what's happening. Think about it. Everything you say you're doing for that baby is just to make *yourself* feel better. You don't know what plans other people might have made concerning the baby." She felt her head close off. "Maybe the baby would be better off if somebody would just adopt her. Then the police would leave her alone. They'd leave your daughter alone, too."

"Somebody like you, right?" Nettie Lee said sarcastically. "When I decided to tell, I wasn't thinking anything about myself. I was thinking about Tookie, what *she* needed. I came to the hospital because I wanted to be close to her, to be here if she needed me. Now all I want to do is tell them her name and take her home when she gets well. I want to raise the baby for Yolanda. Maybe she ain't never coming back, but I know I ain't done nothing wrong. And maybe I am selfish, I don't know. But this feels like love to me. I love her."

Martha was struck by the sincerity of Nettie Lee's plea. And yet, what Nettie Lee had done was wrong. Babies needed to be nurtured, held close, watched over, not thrown in a toilet. They weren't responsible for the problems they were born into. If a mother couldn't care for her baby, she needed to give it up, step aside and let another woman take her place. "If you really want to help the baby," Martha finally said, "tell CPA where Yolanda is. Force her to get treatment."

"Even if I knew, I wouldn't tell. You know what they'll do to her. They'll put her in jail. If I take this baby, then Yolanda can still get help without turning herself in. When she gets herself straightened out, she can come back home and her family will be waiting for her."

"What makes you so sure she can do it without going in a program like Miss Hunter was talking about?"

"I didn't say she wasn't going to a program, I just said nobody had to know that she's this particular baby's mother. That's all. She could go to a drug program somewhere else. Or here, if she kept her mouth shut."

"That's not likely." Martha shook her head. "If you tell CPA you're the baby's grandmother they probably will give her to you, but they'll also be looking for Yolanda, because now they'll know where to look. Your house. Didn't you think of that? Yolanda won't be able to come back home as long as you've got the baby in your house."

"So what are you saying now, that I ought to keep my mouth shut about being her grandma and let *you* take her? Don't you know that whole notion you got about adopting my baby is just a dream? You're too old to be adopting a baby. There ain't no agency that's going to let you do that. You know that, don't you? That Miss Hunter is just humoring you, pretending like she's taking you seriously. And what if it was *your* daughter they was looking for? Or your son. What if it was Paul?"

Martha flinched at hearing his name, didn't want to speak of him, but her anger, beating like helicopter blades, impelled her onward. "Paul wouldn't do anything like this. I would have raised him better. I know he wouldn't be on dope if he wasn't—"

"Dead."

"If he wasn't dead." Martha had finally spoken the word. Everyone else had said it—the doctors, James, her family—but she had never been able to even hear it in her mind. *Dead.*

"I know people like you," Nettie Lee said. "All you good for is sitting up here passing judgments, like you Saint Peter and the three wise men rolled into one. As long as you get what you want, everything else is okay. Well, here's what I want—I want to name my grandbaby, just in case she don't make it. And if she does get well and comes home, I'll worry about my problems later. If I hear from Yolanda, I'll worry about that when that happens. But I ain't worrying about you, because you ain't nothing but a waste of my time. If you ain't going to help me, then you can get out of my way." She turned to walk out the door.

"Nettie Lee—" Martha held Gonsalves tightly against her breast, felt his small feet and knees struggle against her. The panic was rising up again, dark and lonely as her empty house. "Forget about me," she finally said. "Forget about what I told you. I know the baby isn't mine, that she belongs with you. All right? But think about what you're doing, if it's worth the risk of losing your baby, just to name her. You know, Paul had a name,

Michael had a name. What good did it do either one of them?" For a moment, Martha clearly hoped Nettie Lee could tell her the answer.

Nettie Lee turned back, was quietly observing Martha. "I'm not like you," she said. "I'm not trying to bring somebody back from the dead. I won't let my baby die without a name, and that's all."

Debbie Foxx opened the supply room door and stuck her head in. She looked at them uncertainly. "So, you've taken the babies for a change of scenery?" When neither one answered she said, "Are both of you free? Dr. Xiang wants to examine the Doe baby right now and change her bandages, too. I'm tied up with Baker, but if one of you will help, the other person can watch. Then that'll be something else grandmothers can do in the nursery."

"I'll do it." Holding O'Neil in the crook of her arm, Nettie Lee left the room.

Before she'd come to the hospital, Martha didn't want to know how people's lives turned out. She didn't want to get involved, didn't want to know that so-and-so ended up being an alcoholic, or so-and-so turned out to be childless. She just didn't want to know the end of their story, because then she could see their lives were passing by, getting used up. It made her feel so sorry for people when she knew they had come to the end, because she knew the end couldn't be changed. And she wanted to change what Paul had meant to her, but for that to happen, her old life had to fall away, had to die. She felt as if she were dying, and she hated it.

Martha watched Nettie Lee and Foxx bend over O'Neil's Isolette, connecting his monitor leads. She knew that in a few moments Foxx would look up and wonder where she was, wonder why she still stood in the supply room, clutching Gonsalves and staring out the door.

Nettie Lee and Dr. Xiang leaned over Tookie's warming tray. The baby lay quietly on her back, arms and legs stretched flat to her sides, the green and red respirator tubes jerking slightly alongside her. Dr. Xiang motioned for Nettie Lee to get the box of exam gloves. Bristles of hair escaped from Dr. Xiang's short ponytail, which she'd secured with plastic-coated rubber bands. Her glasses obscured her eyes. Nettie Lee's feet still bothered her, had been hurting her all morning. Even though she didn't feel up to watching the doctor do something more to Tookie, she did want to see how her grandbaby was doing up close, to help take care of her. She felt a little shaky from her fight with Martha, but now that she had told Martha the truth, she knew she could go ahead and tell the Child Protection Agency.

Dr. Xiang pulled on the thin exam gloves, her fingers slipping delicately into their powdered interior. She held the box out to Nettie Lee, whose large hands made drawing on the gloves less smooth. Dr. Xiang turned to Nettie Lee. "Open the bandage pack."

Nettie Lee pulled the tape from a package wrapped in blue paper toweling. Inside lay a roll of sterile gauze, several gauze pads, white paper tape, and bandage scissors. She put the pack on a table beside the warming tray and watched Dr. Xiang. Holding the bandage scissors in her gloved hand, Dr. Xiang inserted the blunt tip beneath the swath of gauze on the baby's chest and began to cut, her hand working the scissors in a slow squeeze.

Nettie Lee felt her knees weaken. She pinched her right thigh hard through her scrub gown and dress. The scissors cut through the last of the bandage, just under the notch in the baby's throat, exposing the incision, precise and slightly puckered around the black sutures. The baby's chest undulated gently, her heart visibly beating beneath her ribs. Dr. Xiang warmed her stethoscope's disk in her palm for a few seconds, then placed it on the baby's chest, listening closely, her eyes hidden behind her glasses.

"May I?" Pointing to the stethoscope, Martha stepped up close to the doctor. Nettie Lee hadn't seen her standing behind them.

Martha listen to the baby's chest, a frown forming between her eyes, as if trying to gather meaning from the beating of the child's heart.

Dr. Xiang explained what Martha was hearing. "The first

heart sound means the blood is pumped to the lungs and body. The last heart sound means the heart is filling with blood again. That continuous sound you hear is a murmur—it sounds like a sheet of aluminum flapping on a clothesline."

"I can't hear that," Martha said. "It just sounds too fast to me."

"Smaller the person, faster the heart," Dr. Xiang said. "Other grandmother wants to listen?"

Nettie Lee took the stethoscope from Martha's hand and adjusted the earpieces. They clamped into her ears tightly. She bit her lips between her teeth. She rested the disk on the baby's beating ribs and listened hard. The heartbeat pulsed against her ears, loud and quick, more pressure than sound. The intensity of the beat, its presence inside her head, made it hard to distinguish from her own heart. She felt a touch at her elbow.

"Let's finish." Dr. Xiang lifted the baby's body with one hand, drew the soiled bandage from beneath her with the other. She painted the wound with a 2×2 soaked in red Betadine. "Gauze pads?" Nettie Lee tore open a square package of two pads and extended the open pack to Dr. Xiang, who placed them against the wound. "Okay, give me the roll." Nettie Lee unwound the roll of gauze a little, handed it to Dr. Xiang. "Can you hold her up? Just enough for me to put my hands under her."

Dr. Xiang steadied the gauze on her chest, then Nettie Lee slid her hand beneath the baby's head and scooped her gently off the tray. Her head and back lifted, but her arms and legs sagged downward. The heart monitor began to beep more quickly; then the alarm whined. The green line it traced zigzagged erratically.

"That's okay," Dr. Xiang said, passing the gauze roll quickly from hand to hand, beneath, then over her, wrapping her chest. "Done."

Nettie Lee laid the baby back on the tray, straightened the respirator tubes beside her, and placed her feet on a rolled-up washcloth to take the pressure off her heels.

Dr. Xiang looked at the monitor. "Incision is healing well.

Baby's just so-so. She needs more time." She pulled a chart from the metal stand and began to write.

In the afternoon, Nettie Lee got on a bus headed downtown. Since morning, the sky had completely clouded over; warm snow continued to fall. She watched through her window as the bus passed the large hospital parking lot and a line of cars turning into the slushy entrance, where a security guard handed out stubs. The lot stayed full. Either staff were coming to work or people were visiting their kids. As the bus pulled into the right-hand lane and turned, the hospital receded, replaced by a residential area of small homes, Christmas trees still behind picture windows, new snow melting on sidewalks already scraped clean.

Downtown, in the city rink, the skaters stumbled in the early dusk. Through the window, Nettie Lee absently listened to their muffled complaints about the sudden warm snow melting the ice, how their skates were digging ruts instead of skimming on top. When the bus pulled up to the corner of Third and Main, she got out.

The county courthouse building gave her a bad feeling. Its dark ornate interior, high ceilings, and massive dusty antique furniture made her think of the dentist's office M'Dear took her to in Chicago, the time she had a toothache so bad she couldn't open her mouth. After seeing the bloody tooth lying on the towel the dentist had draped across Nettie Lee's chest, M'Dear had fainted to the floor. In the courthouse building, the elevator was located down a narrow hall lit dimly with yellowed glass ceiling fixtures, but Nettie Lee found the building directory. The Child Protection Agency was listed as being on the ninth floor, room 927.

The door was closed. The knob felt cool and heavy in her hand, like iron. She turned it and pushed forward, peeked inside, then entered.

In the tall-ceilinged room there were five desks arranged in a haphazard manner, but all of them faced the door. The social workers, a man and four women, sat behind piles of paper; none of the desks were neat. One of the women talked to a middle-aged woman who sat with her coat still buttoned tightly, her scarf still tied around her head, as if she were cold, though Nettie Lee had felt a blast of stuffy heat as soon as she opened the door. She saw Barb Hunter in the corner, tapping her pencil impatiently on her desk, talking into the telephone. "Yeah, yeah," she was saying. She slammed down the phone. Nettie Lee approached the first desk.

"I want to talk to Miss Hunter. I see her back there." She nodded to the corner.

"Let me see if she's free." The woman had a short frosted-blond hairdo, long French-manicured nails. She punched the telephone buttons with her pen. Nettie Lee heard a phone buzz, then Barb Hunter's "Yeah?" from the back of the room.

"Somebody to see you."

Barb Hunter looked up from her desk, frowning. "Who is that?"

The woman looked at Nettie Lee. "Who are you?" She sounded incurious.

"Nettie Lee Johnson."

"Nettie Lee Johnson," the woman repeated into the telephone.

From the back, Barb Hunter said, "Okay."

"Nettie Lee. Hi. What's up?" A computer sat on her desk. She held her hands poised above the keypad.

"I got to talk to you, Miss Hunter, about the baby."

"Which baby are you talking about?" She pushed the keypad to the middle of her desk, rested her arms in front of her.

"Maria Christina Johnson. The baby y'all been calling Baby Doe. The one the TV's been calling Baby X? Well, that ain't her name. I just told you her name."

"Sit down." The tip of Miss Hunter's tongue showed between her lips. "What do you know about her?" Her voice was careful.

"I know I'm that child's grandmother."

Miss Hunter raised her eyebrows, inviting Nettie Lee to move in closer. "Are you?"

Nettie Lee moved back. "Yeah. And I want you to put that down in your computer. And when she gets better and they let her go from the hospital, I'm going to take her home with me. Put that down in your computer too."

Arms crossed on the desk, Miss Hunter seemed to be thinking. "Well, okay. Let's put some of this down." She drew the keypad toward her. "Please give me your full name."

"Like I said, Nettie Lee Johnson."

Miss Hunter tapped the keys quickly.

"And the baby's mother's name?"

"You got to know that?"

Miss Hunter looked up. "Of course. What's her name?"

"I can't be telling you all that. I'm just here to let you know Maria Christina Johnson got a name and a place to go when she gets well. She needs anything, you ask me."

"Well, it's not as simple as that." Miss Hunter looked around the room. She lowered her voice. "The police are looking for the woman who gave birth to that child. You know that. Fortunately, the child didn't die as a result of exposure, but what your daughter did is still a crime. And what you are doing now by withholding her name is also a crime. Okay? I'm not a law enforcement officer, but you cannot withhold this information if *they* question you." She typed on the keypad. "What's your address?"

Nettie Lee felt the world slipping away from her. "I'm not saying nothing else today." She got up. "Maria Christina Johnson. That's the baby's name."

Back on the street, Nettie Lee waited for the bus to come. What should she do, go back to the hospital? That social worker was probably dialing the nursery right now, itching to let the hospital know she'd found out who to blame. What Nettie Lee really wanted was to go home, get into bed, and sleep. Her head felt as wide open as a field, her heart was jumpy, she couldn't keep her hands still. What would happen to Tookie, to Little Barn, to Yolanda? She rested her head in her hands, forced her breath out into her palms. It felt like being in jail, knowing that somebody else had all the power over her life, that she was not the one to make decisions, to guide her own family. She always had to work around *somebody:* the social worker, Martha, Barn, Sweet, Big Daddy Walter. When would she be allowed to handle her life without somebody else thinking they knew better than her what was right? Laws. How can somebody make a law telling her how to take care of her own family? How can they tell her what she is allowed to do for her children and her grandchildren? What did they know about it, besides something they read in some book?

The bus pulled alongside the curb, noisily running its engine. The driver, an overweight harassed-looking woman, hurried Nettie Lee inside and quickly closed the doors against the cold air. As she handed the driver her dollar, she felt a lightening in her chest. "Give me a transfer," she told her, holding out her hand for the ticket and the change. She folded the ticket into her coat pocket and walked up the aisle as the bus rocked away from the curb.

The transfer bus, headed to the west side, was full of people coming home from work and smelled of damp coats. Nettie Lee hung on to a pole near the front, reading every word of a cigarette advertisement, studying the face of the beautiful girl holding a cigarette to her lips. If she kept her mind busy, she could stand the jumpy feeling and her wish to be off the bus.

Through the heads of the other passengers, she saw her stop roll past, but she wasn't looking for her own street. A minute later, she reached over and pulled the cord. The bus stopped at the corner of Summit and Germantown. She hurried up the slushy street, snow falling around her, walking the three blocks to Yolanda's apartment.

Construction work had stopped on the Hip Hop's Chicken Joint, no doubt because of the snow. Behind the chain-link fence, the building, almost completed, stood under a covering of snow, the ground unevenly shrouded in white. In the back corner of the lot, the Port-a-Potty stood like a deserted lean-to shack, snow on the roof, surrounded by deep snow turning blue-white in the dusk. Nettie Lee hurried past the site, on to Yolanda's apartment.

The door was closed but unlocked. She turned the knob slowly, unsure of who might be there now. It had been almost two months since she'd last been inside.

The heat was running and it felt good. She had gotten cold from riding around all afternoon. She felt on the wall for the light switch. A ceiling fixture came on. The living room looked just as it had the night she'd been there—mirrors busted out, broken glass on the floor, deserted. In the bedroom, the covers were still tangled on the bed and stained brown with blood. Benji and them must have gotten scared and left when Yolanda did. Just took off and left their furniture and stuff behind. Nettie Lee walked back to the living room and sat on the couch. A smell like baby piss came out of it. If somebody asked her what the smell of life was, she'd have to say it was just like this—baby piss. The smell of baby piss was as natural as the smell of sex. All the odors we try so hard to cover up, but they're all still there. And they don't mean anything bad. They're just the smells of life. It was the other odor in this room that upset her: the stale burnt smell of weed and crack and Benji's nasty cigarettes. All that man-made misery. Woman-made misery, too. As much as she wanted to *do* something about it, as *close* as she was to it, she didn't feel close to it at all. She was right in the middle of it, but she couldn't touch it, couldn't change it. She rubbed her fingers on Yolanda's couch and got the sensation that her hands were numb, didn't belong to her. Her body felt light, not hers. Her head was full of air.

She got up from the couch, walked into the kitchen, and began searching through the cabinet drawers, not sure at first what she was looking for. Her fingers pushed aside a jumble of silverware, corkscrews, spatulas, odd knives. She pulled open another drawer; a cockroach ran out onto the counter. Then she thought of it: the pipe. She wanted Yolanda's pipe—and anything else she could find that kept her daughter away from her and her own children.

She didn't find it in the kitchen drawers. Inside the refrigerator, a litter of food lay rotting. What smelled like tuna salad in a big mixing bowl sat on the middle shelf, milky and foul. She almost closed the door before she saw it—a small collection of dirty-looking rocks, three or four, in a Ziploc bag. She took it off the shelf and put it in her coat pocket.

In the bedroom, Nettie Lee pulled bureau drawers out of their tracks and dumped them on the floor. The drawers were stuffed with Yolanda's expensive clothes from Barn—silk panties and brassieres, black stockings woven with gold thread, nightgowns in turquoise, emerald, and coral, and stretchy Lycra outfits, leggings, exercise leotards. Junk, Nettie thought. Just junk.

She went back to the kitchen for plastic garbage bags. She started in the bedroom and stuffed everything—every piece of clothing, every ashtray, every poster, the sheets from the bed, the shampoo and deodorant from the tub, the crack in her pocket, everything that looked like Yolanda's—into the bag and tied it with a twist tie. She filled two bags.

She bumped down the stairs with the bags, took them to the alley, lifted them into the dumpster, and let the lid bang shut.

Then she walked the three blocks back to the corner of Summit and Germantown and waited in the dark for the bus to come and take her home.

CHAPTER 11

Was that Nettie Lee sitting out there in the cold on a *bench*? Martha stepped off the bus. She brought her gloved hand up to her throat, zipped up her parka, hurried to the wooden bench in front of the hospital. Sitting stiff-shouldered against the wind, Nettie Lee seemed to be unaware of the early morning traffic moving just past the curb. She looked up when Martha sat down.

"Anybody been looking for me yet?" Nettie Lee said.

"Anybody like who?" Martha wasn't sure she wanted to hear the bad news. She was so tired of fighting.

"The police."

Martha paused. "Well, not that I know of. I haven't been inside yet." She watched Nettie Lee's face. "So, why are the police looking for you?"

Nettie Lee looked out into the street.

"What happened yesterday? You go over to Child Protection?"

"Yeah."

Martha didn't feel angry. She had known Nettie Lee would go. In fact, watching Nettie Lee leave the nursery yesterday afternoon, she had silently prayed for Nettie Lee's strength to complete her task. "And what did they say?"

"They said they want to know where Yolanda is at."

"Did you tell them?"

"I couldn't tell them nothing, even if I wanted to. I don't *know* where she's at."

"Why are you sitting out here, where anybody who's got eyes can see you?" It seemed foolish to her, and moreover, it worried Martha that Nettie Lee obviously felt herself to be in danger, yet didn't seem to care.

"What's the point of hiding? I go inside, they might be there. I go home, they might be there. Ain't no place to go. I'll just sit out here till I figure something out."

"You'll catch your death." Aware again of how cold it was, Martha shivered and pounded her gloves.

"That could be a solution to my problems."

Martha spoke sharply. "I don't want to hear talk like that. You're a strong woman. Don't you forget it."

"Maybe I'm not so strong."

Martha sat down beside Nettie Lee. "Did I ever tell you about the strongest woman alive?"

Nettie Lee shook her head and looked away.

"Oh yes. Vendetta had quite a reputation around town. They say her physical powers were enormous, but her strength didn't stop there. Her creativity was unequaled. God called on her to solve problems He was too busy to handle, with all the troubles in the world, you know. She could fix anything. If one of His creatures got broken, or had a special need, Vendetta would find a way to piece it back together again. That's why you see so many odd-looking creatures walking the earth, like rhinoceroses and porcupines and beavers: she fixed them so they work.

"God admired Vendetta so much He made her His assistant. He started thinking maybe He should make all His folks strong like her; she had a little something extra they didn't have. But Vendetta had gotten used to being the strongest woman in the world and was jealous. She told God, 'Before you start handing out my power, make sure the folks deserve it.' She thought that would fix things.

"God got to work in His laboratory and isolated the little piece of something that gave the woman her strength. He held it up to the light and called it Mabel (he liked to give everything a personal name). God took Mabel and flung it high up on a mountaintop where everybody could see it, but not everybody could get to it. He wanted folks to have equal access to Mabel, but He had promised Vendetta He would accept only the best of the best.

"All people, all races, young and old and in between, knew there was something powerful on top of the mountain, but try as they might, nobody could get the nerve to go see what it was. The young man said he was scared of it, the middle-aged man said he was, too. The little girl and the young woman said they felt it was none of their business. There was a rumor going around that if Vendetta heard you mention Mabel, she would turn the moon upside down and snatch the stars out of the sky. Everyone left Mabel alone.

"There was only one person brave enough to climb the mountain, a little old woman who wasn't afraid of anything that claimed a home on the earth. She put on her sneakers and climbed straight up. When she got ahold of Mabel, it started to explode. It bucked, it kicked, it threw her to the ground, it singed her flesh, it knocked her down the side of the mountain. Finally, after tumbling all the way to the bottom, she came to rest in a heap, Mabel thumping beneath her.

"God knew what she was up to the whole time. He heard her thoughts when she got the idea to steal a little piece of Mabel. He saw her trudging up the mountain, climbing over all kinds of obstacles, and, finally, He saw her wrestle Mabel to the ground. Then He spoke to her, and He wanted to know, 'Why do you think you need to steal Mabel from Vendetta, the strongest woman in the world?' She looked up from where she lay in a heap at the bottom of the mountain, her hair going every which-a-way, her clothes torn up, just barely hanging on to Mabel. 'Lord,' she said, 'I'm not opposed to sharing this thing.'

"He gave her a big piece. Bigger than Vendetta's. The old woman had proved she was strong enough to take it."

They were quiet for a moment, looking out to the street.

Nettie Lee said, "Funny, ain't it? But it does seem like God gave strength to the old people. The young ones got their bodies and their passions. They going to fix the world *today,* or they going to destroy it. But they don't have the sense it takes to do either one. Nobody does. We're all just running around here like what we think we want is important, when all the foolishness in the world don't mean nothing." Nettie Lee looked bemused. "I guess every old woman still going gets frustrated, knowing what she could do with all the wisdom she got in her, if only she could get ahold of just a little piece of that energy, that passion the young people got. Just a little piece. Lord, I am so tired of trying to clean up after Yolanda. I can't do it any more."

"People have to figure things out for themselves."

"Yeah. But I feel undone every time I got to watch Yolanda rediscover the wheel when she's got a decision to make. If I say to her, 'Honey, don't do that,' she acts like I'm no part of the world. According to her, I've never fallen in love, or been hurt, or had dreams. And I still have dreams. I guess I gave up thinking that the future was so boundless it didn't matter what I did right this minute. I always used to figure I could go back and correct my mistakes later. But later is too late. There ain't nothing going on except *right now.* We got to do the best we can *right now.*

"Sometimes at night I start thinking about how there is only so much time each person has. When you're young, time passes slow and you can't help but waste most of it, trying to get to the good parts—like Christmas, or summer, you know. All those special times for a child. All the time you're growing up, people keep asking you what you want to be, and you say something like the first woman president, or an astronaut, or, you know, whatever a child has on her mind. And you don't really think you *can't,* because you think the future is so big that somewhere along the way you'll start doing all the things that will get you there—until one day there you are: an astronaut. You know what I'm saying?"

Martha nodded.

"Well, I'm sitting there and I think, No more astronaut. But then I look at Little Barn and I think, He could be the astronaut or the president. Then, just as quick, I realize that's not going to happen. I mean, look at me. Look at his mama. What do we have? What's Little Barn ever going to have? Or Tookie? What's the future going to be like for her?"

"You sound just like your daughter."

"I heard *that.* But sometimes I get to thinking she's right."

Martha said, "It'll all work out. Sometimes when you get to the end of one thing, you realize it's really the beginning of something new." She hoped that was true, hoped there was more for her in the future.

"Yeah, I know what you mean," Nettie Lee said. "But I feel like the world is passing on by, and I'm just sitting here watching the parade." She got up. "Come on. This is a hell of a way to spend New Year's Eve. At least it's warm inside."

Nettie Lee walked back into the hospital with Martha at her side. Martha's slew-foot walk had grown familiar, was a comfort to her. Her white Reeboks and khaki Dock pants even seemed right. That was Martha—no frills. She found herself being soothed by the predictability of Martha's step, her plainness and reliability, her controlled shuffle.

As the nursery doors opened, Debbie Foxx looked up from Baker's Isolette. She held Baker in her hands like a small package, hands on his butt and under his head. She cupped him to her chest and walked quickly to Nettie Lee, her face grave. "May I see you in the conference room?"

"Right now?" Nettie Lee watched Debbie's face. Debbie didn't change her worried expression.

"Yes, right now. Let me put Baker back." From the Isolette she said, "Go ahead. I'll be there in a minute."

Nettie Lee sat at the long conference table and folded her arms across her chest. On the side wall, a small heater, the size of a shoe box, glowed red. She got up and sat near it to warm herself. Winter was dragging on and on. Debbie came into the room, closed the door, and sat down in the chair next to Nettie Lee's.

She sighed. "I just don't know what to say except I'm pretty surprised about everything. And really sad. I thought I knew you, Nettie Lee, and now I find out I didn't know anything about you." Her voice rose. "I just went on my instincts. I trusted you. I don't know why you did this."

"What do you mean?" Her heart leaped in her chest, and she knew what was coming.

"I'm talking about you and Baby Doe." Debbie's voice rose to a peak. She searched for words. "How could you come in here every day, pretending—" She sat back in her chair, blew out a defeated *huff* of air. "I told Barb Hunter I wasn't going to do this. I said I would not accuse you of doing anything wrong. I know what you did has a good reason behind it. Doesn't it?" She slapped the table. "Oh, Nettie Lee, you're in big trouble. I've got to tell you to leave and don't come back."

"Why? Is what I did so wrong you can't understand it?" Nettie Lee wiped at the burning in her eyes.

"You deceived us!"

"What's so terrible about that? I didn't do anything to hurt you or any baby in here. I came in here to help the babies. Especially my granddaughter."

"You lied!"

"Ain't you ever told a lie before?"

"Not when I was working with people who needed to hear the truth."

"Y'all didn't need to hear the truth."

"Nettie Lee, we've been looking for relatives for this baby for over seven weeks. *Seven weeks.* And every day you came in here you acted like you didn't know anything. And we would still be looking, if Barb hadn't checked out your story. How could you have been silent for so long?" She put her hand to her forehead. Nettie Lee watched her hand tremble. Debbie's wedding ring, a yellow cat's-eye set in a gold band, held her gaze. "The hospital looks like a fool."

"That's what you so worried about?"

"Of course not, but—yes!" She rested her head in her hand.

"Look, do you know what this could do to us? The insurance problems we'd have? The media circus? If it gets out that somebody the police are looking for—and, yes, that's *you*—if somebody the police are looking for is working right here in the nursery with Baby *X*"—she looked disgusted to say the name—"they're looking for the baby's relatives and you're right *here*—well, how do you think that makes the other parents with babies here feel?" She spat out a small laugh. "This can't go any further than it has. Now look, I'm on your side. I mean, I think what you did was wrong, okay? The lying. But I do believe you did what you thought was right at the time. So all I have to tell you is that you're to leave and not come back. And security will respond if they see you in the hospital or on the grounds. Okay?"

Okay? No, it was not anywhere close to being okay. From the crack in the door, Nettie Lee heard Debbie's name called in frantic yelps.

"Oh, for heaven's sake." Debbie opened the door.

The redheaded nurse was yelling from Tookie's warming tray. "Page Dr. Xiang, stat. Page respiratory. Page the lab." She turned toward the conference room. "Debbie!"

Debbie was already out the door.

From her rocker, Martha had watched Nettie Lee and Nurse Foxx go into the conference room and close the door. She held O'Neil in her lap. His head, heavy as a stone, rested in her palm, while his feet kicked out against her stomach. He was tired, Martha thought, worn out from sucking his formula. Now he was using his feet as an engine to keep his mouth going. He'd be finished soon; then she'd put him back to bed for a long morning nap. Did anybody sleep as deeply as a baby? Not O'Neil, of course. He was restless as a flea, but in general babies slept well, she thought.

She wondered what Nurse Foxx wanted to say to Nettie Lee. Probably the social worker, Miss Hunter, had told Foxx what Nettie Lee had said to her yesterday. She had to admit it, Nettie Lee had already suffered all she needed to. What would they do to her now?

Martha heard Callie Hart yelling for Debbie Foxx. When she

looked up, Callie stood by Faith's, no, *Tookie's,* warming tray, grasping the stethoscope around her neck, yelling for respiratory therapy.

In the background, Martha heard the intercom operator, in a calm droning voice, page Dr. Xiang to the NIC nursery, stat. Code Blue.

Martha tried to see what they were doing. The doctors, the nurses, the technicians crowded around Tookie's warming tray, their backs to Martha. At the head of the tray, a girl with an Afro hairdo and wire-rimmed glasses squeezed oxygen into the baby with a little see-through green bag. Dr. Xiang cut the bandage and pressed her fingers into Tookie's chest, pushing the ribs against her heart, forcing out blood, releasing the pressure to let it flow back in. For every third push Dr. Xiang made, the girl squeezed her bag quickly; the baby's chest rose and collapsed. The handling of the baby was gentle, precise, an economy of motion. But around the tray sprawled a storm of noise, confusion, swearing.

Martha thought she would go crazy if the heart monitor didn't quit screeching. It hurt her ears, made her brain race. *Stop it, turn it off. Save the baby. Get the heartbeat back.* Foxx wheeled over the crash cart, a red tool chest full of equipment. Nausea turned Martha's stomach. Callie switched on a high-intensity lamp above the warming tray, pulled it to shine on the baby. "Out of the nursery," Mary Pangalangan was calling from across the room. "Medical personnel only. Everybody else out." Mary touched Martha's arm. "You have to wait outside until this is over," she said. "Sorry."

Nettie Lee sat in the conference room and looked out into the nursery. She saw the double doors burst open, the doctors run in. Poor Tookie, poor baby, poor child. She bowed her head to pray. *Our Father, Who art in heaven, hallowed be Thy name. Thy kingdom come. Thy will be done on earth as it is in heaven. . . .* She couldn't finish.

Debbie Foxx was crying, and that was what made Nettie Lee cry. To see that young woman, a model of control, a professional nurse, shed tears on behalf of her granddaughter, who never knew her mother— *Oh, quit! Shut up. Stop the show, honey. Can't nobody going feel as sorry as you do. Nobody.* Debbie was wiping her eyes, asking her, "Do you want to say good-bye?"

Nettie Lee moved to the warming tray. Dr. Xiang looked up, eyes reddened, and nodded her head. "I am deeply sorry for the grandma." She moved off. Mary and the redheaded nurse, Callie, touched Nettie Lee's arm as they passed. The warming tray stood by itself now, the monitors shut off. Nettie Lee looked at Tookie through a blur of tears. She lay on her back, wrapped in one of the rough white receiving blankets. Debbie probably thought of it, Nettie Lee told herself. She touched her finger to Tookie's face, which looked composed now that the respirator tube was gone. A helpless feeling welled inside Nettie Lee's heart. "I asked myself what I could have done for you, asked myself that question every night. I asked God what I could have done. And I guess I just never did figure it out. But you know something, Tookie? You never was alone."

Standing behind Nettie Lee, Debbie said quietly, "María Christina Johnson. Time of death: nine forty-seven A.M." She wrote it in the chart.

Martha stood outside the nursery doors, watching the hospital personnel leave. First the X-ray tech, then several respiratory therapists, and then the lab techs. Where was Nettie Lee?

When Nettie Lee came out, eyes puffy and red, hands full of bunched-up tissues, Martha's eyes filled with tears. She circled Nettie Lee's shoulders with her arm, walked her into the scrub room.

"It ain't no use being here. I'm leaving."

"You go home and rest."

"It ain't about rest, it's about leaving." Nettie Lee took off her yellow gown. "I ain't got no business here. I got to go home and take care of what I got there."

Martha watched her get on the elevator and then it went down.

Martha stepped on the automatic door pad. It was late afternoon, time for the four o'clocks. Without Nettie Lee to help her, Martha would spend less time with each of her babies.

With relief, she saw Mrs. Baker scrubbing at the sink. That's one baby taken care of, she thought. She pulled a scrub gown over her slacks and shirt, then lathered up her hands. Through the window, she could see LaRone already sitting in a rocker, feeding Daquille a small bottle of milk. Martha would attend to Gonsalves, O'Neil, and Perez. Foxx and the student nurses would have to feed the rest. Martha dried her hands and walked into the nursery.

Tookie's warming tray was gone, leaving a space in the horseshoe, a dirty area on the floor, sticky with spilled IV solutions and meds. Martha's chest suddenly felt larger, as if the bottom had dropped out. How would this work, rocking the babies after Tookie was gone? She'd never considered what it would be like to lose another baby, to walk in here so soon after a loss, a death. *Her baby's death.*

LaRone looked up. "Hey, Martha." Daquille's dark eyes focused on his mother's face. "I'm taking him home today. Soon as I give him this bottle." She jiggled it against his lips. "He wants to eat slow today, like he knows I'm in a hurry."

"I thought you were taking him this morning."

"I was, but I had to wait for Shavonne and her friend to pick me up. They just got here."

As if to prove her right, Shavonne appeared at the nursery window. She waved her hand in a hurry-up motion. LaRone made an exasperated face at her, shrugging her shoulders and nodding toward the baby in her arms.

LaRone said to Martha, "I know she can see I got this baby to feed. She's not blind."

"Well, I'll go tell her to come in."

Out in the hall, Shavonne leaned against the window, pointing out babies to a tall boy who looked to be about nineteen or twenty. His head was shaved completely bald, but he kept running his hand over it as if he still had hair. "See that one over there? I think that's the one that got left in the outdoor toilet." She was pointing at Perez. "They still looking for the woman that did that." The boy seemed squeamish, looking down the hall as Shavonne spoke, unable to study any of the babies. He said, "Let's just get LaRone and step. I'll be looking at all this hospital stuff soon enough." Martha assumed he meant Lamaze classes. She stood a few feet from the two of them.

"Are you waiting for LaRone?"

The boy swung quickly in Martha's direction, accidentally stepping on one of Shavonne's shoes, large patent leather chunks that reminded Martha of the boots her father wore at the foundry. Shavonne glared at him. "Get off of my foot!" She turned to Martha. "Yeah. How long's she going to be?" The boy put his arm around her shoulder, drawing her close to him, but she shrugged him off. "Fool, don't touch me! I told you I got bad indigestion, and here you are trying to squeeze me like some kind of squeak toy."

"After LaRone feeds the baby, she has to sign him out in the business office, unless she did that already."

"So how long is that?" Shavonne's face was a wide blank.

"An hour or so."

The boy blew air between his teeth.

"I *told* her to be ready when I came." Shavonne sighed. "Okay, tell her I'm going down to the cafeteria for a Coke or something." She turned to the boy. "You coming, Joe?"

"Whatever."

They walked to the elevator. Shavonne's gait had a side-to-side shift, Martha noted.

When they reached the elevator Shavonne called back to Martha. "Tell LaRone I said to hurry up. If she gets done faster than an hour, we'll be waiting for her in the cafeteria."

Inside the nursery, LaRone sat in the rocker, patting up burps from Daquille. He sat on her lap in a loose hunch, eyes blinking wide with each pat. He gave a small lift of his brows when the trapped air found its way out. LaRone's nails were done red, with wispy gold lines painted on a diagonal. Her long thin hands were jeweled in delicate gold rings and bracelets, which tinkled as she patted her baby's back. She'd obviously dressed up for her son's discharge from the hospital.

"They'll be in the cafeteria," Martha told her.

"They can wait," LaRone said. "They don't have anything better to do." She leaned Daquille back into her left arm, put the nipple into his mouth. "What happened to the baby that used to be over there?" She nodded to the empty space where, now, a woman wearing a pink housekeeping uniform wiped the oxygen nipples and gauges on the wall next to which the warming tray had stood.

"She passed away."

"When?" After Martha told her, LaRone said, "I know you liked her a whole lot. I saw you over there looking like you wanted to rock her. I used to think it was just like a grandmother to want to rock a baby, no matter what was supposed to be wrong with it. It's like they can't help themselves." LaRone started rocking. "She was really sick, though. Maybe she was suffering the whole time and now she's at peace."

"I think that's true." Martha did believe it.

"You're going to miss her a lot, aren't you?"

"Yes."

"Well, anytime you want to, you can come and visit my big old baby. He'll miss his grandmas if they don't come and see him." She looked around the nursery as she rocked. "Where *is* Nettie Lee? I haven't seen her today."

"She was here earlier, but she went home." Martha thought of Nettie Lee's long bus ride home.

"Is she sick?"

"Yes. I think she must be."

"Well, that's too bad," LaRone said. "I hope she feels better soon."

"I hope so, too," Martha said. "I'm worried about her."

A little while later, Shavonne and her friend Joe came back to the nursery windows, waving LaRone out into the hall. They talked to her for a few minutes, then LaRone went to the business office.

After she came back from signing the papers, she stood at the nursery doors while Debbie Foxx and Martha handed over Daquille and all his equipment: the mandatory car seat, which LaRone was to return the next day, free samples of formula and diapers, a comic book describing how to care for a preemie, and the doctor's instructions for a follow-up clinic visit in one week. Martha handed the packages to Shavonne. Joe took the car seat.

Foxx placed Daquille, bundled in a navy blue bunny suit, into LaRone's arms and hugged them both good-bye, then said to Joe, "Go get the car. They'll wait for you at the lobby entrance." He left. Foxx went back into the nursery.

"Look how fat his cheeks are," Shavonne said, filling the pause between Foxx's leaving and Martha's saying good-bye. "He's going to pork out once you get him home."

"Want to hold him?"

"I don't care." Shavonne held out her arms. Martha saw them tremble as LaRone gave the baby to her. Shavonne held him against her coat, pressed her face against his. "He's so warm. He's like your own personal heater. I'm going to take him for a walk." She started for the elevator.

Martha took LaRone's hands in hers. Now that it was time to say good-bye, she felt saddened by how much she would miss the girl. "Well, you take care of your baby. And call me sometime. Wait a minute." She took a piece of paper from her pants pocket. "Here. That's my number. But you can get me here at the hospital if you lose it."

LaRone took the paper, circled Martha's shoulders in her arms, and gave her a quick squeeze. "Thanks, Mom." She picked up her supplies from the floor, then turned away and hurried toward the elevator, where Shavonne waited with a young man from Transportation who would escort them to the car. The elevator doors opened. "Shavonne! Don't you go too far with my baby!"

"Well, hurry up then."

Martha watched the elevator doors close, then she slowly walked back to the nursery.

CHAPTER 12

When LaRone Cruz picked up the phone and heard Martha's thin voice asking after Daquille, she was a little surprised. After all, she'd only had Daquille at home for a month. Since Martha was calling so soon, LaRone thought Martha didn't trust her to take care of her own baby. But Martha went on to tell her that *she* needed help with a problem, and the problem was Nettie Lee; that made LaRone feel very good, although what Martha had to say about Nettie Lee shook her. Martha told her that poor little Baby X was Nettie Lee's grandchild and now her heart was broken. LaRone let Martha's voice trail away for a moment. The whole time she worked as a grandmother, Nettie Lee had kept this secret. It was weird that LaRone hadn't known anything about it, since she thought of herself as a bullshit detector. If you had something to hide or you didn't want somebody telling you the truth, stay away from LaRone, because she could see right through you. At least, that's what Shavonne always said. But LaRone had never thought bold, bossy Nettie Lee had any problems. She guessed she just hadn't been paying close enough attention to what was happening in the nursery.

In fact, she had been afraid the entire time she was there—too much going on with all the hospital equipment, and the noise, and her not knowing if she really could take care of a preemie. Now that Daquille was home, he was on her mind constantly: feeding schedules, morning baths, growth charts. She made sure he gained several ounces a week, to keep up the pace the nurses set for him at the hospital. So far, he had gained twenty ounces, one more than she had expected. She had her fears, though, and she tried to deal with each one. She was afraid he'd die in the middle of the night, stop breathing the way Martha's baby had, a terrifying thought. She kept Daquille in bed beside her at night, softly breathing while she dozed. Days, she just cooled in her La-Z-Boy, Daquille asleep on her chest, while she watched *Supermarket Sweep* and *Oprah, All My Children* and *Montel.* And she was afraid he might get killed by a stranger, like Martha's brother, or he might get a girl pregnant, like Byron did to Yolanda. Really, she admitted, like Daquille's father did to her. Sometimes she had so much to think about, her mind just raced, and she couldn't concentrate on one worry long enough to play it out before another worry broke in.

LaRone promised Martha she would go with her to visit Nettie Lee, maybe cheer Nettie Lee up by letting her see Daquille. Then again, she thought, seeing LaRone with fat old Daquille might make Nettie Lee feel bad, might remind her all over again that her granddaughter had died. When LaRone finally said, "I don't know what to do," Martha said, "Let's just go for a visit. See how she's doing. All right?"

They met at the bus stop in front of the hospital on a Sunday morning, the last day of January. LaRone got there before Martha. She stood beside the bench with Daquille, whom she had strait-jacketed into a snowsuit. The weather was good, blue sky, a few clouds bunching together on the horizon. The January thaw. It was cold but not the coming cold of February, with its stiff winds and below-zero temperatures. The air felt almost mild. In fact, that morning it felt warm enough to snow. Traffic past the hospital was busy as usual, several buses moving heavily among the cars. When Martha's bus from the north side pulled up a couple of minutes later, LaRone watched her step off, bundled in a green ski parka with fur around the hood. Martha spotted them immediately, a smile on her face. She flipped up the parka hood as she walked to LaRone, then gave both her and Daquille a furry hug. Too cold to sit, they stood close together at the bus stop, waiting for the bus that would take them through downtown into the west side, where Nettie Lee lived.

They got on their bus. It was weird seeing the shops and, after a few miles, watching the houses on Germantown roll by so quickly, then roll away. She had made this trip every day for a month visiting Daquille in the hospital. Until then she hadn't taken the bus anywhere, but depended on friends to give her a ride to wherever she had wanted to go. When they got off at the corner of Germantown and Broadway, LaRone realized they weren't too far from her own apartment. Her street was actually quite close. The neighborhood suddenly looked small to her.

They walked the two blocks to Nettie Lee's house slowly. After crossing the first street, Martha stopped on the sidewalk and held out her arms.

"Want me to carry him for a little while?" She was slightly out of breath. LaRone could hear a faint wheeze behind her words.

"It's all right," she replied. "He's not too heavy. Besides, we got a whole 'nother block to go." She hitched Daquille a little higher on her shoulder, his pink-cheeked face slack with sleep.

Careful to avoid stumbling on the sidewalk, made uneven by tree roots from a line of huge old catalpas growing next to the street, they made their way past houses that looked ridiculously small compared to the overgrown trees and shrubs beside them. Nettie Lee's house was in the middle of the block, very neat white clapboard and brick, just as small as all the others. LaRone thought she'd like to live in a house again one day. Maybe she'd get married or maybe she wouldn't, but someday she would buy a home for herself and Daquille.

When LaRone knocked on the front door, a little boy of about four immediately opened it wide and looked up at them. From inside the dark house, LaRone could hear Nettie Lee calling.

"Little Barn! What'd I tell you about opening the door without asking what they want first?"

"What do you want?" His voice was loud in a rehearsed show of confidence.

Nettie Lee came up behind him, wiping her hands on a paper towel. When she saw LaRone and Martha standing on her porch she smiled broadly and shook her head, reaching across Little Byron to hold the screen door open wider.

"Well, ain't this just something, you two coming here to see me." She motioned them through the screen door. "And look at that. You brought the baby!"

LaRone let Martha go in first, then followed her. Little Byron pulled on her coat.

"Hello," LaRone told him, bending down slightly.

He pointed to Daquille. "I was having a baby sister, but she died at the hospital."

"I'm sorry." LaRone felt at a loss to say more. "Did you get to see her?"

"No. Grandma saw her. She said she was the beautifulest baby in the whole world. But I don't believe her, because she said that about me too, and we can't both be the best."

"Well, you not a baby anymore," LaRone explained. "That's why your sister could be beautiful too. Now you're grown up and handsome, see?"

He seemed to think about this. "I guess so."

Nettie Lee took their coats and had them sit on the couch while she went into the kitchen and opened and closed cabinet doors. Little Byron sat at LaRone's feet, playing with her bootlaces.

"These are pretty," he said. "How much they cost?"

"Not too much," LaRone said, though she really didn't care if he knew. She just thought Nettie Lee wouldn't want him to get an answer to a question she would think was rude.

LaRone pushed her back against the couch cushion for support. Since she'd had Daquille, her back seemed weaker, always hurting her. Directly in front of LaRone sat Nettie Lee's television. It was one of those old-timey TVs from the sixties, a huge console model that married people got, with big knobs that turned and a curved picture tube like a fisheye lens, skewing their reflections. In its dark face, LaRone could see all the way into the kitchen behind her without moving her head.

Daquille slept inside the crook of her left arm, neatly bundled in flannel pajamas and a blue receiving blanket, held close against her heart. He felt heavy for his small size, a fact that always surprised her when she picked him up. Yet his weight made her feel grounded, rooted to the earth. Now when she walked her footsteps were heavy, freighted with responsibility. But when she thought about it, she realized she felt silly with happiness. Here in Nettie Lee's living room, sitting on her couch, she felt comfortable, at home. Years ago that's what her father would tell people who came over: "Make yourself to home." She used to think of his words as merely a polite way of talking to company—until now. Since Daquille's birth she thought differently about so many things. *Make yourself to home.* That's what Nettie Lee had said when she closed the door, and that's exactly what LaRone was doing.

It was LaRone's idea to tell a story. She'd had some things happen to her too, just like Martha and Nettie Lee had. Besides, it was kind of like a gift you could give somebody, if you dug way down deep in yourself and let people know what you were really like, what you really thought about inside your head. Once, after Daquille had been in the hospital for four weeks, she had tried to tell Shavonne about some of the things that worried her. She'd had a fantasy, like a daydream about Daquille, and she had started to talk about it one evening when she was at Shavonne's apartment. It was pretty bizarre, the feeling she had that day.

She was lying on the couch at home with her legs hanging across the arm, reading the Dr. Spock book she got from her parenting class. Her nose was dried out, since the register had been blowing hot air all evening. She was reading the chapter on the newborn baby, what it could do, the reflexes it had, when the heat finally got to her and her eyelids drooped down far enough that she couldn't drag them back up. She wasn't asleep, just thinking about being asleep. An idea started circling her mind, picking up details as it went round, and she could suddenly see her life as having a beginning, a middle, and, somewhere far off, an end. It was as if she could hold her whole life in her mind at one time, and though she couldn't quite put her finger on it, she knew Daquille had something to do with her new ability, as if he were an anchor dropped in the middle of her life, and now everything was held down so she could examine it, see how one part related to all the others. That night she went over to Shavonne's and told her about it, about how she could see her life, really *see* it, but Shavonne had got tired of listening and turned on the TV.

"Go on with your story," Martha said. She sat beside LaRone on the couch. Martha was a trip. She could be counted on to wear the same type of clothing every day, no changes: the same oxford shirt with a ski sweater over it, the khaki pants, and the white Reeboks with ankle socks. Martha crossed her legs and accepted a glass of water from Nettie Lee, who bustled back into the kitchen. Nettie Lee looked okay. It wasn't as if she looked depressed or crazy since the baby died. Her house was picked up. Little Byron looked okay.

Nettie Lee came out of the kitchen with a plate of Rice Krispies marshmallow squares. "Y'all want a Coke or something?" she asked, putting the plate on the coffee table.

Martha said, "I guess it's too early for me." She turned to LaRone. "We're both waiting for you, dear."

"I want one," Little Barn said. He took a piece off the plate, then lay on his stomach under the coffee table and played with little turtle figures in ninja outfits.

LaRone breathed in; maybe storytelling wasn't as easy as she had thought. "Well, I'm going to tell you my story, and remember, I never did this before, okay? In my story that I call 'Looking at the Future,' I put all the things I want to happen. I guess some of it's sort of corny." She looked at Daquille, her throat a clenched fist. Why was it so hard to let go of words?

Nettie Lee broke into her thoughts. "Don't worry about us, honey. Just go on ahead and tell the story. We just eavesdroppers."

"I have to disagree with that." Martha shook her head. "We *do* matter. You know the only reason you tell a story is so somebody will hear it." She smiled at LaRone. "But don't let that worry you, dear. Go ahead and tell your story."

LaRone felt worse. Now her stomach was looping in circles. She started again.

❦❦

I call my story "Looking at the Future." No, that doesn't sound right. Wait a minute. I got a better title. Okay, this is called "*Creating* the Future." Hear the difference?

Well, there used to be this girl who had a mother from Hong Kong and a father from the United States, and they met during a war, so this is a romance story. He was nineteen and just got his high school diploma, but he couldn't get a job that summer. *Give him a name?* Roland, that's his name. After they graduated, the girlfriend Roland had all through high school left to go to college in the fall, to a city he never heard of. *What was the city?* Yellow Springs. *Yeah, I know where that is too, Martha, but he didn't. And anyway, I think you two should quit interrupting me. I kept quiet when you told your stories.* The August after he graduated, the song he cried to every night was the Supremes, singing, "Where did our love go?" That song can still make him cry. His grandmother cried the day he left for boot camp. He told her, "Ain't no need to be crying. No need to be sad at all. If only one man comes back alive, that's me." He meant that, but where he was going, the fighting was really bad.

The girl's mother, Lisa—that's her American name; she never told him her Chinese name—she was seventeen and fell in love with the American soldier because he was so big and black. *Don't laugh at me, Martha! That's true.* She loved him because he was big and black. And strong. She never saw a man who could carry as much as he did on his back, all the shit they had to lug around when they marched from village to village. He was big then, weighed around two hundred and thirty pounds, six-three. He was a really big dude. And black. Very black.

So Roland is over in Vietnam. He has to march through jungle, hack out a way for himself just to be able to put his foot down on the ground. And when they're not in the jungle, they are tramping through rice paddies, up to their shins in sticky mud. He's part of the infantry; doesn't that make you think of babies? But anyway, they're the soldiers who fight hand-to-hand combat, the ones who have to kill while looking the enemy right in the face. He gets there in May in 'sixty-eight and leaves in April in 'sixty-nine. He marches until his feet are permanently messed up. He wears shades the whole time, day and night. They're so dark he can hardly see with them on, but they cover his eyes, stop the other soldiers from seeing how scared he is. It's hot and wet. A hundred and ten degrees. The rain comes down for endless days. His feet are rotted, always sucking through mud. This place is like *Raiders of the Lost Ark,* okay? That Indiana Jones movie? *You didn't see it?* Okay. Well, all the bushes and trees and bugs and shit are bigger than they're supposed to be. What's a little bush here in America is like a tree over there in Vietnam. There's snakes and shit all over, too. He's trailed by leeches, little brown ones that smell you from far away, then head your way in gangs, crawling right on top of the mud like they just got word *you're* the target. That's what he hates the most, those leeches. The whole time he's there, ringworm crawls across his body on his chest and his thighs. He scratches himself like a chimpanzee, checks his buddies' heads for lice, checks their backs for bugs, but they got to feel their own crotches for the leeches. He's macho. He's so macho that when Jimi Hendrix sings that song "Purple Haze," Roland hears " 'Scuse me, while I kiss this guy." It turns him off Hendrix for a while. He acted sillier than Shavonne. Anyway, the leeches—sometimes he doesn't even know they're on him until they get fat with his blood and drop off into his pants, where he's got them tucked in his boots. He empties out his pants every night, before he eats.

After Roland's platoon was in country for six months, one dude clocked out. Roland watched him shoot his weapon in the air, just shooting at the sky, like he saw Charlie up there. Just totally went off, right in the middle of the field, too tired to think straight.

They called a helicopter to come in and take him away. At first, Roland felt sorry for the dude, but the longer Roland stayed in the field, the more he envied him. He started thinking the poor bastard was lucky to go insane. At least his feet could dry off in the hospital; at least they could pull the leeches off him for good. The thing was, Roland was over there fighting this war that everybody hated back home. He felt lonely. Depressed. He stunk. He was always funky from laying in the mud, slogging through the swamp. And scared. It was always something to be scared about. His mouth tasted like lead from the day he got there. That's the taste of fear. Most of the time he didn't know if he could live through the day. Every day he just prayed to make it home.

Roland wasn't like some of the dudes there, collecting teeth and thumbs, scoring all the Vietnamese jinny they could. He tried to learn the Vietnamese customs, like don't cross your legs when you sit and, if you do, don't point the soles of your feet at the person you're sitting with. Don't rub a kid's head, don't hold hands with a female in public. He respected their culture. It wasn't like now, when you hear about Iraq, how the American soldiers in Desert Shield, the women, think the Muslims are stupid for the way they treat their women—you know, our women soldiers said too bad the Muslims don't like American female soldiers in T-shirts. Our women said too bad they think T-shirts are slutty, because we're from America, and we can wear what we want, anyplace, anytime. But see, I understand what the Muslims were saying, the point they're trying to make. Everything is not about personal freedom. Nobody wants to think about that, because when somebody tells you what to do, it makes you feel small. But some things are bigger than just one person—family, and children, and community, spirituality. To me, that's more important than everybody going out and doing whatever they want, whenever they feel like it. You don't have to agree with me; I just wanted to say that.

Okay, so one day Roland's out on patrol, on a five-man LURP. They're scouting out the Viet Cong, staying away from the NVA. Then Roland first sees a girl. She's trying to hide underneath her hut. She had dug out a shelter under the side to crawl into when the looters came through—NVA, Viet Cong, Republican Army, or American. She probably dug it with her hands, patted up the mud into a hard shell. The first part of her Roland sees is her behind trying to wiggle through the little opening. The sight of that girl trying to hide from him, like he's dangerous, makes him trip. He's got to convince her he would never hurt her. He's got to touch her, he thinks, just one time, without her being afraid of him, just to prove to himself that he's harmless.

He knows he's being really stupid, that he could get killed, shot by her, but he tries to crawl into the hole after her. He's loaded down with stuff, though. He can't get in. He takes off his pack and shit, leaves it on the ground by the hut. He takes off his helmet, sticks his head in the hole, and he's so big he can't get any further. It's dark and quiet, like there's nobody in there, but he knows that can't be true. He saw her crawl in. Staring in the dark, he turns his head all around, until he can finally make out the barrel of a gun coming at his face, aiming right for his eyeball. He backs up quick, but can't get out of the way, here it comes, he gets *poked.* But it's not a gun. It's her finger. He jerks his head out. It's still quiet like a tomb in there. He gets off his knees and stands up and rubs his sore eye.

One of his buddies is standing behind him, this white dude they call Puny Son because he's so small. Puny Son carries the M-60, the heavyweight bad boy. He's loaded up with extra ammo and knives, wears his shades like Roland does, walks the pimp walk like he's got big balls too. Puny Son is looking at Roland and says, "Hey, bro, what you tracking?" Roland adjusts his shades to the proper angle, says there's a gook under the hut, but go on, he'll take care of it. The buddy says, "Stand back, motherfucker," and shoots his weapon into the hole like he's flushing out rats from a garbage pile. Roland watches the straw blow into pieces, the mud chips fly from the igloo, the bullets tear into the hut. Well, nobody's coming out of that hut. That hut has been wasted. Except the girl crawls out. She's so scared that when Roland puts his hand out to her and coaxes her to come to him, she takes it. Mission accomplished. It's like she's so shocked, she's crazy. Then the buddy gets mad and says since he did the shooting, the girl is his. But Roland says, Naw, he saw the girl first, so she's *his.* She spits in Roland's face.

She's crying so hard she can't see where she's walking, but Roland's got her by the arm and he's careful to walk slow and be gentle with her, except that he's got to drag her, but he's trying not to freak her out. They walk through the village, into the jungle on the trail he's been hacking out. He's hacking on through, and she's dragging, making him pull her. Then, right in front of them, a VC pops out of the brush and shoots like crazy. Ambushed. Roland tries to shove the girl behind him, protect her so she won't get hit. But she falls to the ground right away. He lets her go. He rolls and crawls into the brush. Takes a lucky shot at the VC, shoots him in the face. He stands over the body and the VC looks like, instead of getting shot, he got a plate of spaghetti thrown against the side of his face. Roland tries to say "Gook dog" out loud, then walk away, but the words won't come out of his mouth; he can't move, can't escape looking. Instead he says, "I'm sorry, man." He tries to find the girl, but she's gone. He doesn't know what happened to her.

He needs an R and R. Says he has to get away from the country, go to the city to clear his head. He's not a country boy. He wants to see tall buildings and street corners with people talking, like what he's used to. He's had his six months in, so they send him to the R and R center in Cam Ranh Bay. When he gets there, it's like he's at some kind of funky travel agency. They say, "Where do you want to go, Thailand? Or maybe Australia or New Zealand—get yourself a round-eyed girl?" But he's set his heart on Hong Kong, the city all the brothers talk about. "You *got* to go to Hong Kong," the brothers say. "That's where it's happening, most beautiful women in the world." Roland says Hong Kong is where he wants to go.

It's all that and more. Beautiful city built against a rocky cliff looking out over the ocean. Flying in over the city, it's so pretty he starts to cry again. Then he feels like he always wants to cry.

Tears are right behind his shades every minute, waiting to drop out.

He checks into the hotel. It's big and old and fine, and it doesn't cost too much. Most important to Roland, it's clean. He takes a bath, washes the red dirt out of his skin. Now he's set. He's ready to get him a girl, since it's been so long. Even though they've been telling him about VD, he's not too worried about catching anything. The VD back then was gone with penicillin.

His first night there, he goes to a club called Maman's, stands in the doorway. It's dark. All he sees for a minute are heads bobbing around. He can hear a band playing upstairs. Mama-san grabs his arm right away, pulls him over to the bar, where his eyes adjust, and he see there's girls sitting on stools, drinking. Mama-san whacks him on the arm with her flyswatter and says, "Who you want?" Roland looks down the bar at each girl. One is too short, one has a flat chest, one looks at him and spits. While he's looking, a girl, long-haired and smelling like Windsong, his high school *girlfriend's* perfume, comes up behind him and starts freaking him. Mama-san whacks her and fusses at her in Chinese. She says something to Mama-san that sounds like spitting and goes upstairs. Then Roland sees a girl standing at the bar who is very fine. She squints, gets a good look at him, bunches her hair into a ponytail, then flings it loose into the air, so he points to her. She goes to sit on a bar stool. Roland bends down to Mama-san. "That one," he says, tears itching his eyes. Mama-san sticks out her hand. "That one, you sure?" She is curling her lips down. "Ten dollars, you take her for walk. No refund." Roland doesn't want to walk, but he figures this is the way things are done and flips open his wallet. Mama-san smiles when she grabs his ten-dollar bill, frowns when she fusses at the girl to get off the bar stool and be quick about it.

"We go to your room and talk about price," the girl says. "I cost a lot of money. I have medical card."

They go outside into the daylight. She is really beautiful, about seventeen, hair very long and clean. Her skin is not white but still pale, but that's all right with him. He prefers dark girls, but she is still beautiful. She has long pale fingers, brownish at the knuckles, unpolished nails—a natural woman. He looks at her hands and he's sure they have never touched anyone before him. He knows they are the hands of a virgin. Looking at her hands makes him choke. He is eating his own heart.

In his room, she says she wants fifty dollars a night, and she'll stay with him his whole week. He says, "Ten dollars," but his heart isn't in it. He wants to bargain, save money, cut a deal, but he can't talk. She pretends like she didn't hear him. She says, "Fifty dollars is my low everyday price, but because I like you, I'm going to give you discount." This makes Roland laugh and ask, "What's your name?" She tells him Lisa. "Well, Lisa," Roland says, "you all right." She lifts his shades, looks at him, wipes under his eyes with her fingers, licks his tears from her fingertips.

He starts telling people in the hotel they're married, just to try it out on himself. He likes the way Lisa Cruz sounds. He says he'd like to hear her birth name too, but she tells him, no, she wants to be an American, she wants to forget her Chinese name. He tells her he loves her and they'll get married later, maybe in Saigon. He goes to the embassy in Saigon to do the paperwork for an American marriage. The papers come through. He waits out his last six months.

His time gets short; then it's his turn to go home. He will fly from the field to Cam Ranh Bay, to Hong Kong, to the States. Just as he's getting in the helicopter, Charlie hits them, just to bug them, and he gets shot in the leg. It's the first time his luck doesn't hold. They send him to the hospital in Saigon instead of home.

In the hospital, he has time to think about things. What is he doing bringing Lisa back to the States, with America so prejudiced? Is he crazy? With everybody so "nigger this" and "gook that," what will happen to her there? He can't hurt her that way.

She visits him, his new wife. Her manner is bold; she will not sit still for talk about prejudice in America. America has many riches and freedoms. Has he taken a look around to see where he is now? He wants to stay here? Is he crazy? What she doesn't say right then is she's pregnant. She's having a kid in seven months. And she's not having it in Saigon. What will they think of her kid here? Part Chinese, part American, part black. She is going to America.

His leg heals up. They fly home on a commercial plane.

Now he's back in the world. They take his weapons away—his grenades, his smoke bombs, his knife carried strapped to the inside of his forearm—they take it all away. He's walking the streets in Dayton without protection. He never had a gun or a knife before Vietnam, never even picked one up. Before the war he said he was a lover, not a fighter. When they find out he fought in Vietnam, friends *and* strangers treat him like a traitor, like he's a killer. You know, now that he's back home all he wants is his propers, and all he gets is disrespect. Now his shit is to the curb.

Roland and Lisa have their kid. Born in Dayton, Ohio, a tiny baby girl with not much hair and almond eyes. Too beautiful to be true. Then Lisa goes away when the girl is five, leaves town alone, no help. Roland explains and explains, says she just couldn't handle being away from everybody she knew and loved back home in Hong Kong. Couldn't handle being away from her real life. Maybe, Roland says, she couldn't handle *him.* He felt like somebody else when he came back to the States. Maybe he wasn't acting his best. Maybe he scared her, because he was sure scaring *himself.* Maybe this, maybe that. All the girl knows is she doesn't have a mother anymore, and she is sad.

Roland raises his girl until she's fifteen. Then she runs away from home, away from Roland and his rules, his boring house where she has to do everything his way or it's not done right. She doesn't wash the dishes clean enough, the floor isn't vacuumed in the corners, she stays up too late, watches *him* watch TV and drink whiskey, when he wants to do all that stuff alone. She's too old now—when she looks at him, she knows he can see himself, see what's left of the strong man he used to be.

Fifteen is the year she runs away to live with her boyfriend. They have two roommates. Together, she calls them the Three Pigs. They've always got people over, drinking, smoking, talking, always talking. All they do is run their mouths, never get up and *do* anything. But she falls in with them, parties too long and too hard.

She's got no job, got no money, no food, no nothing, so she shoplifts. Now she's got leather skirts and cute shoes, cigarettes, and, if she don't mind buffing, dope. Crack. She smokes the shit, stays high all the time, gets pregnant with her boyfriend's baby. Marry him? She's not with that.

She thinks about abortion for days. Should she do it? No. Yeah. Why have a baby to mess up her life?—what little life she's got. Her boyfriend promises everything she wants to hear: he'll get a better job, he'll stay with his little family. She starts thinking maybe she'll go back to school. But one day pretty soon she's washing the clothes, pulling them out of the dryer at the laundromat. A piece of paper falls out of the clothes pile, washed and dried, soft like leather. She reads, *The Women's Center, ten o'clock.* Not his handwriting. Why does he have an appointment with the abortion clinic and she doesn't? Whose abortion is this an invitation to? Turns out he had a woman on the side. Did to *her* what he did to her. He's not just a dog—there ain't a name for what he is. Now she decides she will get an abortion too. Kill his kid.

She gets up the morning of her appointment. Her hands are shaking, and her mouth tastes bad from morning sickness. She thinks, Now is the time to put all my problems behind me. Now is the time to get rid of this one last thing holding me back. If I get rid of this kid, I can go to school, I can find a new man, without having a reminder of the Pig looking me in the face. I can plan a future, think about what I want out of life. I can do all that if I just wipe the slate clean and start all over again. I can wake up tomorrow and this will be just a memory.

She puts on her jacket, digs around in the pocket for bus fare, but she's one dime short. There's no money in her purse, nothing in the brothers' dirty-laundry pockets, only two pennies in the couch. Can't leave the house with no money. What's she going to do, walk to get the abortion? She gets frustrated, throws the cushions on the floor, thinks, Forget this. I don't have to walk nowhere. I can start new right now. I can start a new life right where I stand, right now.

She takes off her jacket, takes off all her clothes, runs hot water in the bathtub, gets in. She scrubs her body up one side and down the other, puts her clothes back on, then walks home.

Roland used to say to her, all through growing up, all through grade school and high school, until she moved out, "No matter what is going on in the world outside that door, this house is different. This house sits on the seventeenth parallel. Ain't no fighting here."

When Roland opens the door, he lets her look at him for a long time. He's big, black, strong. Better than she remembered him. He wears his funky frayed combat fatigues from twenty years ago, and a T-shirt with a picture of MLK on the front. She has to smile at that. She don't remember his stomach being so big, or his face being soft around the jaw like that, but he is definitely her daddy. She reaches out to him. Her hand looks scrawny and pale when he covers it with his. His calluses slide across her palm when he pulls her to his chest. He says, "Welcome home, Baby Girl. How long you staying?" She says, "I can't stay, Daddy, but I can visit. I came to tell you some news."

His eyes are quiet; he listens. She can't tell what he's thinking, but she rushes ahead, her tongue slipping and saying things she didn't know she was about to say, like how scared she is, how much she needs his support. And she says the things she was planning on saying, too. She tells him how she's going to go to beauty college, how she's moving to California, how she's giving up smoking and using, eating healthy food, exercising, taking vitamins, going to bed early, whatever she can think of to help her baby. He nods his head, lets her talk all afternoon, all night, while he drinks from his glass of Old Crow.

Strong now from talking to her daddy, she moves away from the Pigs, goes on welfare, buys groceries, only shops when she's got the money to pay for what she wants, which is practically never. She tries hard, but she backslides. She can't stop wanting that pipe. It's not that smoking feels that good, it's just she feels so bad without it. She gives up crack. She takes it back again. All the while she's worrying about her baby, worrying what she's doing to him, how can she be so reckless? But worrying makes her feel worse, so she smokes more to get away from the worry.

She can't stop. Hope gone, she tells the doctor at the clinic what she's been doing, and he says they'll give her one chance and one chance only—she's got to go into treatment *now.* She's five months along.

One night she's paining in her back and stomach, blood is all in her panties. She's only seven months pregnant, but she knows it's labor. What's she going to do? Ashamed that she's so alone, that there's no father for this baby, she gets on the phone, calls up Roland. He comes, wearing his combat fatigues and a worn-out Nike shirt that says JUST DO IT. It makes her laugh a little bit. He gets them a cab to the hospital. Even though she saw the Lamaze movie, *The Birth of a Family,* where they show the baby being born, blood and all, she is in no way prepared for the doom that comes down with the labor pains. She feels them coming after her, can't get away from them, and that rap song "Here Comes the Hammer" is busting through her head so loud she thinks Roland can hear it coming out her ears. She wants to run from the pains, to outdistance them, but she also wants to lay right where she is and curl herself into a ball around the pillow. She stuffs the sheet in her mouth and chews it and cries.

Roland says, "Straighten out, sit up, *look at me.*" He says, "Here you are, now do what you gotta do." He helps her with the breathing. When the baby is ready to come out, he says, "You want me to go wait outside?" She says, "No, Daddy. Stay here. Don't leave me!"

The baby weighs three pounds, two ounces. He comes out ugly and beautiful and real, like a slap in the face. She looks at him laying in his incubator, jerking and shaking, and she knows he's suffering with drugs and she did it to him. She looks down on him, trying to feel love, but she's not feeling anything. She got no respect for herself. She let go of her baby before it could live on its own. She's not a normal mother. She ain't shit.

She goes home and lights up her pipe, but the smell turns her stomach like vinegar. Then she throws the pipe out, looks in the mirror. That weak, scared person looking back at her makes her cry. She decides.

At first she won't go nowhere near the hospital. The social worker calls her, asks her what's going on, where is she at, does she know her baby needs her? Let the doctors fix him up, she thinks. When they get him in good shape, she'll go. Until then, she's staying away. If the baby sees her now, he might take a turn for the worse. She'll walk into the nursery; the baby will know it's her and die.

After a week goes by, she decides to take a chance. She goes to the hospital to hold her baby.

There's two grandmothers there. "They're just like your own mother," the nurse tells her. But these two ladies don't look nothing like her mother. She thinks maybe one of them looks like Roland's mother. The first time she goes in, the funny, loud grandmother is rocking *her* baby, holding him like he's just a regular old baby, singing to him. She is shocked. He looks normal, just being little is all that's wrong with him. She gives him the name she's been saving in case he lives, Daquille Roland Cruz. The next day when she comes in, the grandmother who is quiet and serious is holding Daquille. Then he starts to jerk, just like right after he was born. He's jerking and shaking. She is so scared. The grandmother puts him back in his incubator, stands beside him. The nurse says it's a drug seizure. For an hour the grandmother stands there beside her and the baby, not bothering him with her worries, not singing him any songs, not even touching him, but still letting him know she's there. Letting *her* know she's there for both of them. She feels so calm standing beside the grandmothers. Then she knows that sometimes all you can do is keep watch over your baby. Just keep your eye on him.

When the hospital tells her the baby can go home, she really starts tripping, but she won't ask for help. She doesn't want the grandmothers getting disappointed in her. She's fronting. But they figure that out, and they show her how to give the baby enough milk, how to get the gas out of his stomach so the milk stays down. They show her how to wash him, give him the amount of closeness he needs when he needs it—not too much when he's stressed out and tripping, more when he is ready for it. They help her stay with it. She takes him home, and some days it's all she can do to take care of him. Some days she is so tired she can't do nothing but feed him, take care of him, rock him to sleep.

Then last night she has a vision. She is laying on the couch watching cable, when she gets a flash of herself in a few years. Her clothes are like a business suit and she's walking through some kind of building through double doors, to the outside. It's morning and birds are out. There's flowers growing around the building. It reminds her of when she was little, when Roland took her through his August garden to see his flowers, his basil and marigolds.

The vision seems kind of iffy, like it might go away, so she cuts off the TV and lays back on the couch to get a good look at it. First thing she sees is herself—clean and hopeful, her little boy holding her hand. She takes him down the street, past the buildings and cars, houses and yards, into the country, and finally they end up in a meadow. They sit in the grass, in wild onions, and they talk about everything she can think of that she wants him to know. He asks her all the questions on his mind, and she's got answers. They get up, she takes his hand again, and takes him back to the city. By the time they get there, he's turned into a man, and it hurts her to see him so big. She wants to cry, looking at his mustache, listening to him talk with his deep voice. He goes into one of the tall buildings. She's real sad when she walks away. Just before the vision wants to quit, I make her look up and see him in a window high up in the building. He waves, and he keeps on waving until I can't make the vision go on anymore.

❧ ❧

"And that's my story," LaRone said. "I don't know what it all means, but I'm not into analyzing anything. I can't compare my story to anybody else's. I'm just happy if I can have dreams like that. And I just want to keep on dreaming."

"That's beautiful, honey." Nettie Lee got off the couch and hovered over LaRone, arms outstretched. "Give Grandma the baby."

To LaRone, Nettie Lee smelled as warm as a patch of garden dirt. Her soft arms looked strong as they lifted her baby.